"I WOULD SAY YOU WERE BORN ON THE TWENTY-NINTH OF SEPTEMBER."

Her eyebrows shot up. "How did you know that?" She smiled. "You *do* know something of the stars."

He could not resist. Leaning forward, he tapped her chin. "I know something of Saint Michael's Day. Michaelmas." He enunciated her name slowly, in careful English. "Whatever I learn about you will not come from a chart," he said somberly. "It will come from being with you. Watching you. Listening to you." His voice became husky, and he leaned in close. "Touching you." He should not have said that so boldly, he knew, but just then he felt as though he could not hold back the words, or the thoughts, or the feelings she stirred in him.

She lowered her lashes as if in sudden ecstasy, and he felt its twin in himself, a plummeting rush of desire. He wanted to feel her lips beneath his again, wanted to touch the silk of her hair and skin, wanted more, so much more.

And could not have it. Heart thumping heavily, he fisted his hands against the powerful desire to take her into his arms. Uncertain how he had gotten caught in this current, he fought it like a drowning man.

Lady
Miracle

Susan King

A TOPAZ BOOK

TOPAZ
Published by the Penguin Group
Penguin Putnam Inc., 375 Hudson Street,
New York, New York 10014, U.S.A.
Penguin Books Ltd, 27 Wrights Lane,
London W8 5TZ, England
Penguin Books Australia Ltd, Ringwood,
Victoria, Australia
Penguin Books Canada Ltd, 10 Alcorn Avenue,
Toronto, Ontario, Canada M4V 3B2
Penguin Books (N.Z.) Ltd, 182–190 Wairau Road,
Auckland 10, New Zealand

Penguin Books Ltd, Registered Offices:
Harmondsworth, Middlesex, England

First published by Topaz, an imprint of Dutton Signet,
a member of Penguin Putnam Inc.

First Printing, September, 1997
10 9 8 7 6 5 4 3 2 1

 REGISTERED TRADEMARK—MARCA REGISTRADA

Printed in the United States of America

for our own little selkie

ACKNOWLEDGMENTS

Grateful thanks are due to Ted Wells-Green, M.D., for generous counsel and a great imagination; to Eileen Charbonneau, for spiritual midwifery; to Mary Jo Putney, for celestial wisdom; to Janet Beall, for friendship, ideas, and silliness; and to my son Jeremy, who did more research for this book than he knows.

Prologue

She walked among the wounded like sunlight gliding through shadow. Mists floated over the field, obscuring the bodies of those who had fallen in that morning's battle, but Diarmid Campbell saw the young girl clearly. He watched her, his fingers still as they gripped the scalpel, his attention captured for an instant.

Her pale gown and golden braids seemed to shimmer in the veiled light as she moved. Surrounded by mist and mud, she looked ethereal and graceful as she bent toward a wounded man and touched his forehead.

Like an angel come to find the dying souls, Diarmid thought. Then he shook his head to clear his battle-weary mind. No blessed vision on this cursed field, he thought, just a fair, slight girl carrying a basin of water and a handful of bandaging cloths. Obviously she had come with the local women to help in the aftermath of the battle between English and Scots.

Diarmid wiped the back of his hand, red with other men's blood as well as his own, over his sweaty brow. Then he bent to examine an arrow wound in a Highland man's shoulder.

The man grimaced. "Does a beardless lad do the work of healing women?" he asked in Gaelic. "I saw you fight, lad. That I know that you can do, and your brother with you."

"I have not yet reached my majority, that's true," Diarmid said mildly, "though I did study with the infirmarian at Mullinch Priory. And I have repaired hundreds of wounds more serious than yours."

"*Ach,*" the man growled. "Do the work and be quick."

Diarmid grasped the wooden shaft, set his mouth in determination, and swiftly yanked out the embedded iron tip. As the man gasped, Diarmid drenched the fresh wound with wine poured from a flask. Then he readied a silk thread and a needle of gold, cleansed them and his fingers in a trickle of wine, and stitched the flesh together rapidly. Wrapping the shoulder with a strip of linen torn from the man's shirt, he looked up.

"Change the bandage often and pour wine or *uisge beatha* over it when you can," he said. "And pour yourself a dram too." The Highlander nodded his thanks.

Diarmid stood, swiping again at the blood that seeped from the cut over his left eye. He would have to ask Fionn to stitch it closed for him, though his brother had no gentle hand for such work. For now, he would continue to ignore that as well as the aching gash on his left forearm, injuries received in the battle.

He ignored too the lurking fear that he did not know enough about treating these wounded men, the fear that he could cause severe pain or even death through error or ignorance. He flexed his hands tightly as he walked across the field, and resisted the fatigue that dragged his steps.

He had not treated hundreds of battle wounds, although he had told the Highlander that to reassure him. He had learned some herbal lore and the ways of the body in illness and injury from a capable infirmarian. But Brother Colum had had scant experience with battle wounds, and he had died before

Diarmid had been able to absorb all that his curiosity urged him to learn about healing and the design of the body.

Most of what he had learned since had been gleaned through experience, in grim circumstances outside the peaceful monastery infirmary. During the past year, while fighting beside fellow Highlanders for King Robert Bruce, Diarmid had routinely helped the wounded. Despite his youth, he had earned a reputation as a capable surgeon. Necessity had proven a demanding teacher.

That morning, his skills had been in constant demand. An English patrol had routed the small band of Highland men, whom Diarmid had accompanied, leaving many of the Scots injured or dead on the damp ground. Some of the men were Diarmid's own Campbell kin, though he and his brother Fionn had been spared.

He had done his best to repair flesh and set broken bones swiftly and efficiently, but he had not been able to save every man who needed his skills. A quick hand, a keen eye, and a little training were hardly enough against the power of death. He shoved a hand through his tangled brown hair in mute frustration.

Glancing around, he saw the girl again. She glowed like a shaft of pale sunshine in the gray mist, a fragile thing, far too innocent and pure to be in such a sad, bloody place. As Diarmid watched, some of the wounded men called out to her or stared, as if she was a saint drifted down from heaven.

But Diarmid had no such illusions. The monks of Mullinch Priory had believed in miracles, but they had been sheltered men. At nineteen, Diarmid was well acquainted with the harshness of the temporal world. He had been educated by monks, but his father had trained him to be a warrior and a laird. He had witnessed death and devastating injury, and had dealt them himself. Wielding a broadsword was as familiar to him as using a scalpel.

Just now he wanted to use neither. He thought of Dunsheen Castle in the western Highlands, standing proud on its green isle, surrounded by water and mists and mountains. His new role as the laird there was challenge enough. His kin, his tenants, his herds, and his late father's trade business all needed his guidance in one way or another; he dreamed of being at Dunsheen again, and also longed to sail a new, sleek galley on trading voyages. But those matters would have to wait while war raged.

Diarmid sighed as he walked across the field. Others moved through the wispy fog too: injured men, whole men, and a few women who had come with a priest to offer help and succor. The cries of the wounded echoed in the mist, chilling his soul.

He saw the blond girl kneel in the mud and lean forward to cleanse a man's bleeding arm. She had a serene, assured manner, as if raw wounds and agony did not frighten her. Diarmid stopped and watched from a distance.

"If angels exist, they look like her," a voice murmured behind him.

"Ah, but angels are rare on battlefields, brother," Diarmid said, and turned.

Fionn Campbell nodded, his profile handsome and strong, framed by rich waves of brown hair. Diarmid knew, from images in still streams and polished steel mirrors, how much he and his younger brother resembled each other.

Fionn glanced at Diarmid, his gray eyes somber. "We have no time to contemplate the heavenly host. Come look at Angus MacArthur over here. When one of the local wisewomen tried to repair his leg wound, it began to bleed heavily."

Diarmid followed Fionn's tall, spare form, and knelt in the damp grass beside Angus MacArthur, their father's distant cousin. The older man groaned and shifted as Diarmid examined the deep wound in his thigh, made from the wide sweep of an English broadsword. Angus had once been his father's *gille-ruith*, his runner; the man's legs were as strong as iron. But the blade had bitten deeply into the tight muscle, nearly cleaving the bone.

Frowning, Diarmid wadded the cloth that Fionn handed him and pressed it against the gushing wound for a few minutes. When he saw little improvement, he sighed heavily and glanced at Fionn.

"Steady his leg," he directed. "I need to search the wound. If an artery is torn, I must attempt to repair it."

Fionn supported the thigh while Diarmid probed. "After this, you should tend to your own wounds," he told Diarmid. "The gash in your arm is bleeding through the bandage. And that cut over your eye is wide open again."

"My wounds will do for now. Later you can sew them shut."

"You will risk your life twice in one day, then," Fionn said wryly. "Ask the angel to tend them, if you would survive."

Diarmid huffed a flat, humorless laugh and worked silently.

Fionn gazed over the field. "I've been watching the girl. She seems to know how to help these men. Perhaps she is an herb-healer, or even a nun. Now that would be a shame. She's truly fair, that one."

"She's too young to be a nun, or a skilled healer," Diarmid said as he bent over his task. He worked quickly and gently, but Angus MacArthur passed out with a heavy sigh. Although that made Diarmid's work easier, it increased his concern.

"I mean to speak with her," Fionn said. "I wonder who she is. She has a sweet way about her. I will need a wife soon enough, you know. A fair one who could tend my battle wounds would be a blessing."

"Mm," Diarmid answered distractedly. He concentrated on applying heavy pressure, but the folded cloth grew red far too quickly. He swore under his breath. "I need a strip of linen. Now!"

Fionn tore a long piece from the hem of his own shirt and handed it to him. Diarmid wrapped the cloth high on the leg, twisting it and holding it tight.

"If I cannot halt the flow—" He stopped, gazing at the unconscious man's pale face. The outcome was obvious.

"What did Brother Colum teach you in such cases?"

"Not enough before he died." Diarmid loosened the bandage, then tightened it again. "Pressure will do, or a tight band. Certain herbs will ease bleeding, but I have no simples or potions. I should have found a wise-wife to beg a few herbs."

"None of us knew that an English patrol would attack us out here. We were assured that we could pass through this part of Galloway without threat. But we had the assurance of Englishmen," Fionn added. "Will the blood band work?"

"I will make it work," Diarmid said fiercely. After a moment, he nodded. "It seems to be slowing some, thank God." He lifted the wineskin that hung at his belt, pulled the wax stopper free, and trickled wine over the wound. "Hold the leg," he said quietly.

As Fionn complied, Diarmid readied the needle with silk and dribbled wine, and began to pull together the deepest layer of muscle. He swore as blood pooled freely where he worked, making it difficult to see what he attempted to repair.

Leaning over his patient, he did not notice at first the slight figure who knelt beside Fionn. When he glanced up, he saw the girl.

"Be gone," he said curtly.

"Let me help," she said. Her voice was young and soft, and she spoke in Gaelic, as he had, but he hardly noticed. A mix of voices floated over the field: Gaelic, northern English, French, and the droning Latin of the priest. He understood them all.

"You can do nothing here," he said. He drew the

needle in and out, in and out. Fionn and the girl watched.

Diarmid swore softly as the silk slid from the golden needle, and swore again as the bleeding continued. He would have to find the opening in the artery or Angus MacArthur would die soon. He rethreaded the needle and instructed Fionn to loosen and then tighten the blood band.

The girl leaned forward suddenly and laid her slender hands over the gaping, ugly slash. She drew in a deep breath.

"Girl!" Diarmid snapped. "Stop!"

"Hush." At her firm command, he glanced at her in surprise.

Small and slight next to Fionn's muscular, plaid-draped physique, she spoke like a queen. Eyes closed, back straight, she lifted her delicate golden head to the dreary, misted light.

She looked like a shining sword, beautifully shaped, hilted in gold and bladed in silver. Flawless and strong, an angel come to earth. Diarmid blinked in astonishment.

Then he recovered his wits. Angus's wound required urgency from him, not awestruck dreaming. He reached out, meaning to lift the girl's hand away. But he paused, his hand hovering.

Heat radiated from her fingers. She appeared to be praying, or in some sort of meditative trance, her eyes closed, her thick gold-tipped lashes still. Her small hands were cupped over the wound, fingertips and palms staining deep red.

"Holy Mother of God," Fionn breathed after a moment.

The girl withdrew her reddened fingers, sliding them into her lap. Diarmid looked at the wound. The gushing flow had slowed considerably. He could see the slice in the artery.

Diarmid stayed silent, uncertain what he had seen, and lacking time to wonder at it. He repaired the tear and asked Fionn to heat the tip of his dirk so that he could cauterize the sealed artery. Then he closed the wound, easing the layers of muscle back together.

While he worked, he focused on what he saw now, what he must do next, until he finished the task. Finally, he accepted the clean cloth that the girl handed him and wrapped it over Angus's leg.

He looked at the silent girl, who knelt an arm's length from him, her bloodstained hands in her lap. "He will live," he said quietly.

She nodded, a vulnerable little shake, as if her delicate head were a trembling flower on a slender stem. She rose to her feet, and wavered unsteadily.

Diarmid stood too, taking her arm to offer his support. "What was it you did?" he asked.

Her eyes were wide and round as she looked up, blue as a summer sky and fringed by gold-tipped lashes. Innocent, youthful eyes. Yet he saw wisdom in their depths, awareness, as if the bright soul that looked out at him had lived a long, long time.

"What is your name?" he asked softly. "I am Diarmid Campbell of Dunsheen."

"Michaelmas," she said. "Michaelmas Faulkener."

He frowned at the odd English name, but recognized that her surname belonged to an English knight who was now one of Robert Bruce's most loyal advisers. "Are you kin to Gavin Faulkener?"

She nodded. "He is my half brother. I came out here this morn with my mother and our priest to help. Kinglassie Castle is but a mile from this place. We heard the shouts of battle just after dawn," she added. "I must go. My mother will be looking for me."

Diarmid did not let go of her arm, his long fingers rust-red against her pale sleeve. Her bones felt fragile beneath his touch. "*Micheil*," he said in Gaelic, unfamiliar with the sound of her strange English name. Michaelmas. He realized that she must be named for Saint Michael's Mass, a feast day, the twenty-ninth of September. "Your name is *Micheil*?"

She nodded at the Gaelic equivalent. "Michael will do."

"Tell me what you did, Michael. I have never seen the like."

"You're hurt." She reached up and touched the cut above his eye gently. He felt her fingertips tremble against his brow.

He looked down at the pale golden crown of her head, with its silky parting, and felt a distinct heat seep into his wound, like the warmth of sunlight or wine. A moment later he felt the heat throughout his body, as if he sat close to a fire.

As if this girl had fire in her touch.

She took her hand away. He lifted a finger to the cut and looked, seeing only a thin line of blood on his fingertip. The stinging ache had diminished. He exchanged a quick glance with Fionn, who watched them intently.

"Sweet Mary," Diarmid breathed. "Girl, how do you come by such a gift?"

"My mother calls me," she said. He heard a voice sound from a far corner of the field. "I must go."

"Michael—" Diarmid reached out, but she stepped away.

"I must go," she said.

Diarmid saw the stocky priest walking toward them, accompanied by a slender, dark-haired woman who called out the girl's English name.

Michael glanced up at Diarmid. "You must never tell what you saw me do," she whispered. "My family knows, and our priest. But I want no one else to know. Promise you will never speak of this."

Diarmid blinked in surprise. "You have the word of the laird of Dunsheen," he said.

"And his brother," Fionn added.

"Michael—" Diarmid began.

"God keep you, Dunsheen," she said. Then she spun away from them and ran lightly through the muddy field, lifting her skirts high, her thin legs nimble as she skimmed over rocks and tufted grasses.

"What in all this world and the next just happened?" Fionn asked after a moment. "I feel as if I've been struck by lightning."

Diarmid did too. He watched silently as the girl greeted the slender woman and the priest, and walked away with them.

"We've seen the making of a saint, brother," Fionn continued. "*Ach,* she will not wed me or any man. She'll become a nun, that one, and be beatified one day."

"Then she's better off in a convent, if what we saw is real."

"Real? For a lad taught by monks, you're a thorough skeptic. You should see the cut over your eye. I swear on my life and soul, it looks like it's been healing for days. We've seen a saint, man."

"Perhaps," Diarmid said. He touched the tender spot over his eye. "Her family is wise to protect her. If others witness what she can do, she could be named a saint—or a heretic."

"Pray, then, that her family keeps her well hidden." Fionn clapped his hand on Diarmid's shoulder. "But before she left, you should have asked her to tend to your arm. Now you have none but me to sew it for you."

Diarmid shot him a wry glance. "Let me find some strong wine first." Fionn grinned.

Diarmid turned as someone called out for him. As he walked away, he glanced across the field once again. The girl had disappeared into the shifting mists, but he would not forget her.

She had shown him a golden miracle on this bloody field.

Chapter One

The cry echoed again, eerie and poignant through the darkness. Diarmid straightened in his saddle and looked around. He heard the sound once more, and judged it to be some small, young creature, probably lost or hurt. But a strangely wistful quality in the cry reminded him of the legends of the *daoine sìth*, the fair folk, said to inhabit so many of the hills in the Scottish Highlands. Smiling ruefully, he dismissed the fantasy with a shake of his head and rode on.

A few moments later he heard it again, a whimper this time. Diarmid halted the horse to glance at the surrounding hills that slanted beneath half a white moon. He was certain no one else would be out here on a cold spring night, when rising winds and scudding clouds threatened rain.

Satisfied that he heard only the whine of the wind, he urged his sturdy black mount along the grassy moonlit track, proceeding cautiously through unfamiliar territory. Years had passed since he had come this way, but he was sure that Sim MacLachlan's small castle was near here. Although MacLachlan and his kin would not be expecting the laird of Dunsheen, Diarmid looked forward to an offer of broth, a seat by the hearth, and a good dram.

Highland hospitality would prevail as it did at Dunsheen, a long day's ride from here. Diarmid would

attend to the matter that brought him here, and after
a night's sleep beside the MacLachlan hearth, he
would ride back in the morning.

He shifted the reins to his left hand as he rode, but
the cool air aggravated the troublesome weakness in
that hand. As he clenched the leather strips, he felt a
dull ache.

The soft keening came again, louder now, a
trembling sound that slid down his spine like ice water.
The horse whickered nervously and slowed. Alerted
to danger, Diarmid placed his hand on the dirk in his
belt and sensed the weight of the broadsword strapped
to his back. One swift movement would bring the hilt
into his right hand.

Certain that the cry emanated from a nearby hill,
he cautiously dismounted in the pale moonlight and
climbed the slope with long, agile steps. On the hill's
rounded peak, he saw a bundle of rags blowing in the
wind. Something moved in their midst, and the whimper echoed again. Diarmid went toward it, crouched
low. He stopped then, and stared.

A child sat on the crest of the hill, a small, slight
thing, shivering inside the folds of a plaid. The wind
stirred the tangle of pale hair around its head. After
a moment, the child turned and stared at him.

Diarmid moved forward. The child cried out and
scuttled away, using its scrawny arms to slide back on
its behind, but it did not run. The creature—he
thought it a female—stared back at him, breathing
rapidly.

He looked into light-colored eyes and at an elfin,
moon-pale face, and wondered if he indeed faced a
child of the *daoine sìth*. But the wobbling of her lower
lip was utterly human; she was a child, lost and frightened, clutching a plaid around her, her tangled halo
of golden curls quivering in the wind.

She gave out a soft, fearful sob. That small sound
rocked the foundations of Diarmid's soul. He hunkered down beside her.

"Are you lost, little one?" he asked gently.

She stared at him and shook her head.

"Not lost?" Diarmid frowned, puzzled; she was far too small to have run away on her own. "How is it you are out here alone? Is your mother or father nearby?"

Silent, she gazed up at him. When a draft of cold wind cut between them, she shivered.

"You're chilled," he said, and drew the plaid up to shield her head. Then he held out his hand. "Come with me. I'll take you home. Tell me where to find your kin. Come, now." He stood, and waited for her to stand.

She looked up at him and held up her thin arms, sleeved in rags. Her delicate hands opened in a trusting gesture, as if she wanted him to lift her.

"*Ach,* you're tired." He bent down, slipped his arm beneath her legs, wrapped in the wool, and picked her up.

He might have balanced a sack of feathers. She put her arms around his neck so lightly that he hardly felt her grip. He turned and began to descend the slope. The child rode in his arms like a moonbeam, weightless, fragile, pale and silent. After a moment she rested her head on his shoulder.

"What is your name?" he asked. She blinked up at him with smudged, somber eyes, and did not answer. "I am Diarmid," he said, hoping to encourage her to share her name.

"I heard a wildcat," she whispered.

"It will not harm you," he replied.

"I waited for you. I was cold," she added plaintively.

He frowned. No one expected him in this place. "You waited for me?" he repeated, perplexed.

She nodded "And you came."

His frown deepened. He had ridden here at his sister's urging to visit the small girl-child who fostered in Sim MacLachlan's household. He remembered a healthy, sturdy child with fat blond curls and the

charming, crooked smile of the Dunsheen Campbells.
This little one was fair and young, but far more delicate than the child he recalled.

Certainly Sim MacLachlan, who had the safekeep-
ing of Brigit Campbell, would never allow any harm
to come to Fionn's daughter. Diarmid himself had left
her in Sim's wife's care as an infant, and yearly paid
a handsome fee to help with her fostering.

She tilted her head to look at him. "Are you the
king?"

"King of Scots? I am not." He almost smiled.

"King of the *daoine sìth,*" she said. "They're my
kin. I am a changeling child." She said it casually, as
if she told him the color of her hair, or the number
of her toes.

He stopped. On this moonlit, windy night, he could
almost believe that he held a child of the fair folk.
The waif's eyes seemed to glow with a magical depth,
and her small voice sounded otherworldly. But the
cool pressure of her little hands on his neck, the faint
unwashed odor of her hair, the bony, fragile feel of
her were far too real.

"Someone has filled your head with tales," he
muttered.

"Old Morag told me my kin are the fair folk,"
she insisted.

"You listen too much to this Morag, whoever she
is."

"She is Simmie's old grandmother."

"Sim MacLachlan?" he asked.

She nodded, her eyes huge and clear in the eerie
light.

A chill of dread rushed through him, but he dismissed it abruptly. At the horse's side, he bent to set
the child on the ground. Her arms tightened around
his neck.

"Do not let go," she said. "I cannot walk."

Holding her feathery weight, he was suddenly aware

of the limp drape of her legs over his arm. "You cannot walk?" he repeated, stunned. "Are you injured?"

"I have a curse on me. Old Morag says I am a changeling. She is a wisewoman." She nodded.

"I hardly think that," he growled.

"She told me that if I stayed out here, all would be well."

He narrowed his eyes. "Old Morag left you out here alone?"

She nodded. "She said I should wait for the *daoine sìth* to come for me. And you came. So you must be one of them." She tilted her head. "And you are tall and strong, like a king."

He huffed impatiently. "I am no *sìtheach* come for you."

"*Ach*," she said, sounding almost wise, "you are." She smiled, elfin and charming.

That slanted little grin struck him through to his heart. She bore the distinctive smile of the Dunsheen Campbells. Silently, carefully, Diarmid set her at the front of his saddle and swung up behind her, stifling his rising fear with slow movements. This could not be his niece; the resemblance was merely a coincidence.

Whoever she was, he meant to find out who had left her alone on a windy hilltop. He knew that many Highlanders believed that healthy human infants and children could be stolen away by the fair folk, and sickly supernatural offspring left in their place. The changelings were sometimes abandoned on hilltops in hopes that their otherworld kin would reclaim them.

Someone had abandoned this child, believing her to be a changeling, perhaps because of some weakness in her legs. The thought of such cruelty and ignorance chilled him. And the thought of who she might be made his hands tremble with dread and anger. Taking the reins, holding her secure in his lap, he looked down at her.

"Tell me your name," he said.

She lifted her chin proudly. *"Brighid,"* she said. "Brigit. It means strength."

"Brigit Campbell?" His voice was barely above a whisper.

She nodded, blinking up at him. He saw then that her moon-colored eyes would be gray in sunlight, like his, like his sister's. Like Fionn's. He saw the ghost of his brother's handsome face in her small countenance. Fionn's daughter, Diarmid's own charge since his death, looked at him.

Shock coiled into rage as he realized that his niece had been mistreated. And then rage hardened to a burden of remorse and guilt. He had promised Fionn that he would protect this child as if she were his own.

He held the proof of how well he had honored that vow.

"Where is Sim MacLachlan?" he growled.

Brigit startled in his arms like a hare. He saw that he had frightened her. "Simmie is dead," she answered. "They're all dead now. But for Old Morag. She took me to her little house."

"I am your kin, child. I am your uncle, Diarmid Campbell." He drew a deep, shuddering breath. "You will come home with me to Dunsheen Castle. But first I will have a word with this Morag. Is her house near here?"

"It is," Brigit said. "But she will be sleeping."

"Then we will wake her up," he said fiercely. Holding Brigit secure in his arms, he urged the horse ahead through the rising wind.

September, 1322.

Dawn streaked the sky, a flash of wild rosy brilliance that soon faded into morning as Diarmid rode beside Mungo MacArthur, his friend and *gille-ruith.* As their horses climbed a low hill, Diarmid watched the morning light spread over the lavender shoulders of the distant mountains. Far beyond those peaks lay the western coast and Dunsheen Castle, several days' ride from these Border hills where King Robert's army clustered.

He and Mungo had been part of that raiding force for months, but days ago they had finally been granted permission to return home. The price of that release was far higher than Diarmid had ever anticipated. But he would have agreed to almost any request as long as the task brought him home.

He had heard no word from his brothers or his sister since he had left Dunsheen in July. He knew nothing of Brigit's health since then, when Robert Bruce had summoned him to the Border hills to join his raids on the English. Diarmid owed fealty and service to the crown, which took the form of either knight service or the loan of his fast multi-oared galleys, according to the king's needs. He had been given no choice but to ride out.

He spurred his horse and cantered down the hillside, taking the next slope at a fast pace. Mungo, less agile on horseback, for as a ghillie he was more used to running wherever he went, finally caught up to Diarmid.

"You are in a hurry, Dunsheen," he panted.

"I need to get home," he said. "And first I have an errand in Perth. That will delay us another day."

Mungo grunted, his brown eyes narrowed speculatively as he watched Diarmid. "You seem very certain this woman in Perth will come with you to Dunsheen."

"She will," he said. "She has the soul of a saint. She will not refuse my request."

"Who would ever have said that the laird of Dunsheen would eagerly toss away his games of war to see to the needs of a small girl-child?" Mungo mused.

Diarmid slid him a wry glance. "You have four children, man," he said. "Do not tell me you would not do anything for them if they were ill. Brigit has improved little since the night I found her abandoned. I hoped that rest, good food, and herbal doses would help her limbs to regain strength."

"True, if it were one of my own, I would do the same, but you have hired several herb-wives and even a physician to treat her," Mungo said. "And each one has said the same thing. She will not walk, Dunsheen," he added gently, his voice gruff.

"One woman predicted she would waste away until she could move nothing but her head," Diarmid said bitterly. "Another says she will not live through two more years, and should be put in a convent. And the physician," he added angrily, "the educated man, wanted to bleed her daily and amputate her legs so the weakness would not spread. Should I listen to them?"

"You threw the physician out. There is no need to listen to nonsense," Mungo agreed. "But no one knows what caused this for her, and no one—not even you, with as much medical knowledge as anyone—knows how to treat it."

"She is my responsibility," Diarmid growled. "I will see her healed." He would find a way—she was his niece, his ward, the soul of the promise he had made to his brother and had not kept. The awareness of that tugged at him constantly.

"Is this fierceness because of what Brigit believes of you?"

"That I am king of the *daoine sìth*, and capable of magic? In part," he admitted in chagrin. "I cannot dissuade her from insisting on it. She has faith in me."

"She adores you. And you, Dunsheen, refuse her nothing."

"Nothing at all. I am lost each time she smiles at me."

Mungo chuckled. "I know. I have daughters. But you made a hasty promise to her, Diarmid, when you left last summer."

He nodded, knowing the truth in Mungo's admonishment. One night, as Brigit cried with pain, she had begged one promise of him. Now he must find a way to fulfill an impossible vow.

The child wanted magic. Convinced that her uncle was king of the fair folk, she believed that he could summon magic to heal her. And he, like a besotted, desperate fool, had agreed.

He sighed, feeling the fresh autumn air blow his long hair and his plaid. He wished it could blow away all of the troubles that sat upon his shoulders. He needed a little peace in his life; he met only turmoil wherever he turned of late. Now king and crown demanded his time and challenged his honor in a way that he strongly disliked.

He breathed in the smells of pine, of distant chimney smoke, of burbling water, and listened to the quiet thud of the horses' hooves and the sweep of the wind. The immediacy of those sensations smothered the remorse and dismay he felt, and reminded him that he had a sworn duty to his king as a Highland laird.

Diarmid looked at his left hand, fisting it slowly, flexing the fingers, feeling the ache and stiffness in the old scars there. He studied their familiar ugliness while he thought about what King Robert had asked him to do.

Mungo, as he often did, seemed to know the turn of his thoughts. "This task the king and his adviser gave you at least allowed you leave to return to Dunsheen. You wanted that."

Diarmid nodded. "I was reluctant to agree, but Gavin Faulkener convinced me of their need for my help. He is a capable, good man, and I trust his judgment."

"He is an Englishman, is he not? Interesting that he is now one of Bruce's closest advisers. Bruce has gathered many strong men around him with true hearts and clever minds. He includes you among them, Diarmid. That is a rare privilege."

"And now I know that the king's favor demands hard work and unwavering loyalty. And poses difficult choices," he added. He shoved his fingers through his unruly brown hair. "So I agreed to report any sign of treason in my own sister's husband."

"But Ranald MacSween claims utter loyalty. He holds Glas Eilean for the king, and guards that seaward entrance to the Isles with much dedication."

"Which the king now suspects may be false. If Ranald is a traitor, my sister may suffer for it."

"Sorcha will not be blamed. You and I would never allow that to happen."

"But she will suffer in other ways, and you know it," Diarmid said sharply. He sighed and rubbed his bristly, unshaven chin. "What choice did I have? English ships barricade the waters on the western coast and cut off our trade routes. The Highland people are dependent on exports of grain and other goods. My own galleys have engaged in sea warfare, and we are now forced to trade only through Irish ports. This has to stop. The king has heard a rumor from an English source that Ranald is less than loyal. Glas Eilean is a key sea fortress."

"Invasion is too great a risk," Mungo said. "If there is a plot in the western Isles to harm Scotland, it must be exposed."

"The king wants MacSween watched. He lately granted Glas Eilean's charter not to MacSween but to Gavin Faulkener, who gave it to his half sister, hoping to attract a strong Highland lord as her husband. Gavin cannot oversee the holding of Glas Eilean himself."

"Ranald must be furious about this. Who is Faulkener's sister?"

"Her name is *Micheil*," Diarmid said.

Mungo gaped at him. "This woman in Perth—the one who you say healed my father's wounded leg years ago—she is Gavin Faulkener's half sister? And the owner of Glas Eilean?"

Diarmid nodded grimly.

"You did not tell me who she was. Typical of you

to hold your thoughts close." Mungo blew out a long breath. "A fine mess this is. No wonder you mean to fetch her and take her to Dunsheen. A lot of birds in hand here. I suppose Gavin knows you are already wed?"

A muscle tightened in Diarmid's cheek. "He knows," he said curtly. "I suggested one of my brothers as a husband for Lady Michael."

Micheil. Her name, whenever it was spoken, burst like a flash of light in his mind. Just as MacSween held some unknown key to Robert Bruce's dilemma, Michael held a key too—one that could fulfill Diarmid's vow to a small child.

Magic. The only true magic he had ever seen had come from Michael's hands. He meant to find her for that reason.

"And she is in Perth? She is still a healer?" Mungo asked.

"Very competent, from what Gavin told me. She has had some further medical training in Italy, where she was wed and widowed." True to the word he had once given Michael, Diarmid had never told anyone what he had actually witnessed on that battlefield. Mungo and his father Angus, whose leg she had healed, simply believed her to be a precociously skilled healer.

"By all means, man, we must find this woman," Mungo said.

"I agree," Diarmid said smoothly. He cantered ahead in the direction of Perth, where an angel dwelled.

Chapter Two

No sunshine once again, Michaelmas thought, and sighed in disappointment. She had spent nine years in Italy, and, since her return to Scotland, sometimes longed for warm sun. Standing in the doorway of the main hospital building, holding a stack of clean, folded sheets, she lifted her face to the cool autumn breeze. The hems of her widow's black surcoat and gown fluttered around her feet, and the air ruffled the linen wimple that framed her face. She shivered slightly.

"Lady Michaelmas, bring the sheets, if you please." An imperious female voice cut into her thoughts. "The sisters have stripped four of the beds to be remade."

"I am coming, Mother Agnes." Michaelmas began to turn, but a shift of the light caught her attention. She glanced back.

In the distance, where blue hills rose above the rumpled curves of a brown valley, she saw two men riding horses along a riverbank. Narrowing her eyes, Michaelmas watched their progress, recognizing the wrapped plaids of Highlanders. Their sturdy mounts headed toward the hill on which the small hospital complex stood.

Saint Leonard's Hospital, its buildings enclosed within a low stone wall, overlooked the river valley. Michaelmas had often stood in this doorway to watch arrivals. The master physician came every day, and the apothecary rode in twice a week from nearby Saint John's Town, which some called Perth. Visitors came too, as well as those in need of medical help or the charity of clean beds and food.

She frowned as she watched the two riders, wondering if they were returning to their remote hills through this valley. Several Highlanders had come here in the last few weeks, wounded in the recent raids that King Robert and his army had made against the English.

The taller of the two men rode a black horse and moved with singular grace and rhythm, his dark hair flying loose, his posture strong and proud even from this distance. He would not be the wounded one, she guessed. Perhaps his companion, who rode more awkwardly, needed treatment.

Perhaps they sought one of the wounded Highland men who were recovering at Saint Leonard's. Michaelmas, fluent in the Gaelic language, had been acting as their translators.

That much she was allowed to do. Regardless of her medical training, she was not permitted to treat patients. The prioress, the priest, and the master physician agreed on that, although she still tended patients when no one was nearby to witness it.

"Lady Michaelmas, we are waiting!" the prioress called.

She turned quickly. "Coming, Mother Agnes!"

"Close the door! You know that Master James does not like his patients to be exposed to the outside air!"

Michaelmas hastily shut the door, then hurried along the main aisle formed by twenty-four beds, twelve to each side, in the whitewashed common hall. In a dim corner of the wide room, Mother Agnes watched her with a pinched expression, then spoke with the two novices who stood with her. A moment later she left by the door. Michaelmas breathed out a sigh of relief.

A few of the elderly patients, lying in pairs in the beds, reached out toward Michaelmas as she passed. She smiled and greeted each one, but hurried along. She had spent too much time in the courtyard fetching the clean sheets from the drying ropes. The laundress had been busy scrubbing loads of soiled clothing, and had not yet gotten to that task.

"I ask your pardon, Sister Marjorie, Sister Alice," she told the novices as she laid the heavy stack of sheets and towels on a table. "I hope you told the prioress 'twas my doing that the beds were not yet made up this morn."

Marjorie shook her wimpled head and picked up a sheet to spread over one of the straw mattresses. "Och, the Mother Prioress wasna so grieved about that as she was by what Father Anselm reported about you."

Michaelmas sighed as she helped Alice fold and tuck a set of crisp linen sheets over another mattress. "What did he say?"

"He told the prioress that he saw you examine Mistress Jean and the Highland men yesterday in the manner of a physician," Alice said. "And he said that the patients were calling you that name again. Mother Agnes wasna pleased."

"I can imagine," Michaelmas said wryly.

" 'Lady Miracle' befits the mother of our Savior, the prioress says. She said"—Alice pursed her lips and folded her hands in imitation—" 'Tis no name for a mere nurse and a Saracen's widow, who has scant hope of attaining the gifts of heaven because of her sinful marriage.' "

Marjorie laughed. Michaelmas said nothing, only snapping open a folded sheet vigorously, annoyed not with the mimicking but by the prioress's statement, which she did not doubt was truly reported.

"Och, but she isna a mere nurse," Marjorie said indignantly. "She's a physician! And Lady Miracle is a fine name for our Lady Michaelmas. She has a touch as sweet as an angel."

"Mother Agnes is envious," Alice said. "She dislikes your marriage, your widowhood, and your education."

"Och, you shouldna be making beds and giving baths, and dosing the patients with medicines prescribed by Master James," Marjorie said. " 'Tis fitting work for us, but not for you."

Alice punched a heather-stuffed pillow. "You could help many more here if they didna put such restrictions on you." She blinked at Michaelmas curiously. "Was your husband a pagan sinner? Could your marriage truly keep you from heaven?"

"Ibrahim was a fine physician and a kind man," Michaelmas said as she smoothed the covers on one bed and moved to another. "He was a Saracen, but his mother was a Christian lady."

"But now you're widowed, and so you must make your way in the world," Marjorie said in sympathy. "Will you accept membership in the barber-surgeon's guild, since it was offered?"

"I refused it. The guild will only allow me to extract teeth, let blood, and repair small wounds. They willna even allow me a license to practice midwifery unless I apprentice for four years first."

Marjorie looked appalled. "You know as much as any midwife, I vow, from what you've done for the few women who have come here for assistance."

Alice unfolded another laundered sheet. "Father Anselm told the prioress that Lady Michaelmas is to be restricted in all nursing duties until their investigation of her is ended."

Michaelmas sighed. "I have been arguing for my physician's license for months now. They will never grant it to me."

"Will you go back to your brother's home?" Alice asked. "You do not need to beg favor from the master physicians in Saint John's Town. You can marry well, my lady."

Michaelmas frowned. "I do not wish to marry a Highlander, as my brother wishes. I have skills, and I want to use them."

"There must be a hospital somewhere that would welcome a female physician," Marjorie said.

"That hospital may not be in Scotland," Michaelmas said, discouraged. "But enough of this, my girls, we have duties." She gestured toward the patients who had been squeezed into other patients' beds until their sheets had been changed. The two girls turned to escort those men back to their beds.

"Alice, please fetch this morning's doses from the infirmary," Michaelmas directed. "I'll help you give them out. And Marjorie, you can begin to wash hands, faces, and feet. There should be plenty of warm water in the kettle by the hearth. Let them rinse their mouths too with minted water, if you will." The girls nodded and walked away to begin their tasks.

Michaelmas turned toward an old woman who lay in a bed alone, a knitted cap on her scant white hair, several blankets tucked up over her bare, bony shoulders. Her eyes were closed, and her head trembled with age.

"Mistress Jean," she said. "How do you fare this morn?"

The woman opened her brown eyes, their color flattened by age to a muddy hue. "Lady Miracle! Ye're still here. I thought ye might leave us with the trouble the prioress gave ye."

"*Ach,* Jean, would I leave without a farewell to you?" As she spoke, Michaelmas circled the woman's wrist to measure her pulse beat.

Jean's face folded in a quivering smile. "Och, I might leave ye first, dearling. I'm verra old." She closed her eyes.

Michaelmas stayed silent, counting, waiting, measuring the pattern of the beat. The weak pulse beneath her fingertips fluttered like a butterfly moving its wings against a cage. Ibrahim had taught her to recognize the rhythm of an aged heart slipping toward its final silence. Only weeks, perhaps days, were left to Jean.

She laid down the woman's arm gently. "What treat

shall I bring you at midday dinner, Jeanie?" she asked. "How about some sweetmeats? But you must promise not to tell Mother Agnes."

"Och, more trouble wi' the prioress? She was angry when ye told her I needed a bed to myself. She's like a hawk, that one, hunting after ye. She'll bring trouble, I warn ye."

"Dinna fret for me," she said gently. "Here comes Alice with the sage electuary that Master James prescribed for you."

Jean wrinkled her nose in distaste, then popped open her eyes. "Ooh, who's that?" she asked curiously, looking toward the door. "Two young savages!" She sounded delighted.

Michaelmas spun in surprise. Two Highland men stood in the threshold of the common room, looking around silently. Their bulky green-and-black plaids, unkempt hair, and bare legs looked startlingly savage, just as Jean had said. These were the men she had seen riding through the valley.

The gaze of the taller man met and held hers across the length of the room. The raw power in his light-colored eyes made her look down hastily; she took in his laced hide boots, his muscular legs, his wide leather belt, where a dirk glimmered.

Her gaze traveled upward as if drawn by the strength in his glance. She noticed his leather vest and wide linen-covered shoulders beneath the draped and brooched plaid, noticed the strong column of his throat beneath dark stubble. His face was striking, lean and hard with well-balanced features, the whole framed by long, untidy brown hair.

Then he turned, breaking the riveting contact of their gazes, and murmured to the man behind him. Dressed in a similar plaid patterned in green and black, the second man was perhaps a little older than the first; he looked equally wild, with a craggy face, limp brown hair, and a formidable scowl.

"They must be more Highlanders come here from

raiding the English in the south," Alice muttered as she joined Michaelmas, carrying a tray with medicines in wooden cups. "They seem hearty, though. Perhaps they seek food and shelter. That one is looking straight at you, my lady," she said. "Do you know him?"

"Not at all," Michaelmas said.

"Och, they're handsome lads, let them in," Jean crowed. Alice laughed and handed her a cup.

Michaelmas turned and went toward the men, folding her hands demurely and holding her wimpled head high. "May I help you?" she asked in Gaelic. "If you have come to visit the other Highlanders, they are over there, at the far end of the room."

"We do not know them," the taller man said in Gaelic. His voice was deep, strong, and surprisingly soft. "I have come to see you, if you are *Micheil,* half sister of Gavin Faulkener." He looked at her, and inclined his head politely.

She blinked at him in momentary surprise, then realized Gavin must have sent these men with a message for her. Aware that no direct Gaelic equivalent of her English name existed, she did not correct his error. But the familiar, easy manner in which he said *Micheil* stirred a long buried memory in her that she could not quite grasp.

"How is it you know me?" she asked. "Did Gavin send you?"

"Your brother told me where you were," he replied.

"Is he well? Do you have a message for me?"

"He is well, but I bring no message. I came of my own will to ask you to look at a patient."

Gavin must have told the man of her medical skill, but her brother was unaware of the difficulties she had encountered here. "I am not permitted to practice medicine here. You need the master of this hospital. He will be here later." She nodded farewell and hurried the length of the room, aware that the tall Highlander's intent gaze followed her.

She stopped by two beds where four injured men lay, whose limb wounds had required the attentions of a surgeon. She checked the bandages and felt their heads for fever. One man's brow seemed overly warm, and his leg incision was pink and hot. She turned as Alice approached with another wooden cup.

"Mother Agnes sent this for the surgery patients to drink," Alice said, handing the cup from one man to the next. " 'Tis herbs for pain, in wine and sugar. And she says that you shouldna change their bandages. She will do that herself later."

"Well enough," Michaelmas said. "But tell her that this man needs a potion for fever. His wound must be cleansed, for 'tis beginning to fester. It may require lancing."

"Master James will decide that," the prioress's stilted voice replied. "He says festering is helpful."

Michaelmas turned swiftly. Mother Agnes stood behind her, hands folded over her ivory rosary, her sharp gaze fastened on Michaelmas. Father Anselm, a small, dark man, stood beside her.

"Mother Agnes," Michaelmas acknowledged. "Father Anselm, greetings." The priest nodded, his brown eyes grim.

"Arabic physicians advise the cleaning of seeping wounds," Michaelmas said. "In this case, it would be the wisest course."

"Alice, see what those Highland men want here," the prioress barked. Alice nodded and backed away. Mother Agnes turned to glare at Michaelmas. "Lady Michaelmas, let me remind you that medical advice is not needed from you. We have a competent physician. If you cannot cease to examine the patients, you will be dismissed—or worse."

"Worse?" Michaelmas asked.

"You risk excommunication by your actions," Father Anselm said. "And you risk lives. What if you made an error? Master James is continuing his inquiry into your behavior."

Michaelmas clasped her fingers in front of her, waiting for the priest to continue. She stole a glance at the doorway, where the two Highlanders still stood. Alice spoke to them, and the taller one waved her away briskly. They stood in the threshold like two powerful guardians. Michaelmas looked away, feeling oddly safe.

"We know that you secretly feel pulses and touch the limbs and torsos of both women and men," the priest said. "You look at the patients' private water in glass phials in the manner of a physician. This behavior is abhorrent to us."

"I have the right and the knowledge. You have seen my letters of diploma, signed by the master physicians of Bologna," Michaelmas said.

The prioress's mouth pursed haughtily. "You have some knowledge of the diseases of women and children, I admit. But you should never examine men as you do."

"And you argue with Master James over his treatments," Father Anselm went on. "He was educated in arts and medicine at both Oxford and Paris, and does not require your opinions."

"I assisted my husband in his medical practice," Michaelmas retorted. "Ibrahim Ibn Kateb had a fine reputation, and his medical treatises are well respected. He regarded me as an equal colleague. I hoped that you would honor that."

"That is vanity," Mother Agnes said. "And you are excessively stubborn. Both vices will cause you to make ignorant errors. We cannot allow you to practice anything here."

"Let me help," Michaelmas protested. "I came here to help."

"Sickness is a means of overcoming sinfulness," Father Anselm said. "Physicians are the instruments of God's forgiveness. Only the most skilled *men*"—he emphasized the word—"are worthy to be God's healers. Women commit errors through their vain, impulsive, and inconstant natures."

Mother Agnes nodded in agreement. "Offer your feminine gifts of compassion and service, as I do, and leave the treatments to qualified men."

"A report came to me," Father Anselm said. He scowled as he spoke. "While you were in Italy, you apparently laid your hands upon an ailing woman and called upon the power of God to come through you as divine healing. That shocking deed brought charges of heresy upon you."

"I did not do what they claimed," Michaelmas said stiffly. "That was years ago. The charges were cleared."

"The name 'Lady Miracle,' which you encourage among the patients, reveals your vanity," the prioress said. "Only God can perform miracles. Anything else is a heinous sin."

"How can any effort to heal be sinful?" Michaelmas asked. Her heart beat heavily as she resisted raw fear, stirred by the dark memories of her experiences in an Italian judicial court.

Since that time, she was careful to touch patients only to examine them. Ibrahim had repeatedly warned her never to use her healing gifts again, and to rely only on her medical skills. He had hoped that such restrictions would protect her. He had not understood her gift, and had urged her to abandon it.

And she had. These revived accusations were deeply hurtful. She had tried to forget the fear and pain in her past.

"Perhaps you believe yourself a saint," Mother Agnes remarked acidly.

"I am no more a saint than you," Michaelmas said angrily. "And I will thank you to keep your opinions to yourself." She whirled and walked away, her hands and knees trembling.

The tall Highlander still shadowed the outer doorway as she approached. His height and breadth, his

sheer powerful presence, blocked her exit. But she
kept on advancing.

Her gaze rose to meet his light eyes. They were the
color of storm clouds, or like the northern sea. His
glance pierced and held her own, as before. Then he
angled in the doorway to allow her passage.

"My pardon," he said. His voice was mellow and
hushed, like velvet wrapped around deep sound.

She pushed past him silently. Her shoulder brushed
against his wide, solid chest. He smelled of maleness
and wood smoke and fresh air, a robust blend of
strength and comfort and freedom.

Glancing back, she saw that he watched her steadily,
his cool gray eyes aware, as if he knew her well. She
gazed back at him, but did not slow her step. Startled,
she bumped into the second man, who hastily stepped
out of her way.

Michaelmas stalked past him into the courtyard.
Black wool flapped around her legs as she strode rapidly away from the common building and crossed the
yard. Fisting her hands, breathing like a bellows, she
headed into the wind, pushing through its force, glad
to feel it give way.

"She's overbold for a nun," Mungo said. The
woman had glided past them like an indignant queen,
head held high.

"She's no nun. Her brother said she was a widow."

"Widows take vows quick enough. Well, then, if
she's no nun, go speak to her. We could be heading
home right now." Mungo tapped a foot impatiently.
"Go on, man—though she looks to be a fearsome little
wench. She makes me quake. I would be afraid to ask
her the way to Perth, much less to come to Dunsheen
with us."

"I am not afraid of an angry little widow," Diarmid
said as he watched Michael cross the yard. Her wimple
and black surcoat flapped wide with the fury of her

retreat. She shoved at some bedsheets hanging on ropes, and disappeared behind them.

He recalled, from eleven years earlier, a gentle slip of a girl, flawless in form and spirit, who had knelt in the mud and chaos of a battlefield. He would not have seen that gifted child in the outspoken, temperamental woman who had just passed him.

But he would have recognized her eyes, blue and deep as a summer loch, edged in gold lashes, and he knew the hair bound under her veil would be pale as moonlight. He frowned, wondering what to say when he approached her.

"Go on, man," Mungo urged. "But I'll wait here." He leaned a shoulder against the wall. Diarmid turned and strode through the courtyard toward the flapping sheets.

Michaelmas yanked another clean, dry sheet off of the laundry rope and folded it with brisk, angry motions. She fumed as she grabbed, and thought, too late, of replies she should have made to the prioress and the priest in her own defense.

She had been a fool, she told herself, a dunce-headed fool, to come here to Saint Leonard's. How could she have thought that the English master physician and the hospital corporation of priests and surgeons—many of them English or English-trained— would respect her knowledge and her education? She might never be viewed as a *physicus* anywhere outside of Italy. Unlike France or England, women were allowed to study in Italian universities and were commonly awarded status as full physicians.

Apparently they were not regarded well in Scotland. She kicked at the basket and moved sideways to reach another sheet. Somehow—perhaps through a letter from the clergy of Bologna—Father Anselm had learned about the trial, so long ago in Italy.

She closed her eyes briefly against the ugly memories. She had never even told Gavin what had hap-

pened there. Ibrahim had assured her that the
experience would never haunt her again. But Ibrahim
was not here to protect her this time.

She folded the sheet vigorously, fighting tears. She
would have to go home after all, and relinquish her
dream of practicing her learned arts in Scotland. The
hospital corporation and the physicians' guild in Perth
had denied her a physician's license, offering her only
membership as a sister of the barber-surgeons' guild,
where she would be restricted to pulling teeth,
stitching cuts, and letting blood from those who did
not need it done.

Ibrahim would have helped her to fight. But she
could not do this alone. She no longer had the protection of his name and his reputation. Her husband had
provided, in their sunny apartments in Bologna, a
haven of books and stimulating discussions between a
student and a teacher, and later the equal respect of
a professional colleague. But he had never told her
that she would not find that kind of peace or freedom elsewhere.

And he had not told her that he was ill enough
to die.

She blinked away tears of old grief and frustration,
and yanked another sheet from the rope above her
head. Sighing heavily, she wished that she had never
come to this hospital. Her duties here could be per-
formed by any servant.

She pulled another sheet from the line, folded it,
then snatched at one more. And shrieked.

The tall, broad-shouldered Highlander stood behind
that sheet. Startled, Michaelmas dropped the clean
linen.

"What do you want?" she demanded, more harshly
than she had meant. Her heart pounded and her hands
shook, and she felt no inclination toward courtesy. He
tipped a brow at her silently, and bent to retrieve the
fallen sheet.

"Give me that," she said, and snatched the length

of linen away from him to shake the grass from it and fold it quickly. She dropped the cloth into the basket and looked up at him. "Why did you follow me out here? Be gone."

His lopsided, fleeting grin had a curious softening effect on her irritable mood. "I came for you," he said. His voice was compelling, fluid, and deep. "You are the healer I seek."

She stared up at him. "Healer?" she asked. "I am not an empiric healer, or an herbalist, or a midwife. I am a trained physician, but I am not licensed in Scotland. You must ask someone else."

"I did hear that you are a trained physician," he said.

"I have a certificate from a university in Italy." She lifted her chin defensively.

He tilted his head, watching her. Gray and clear, his eyes were like pieces of the silvery clouds behind him. His hair, the rich brown of chestnuts, roughened by tangles and in need of trimming, whipped about his head and shoulders in the brisk breeze. A few of the fine strands caught on his stubbled beard.

Sheets and towels fluttered and swung around him as he gazed at her steadily. Strength and determination emanated from his eyes, as well as from his confident, powerful stance.

"You must be a fine physician, indeed," he said quietly. "I want you to come with me."

She blinked. "Who are you? Did Gavin ask you to do this?"

"He did not. I am Diarmid Campbell of Dunsheen."

She narrowed her eyes. Then she gasped, a tiny inhalation of recognition, as she recalled a battlefield near Kinglassie. She had been but thirteen years old when she had watched a handsome young Highlander repair a bad wound in a man's leg. She remembered his graceful, capable hands and his deep concern for the man's welfare. She remembered how she had admired his skill.

Diarmid Campbell of Dunsheen had called her *Micheil* then, in a tender way that she had liked. He had watched her lay her hands on the wound and staunch the flow of blood. He knew about her gift. She felt her heart lurch uneasily.

But the tall, slender young surgeon she recalled had changed, matured into a handsome man, with a wild, barely restrained power that seemed more than muscular. His steel-colored eyes, his deep, quiet voice, were commanding, even intimidating.

She looked closer, at the tiny creases around his eyes and mouth. Over the years he had hardened, changed as much as she had. They were strangers, separated by the events and growth of years. But the bond of a single moment still linked them.

She read his awareness of that in his eyes, and looked away, busying herself with the laundry. "Greetings, Dunsheen."

"We met once, long ago," he said. "You must remember it."

She pulled down a towel and folded it. "I—I think so. You are a surgeon, are you not? I was very young."

He frowned. "Surely you recall more than that."

Panic gathered in her, squeezing her breath. She had strived for years to keep her gift secret. Fear rose in her like bile, and her hands shook as she worked.

"Diarmid Campbell of Dunsheen"—she spoke formally, haughtily, to subdue her fright—"what medical service do you need? Is your wife with child? Are your children ill, or do you have an elderly parent who needs an examination? We have a physician here, and nurses, and in the town there are many barber-surgeons." She heard herself babbling. Why had she said that? The man was surely a competent surgeon himself, and had no need of the guild.

"I have an ailing child," he said. "You can help her."

"A child?" She looked at him with interest, in spite

of her tumultuous thoughts. "Much of my study involved the diseases and conditions of childhood," she said, glad of an objective topic. "Is the child fevered, or injured? Did you bring the child here?" She glanced past him.

He folded his arms across his chest and looked down at her. A gust of wind picked up the hem of a sheet, which flapped over his chest. "She is at Dunsheen. She is unable to walk."

"How old is she?"

"Past five years."

She frowned. "Was it a birth injury, or has she been hurt? Surely someone has tended to her already."

"She has been seen by a physician and three herb-wives," he answered. "None of them have helped her, and none of them know what causes her ailment. You must look at her."

"Bring the child here, and I will examine her."

"I cannot bring her here. You will come with me."

"If Dunsheen is not far, I suppose I could—"

"It is in Argyll, in the western Highlands."

She stared up at him. "I cannot travel there with you!"

"You can. You will. I want her made whole again." His voice had a soothing quality despite his demanding words.

"No physician can guarantee a cure!"

"That is not what I want from you." His keen gaze held hers. "I need a miracle of you," he said softly.

Michaelmas stared at him. "A—a what?"

"A miracle." He said the word simply. Expectantly.

Chapter Three

"A what?" she asked again. Michael blinked up at him as if he were mad, or as if she were distinctly hard of hearing.

"A miracle," he said patiently. He saw, in her pinkening cheeks and the awareness in her blue eyes, that she knew exactly what he meant. He folded his arms over his chest and waited for her agreement.

She spun away to crease the sheet she clutched. "I am sorry your daughter has been injured. If you will bring her here to Saint Leonard's—"

"I will not," he said. He had no time to explain to her who Brigit was, or what the child had suffered. That would come later. "I will not have her poked or lanced or bled any further. I came here for you, *Micheil*. Only you can help her now."

"I do not understand what you mean," she said, her voice brittle. "Speak to Master James. He will be here in the afternoon to see the patients." She pushed through the fluttering row of sheets and towels.

He followed her with one long step and grasped her arm, spinning her so that her skirt swirled around her and her veil drifted over her cheek. She shook its folds back, lifted her head, and faced him. Her eyes were vivid blue.

Sheets and towels shifted around them in the wind, scented with lye, lavender, and cold air. The white walls enclosed them intimately. Michael gazed up at him, her breath heaving softly.

"Let go of my arm," she said.

"I came here for you," he said. "Only you can help Brigit."

"Any competent physician can help her. You do not need me."

"I do need you," he said, feeling a mounting desperation, although he was loath to show it.

"You have medical knowledge yourself," she argued.

"Not enough. I have examined her as thoroughly as I know how. But I can find no injury, no illness, only withered limbs."

She sighed. "Some there are who were never meant to walk," she said gently. "God works his will—"

He huffed impatiently. "Give me no lectures. Brigit will be well. You must see to it. You must," he added, unable to stop the soft plea. He still held her slim wrist in his hand, and could feel her rapid pulse beneath his fingers. She shook her head and tried to pull away, but he held her, firmly.

"Let me be!" she burst out.

He had not anticipated adamant refusal. He had expected a gentle young woman who would quietly agree. He had expected a saint. But she had a surprising dash of warrior spirit in her.

"Lay hands on her, Michael," he said. "You can heal her."

"What you demand is heresy. You are a madman!" she snapped. "The frenzied patients are kept in another building. I will have someone escort you there!" She jerked away from his grip. "Now leave me be!" Turning, she shoved at the laundry that blocked her way. Sheets flapped all around her as she pushed through.

Diarmid stepped after her, and watched her walk toward the common hall. She passed Mungo, who leaned against the wall. He straightened in surprise as she whisked past him.

She stepped over the shadowed threshold, and glanced back toward Diarmid. He held the white lin-

ens curtain-like and watched her as she turned away
and disappeared into the building.

Best to leave her alone for now, he told himself.
She would think about his request. He would come
back later and speak to her again. She might deny her
ability, but they both knew what she could do.

He had failed Brigit once before. He could not fail
her again. If he had to drag the little widow back to
Dunsheen cursing and kicking, he meant to do it.

Candlelight illumined the corner of the common
room, where Michaelmas sat by Jean's bed. Sounds of
breathing, both restless and peaceful, filled the large,
dim chamber. The hour was late, since the bell for
matins had chimed long ago.

After giving doses to the patients who needed medications and ointments, she had checked the surgery
patients again. One man was still fevered, and she
would watch him carefully, but the rest seemed content. With few exceptions, the patients in the common
hall were elderly and infirm rather than seriously ill,
and so the hours after midnight tended to be quiet.

She sighed, leaning her back against the wall as she
sat on a wooden bench beside Jean's bed. As she
watched golden candlelight flutter over the walls, she
heard Jean stir restlessly. Michaelmas glanced at her,
then relaxed when she was sure that the old woman
slept soundly.

After supper, when Jean had complained of pain in
her chest and arm, Michaelmas had been glad that she
had already agreed to sit with the patients in the night
hours. Marjorie or Alice would come later, but for
now she wanted to watch Jean more closely.

She closed her eyes and listened to the quiet sounds
around her. Varied snores mingled with the rush of
the outside wind. Across the room, one of the Highlanders mumbled in Gaelic in his sleep, and grew
quiet.

The soft language reminded her of Diarmid Campbell. She had thought of him often, astonished and alarmed by his impossible demand of her. He knew the secret that she guarded. If Father Anselm or the prioress discovered it, they could bring charges of heresy against her again. She could not endure that, particularly in her own homeland.

Fear gave her these thoughts, she told herself; surely that horror could never happen to her again. But if she went with Diarmid Campbell to his castle in the western Highlands, no one else would learn what he knew about her. She could examine the child, using only her medical knowledge, and propose a treatment. Then she would return to Gavin's home at Kinglassie.

Certainly she could no longer stay here at Saint Leonard's Hospital. Her dream of using her skills to help others had been rejected and ridiculed. She was not wanted here.

Shifting on the hard bench, she thought about sending word to her brother that she was ready to be escorted home to Kinglassie Castle. Diarmid Campbell had mentioned that Gavin had told him where to find her. Several weeks ago, her brother had sent a letter by messenger; at the time he had been somewhere in the Lowlands, traveling and fighting alongside the king.

Frowning, she tried to recall Gavin's last letter. Her brother had discussed at length the dilemma of Glas Eilean, her Highland property. Gavin had the king's permission to take the castle under his own control, but the captain who had held it for years refused to relinquish it. Gavin also mentioned that he would continue to look for a Highland laird to suit her—and the needs of that castle, she thought bitterly.

Gavin had received several offers for Michaelmas's hand in marriage since she had been widowed, from Highland chieftains, a Lowland knight in the king's service, and even an English baron. She had turned them all down, although she knew that her brother favored a Highland union for her.

She had never seen Glas Eilean Castle, but she
knew that its seaward position gave it great political
and strategic value. She was sure that any man interested in marrying her wanted Glas Eilean above all
else. But she had no interest in another marriage. As
a widow and a physician, she wanted a peaceful, inde-
pendent life in which to establish a practice. That path
had proven more difficult than she had thought, but
she did not care to give control of her life to a man
she might barely know.

At least she knew that Diarmid Campbell did not
intend to seek her hand—and her charter to a castle
in the Isles. He must be wed, since he was here only
to ensure his child's well-being. His fatherly devotion
was admirable, if his methods were unusual.

She could not erase from her mind the image of
him standing amid the white sheets, his stance powerful, his gray eyes like slices of shining steel. The aura
of force that surrounded him was undeniable. And if
the arrogance he had shown her was typical of him,
she had done well to refuse him.

Still, she had glimpsed in his eyes a deep vulnerability, and real kindness. His concern for the child stirred
her sympathy. She wanted to help the girl, but she
could never agree to—or accomplish—what he asked
of her.

Beside her, Jean shifted again, still restless. Michaelmas leaned forward and took the old woman's arm,
placing her fingertips lightly over the pulse in the
wrist. She counted silently, feeling the weak, erratic
pattern of beats.

Jean opened her eyes. "Lady—" she whispered.

Michaelmas smiled and set her arm down. "How do
you feel?"

Jean flexed her fingers uneasily on the blanket. "My
arm hurts . . . and my chest . . . " She rubbed at her
breastbone uneasily.

"Let me listen." Michaelmas bent forward and
placed her ear against Jean's chest, listening to the

sounds inside: an uncertain heartbeat and faint crackling noises in the lungs. "I'll fetch the infusion that Master James has prescribed for you," she said. "You've had a dose already this night, but another willna harm, and may help."

Jean touched her arm. "Och, lass," she said. "Someday soon the medicines willna help me, and I will go, and be glad." Her dark eyes were vivid. "My husband went long ago. I miss him."

Michaelmas watched her uncertainly. "Jeanie—"

"Give me yer hand." Michaelmas held her hand out. Cool, fragile fingers covered her own. "Listen to me—ye've a gift for healing, lass. I've felt it often in yer touch. Lady Miracle. 'Tis a proper name for ye."

"Jeanie, hush. Rest."

"I want to say this," Jean whispered. "I heard what they told ye today. Dinna let them frighten ye. I have a feeling about ye, lass. I think ye have a gift from heaven, and if so, it must be used."

"The only gift I have is my education and my training," Michaelmas replied. "I will fetch the medicines."

Jean squeezed her hand. "Deny it, but I know ye have it. My mother had a healing gift. She used to say that she always let heaven guide her in her healings. Remember that." She smiled, then drew a breath. "I'm tired, lass. And thirsty."

"I'll fetch water." Michaelmas rose, her thoughts whirling. How had Jean known about the healing touch? She crossed the room to a cupboard, where she took out a painted ceramic pot. Master James had prescribed an electuary for Jean, several herbs blended in syrup; to that, Michaelmas added a few drops of an infusion of foxglove. She ladled water from a bucket into a wooden cup, and returned to Jean's side. After Jean sipped the water and took the medicine, she laid back and soon slept.

Michaelmas sat silently beside her friend, aware that death might come soon, and sure Jean would welcome it peacefully. No method she knew, no herb would heal a failing, aging heart. Only time and heaven decided how much time remained. Ibrahim himself had told her what could be done—and what could not.

He had reminded her often that wisdom resided sometimes in doing little. A physician must be a careful judge, he had told her, and an extention of God's mercy. Death was not always to be feared, for it was sometimes a blessing.

She wished that her husband, with his calm ways and his deep fund of knowledge, could be here beside her. But he had been almost as old as Jean when he had succumbed to a similar disease of the heart. He too had been ready, although Michaelmas had not been ready to lose him.

Jean's words echoed in her mind, strangely in keeping with what had occurred already today. The Highlander had wanted a miracle from her hands, and the prioress had cruelly reminded her that she had once been accused of heresy for that very act.

Michaelmas had possessed the healing gift since childhood, inherited from her Scottish mother through an ancient Celtic bloodline that went back to Saint Columba. Gavin had the same unusual ability, although none but his wife and closest family members were aware of it.

Michaelmas had often felt the power sweep through her like a flood of warmth in her hands. Now she clenched her fingers tightly in her lap as if to stop any force that might gather there. She was not sure if the healing touch still existed in her, but enough fear rushed through her to banish any urge to use the gift.

Tears stung her eyes. She could not do as Jean advised, and just let heaven and the gift guide her. Over the years, she had deliberately neglected the heated force in her hands until she felt only a shadow of what once had been. She had replaced it with the educated, soothing touch of a physician.

Once, long ago, Gavin had told her of his struggle to accept his own healing ability. Michaelmas had been a young girl then, and had felt no such conflict within herself. Her own trial of spirit came later. She had never told Gavin about the trial or the awful terror that came afterward. He did even not know that she had promised Ibrahim to abandon the healing touch.

Leaning her face into her hands, she began to cry, a hot stream of tears for herself, for Jean. Her friend was wrong. The Highlander was wrong too. Lady Miracle did not exist.

He watched her though the shadows, as he leaned a shoulder against the wall just inside the door. She had not seen him slip into the common room, for she had been occupied mixing medicines and speaking with an old woman, a patient.

Earlier, he had overheard one of the novices mention that Lady Michael would sit with the patients after midnight. He had left his pallet—a plaid thrown on the ground beside his horse, outside the hospital enclosure—and had come here hoping to talk to her again, more peaceably this time.

She sat with the old woman, who slept now. Michael's face in candlelight was delicately planed, smooth as cream and roses. Her slight form and countenance were simple and serene; she was the image of a saint in that veil and black gown. He remembered her hair as a young girl, pale as moon glow, and longed to see it.

He frowned and admonished himself for letting his thoughts stray into fancy. He ached to talk to her, but he did not want anyone nearby to wake or listen. Perhaps he would wait until she left the room. This afternoon he had frightened her, but he meant to try again to convince her that he was no lunatic, and that he truly believed that she could heal Brigit.

He had to let her know how necessary she was to him, to Brigit. And he thought of his sister Sorcha, whose pain was not physical but of the heart, a tragic suffering that was a constant part of her life: one child after another, lost at birth. He wondered, standing in the shadows, if the little widow could bring her miraculous powers to Glas Eilean too, where Sorcha awaited the birth—and the loss—of yet another babe. No one could save those lost children, but perhaps Michael would know some way to heal his sister's grief.

But he had no time to explain all of this to her in ways she could understand, and he knew he lacked the talent to cajole and charm. Blunt, honest, direct— he was little more than that, he knew. No wonder he had frightened her. Sorcha, if she had known his plans, would have advised him how to phrase every statement tactfully and graciously. Not that he could carry any of it out on his own.

He sighed, determined to try his best to make Michael see his sincerity and his total belief in her power to heal. Once he had been a healer too, but with other means—surgery, bonesetting, wound repair. All that had been eliminated from his life with one vicious swipe of an Irish broadsword.

He saw Michael drop her face into her hands as if she sobbed. Startled, disturbed, he moved out of the shadows on an impulse to comfort her. Then he stepped back, realizing the foolishness of that desire. He would likely only frighten her more deeply.

A creaking noise brought his attention to the far end of the room. The two young novices entered and came toward Michael, who hastily wiped her teary eyes and rose to meet them. Diarmid drew back and stayed still. After speaking to the two girls quietly, Michael walked the length of the room and lifted her cloak from a wall peg. She passed by his blackened corner without a glance—he could have touched her sleeve, and smelled the faint scent of roses and mint as she went by. She opened the door and stepped outside into the moonlight.

He slipped out after her, hoping for an opportunity to meet her as if by chance. But the courtyard was not empty, despite the late hour. A group of monks were on their way to the chapel, and one of them stopped to talk with Michael.

Diarmid watched from the shadowed overhang of an arcaded walkway. Michael walked quickly past him again and went into the wide doorway of a low building, probably the women's sleeping quarters. He waited, saw no light, and ran around behind the building, where he saw a candle flame flare in a ground-story window.

He did not like skulking about in shadows. He preferred honesty and a straightforward approach, but he did not wish to cause a scene with her in the middle of the moonlit courtyard. The woman had him doing things he never would have dreamed of—begging for miracles and hiding in corners like a lovesick boy, desperate for a chance to speak with her.

He had spoken his mind to her already, approaching the matter as he generally did, stating his request logically and expecting agreement. Knowing that trait for a fault at times, he was not certain how to summon the tact he needed for this delicate, important task.

He would just have to blunder ahead and hope for the best.

Michaelmas felt as if someone watched her, and she spun quickly. The monks had gone on to the chapel, and she saw only vague night shadows beneath a bright moon. As she reached the women's dormitory, which housed the nuns, servants, and noblewomen who stayed here, she slipped inside and shut the door, making her way down the dark corridor to her own small cell.

Sighing loudly, she lit a candle from a glowing coal in the hot brazier and set it on the small table beside her bed. She thought about resting, longed to, but felt too agitated for sleep just now. Too much had happened today. She began to pace the small, square

chamber, passing her narrow bed and the carved
wooden chest that held her belongings.

Her skirts swung softly as she went to the window
and unlatched the leather loop that held the shutters
closed. Blue moonlight and cold air spilled into the
room as she looked out over the hospital gardens and
the low enclosing wall that surrounded the complex.
A chilly breeze ruffled her linen wimple, but the cold
felt good, fresh and stirring.

She sank down upon her flat bed, feeling weary but
anxious, wondering if she would be able to sleep at
all tonight. She had decided to leave Saint Leonard's,
a decision she should have made long ago, if she had
not been so determined to gain her license.

Now she wondered how soon she could get a message to Gavin. But she would have to know where he
was to do that. Kneeling, she opened the lid of her
wooden chest and reached inside to find the casket
that held her correspondence.

After Ibrahim's death, she had sold the house with
all of its books and furnishings, and had left Bologna
with only this large, carved chest. The smell of cedar
reminded her of her home in Italy. She bit her lip
against the memories and ran her hands through
stacks of folded clothing layered with dried roses, over
the casket holding her few pieces of jewelry, and over
bundles of steel and iron instruments wrapped in silk
and wool, as she searched for the small silver casket
that held her letters and papers.

Several books filled the bottom of the chest, their
leather covers protected by silk cloths. She had read
and studied each volume countless times. Touching
the largest book, she blinked back tears, missing
Ibrahim and his wise counsel.

She would have to help herself now to make a new
life. She found the silver box that contained Gavin's
last letter. She tilted the parchment page toward the
candlelight and squinted at the French words, shaped
in Gavin's precise writing hand. His calm personality

seemed to exist in those small letters, quiet and comforting and capable.

Quickly scanning the letter, she read again his mention of the captain of Glas Eilean, Ranald MacSween,
who had refused to give up his position. Gavin had
sent men there by sea to take over the fortress until
Michaelmas married. But his sergeant had been killed
in a battle at sea below the cliffs of Glas Eilean, and
the rest of his men had retreated.

"I have sent word to Ranald MacSween to abandon
the castle," Gavin wrote, "or I will come there myself
with a contingent of men to dissuade him. I am not
free to do so just now, for the king commands me
elsewhere. But I pray that this man understands that
the wrath of his king will turn toward him if he refuses
me access to my sister's castle."

She gripped the page and read on. She did not want
Gavin to risk his life over some remote castle, and its
more remote role in her life. She would give away
that castle if she could, for it only caused men to fight
and die, and at the least made strangers hungry to
marry her just to gain control over its cliffs, which
faced the southern approach to the Isles.

Running her gaze down the lines, she searched for
some hint of how to reach Gavin. But he only said
that he was still in the Borderlands with the king and
would not be free to ride to Glas Eilean for weeks,
perhaps months.

Her fingers trembled as she replaced the letter in
the casket and closed the lid of the great wooden
chest. She stood, her back to the open window. The
chill night breeze felt crisp, cutting through the fog of
fear and confusion in her mind.

She undid the linen wimple and veil pinned around
her head, with its pleats and snug chin covering that
denoted her widowhood. Then she took off the gold
brooch pinned to the shoulder of her surcoat. The
piece was quite old, a beautiful circlet of knotwork
gold with a straight cross pin, studded with small gar-

nets and sapphires. Gavin and his wife Christian had
found the brooch in a horde of ancient gold, hidden
deep inside Kinglassie Castle. She had treasured the
pin since childhood as a symbol of home and safety
and love, thinking of it as her own luck charm.

She sighed as she laid it down, thinking that the luck
in the golden brooch would have to be quite strong to
help her find the home and safety and acceptance she
longed for in her life.

She slipped out of her black surcoat and black serge
gown—common dress for a widow in Italy, though
not so common here—and stood in her long-sleeved
chemise of heavy, creamy silk, and her low leather
boots. Each movement was deliberate and calm, as if
this was any other night when she readied for a few
hours' rest after staying late in the ward.

But her heart beat in a heavy, panicked rhythm.
She did not know what she should do on the morrow.
She wanted to send word to Gavin as soon as she
could, for she did not feel that she could stay here
peacefully much longer. Perhaps she should send word
to Kinglassie instead, and ask her mother to send a
friend or a servant to come for her.

Striving to calm herself by focusing on one small
task at a time, she undid the tousled braids pinned
over her ears and combed her fingers through until her
long tresses slipped, pale and sleek, over her shoulder.

"*Micheil.* Here, at the window." The voice was deep
and soft, the words Gaelic.

She jumped, deeply startled. Spinning, she saw a
large shadow at the open window.

Diarmid Campbell, his head and broad shoulders
framed by the simple arched window, looked at her
in the moonlight.

"Michael," he whispered. "Come here."

Chapter Four

"What are you doing here?" she whispered. She went to the window and swung the shutter wide. Her window faced the back of the hospital enclosure, on a ground level, so that Diarmid had no difficulty looking inside. She scowled at him.

"I wanted to talk to you," he answered, with the same calm manner he had displayed in the courtyard. Then, too, he had made an outrageous statement as if it was ordinary.

She gaped at him. "In the middle of the night?"

"Go to the door," he murmured, and was gone. She leaned forward to peer through the window, and saw him disappear around the corner of the building.

She ran to the door and waited, hands pressed against the wood, her heart thumping. Within moments she heard a soft knock. She unlatched the door and opened it a crack.

"Let me in," Diarmid said.

"Be gone," she hissed. "You are mad."

"*Ach,* I will not harm you. I need to speak with you."

"Speak through the door. Or go back to the window."

"Will you have everyone listen, then?" he asked. "The monks are on their way back from chapel."

Sighing in exasperation, sensing his sincerity and recalling that he was a friend of her brother, she let him enter the room. His wide shoulders and wider stance seemed to fill the small cell as she shut the door behind him.

Aware that she was clad only in the silk chemise, she folded her arms over her breasts and watched him uncertainly, suddenly afraid, wishing she had not let him in so quickly. But impulse and a tendency to trust too easily had always been flaws in her character.

He moved toward her. She stepped back. "What do you want?"

"I want you to come with me."

She nearly laughed, not in mirth but in frustration at his bold stubbornness. "I have already refused you. And I have decided to leave here as soon as my brother can fetch me home. I will be going to Kinglassie, not the western Highlands."

"I can offer you an escort."

She lifted her brows, intrigued. She had not thought of that. If she could leave with him, she would be home in a matter of days. "If you mean that, wait until I send word to Gavin and let him know where I am going, and with whom."

"I mean to leave now."

"In the middle of the night, like a thief?"

"Just in a hurry to be home," he answered. He kept his hands fisted on his plaid-draped hips, his wide-spaced legs knotted with muscle in the dim light. He reached past her, grabbed her black gown, and tossed it to her. "Get dressed. I have decided to take you out of here."

She clasped the woolen garment to her chest. "Take yourself out of here—*ach!*" She glanced toward the door and saw the other Highlander peering around the edge. She glared at him. He blinked at her and at Diarmid, who growled low, and then the man closed the door hastily. "Both of you be gone from here!"

"I heard what the prioress and priest said to you today," he began. He tipped his head and looked down at her. "You have some trouble here, it seems. They do not care about your welfare."

"And you do?"

"I do," he said firmly. "And I offer you a chance to do as much healing as you like. Go on, get dressed." He gestured.

She lifted her chin defiantly. "I will not go with you."

He folded his arms, and let his glance travel slowly down her body and up to her face. "Will you not? Your brother would be glad to know I took you out of a situation where people mean you harm. You are not safe here."

"I am hardly safer with a lunatic Highland man!"

"Well," he drawled, "if you wish a hearing and the threat of excommunication, then certainly stay."

He could not know the effect those words had on her. She felt an immediate urge to run out of here with him. But she only shot him a cool, silent glare and yanked the heavy gown hastily over her head, thrusting her arms through the sleeves. She would not stand half naked in front of this man any longer. He handed her the surcoat, and she pulled that on too, and turned to find the golden brooch and pin it to her shoulder. Then she picked up her wimple and began to fold it over her hair.

"Tcha," he said, a soft sound of reproval. "Do not cover your hair. Like moonlight itself, it is."

She paused, startled by his surprisingly gentle words, then hastily draped and pinned the wimple and veil over her loose hair, then settled a band of braided black silk over the crown of her head before she faced him. "And what makes you think that I would leave with you?" she asked, determined not to give in so easily—although she was sorely tempted.

He slid her a glance without comment, then crossed the small room in two long steps and lifted her hooded black cloak from a wooden peg on the wall. He returned and dropped it over her shoulders, and stood so close that she felt his warmth in the dark, heard his quiet breath.

"How do you think to get word to your half brother if you stay?" he asked, keeping a hand on her shoulder as if to escort her out momentarily.

She stared up at him. "You can bring word to Gavin. You know where he is. I will wait here."

"Come with me," he said.

"I will not leave in the night like a criminal."

"Would you stay here and be accused like one?" She blinked up at him, disconcerted by the truth in his words, and uncertain how to answer. "Michael." His fingers pressed her shoulder. Her heart thumped at the vivid contact of his warm fingers. "Listen to me. This is a hospital and a house of charity. But the people here suspect you already. If they discover what you can do—" He drew a breath. "Come with me."

She watched him, held there by his light, gentle touch. He stood over her like a tall, broad, commanding shadow. Moonlight cascaded over his shoulders and glinted through his tangled dark hair. He seemed somehow unreal, a handsome, magical warrior conjured from moonlight and promises to save her.

"Michael," he murmured. "Come with me."

The strange spell of the moment held its force. She did not answer. Then she looked away, breaking the lure of his touch and his penetrating gaze. She wanted to go, fearing he was right, and yet the thought of fleeing with this wild Highlander was foolish. Sending for Gavin was the most sensible course.

"I will stay," she said finally. "Be gone."

Diarmid sighed slowly, half turning. Then he swore under his breath and spun, scooping her up and over his shoulder like a sack of beans. She gasped out as air was knocked from her lungs.

In the time she needed to regain her breath, he stepped to the door, kicked it open, and strode outside. She gathered a scream and let it burst forth.

Just as she uttered the cry, the bell for lauds began to ring, drowning her out. She pummeled at Diarmid's back as he carried her through the moonlit yard and around the corner of the building toward the low wall that surrounded the hospital enclosure. There he set her on her feet.

Before she could scream again, the other man grabbed her from behind and clapped a large hand over her mouth. "Hush, now, Mistress Physician, if you will," he whispered. "We do not mean to harm you."

She struggled while he held her, and looked wildly past him to see Diarmid Campbell throw a length of thick wool over her head. Swathed in darkness, she grunted in surprise as Diarmid grabbed her up again and threw her over his shoulder.

She arched and kicked ineffectually at him. The arm around her legs fit like an iron band, and the hand that steadied her lower back was just as strong. Trussed upside down like a side of beef, struggling against the smoke-scented plaid that cut off fresh air, her efforts soon exhausted her.

A series of bumps and shifts told her that Diarmid had climbed the low stone wall and was striding down the slope away from the hospital. She struggled again, and screamed.

"Hush, girl," he said. "Hush."

She did not. She began to utter full-bodied curses in Arabic culled from Ibrahim's servant man, whose oaths and condemnations, uttered to vendors, had taught her a great deal. She was surprised at her own vehemence.

"I do not understand what you say, girl," Diarmid said, sounding amused, "but I can feel the sting of it."

"I said you have the breath of a camel and the heart of a snake," she hissed.

"Tcha," he said, and strode on. She thought he laughed.

"I told you she makes me quake," his friend said.

Diarmid began to lope, an easy running stride that pushed his shoulder into her midsection and forced the breath rhythmically out of her.

Within moments she felt herself lifted onto a saddle
and seated sideways, her knee resting on the saddle
pommel. The horse shifted beneath her as Diarmid
secured her to the saddle with ties around her waist.
Nearby, another horse shuffled and snorted as Diarmid mounted into the saddle.

When the other man yanked away part of the plaid,
she gasped in fresh, cold air. Her horse stepped forward, led by the second man, who held the reins and
walked ahead.

Twisting to look over her shoulder, she saw that
they had descended the long slope and now crossed
the valley. The eerie brilliance of the moonlit sky revealed the glittering river and steep hillsides that
soared to each side.

Diarmid rode beside her, his profile clean and
strong in the moon glow. She glared at him.

"I am not merchant's goods to be stolen away!"
she snapped.

His glance was sharp. "And I am no thief."

"No thief, but a lunatic!"

The man who walked chuckled. "*Ach,* that's the
physician's word on you, Dunsheen," he called over
his shoulder. "I've told him the same myself, I have,
Mistress Physician."

"And you are no better, for helping him," she
said pointedly.

He looked hurt, tugged at the reins, and walked on.

"*Ach,* go light on Mungo," Diarmid said. "He only
did what I asked."

"You asked him to help steal me away like a sack
of meal?"

"Well, some of it was his idea," he admitted.

"Is he your brother?" she asked, watching Mungo's
long back and strong legs as he loped ahead of her
horse, reins in hand.

"A cousin, and a good friend."

"And a *gille-ruith* whenever he needs one,"
Mungo added.

She glanced at Diarmid. "Your runner? Are you a chieftain of the Campbells, to have your own ghillie?"

"A laird in Clan Diarmid, which some call Clan Campbell," he explained. "Mungo's MacArthur kin have long been ghillies for the lairds of Dunsheen. He carries messages for me, and accompanies me when I travel."

"Then this is his horse I ride," she said.

"No matter, mistress," Mungo called back to her. "I can run the way to Dunsheen, and be no worse for it."

"How far is that?" she asked Diarmid.

"The width of Scotland and north. Loch Sheen lies along the western coast near the Firth of Lorne."

"But such a journey could take days," she said. She knew the area only because Gavin had once drawn a map to show her the location of Glas Eilean, which lay off the Isle of Isla in the lower Hebrides, near islands held mostly by MacDonalds and Campbells.

"Mungo and I travel quickly," Diarmid said. "I hope you are a sturdy rider."

Alarmed by the prospect of traveling across the Highlands with them, she glanced over her shoulder. The dark silhouette of the hospital on the hill was fading. Her sojourn there, as frustrating as it had been, was finished—and her future was wholly uncertain with the Highlanders.

"I want you to take me to Kinglassie in Galloway," she said, trying to sound firm. "My brother will reward you well."

Diarmid hardly blinked an eye. "I did not collect you to trade you for gold. You'll come with me to Dunsheen. That is my price for rescuing you."

"Rescuing me! I was not in danger!"

"You would have been soon enough," he answered smoothly.

She fought rising panic, the result of fatigue and her mounting apprehension. "But I cannot go with you to Dunsheen Castle!"

He glanced at her. "Have you another commitment?"

"You do not have my consent to do this!"

"You have been rescued or escorted, whichever you prefer, not stolen. I mean to hire your services. What is the current fee charged by physicians in Perth? A few shillings for a visit, or a retainer of several pounds a year?"

She blinked at him. "Fee?"

"Fee," Diarmid said.

Mungo looked back. "I heard that King Robert pays an Edinburgh apothecary seven pounds a year to tend to him," he said. "That is a high fee, but Dunsheen Castle has plenty of work for a physician." He turned away.

"Seven pounds Scots a year, then," Diarmid said, sounding satisfied. "Do you want it all in one sum, or in portions?"

"Seven pounds a year!" she exclaimed.

"Not enough? Eight, then, for whatever part of a year you stay in order to complete the task," Diarmid said. "That is very generous of me. It should take you only a few moments, after all."

She thought he teased her, but she could not tell, for he kept his eyes on the dark moonlit path ahead. She glanced from one man to the other. "Mungo, what do you mean by saying that there is plenty of work for a physician? Is there a hospital near Dunsheen?"

"One might think so," Mungo drawled.

"*Ach,*" Diarmid growled, and sent Mungo a sour glance before looking at Michaelmas. "I have one healing task for you," he said. "More, if you want. And I will pay whatever you ask."

"I told you I cannot—"

"And I will take you wherever you wish to go when it is done. Is it agreed?"

"But what you want of me cannot be done."

"I told him the same," Mungo said helpfully. "We've all told him to accept that the child is lame for life, but Dunsheen is a stubborn man and will listen to no one."

"Mungo, *dùin do chlab,*" Diarmid said. "Shut your mouth, my friend, and let me talk to the woman without your thoughts on the matter." He looked at Michaelmas. "What is it you want in return?"

She gaped at him. "Want? You have taken me away against my will, in the dark of the night, with no one the wiser, and with nothing but the clothes I wear."

"Then you must want for something," he said reasonably.

She shifted her shoulders, still trapped beneath the folds of the plaid. "My freedom."

He tipped his head politely. "You are not a prisoner. You are an employed physician."

She sighed. Each step the horses took brought her closer to the unknown. She lacked even a fresh gown. If Diarmid Campbell truly meant to take her to his home to act as a physician there, then, without her chest of belongings, she also lacked the practical means to use her skills.

"My books and my instruments are at Saint Leonard's. I need them," she said, and lifted her chin high. "You took me out of there, and so you can go back to fetch what I left behind."

"You will not need charts and tools," Diarmid said.

"I need them," she insisted, "and you must get them for me. I can hardly go back myself, for as you have pointed out, there may be danger there." She hoped that he would turn and ride back; she thought she could persuade Mungo to let her go.

"*Ach,* she speaks like a *ban-righ,* this one," Mungo said. "A queen." He tipped his head in a gesture of admiration.

Diarmid looked intently at Michaelmas. "Is it part of your fee that these belongings be fetched?"

She watched him warily through the darkness, growing more certain that she had little chance of gaining her freedom from this man. But if she agreed to tend

to his child, she would need the information contained
in her books and notes. And Ibrahim's volumes had
great value to her, both personally and in terms of
her profession; if her possessions remained at the hospital, the master physician would take them for
himself.

"Is it part of your fee?" he repeated.

She had no choice. The books were irreplaceable.
"It is."

He nodded and turned. "Mungo."

Mungo sighed. "I know, I know. Women must have
their things," he said, sounding resigned. "Where are
these books that you cannot do without, Mistress Michael the Physician?"

"In my cell," she said. "There are books, instruments, and clothing in a large wooden chest."

"All that?" Mungo looked doubtfully at Diarmid.

"Go to the castle near Perth, on the north side of
the Tay," Diarmid said, reaching up to unfasten the
silver brooch at his shoulder. "The Scots hold it. Show
this to the laird there. He is a friend, and will know
the cairngorm brooch of the laird of Dunsheen. Tell
him that you require a horse to ride and a sturdy
packhorse, and he will see that you get them."

"And how am I to get a great chest out of the
women's sleeping quarters without being seen?"

"You will manage the task somehow, I have no
doubt. Farewell to you, man." Diarmid held up his
hand.

Mungo muttered something under his breath and
handed Diarmid the reins to guide Michaelmas's
horse. "Farewell to you both. Give my greetings to
my children, Dunsheen."

"I will."

"My thanks, Mungo," Michaelmas said. "I will remember this favor of you." The man nodded, then
launched into a smooth, long running stride as he
struck out across the valley.

Diarmid held the reins of Michaelmas's horse

loosely in his left hand, and rode slightly ahead of her beneath the high white moon. The soft thuds of the horses' footfalls and the sweep of the wind filled the silence as they crossed the valley.

Michaelmas watched Diarmid as he rode; his back, long and agile, rocked with the motion of his horse, his dark hair blew freely. He seemed content to ignore her as she followed behind him, and that irritated her unreasonably.

She shifted stiffly to maintain her balance, still bound to the saddle pommel by a rope around her waist. Her arms were snug at her sides and her right leg ached from keeping her seat on the horse. "Diarmid of Dunsheen," she called. "You did say that I was not a prisoner."

He stopped both horses and leaned over to undo the rope and the heavy plaid. "There," he said, tossing the long cloth behind her saddle, "you're free. And now that I have your promise to come to Dunsheen, I trust you will ride beside me willingly."

Michaelmas bit back her first answer, born of a little flare of anger. She had heard of Highland arrogance, but she had met few men from so far north as this one—and none as infuriating.

"I will go with you," she said. "But that is the only promise I make."

He gathered the reins and looked over at her. "I see that you understand what is at risk here."

She felt anger sear again. "And what exactly is that?"

"Your chest of books," he said easily, and launched forward.

Chapter Five

Diarmid sat back on his heels and watched Michael sleep. She lay curled in the plaid on a slope of old heather, sunk deep in the silvery stems as if they were a feather mattress. His spare green-and-black plaid swathed most of her, while a few locks of her hair streamed free, as bright and pale as the dawn sky above.

He wanted to touch those silky strands again. After she had slipped off into an exhausted sleep, he had wrapped her in the plaid and had removed her linen wimple. He remembered the wondrous feel of her hair, like fresh spring air woven into silk.

He looked away, flexing his stiff, disfigured left hand thoughtfully, and used a stick to flip several oatcakes sizzling on an iron griddle. He had made the flat cakes from oats and salt that he carried with him when traveling, mixing them thoroughly with water so that they would be agreeably chewy. He had flinted a stone against the edge of his blade for a fire, so that the girl would not have to eat her morning meal uncooked. And he had been careful not to burn the cakes.

He expected a noblewoman such as she was to turn up her elegant nose at them, but they were food, and filling, and all he could offer. At least he had not mixed fresh blood into them, drawn from the legs of the cattle that grazed nearby. He was certain she would not eat a cake of that sort.

A lark flew overhead, its trilling call echoing

through the crisp dawn air. The girl stirred, gazing at Diarmid through sleepy, half-lidded eyes.

"Good morning to you," he said, and turned an oatcake.

Michael grunted softly, sucked in a breath, and sat up. Her hair, gold spun with silver, hung limp in her eyes; when she shoved it back, it slid down again. She smiled faintly, glancing at him and away. Diarmid pinched back a smile. Half awake, her natural temperament unguarded, she had an innocence that was far more appealing and natural than the indignance she had showed him the previous day.

"I must have been tired last night," she said, her voice thick and a little hoarse. She looked around, frowning. "I do not recall stopping here. Where are we?"

"Dunsheen Castle is a full day's ride to the west— two in poor weather. And I doubt you remember stopping," he added. "You nearly fell off your horse in exhaustion before set of sun. I carried you here."

She ran her fingers through her tousled hair, then stood, gathering the plaid around her. She seemed to hesitate. Diarmid understood what she needed.

"Over the hill will do," he said, turning the cakes. "None there to see you but a few cattle, and no herder." She nodded and walked up the hill to disappear over its rounded crest.

Diarmid removed the griddle from the fire and set it on a rock so that the cakes could cool. He went down the hill to the narrow stream at its base, and drank, filling a skin flask with fresh water before returning to the campfire.

Michael descended the slope, passing him wordlessly. He watched as she knelt by the stream, rinsed her face, and rose to her feet. The first rays of dawn gilded the top of her head like new gold, and glinted along the length of her hair as she deftly made two plaits and bound them over her ears. Then she wrapped the headdress over all. Diarmid felt a sense of disappointment, as if a light had been extinguished.

He scratched his whiskered chin, aware that he too needed to wash, and more, needed a shave and clean clothing. He took one of the hot oatcakes and bit into it deeply. When Michael came near, he gestured toward the food with one hand, his mouth full.

She sat demurely, arranging her black skirts around her before choosing a cake. Nibbling at it with even white teeth, she chewed slowly. He wondered if the food was too coarse for her tastes, or too ill prepared.

Diarmid finished his cake quickly, and devoured a second in the time it took her to nibble through half of hers. He wiped his hands on his plaid and looked at her.

"If you do not care for oatcakes, I am sorry," he said. "I had only that. A simple meal, quick and easy to carry."

She swallowed. "The cake is good," she said. "And I am glad you did not use blood in the mix."

He lifted a brow. "You know that trick?"

She nodded as she broke off a small piece. "I am from Galloway. The people there are more Highland than Lowland. I have probably eaten as many oatcakes as you have." She popped the bit into her mouth and chewed.

He tilted his head slightly. "I would have thought you were accustomed to fine-milled white bread, roast swan, and new ale every morning. And rose water to wash your fingers, and linen napkins for your mouth."

She wrinkled her nose, and swallowed again. "Oats and water will do fine, thank you," she said. "Finely milled bread lacks grit to aid digestion. Roast swan is greasy and can cause gout and stomachache when eaten too often, and new ale every morning can ruin the liver. And Highland water is excellent for hand washing as well as drinking."

"Ah," he said, leaning back on his elbows. "I nearly forgot. You are indeed a physician."

"I am," she said. "And the best guarantee of health is a careful diet. If everyone were careful how they ate, there would be far less work for physicians. You should avoid cattle blood in your oats, Dunsheen. Animals can carry bad humors in their blood, just as humans can."

"I will try to remember that," he murmured. "So they taught rules of diet in this Italian school you attended? What else?"

"Anatomy, diseases, mathematics, astronomy, philosophy—" she stopped, and shrugged. "But you know as much about those subjects as I do, I suppose."

He raised a brow in mild surprise. "Do I?"

"You are a trained surgeon."

He glanced away. "I am not a book-taught, academic *medicus*. And besides, I do no surgery now."

She frowned. "But I saw you work. You were well trained. You have a gift for—"

"Some gifts do not last," he said curtly, and rose to his feet. "Come. We have far to ride today." He held out his left hand to help her up.

His outstretched fingers trembled, and the scars on his wrist and thumb were shiny in the dawn light. In that moment, he realized that he had unwittingly revealed to her why he did no more surgery. Pride alone kept his fingers extended.

She laid her slim fingers gently on his palm and looked up at him, her blue gaze quiet, searching, sympathetic, but without pity. He pulled her to her feet and let go, turning away. Silent and thoughtful, Michael brushed bits of heather from her skirt and gathered the remaining oatcakes.

Diarmid kicked at the small campfire with more force than necessary to extinguish it, as if a few blows could destroy old hurts, old memories. Then he walked away through the silvery heather stems to ready the grazing horses for travel.

*   *   *

After hours of consistent bouncing on the stiff
leather saddle, her bottom felt numb. Michaelmas
shifted uncomfortably and decided that the broad warrior's saddle beneath her was unsuited to a side position. Just now she would like nothing better than to
walk the rest of the way to Dunsheen. She was unused
to long hours on a horse.

She shifted her hips again, and thought longingly of
the comfortable saddle she had owned in Italy, of
carved wood covered with padded, tooled leather,
hung with bells and ribbons and trimmed in silver.
That and a graceful Arabian horse had been given to
her by an Italian duke whom Ibrahim had treated.

But all of that was gone, sold with the rest of their
things, part of her past. She had come back to Scotland to begin a new life among the people and in the
land that she loved best.

Then she sighed, thinking what a poor beginning
she had made in Scotland. She had planned to be a
licensed physician by now, with a few rooms in the
town, ready to build a flourishing practice for women
and children especially.

Now she had no idea in which direction her life
would turn. She looked at Diarmid, who rode just
ahead of her, cutting a path through the deep autumn
grasses that covered the moors. He would determine,
at least for a while, her future.

He galloped ahead, moving easily, as if he shared
sinew and bone with his black horse, both of them
agile, muscled, lean and dark. With a broadsword
thrusting out of the leather sheath at his back, his wild
mass of dark hair, and his body clothed in the thick
folds of the green-and-black plaid, he was the image
of savagery, a man sprung from the race of legendary
wild men said to exist in unexplored parts of the
world.

The Lowland Scots called the people of the northern hills savages and Wild Scots. Looking at Diarmid
Campbell, she understood why. But she also knew that

there was another side to the wild Highlander, and the contrast intrigued her. He was an intelligent, educated man, and had been a capable surgeon.

She frowned, glimpsing his left hand, where he held the leather reins lightly. The scars she had seen were the remnants of an old injury. Without closer examination she could not be sure, but the damage appeared to inhibit his finger agility.

Likely a battle injury, she thought, and pressed her lips together in sympathy. Sad and ironic that he had suffered such a wound. He likely had the strength to grip a sword or a tool, but he might lack the finer skills needed for delicate surgical work.

As she watched him, he suddenly turned and looked directly at her. His gray gaze was so intense, even at a distance, that she lowered her eyes as if to protect her thoughts. Then he turned and galloped onward. The ease and speed with which he rode made her long to move with the same freedom.

As a child in the hills of Galloway, she had known such freedom while playing with her closest friends, all lads, and her younger half brothers. With them, she had ridden astride, climbed trees and castle walls, had sworn mighty oaths, and had fought mock battles with wooden swords. But her years in Italy as the wife of a prominent man had changed her in countless ways. She had lost her spontaneous nature, always conscious of the proper behavior for a lady and a professional *medicus*.

But this brief journey alongside Diarmid Campbell had affected her unexpectedly. The scent of autumn grasses, of heather and pine and clear water, the sweep of the crisp Highland air against her skin, had stirred wonderful memories of the simple happiness she had known as a child.

Watching Diarmid ride ahead, she decided to reclaim at least one of her Scottish ways or be left behind. Yanking her skirts above her knees, she swung her right leg over the saddle and found the stirrups with her feet. Balanced lightly on the horse's back, she leaned forward and rode into the wind.

She caught up to Diarmid in moments, her black cloak whipping out and the skirts of her surcoat and gown fluttering over her bare thighs. The veil and wimple sagged, and she snatched them off, feeling her braids tumble down. The chilly breeze stung her cheeks. As she neared Diarmid and reined in the horse, she laughed aloud, thrilled by those few wild, abandoned moments.

Diarmid turned and slowed, watching her as she approached. His gaze traveled down her body to her legs, encased in black woolen hose gartered above her knees, and then up, taking in her face and pale, untidy hair. He tilted his head leisurely.

"You know how to ride properly after all, I see," he said.

She sobered in an instant, pulling her skirts down to cover her legs and shoving back her hair. "I rode straddle as a child," she answered, glancing away from his compelling gaze toward the steep, rugged hills and the misted blue mountains far beyond them. "How far is Dunsheen from here?"

"At the foot of that tallest mountain," he answered, pointing at a distant peak. "We'll arrive after set of sun. I assume you would rather ride in the dark than spend another night in the hills." He urged his horse forward in a steady canter. Michaelmas pressed her knees into her own mount, keeping pace.

As they rode, she watched the pale ring of clouds that covered the highest mountaintop, and wondered what waited beneath those slopes. She wondered too who else lived at Dunsheen with Diarmid and his little injured daughter. And she wondered if Diarmid Campbell's wife knew that he had gone to fetch a healer for their child.

"Does your family know that you mean to bring another healer to Dunsheen?" she asked.

"My family?"

"Your wife, your kin."

He watched the pathway. "They do not know that I went to Perth to fetch you. I have been in the Lowlands with the king's troops for nearly three months. But my kin will not be surprised that I have hired another healer."

"You have not hired me," she said. "I come willingly."

He laughed, short and curt. "Is that what you call it? As I remember, you accused me of abduction— several times."

"Well, you did neglect to ask for my services," she pointed out. "You ordered me to come with you, and then took me out of the hospital like a sack of meal, without courtesy."

"You were in trouble," he said firmly, "and I saw the need to remove you. I was not going to bother with bowing and waiting on your will. That may do in Italy or France, but in the Highlands, we deal directly with matters." He glanced at her. "And do not forget that I sent Mungo back for your things when *you* made a demand of *me,* without much courtesy yourself. And I did not burn your breakfast," he added. "All that is courtesy enough, I think."

"You deal with matters like a warrior," she said. "But I am not one of your soldiers to command."

He smiled slightly. "I have heard it said that all physicians are warriors against pestilence and injury and death."

"That may be, but I am accustomed to respect."

He slid her a glance. She lifted her chin in response. "Very well," he said. "Come to Dunsheen and look to my niece, Lady Michael." He smiled, lopsided and charming. "If you will."

She could not help but laugh when he smiled like that. Then she realized what he had said. "The child is your niece?"

He nodded. "Brigit is my brother Fionn's daughter. I am her guardian now."

She frowned, remembering his brother from the battlefield near Kinglassie. "Fionn—is he dead, then?"

Diarmid nodded curtly, his profile turned to her.

"I am sorry," she murmured in sympathy. "I thought you spoke of your own child."

"I no longer have a wife. And we had no children."

"I understand," she said. "I was widowed last year."

"I am not a widower," he said. She glanced at him, puzzled. But the rigid set of his head and back discouraged her from asking more. He rode beside her through the cool morning light, strong, silent, and increasingly mysterious.

As she glanced at him, she saw a muscle pump along his jaw and a faint blush touch his cheekbones. She had met his prideful, arrogant side; now she glimpsed again that vulnerable man she had seen before, the one who carried a bitter sadness. He kept his sorrows and secrets to himself and drove forward on some hidden, relentless quest to find a cure for an ailing child.

Wanting to know more, she could not ask; wanting to help, for that was irrevocably part of her nature, she had only one recourse. "I will examine Fionn's daughter for you, since you ask it of me." She hoped her willingness would bring back the lighter mood of a few moments earlier.

But he only nodded brusquely. "I need more of you." Simple words, firmly spoken in his warrior's voice.

She shook her head. "Only that, Dunsheen."

Diarmid stepped his horse closer to hers and reached out to pull on her reins, slowing both horses. He leaned toward her until she angled her head to look at him.

"Promise me what I have asked, and I will give you whatever you want in return," he said. She stared into the silvery depths of his eyes. A tiny shiver slipped down her back, thrill as much as dread. "Whatever you ask, Michael," he repeated softly.

She looked away. "I will not bargain with you on this."

"I can pay you well."

"I do not crave coin." She pulled at the reins, but he would not let go; he controlled her horse for the moment.

"What, then?" he asked. "Land? Cattle? What is it a woman wants?" He frowned suddenly. "Marriage? Your brother wants you wed again. Shall I find you a husband? Would that meet your price?"

She gasped indignantly, although her heart surged. She wondered if he was married himself—his earlier remark had confused her—and quickly dismissed the thought. She would never take a husband as stubborn and demanding as this man.

He took her wrist in his hand, his fingers hard and warm. "I do not beg favors," he said. "But by God, girl, I am perilously close to it with you. And I will not think kindly of either of us if I come to that." He drew a long breath. "I know you can heal Brigit. I want you to do it."

She shook her head. "Take the child on a pilgrimage to a holy place if you are determined to petition God for a miracle. I am no saint."

He turned her hand in his and stroked his thumb over her palm. Shivers ran through her, utterly pleasurable, deeply stirring. "Saint or none, you have angel hands," he said. "The loan of those is all I seek from you. You may ask what you want in return."

"I do not market miracles." She jerked her hand away.

He let her go without comment, and urged his horse to walk beside hers. He did not glance at her, although she looked at him repeatedly. Finally she could bear the silence no longer.

"I would like to help your niece," she said. "But I cannot do what you want."

"You can," he said evenly, looking ahead.

She wanted, in that moment, to resist whatever he

asked of her out of sheer stubbornness. But he asked the impossible. She had learned to suppress her gift until it hardly stirred within her anymore. Quite simply, she could not do what Diarmid asked.

"Miracles cannot be ordered," she said.

"You can do this," he said, unperturbed.

She could not tell him the truth, and she could not convince him. The man was made of stone. She blew out an exasperated breath and slid a dark look at him. "Perhaps I should ask a miracle of *you*," she snapped in frustration.

He smiled, a slight, crooked lift of his lip, as if he welcomed the challenge. "Name it. Within my abilities, of course," he added drolly.

His confident manner sparked her anger further. She grasped at the greatest challenge she could think of immediately. "Win a castle for me," she blurted out. "Surely waging war is within your considerable abilities."

He stared at her. "Do what!"

"Win a castle for me," she repeated.

"One of your choosing, or my own choosing?" he drawled.

"My choosing," she said.

Diarmid shrugged. "That is not much of a miracle to ask. Any castle can be broken."

"Do not break it," she said earnestly. "Win it."

He pinched back a smile. "And if I do?"

"Then, I will try to do what you ask of me."

"Try?" His voice was low and strong.

She shrugged, as he had. "That is all I can promise. Win Glas Eilean for me, and we will have a bargain."

He swore softly under his breath. "Glas Eilean? I know the place," he growled.

Too late, she realized that he would; his own castle was not far from there. He might even welcome the opportunity to take such a valuable property for himself.

Now she regretted speaking so quickly, but she

lifted her chin proudly to mask her discomfiture. "I hold the charter." She slid a glance at him. "I want you to take it from the man who holds it, and give it over to my half brother's keeping."

She waited. He said nothing. A muscle jumped in his cheek, and his eyes seemed to glitter with a cold light. She wondered why he seemed so angry; moments ago, he had been smiling.

"I will not lay siege to Glas Eilean," he said flatly.

She looked at him, startled. She had not expected that answer from him. "Why—why not?"

He did not look at her. "My sister lives there. The man who holds it is Ranald MacSween. Her husband."

She gaped at him as he dug his heels into his horse's sides and rode ahead. If MacSween, the man who had defied Gavin's men, was Diarmid's brother-in-law, then perhaps Diarmid and Gavin were not friends after all, as she had assumed.

She groaned inwardly. She should not have been so hasty to devise a miracle for him to perform. She should not have come with him; perhaps her actions would now make worse trouble for Gavin in his attempts to win back Glas Eilean.

Diarmid rode far ahead of her again. She leaned forward, skirts flying, to catch up to him. "I did not know," she said.

"There are some bargains I will not make," he said, staring straight ahead.

"Then you understand my position. There are bargains I will not make either."

"Ah," he said. "We have no agreement."

"None," she said decisively.

He rode beside her without speaking. As her anger cooled, she glanced toward him. Sunlight glinted bronze through his brown hair, and the muted colors of his green-and-black plaid blended with the hills and moorland around them. She studied the smooth carving of his brow and nose, the clear gray of his black-lashed eyes, the proud lift of his strong jaw, and the firm set of his mouth. Even the small muscle tensing in his lean, whiskered cheek seemed determined.

No agreement. She was relieved, in a way. If he had promised to fulfill her impulsive demand, she would have been obligated to match his request. She was curious and fascinated by him; Diarmid Campbell was a warrior, strikingly handsome, powerful in demeanor, intelligent and deeply private. He was a chieftain with obligations and duties to fulfill.

Yet he set all aside to fetch a healer for the sake of his niece. He would do anything—nearly anything— to help Brigit. She marveled at the depth of such compassion, such devotion, and wondered at its source.

"I think you would trade your own soul to save this child," she murmured pensively. The words, her inner thoughts, were out before she could stop them.

His glance was lightning-fast and unsettling. "Is that your price?" he asked softly, ominously. "That fee I will pay. To whom shall I deliver my soul? Will you take it now, or in portions?"

She stared at him, struck by the intensity she had uncovered with her impulsive remark. Giving her no chance to reply, he leaned forward and urged his horse to a gallop.

Chapter Six

They rode over rolling moorland and climbed steep, rocky slopes, pausing only once to sip clear water and eat the remaining oatcakes. White clouds sailed high before a bright sun as they climbed a long incline topped by oaks and alders. At the top, Michaelmas saw the jewellike flash of a pool between the trees.

She followed Diarmid through the woodland, hoping for a quiet rest beside the peaceful pool that shone between the trees. They dismounted beside the pool, which was divided nearly in two by a huge projecting rock. The water was surrounded by grassy inclines and thick trees. Nearby stood an ancient hazel, its branches covered not with tiny birds, as Michaelmas first thought, but with hundreds of fluttering, knotted rags.

Several people—men, women and children—were gathered at the far side of the pool. Some dipped their hands or feet in the water, others knelt to pray at the pool's edge, while still others tied cloth strips as prayer tokens to the hazel branches.

Diarmid walked toward the water's edge, standing behind the shelter of the massive rock, out of sight of the others. He turned toward Michaelmas.

"This is Saint Fillan's Well," he said. "You mentioned pilgrimage places. This one was along our way. I thought you might like to see it."

"I have heard of it," she said, looking around. "Saint Fillan's is a sacred pool, well-known. I understand that the king himself comes here to pray for health and guidance."

"He does," Diarmid said. "King Robert has a skin condition with symptoms of weakness that recur without warning. Some say the attacks are God's punishment for the burden of his sins."

Michaelmas looked up at him in surprise. "Dear Lord. I did not know. He comes here in hopes of healing himself?"

He nodded. "But that has not happened. The disease always returns." He kicked at the pebbles that lined the shore. "Robert Bruce has worked miracles enough for Scotland and deserves one for himself."

She did not answer, sensing an odd mood in him, harsh and bitter. Bending, she scooped water into her hands, letting it trickle back to its source like a cascade of liquid diamonds. She thought of her friend Jean, so ill and so ready to find her peace in heaven, and wanted to say a prayer on her behalf.

"They say the water of a healing pool must be silvered," she said, and put a hand to her belt; then she remembered that her small silken coin pouch was still in the wooden chest at Saint Leonard's with her other things.

She heard a small splash, and saw Diarmid toss a few silver pennies into the pool. "Let there be no obstacle to healing," he said, his tone dry.

"Thank you." She cupped her hands and dipped them again, closing her eyes to murmur a prayer for Jean, an old Gaelic chant that she had learned as a child. As the water poured through her hands, she repeated the verses three times. Then she straightened and dried her hands on her cloak.

Diarmid picked up a few pebbles and sticks and began to toss them into the glittering sunlit water. Michaelmas looked across the pool, where the other people chatted and prayed; a few settled down to eat a meal.

"I hear miraculous healings sometimes happen in holy places such as this one," she said.

"Pilgrims come to such places because they believe the water has been blessed by a saint, or by divine power." He tossed a twig into the water. "They silver the water with their hard-earned coin, and think that God is watching over them. But the priests drag nets through the pools when no one is about, and buy fine robes for their backs and golden candlesticks for their altars. Any miracles are surely accidental."

His skepticism surprised her; he had demanded a miracle from her readily enough. "Have you brought your niece here?"

"Here, and other places too," he said. "My sister insisted on it." He flung a stone into the water. "I have paid for healing, prayed for it, and watched my sister beg God for it. She has her own troubles, and no healing has come to her either. And Brigit does no better."

Here she recognized the source of his bitterness; he loved these people deeply and wanted them whole. "But you have faith enough in my healing ability," she pointed out.

He huffed a small, hard laugh. "Faith is a precious substance, lady. I use it sparingly." He glanced at her. "I put no faith in a place like this, but I know you can heal Brigit. I have seen what you can do with my own eyes. That kind of miracle I will believe in, not something promoted by coin-hungry priests."

"Perhaps you could bring Brigit to another sacred place. So many swear by—"

His downward glance, a flash of gray like a storm cloud, silenced her. "Do you think to convince me? I have dipped my hand in this water before, when I brought the child to this holy pool," he said. "But neither of us have been healed." He looked down at his scarred hand.

She extended her hand to him. "May I see?"

He hesitated, then agreed. She took his fingers, his

skin warm and dry, and turned them. The base of his
thumb and the wrist were heavily scarred from burns
as well as deep cuts. The scarring ran up the length
of his thumb, but she found that and all of his fingers
strong and flexible when she tested them.

Her physician's curiosity instantly caught, she
turned his hand to study the wide, striated scars, and
ran her fingertips lightly over the grooves. She felt the
steady, strong pulse at the tender spot just below the
wrist bone. As she smoothed her touch gently over
his skin, she heard Diarmid suck in his breath sharply.

"Your touch is gentle," he murmured. "So warm."

She tugged and folded each finger, feeling tightness
in the tendons. "These wounds healed long ago, but
they must have caused you a great deal of pain, and
still ache in rain and cold, I would think," she said.
She touched the deepest scar over the wrist. "This
would have been nearly fatal if the bleeding was not
checked quickly. A sword wound, I would say, stitched
and cauterized. But the surgeon was not as skilled
as yourself."

"A good analysis," he murmured. "Go on."

She glanced up at him. "What happened, Diarmid?"

He shrugged. "A battle wound, as you say."

She frowned, but was not surprised that he refused
to tell her more; he seemed to hold secrets close. She
resumed her examination, manipulating his thumb and
fingers. "There is some muscular weakness here,
though not as much as there could be. Is your grip
impaired?"

"At times," he said quietly. He rounded his fingers
over her arm and squeezed; the iron-like pressure
nearly took her breath. Then a tremble began in his
two shortest fingers, and he let go abruptly. "As you
can see."

She took his hand again and looked at it. Despite
the scars, his long, supple fingers and wide palm were
a beautiful blend of grace and power. Warmth radiated where their hands met, as if a cushion of protec-

tion existed near him. She felt wholly safe with him, and suddenly imagined those warm, strong hands skimming over her body. A shiver slipped through her and blossomed in her lower abdomen.

Heat seeping into her cheeks, she cleared her throat. "There is a surgeon in France who has successfully cut into muscles and tendons of the hand and foot to repair similar injuries. But the technique is very difficult. I do not know how to do it, although my husband understood it."

"My hand will never be healed," he said. "I have accepted that."

"It is healed," she protested. "The body heals such wounds as best it can, and then learns to compensate. You have more strength in that hand than many who have whole, undamaged fingers." She held his hand as she might have held a child's, smoothing it gently, wanting somehow to comfort him; she felt his vulnerability strongly. He curled his fingers over hers, his skin a deeper contrast, his warm touch utterly compelling.

"Michael," he whispered. "Do you remember what you did the day I first saw you?"

She nodded hesitantly, her hand trembling in his. She had meant to comfort him, but his heated, firm touch created the safety of spirit that she had often longed for. The realization nearly took her breath.

She looked up then. His gray gaze, shining like rain, penetrated hers, and she could not look away.

"There was no ancient legend, no silvering needed, no feast day or fasting necessary," he said. "You touched a man's wound, and saved his life." His words, soft and low, blended with the gentle sounds of wind and water. "So simple, so perfect. I never forgot that day."

"I remember it differently," she said. "You repaired that leg wound, Diarmid. Not I."

He shook his head. "Angus MacArthur would have died because I could not stop the bleeding. But you knelt beside him like an angel"—he touched a drift of pale hair that slipped down beside her cheek—"and slowed the blood loss. All I did was close the wound. Afterward—I never saw a man heal more quickly than he did. And you healed my own cut with a touch of your finger."

Beneath his eyebrow, she saw the thin scar that marked the deep cut. She remembered touching it on a misty morning, surrounded by the dreadful moans of dying and wounded men, with the dark scent of blood on her hands.

She pressed her fingertip to the spot again. He closed his eyes briefly, his lashes black against his cheeks, then opened them, a flash of dark silver.

"You are not the only one who witnessed healing that day," she said. "I watched a gifted, capable surgeon, a compassionate young man."

"Much has changed since then."

"What a strange bond we share," she mused. "Neither of us use the healing gifts we once had."

"Ah," he said, softly, sadly, "but you can use your gift, if you will only try."

She looked down, reminded of Jean's words to her. Use the gift, she had said; let heaven guide you. Spontaneous tears sprang into her eyes. "Healing no longer comes to me as it did when I was a child." She hesitated, swamped by a keen sense of loss; the gift itself, mourned.

He touched the side of her face, a gentle sensation that whirled through her body like fire and wind, taking her breath, sweeping away her ability to think. "Do this for me, *Micheil*."

Her heart thumped. Another touch, another look, and she would promise him whatever he asked. The feeling frightened her. She stayed still, gazing up at him, each breath spinning out the moment.

"*Micheil*," he whispered, his palm warm against her cheek, his fingers slipping through her hair. She loved the short name he had given her, the name he said so kindly, so intimately. She loved the feel of his hand on her face. She closed her eyes briefly. "Please, I beg of you—" he began.

"Do not," she whispered. He was too proud, too strong, to beg. She could not bear to hear that from him. Under his steadfast silver gaze, she felt as if she would agree to do whatever he asked.

"Let me think," she said, looking away. "I cannot think when you look at me like that." She rubbed the gold brooch at her shoulder nervously.

"What is that?" he asked.

"Something that Gavin gave me as a child," she answered. "I wear it always. I like to think it brings me luck."

"Do you need luck?" he asked softly.

"Everyone does," she answered, looking up at him. "You do."

A smile quirked his mouth. "They say that it is luck to kiss by a healing well," he murmured. His hand tightened on her shoulder, drawing her closer. "Such a kiss, I hear, brings peace and joy to those who need them." He lowered his head. "Surely we both need that." He cupped her cheek.

Her heart thumped fiercely as she gazed at him. She felt as if she lost the thread of coherent thought, aware only of the press of his hand, the deep thrum of his voice in her ear, the shape of his lips so close to hers.

Aware, then, of his mouth, warm and pliant and wondrous as it brushed hers and lifted away. She took in a little gasp with the marvelous shock that struck through her. Her thundering heart seemed to fill her chest.

"For luck and a blessing," he murmured.

"For that," she agreed breathlessly, yearning to feel his mouth on hers again. She tipped her head up, lips parted, feeling a simple, strong, sudden desire.

He lowered his hand, and she looked away, blushing. "Come ahead, we've far to ride this day," he said. She nodded and turned, as he did. Bending down, she took a moment to tear two narrow strips of cloth from

the inside hem of her silk chemise. She walked toward
the little hazel tree and tied the rags onto branches,
where they fluttered among a rainbow display of hundreds of pilgrim tokens.

"A prayer for yourself?" he asked, behind her.

"For your Brigit," she answered. *And for us both,*
she thought as she walked away.

Hours later, while a vivid sunset bled orange and
red into the indigo sky, they reached a narrow pass
between a soaring, rugged mountain and a gleaming
loch. The wind brought piercing cold, and Michaelmas
gathered her cloak closer around her.

Diarmid, his plaid pulled over his head against the
chill, rode ahead of her in silence. Wind whistled
around them as they left the dramatic vista of the pass.
After a while, he turned. "Dunsheen is several miles
yet, toward the sea. Can you ride that far, or do you
wish to stop?"

Her bones ached with weariness, but she lifted her
head. "I can ride," she said, and urged her horse
ahead of his.

Some time later, she glimpsed the dark gleam of
another loch, heard the rhythmic rush of water, and
caught the faint scent of the sea. She had used her
last reserves of strength to ride this far, stubbornly
resisting the fatigue that threatened to crumple her
from the saddle. Now she felt a new rush of energy
when she saw a castle jut upward as if it surged, black
and whole, from the loch itself. Another glance revealed that the castle and its surrounding wall rested
on a long, low isle.

They rode to the pebbled shore, where Diarmid dismounted and held his arms up to assist her. She placed
her hands on his shoulders, and he lifted her down
easily. But as she stood, her knees buckled beneath
her. She gripped his shoulders, and Diarmid caught
her around the waist.

"Ho, girl," he murmured. "You must be tired.

Stand here for a moment." He leaned her against his chest, his breath stirring her hair.

Muffled against the plaid that covered his chest, taking in the mingled scents of wind and pine, of smoke and man, she closed her eyes, not thinking, hardly feeling anything but the blessed, firm support he offered her.

Then she pushed away, legs trembling. "I'm fine," she insisted wearily.

He murmured assent and took the horses' bridles to lead them into the shelter of a few trees, where Michaelmas saw the shape of a small stable. After a few minutes, he returned and walked ahead of her along the shore, beckoning her to follow.

"Loch Sheen is a sea inlet," he said. "When the tide is low, a sandbar connects the castle to the shore. But tonight we must row across." He led her toward a cluster of tall reeds, where a narrow rowing boat lay moored.

She caught her breath and hesitated. Boats and water made her distinctly uneasy. She did not want to reveal her fears or her unwillingness to Diarmid. Thin water lapped at her feet, and she stepped back uncertainly.

"Michael," Diarmid called. "Come on."

"What—what about the horses?" she asked.

"They are sheltered over there. I will send someone to ferry them across once we reach the castle. Come ahead, now."

"When will the tide be low enough to walk across?" she asked in a meek voice.

"Tomorrow." Diarmid took her hand.

Pulled along, she secretly touched the golden brooch, hoping that its luck would hold once more. Soon she sat on a crude cross bench made of a sturdy pile of brushwood, while Diarmid rowed the narrow boat toward the castle.

Biting anxiously at her lower lip, she gripped the sides of the boat hard enough to get splinters. She looked at the solid black shape of Dunsheen, thrusting ominously up from its flat, dark isle. Brilliant remnants of the sunset glittered in the sky and across the dark surface of the loch like scattered rubies.

The boat bumped over a series of wavelets, and Michaelmas cried out, gripping the wooden rim. Diarmid glanced at her, his features outlined by the sunset light. "What is it?" he asked.

"I—I do not much like boats," she admitted.

"Ah," he said, rowing. "You will have to get used to them if you are to stay here."

That statement made her even more uncomfortable. She would never get used to boats, or being near water. She held tightly, her empty stomach lurching uncertainly, and gulped in fresh air as she tried to focus on the steady, calming rhythm of Diarmid's rowing. Looking up, she saw the castle looming large and imposing on its isle. A light glowed high in a narrow window.

Diarmid glanced up as she did. "There are not many to welcome us at Dunsheen just now," he said. "My brother, Mungo's kin. And Brigit."

"And your wife?" she asked on impulse.

"She is not here," he said curtly.

She cleared her throat. "You have a brother?"

"I have three, all younger," he said. "Arthur will be out to sea, Colin lives inland, and Gilchrist, the youngest, lives here. Our mother passed a few years ago, after our father. Her elderly cousin, Lilias Mac-Arthur—Mungo's grandmother—tends to the household now."

She nodded and shifted on the pile of wood, trying to ignore the insecure sensation of floating, and resisting the terror that pushed at her. She reminded herself sternly that she had survived two long journeys in merchant galleys between Scotland and Italy. This brief trip would soon be over.

"Relax," Diarmid murmured, watching her face. "You're safe."

She only nodded, hands gripping, and did not trust herself to answer.

Soon the dark, soaring castle walls filled the sky, and the boat lurched against a narrow strip of sand and pebbles. Diarmid shifted the oars inside and stood, reaching down to help Michaelmas out. She stepped onto the shore, glad to feel land underfoot, glad she had not thoroughly embarrassed herself.

Diarmid took her elbow and led her toward the castle entrance. She fought against the urge to lean against his strength, and placed one foot resolutely before the next.

At the closed portcullis, he took a small curved horn from its loop on his belt and blew three plaintive notes. Startled, Michaelmas heard a returned shout. Soon metal and wood creaked as the portcullis rose.

"Welcome to *Dun Sìan*," Diarmid said.

"Storm Castle," she repeated, looking up into the teeth of the iron gate suspended menacingly over their heads.

"Some say it is well named," he said, and escorted her inside.

Chapter Seven

"Dunsheen!" a man's voice cried. "Welcome home!" A tall, white-haired man approached them across the bailey yard, carrying a glowing torch.

"Angus!" Diarmid said, grasping hands with him.

"Greetings to you, Dunsheen!" Angus grinned. "A long time gone, you were. And you bring a guest." He looked curiously at Michaelmas. She thought his gaunt face looked somewhat familiar.

"This is Lady Michael," Diarmid answered. "A healer. My lady, this is Angus MacArthur, Mungo's father." He turned to Angus. "Mungo will arrive in a few more days."

Angus nodded. "Lady Michael," he said. "I have heard the name before—*ach Dhia*, Dunsheen, is this the one?" he asked.

"This is," Diarmid answered. Michaelmas sent him a questioning look. "Angus was seriously wounded on a battlefield near Kinglassie," he explained. "He was unconscious at the time, but afterward, Fionn and I told him about the young girl who helped to save his life with her healing skills. Perhaps you recall that day," he added smoothly.

Michaelmas nodded. Diarmid's careful phrasing told her that he had never revealed her secret, even to Angus. He kept his word all these years, just as he had promised her. "Angus," she said warmly, holding out her hands. "How lovely to meet you after so long. I remember you well."

He bowed his head. "Lady Michael, I am honored,

and I am in your debt. If you want for anything, just ask me. Whatever you need. I'll move the very loch for you if you like." He grinned.

Diarmid chuckled as he took her arm. "She might like you to drain it someday, I think," he drawled. "Is there food ready?"

"*Tch,* of course. I'll wake my mother," Angus said. "Come in, the fire is hot and the wine plentiful, and we'll surely find the pair of you some food."

They walked through the bailey toward the high tower that dominated the enclosure, and climbed a set of wooden steps to the arched entrance. Michaelmas heard dogs barking as the three of them walked down a corridor and went through an open doorway. Angus murmured that he would fetch the food, and left them.

Michaelmas heard the strains of soft music as she stepped into the dark, spacious hall, its raftered ceiling lost in shadow. At one end of the huge chamber, where a wide hearth glowed, delicate harp music floated on the air.

A man, the harper, sat by the stone fireplace, his carved wooden harp leaned against his left shoulder, his dark head bowed over the polished neck. He looked up as they entered, but his hands never ceased to strum the quiet rhythms of the song.

As they neared the hearth end of the room, two large black dogs bounded toward them, barking happily. Diarmid petted their glossy black heads, grinning as he bent down to greet them.

"Ah, Padraig, Columba," he said, rubbing their black coats. "These are the guardians of Dunsheen," he explained as Michaelmas extended her hand cautiously to each dog. The hounds nosed at her hand until she petted them, laughing.

Diarmid subdued them with a quick word, and gestured for her to sit in a high-backed chair with a deep cushion. She sank into its support with a sigh, while Diarmid sat on a bench beside a long table.

The harper rang out the last note on the strings, his

long fingers suspended. He looked up, and Michaelmas nearly gasped.

He was, quite simply, beautiful. An exquisitely
sculpted warrior angel, colored dark and warm by
gleaming firelight. She recognized a younger, more
finely shaped Diarmid in his features. He smiled, a
lilting lift of his mouth, but his brown eyes retained a
sad quality that contrasted his classic beauty.

"Welcome, brother." The harper's voice was deep
and pleasant, with a mellow quality similar to
Diarmid's.

"Gilchrist, God's greetings, *bràthair.*" Diarmid
leaned forward to clasp his hand. "How fares it here?"

"Well enough," the harper replied, shifting on his
wooden stool. He wore a wrapped plaid and was barefooted. Michaelmas noticed, with an odd sense of
shock, that his lower right leg was misshapen; as if
sensing that she looked, he tucked it out of view beneath the stool. She saw the wooden crutch, formed
from a tree limb, that leaned against the side of the
hearth.

"My lady," Diarmid said. "This is my brother Gilchrist. And this is Lady Michael of—" He looked at
Michaelmas oddly, as if he just realized that he did
not know her married title.

"I am Michaelmas Faulkener of Kinglassie," she
said. "Widow to Ibrahim Ibn Kateb of Bologna."

Gilchrist raised a brow in curiosity and looked at
Diarmid.

"I've brought her here from Perth, to examine
Brigit," Diarmid said. "She is a physician." Gilchrist
looked surprised once again.

"I was schooled in Italy," Michaelmas explained.

Gilchrist nodded, his dark hair swinging against his
cheek. "Schooled in Italy and bred in Scotland. The
Gaelic flows sweet as dew from your lips, my lady.
Welcome."

She smiled. Diarmid cleared his throat. "She was
raised in Galloway," he muttered. "Of course she

speaks the Gaelic well." He bent down to pet one of the dogs who lay beneath the table.

Michaelmas blinked at his surly tone, then looked up to see Angus enter the room, carrying a cloth-covered platter. Behind him, two women followed. A young girl held a clay jug, and a small, bent-shouldered woman, her hands filled with a stack of wooden cups, came behind her. The girl, perhaps sixteen years of age, kept her eyes downcast as she neared the hearth, her pretty cheeks bright; the old woman scowled, bleary-eyed, as she shuffled forward.

Angus set the platter on the table and whisked back the cloth to reveal slices of beef and a pot of steaming porridge, and the women set the other things on the table. The dogs, smelling the food, sat up, and Diarmid admonished them to keep still.

"Greetings, Dunsheen, and welcome to your guest," the old woman said. "Cold meat and hot oats are all I could manage so late at night, but eat and drink your fill. I had Angus open a new tun of claret." She peered at Diarmid, her white brows lowered over sharp blue eyes. "You need a bath and a shave," she pronounced critically.

Diarmid grinned. "Lilias, I see you are feeling well and full of spirit as usual." He spoke loudly.

"Well as can be, with my joint pains making me so irritable," Lilias said. "I do not much like being woken after I've gone to sleep. But it is good to see you, and your guest."

"And you. Lilias MacArthur, I have brought Lady Michael of Kinglassie to visit, and to tend to Brigit."

"My lady," Lilias said, bowing her head. "Angus told me who you are. I want to thank you for your skills those years ago. You saved my son's life. We are honored to have you here." Michaelmas blushed and smiled, and turned as the girl silently poured out cups of wine and handed them to Michaelmas and Diarmid. She was lovely in a quiet way, with light brown hair and pale blue eyes, clothed in brown, her build plump and lush, strong and tall.

"Iona, thanks," Diarmid said. "How do your brothers and sister fare?"

"They are well, sir," Iona said, blushing as if she were shy, lowering her eyes. "My father did not return with you?"

"Mungo is on an errand, and will be here soon," he said. She nodded and turned toward Gilchrist to hand him a cup of wine. He ignored her, suddenly absorbed in adjusting the tuning of his harp strings with a small wooden key. She set the cup beside him and turned to leave the room. Michaelmas glanced at him, and saw Gilchrist pick up the wine and watch Iona pensively, his cheeks stained as red as hers had been.

Lilias leaned forward and peered at Michaelmas. "Your lady is a pretty thing, but wan-looking, and young." She swiveled her sharp glance to Diarmid. "Is she a nun? Did you take her out of a convent?"

"Out of a hospital, where she worked with the patients," Diarmid said. "And she is a widow, not a nun. And a physician too," he added loudly.

"Such a young girl, a physician? Never," Lilias said.

"She is a book-taught *physicus*," Gilchrist said, raising his voice. "Trained in Italy. She has come to look at Brigit."

"Italy?" Lilias blinked. "Is that in France?"

"Italy is where the pope lives," Angus nearly shouted.

"We import spices from the Holy Land through Italian ports," Diarmid said. "Your cinnamon sticks and pepper come through Italy, Lilias. Most of our spices come from Venice."

"Ah, pepper and cloves," she said approvingly. "A fine place, Italy."

"How is Brigit?" Diarmid asked.

"Sweet as the soul of an angel," Lilias said, her gap-toothed smile joyful. "Eat now, both of you, and then rest. Mistress Physician, tell me what you know about joint aches. My knees and hips hurt me so much at night I can hardly sleep."

"Let the woman eat, now, Mother, and come to your bed," Angus said, taking her arm.

"I am not tired," Lilias insisted. She pointed to her hip. "I have a pain just here, like a knife, and another here—"

"Mother," Angus groaned.

"Are you taking medicines for the pain?" Michaelmas asked.

"Willow only. What would you suggest?"

"Come ahead, Mother," Angus said, steering her away. "You can talk to the Mistress Physician another time. She is tired." He tugged on her arm, and she snapped at him, but left, bowing her head to Michaelmas.

"Good night, Lilias," Diarmid said as they left.

Michaelmas looked at Diarmid. "I did not mind talking to her about her aches," she said.

"You would if you wished to sleep this night," Diarmid said. "She has a multitude of aches, and a description for each one."

Michaelmas smiled and sipped at the claret, feeling its warmth slip inside of her and spread agreeably. Gilchrist began a song, and she settled back in the comfortable chair to listen.

She glanced at Diarmid, who leaned his head on his hand as he listened to the music. She felt herself beginning to relax in both body and spirit, in part from music and food, in part from the warm welcome that she had received at the castle of storms.

As the low light of a peat fire flickered in his bedchamber, Diarmid sank down in the wooden tub left in its usual place near the hearth. While he and Michael had eaten, Diarmid had asked Angus to bring buckets of steaming water to fill tubs in both his bedchamber and in a small antechamber beside Brigit's room, where Lilias had decided Michael would sleep.

He sluiced warm water over his head and shoulders and scooped up soft ash and herb soap from a wooden dish by the tub, scrubbing his head and chest. He soaped his whiskered jaw and accomplished a needed shave, using the sharpest edge of his dirk. Exhausted, he sat back, wanting to collapse into bed after the bath. But he wanted to see Brigit first, though he knew she was asleep.

He sank lower in the tub. He hoped that Brigit would like Michael, for she had disliked the other healers who had examined her. He could not blame the child for her previous reaction. The two wise-wives from the Isle of Mull had irritated him with their strings and stones, chants and smoke, and he had asked them to leave. He shook his head at the memory, sure their rituals had been of no use.

He had also cut short the visit of an elderly physician he had met in Ayr. The man boasted of his Paris education, and began daily bleedings for Brigit, put her on a strict diet of almonds and chicken broth, and gave her a course of laxatives, all meant to correct an imbalance in her bodily humors. He pored over charts that he had brought with him, claiming that her natal horoscope showed that the legs should be amputated, for, as he said, Saturn conflicted with the moon in three configurations.

Within a few days, Brigit was weaker than a newborn. Horrified when he returned from a trading voyage, Diarmid had dismissed the physician angrily. Lilias had added a dose of her sharp tongue, and Angus and Mungo had escorted him to a departing boat, making sure that he fell into the loch at least once.

Finally, just before Diarmid had left to join Robert Bruce, an Argyll herb-wife had consulted with him. She advised heat treatments, a sound diet, and herbal infusions, medicines with which he was familiar. He had adopted her reasonable suggestions, and now she regularly supplied the prepared medicines. Brigit had seemed more comfortable since then, but he was convinced that none of that would cure her.

He sank against the side of the tub and sloshed water over his soapy chest. He was certain that Michael would use far more sense than the first physician, and would likely know more than the local herbwife. And he hoped that she would consent to use her unique power to heal the child. That, truthfully, was all that he wanted to see done.

Michael's image floated through his mind. Her serene face framed in pale, silky hair, her calm voice and gentle touch were easy to recall, as if he had committed their exquisite details to memory. He remembered, too, the soft, sweet taste of her warm lips, causing his loins to surge suddenly beneath the water. Scowling, he reached over and doused his head with the cooled water that remained in the bucket.

He flexed his left hand, remembering how she had touched the scars, examining his hand beside the pool. During those brief moments, he had felt something wondrous and dynamic, like a sweet lightning over his skin. She might deny her healing ability, but he was sure it was still there.

Her gifted hands were the answer Brigit needed, that he needed too. Like a bit of rag tied on a hazel tree for hope, he had placed the last remnant of his faith in Michael's ability. She could help him fulfill the vow he had made to Brigit.

He shoved a hand through his wet hair as if the simple motion could rake away the worry that plagued him. His own medical knowledge told him the cold truth: no treatment could make the child whole. But each time he saw the brightness in her eyes, he resolved to see her well.

Rinsing the water over his shoulders, he thought about the surprising refusal Michael had given him. He had been unprepared for it. Her counter demand had astounded him even more. He shook his head in dismay. He could sooner win the moon and stars for Michael than Glas Eilean. Breaking through its barriers would be no problem. That was not what stopped him. He held back because he feared for his sister's welfare and her health.

He sighed heavily as he stepped out of the tub and dried himself with a linen sheet. Crossing the dark, silent room, he opened a clothing chest and took out a thick, soft woolen tunic of dark green, one that his sister had made for him in the English style. He pulled it over his head, then left the room, silent and barefooted, to find Brigit.

Michaelmas awoke, startled, when she heard the small cry. Soft and whimpery, the sound came again. She heard pain in it, and more. Troubled, she sat up, listening through the dark.

She had been asleep on a narrow pallet bed in a tiny room above the great hall. Cold air leaked through a narrow window, hung with a piece of hide to keep out the strong winds. She slid out of bed, feeling the chill through her silk chemise and the cold impact of the wooden floor against her bare feet. Grabbing her surcoat, she tossed it on over her chemise; although it was improper to go about with a surcoat over a thin undergown, she hardly thought it mattered just now. No one would see her.

She heard the faint, frightened sound again. Opposite her bed, a doorway, covered with a heavy curtain, led to another chamber. The soft cries seemed to come from that room. She picked up the cold candle by her bed and ignited the wick at the iron brazier, filled with glowing peat, that warmed her chamber. Holding the flaming candle, she went to the adjoining door and parted the curtain.

At the far end of a dark, spacious chamber, faint firelight spilled over a bed draped in pale blankets. Michaelmas heard a whimper and a sniffle.

"Who's there?" she whispered. "Are you ill?" She stepped forward. A small girl lay in the middle of the great curtained bed, propped on pillows, her body thin beneath the blankets.

One of the dogs had been asleep by the fire. He rose up and came toward her—the larger one, Padraig, she remembered. He sniffed at her and seemed to recall her as well, for he accepted her pat on his huge head. Then he went back to the hearthstone to lie down.

"Brigit?" Michaelmas asked softly. "Is that your name?"

"It is," the child whispered. "Who are you?"

"My name is *Micheil*," she said in Gaelic, holding the candle high as she looked down at the girl.

"Michael?" The child's eyes, set in a delicate face, sparkled like silver in the light. "Are you the archangel Michael from my prayers?"

Michaelmas smiled and shook her head. "I am not an angel," she said. "I am a visitor to Dunsheen. Your uncle brought me here."

"Is he home?" Michaelmas nodded. "I thought you came from heaven," Brigit said. "Your hair is the color of the moon, and the light glows all around you. You look like an angel, or a lady of the *daoine sìth*, all magical."

"What a lovely compliment," Michaelmas said. "You look magical too. Your eyes are as bright and pretty as stars."

Brigit smiled, a decidedly crooked grin with the deep shadow of a dimple. "I am a child of the fair folk."

"Are you?" Michaelmas was enchanted by the child's bright imagination. "They are a very handsome people."

Brigit nodded. "My kin are of the fair folk, and so am I."

"Are you alone here? I thought I heard someone weeping." Michael looked around the room.

"Padraig is here," Brigit said, pointing to the dog. "He is my special *gruagach*, my guardian spirit. But he did not cry. You might have heard me. My leg hurts a little."

"Ah," Michaelmas said. "Which leg?"

Brigit pointed to her left leg. "This one hurts at night sometimes. I thought Lilias or Iona would come with that dreadful drink." Brigit wrinkled her nose. "Did you bring it?"

She shook her head, and Brigit looked relieved. Michaelmas set the candle on a wooden chest beside the bed and sat on the edge of the mattress. "I know something about aches and illnesses," she said. "Can I help?"

"The wise-wives and the physician said no one can help me. I am a poor soul." She cast her eyes upward innocently, obviously repeating an adult's words.

"I would like to try," Michaelmas said. "Perhaps in the morning you will let me look more closely at your leg. But for now, we can change your position." She took a pillow from the pile behind Brigit's head and slid it under the covers, lifting the girl's thin legs to support her knees on the pillow.

Brigit leaned back, yawning. "That is better. Will my Uncle Diarmid come to see me tonight?"

"He may be asleep," Michaelmas said. She brushed fine golden strands from Brigit's brow. "And so should you be. You will see him in the morning."

Brigit yawned again and turned her head, snuggling down into the mattresses and pillows. She dug under one pillow and came up with a limp cloth doll, which she tucked against her. "If you are not an angel, then you must be a woman of the *daoine sìth*."

Michaelmas smiled as she rubbed Brigit's back. She could feel the girl's tiny ribs and sensed a strong, quick heartbeat. "Why do you say that?" she asked.

"You came out of the shadows like you were under an enchantment. And you said my uncle brought you to Dunsheen. The *daoine sìth* do what he commands, because he is their king." She yawned and clasped the doll, worn and ragged about its edges, in her small arms.

"He is what?" Michaelmas asked in surprise.

Brigit murmured something sleepily and was silent.

"King of the fair folk." Startled by Diarmid's hushed voice, Michaelmas spun around.

He stood at the foot of the bed in shadows and candlelight. Waves of dark, wet hair framed his face and broad neck. She had never seen him clean-shaven before, and noticed immediately the smooth, firm shape of his jaw. As he moved close, she caught the clean scent of herbal soap.

"King of the—what did you say?" Michaelmas whispered.

He did not answer as he leaned over Brigit and touched her head. "Greetings, little one," he said softly.

The child opened one eye. "Uncle, you've come back."

"I have," he said, stroking her hair.

"Did you bring magic for me?"

"Not just yet, *Brighid milis*."

"Did you bring me a gift from Ireland? I do like sweets."

"I know. But I was not on a trading voyage; I was with the king, where there were no sweets. Hush now, and go to sleep."

Michael watched as he soothed her to sleep, fascinated by his deep, soft voice and the sight of his large, powerful hand, so gentle and careful on the tiny head. After a few moments, he straightened and looked at Michael. "Has she been in pain?"

"She was uncomfortable, but I moved her pillows and we talked a bit," Michaelmas said. She picked up the candle and stepped past him, her shoulder brushing against his hard chest in the darkness, her hand grazing the soft wool of his tunic. She meant to go back to her chamber, but paused and turned back, the candle flame flickering.

"Tell me—what did Brigit say about you and the fair folk?"

He rubbed his fingers over his clean jaw hesitantly, and glanced at sleeping child, then half chuckled, as if in chagrin. "She, ah, she believes that I am the king of the *daoine sìth*," he murmured. "She thinks that I can make magic." He cleared his throat. "And she believes that she is a changeling, a child of the fair folk." He smiled faintly.

Michaelmas stared at him incredulously. "But why?"

He sighed. "I had the guardianship of her when her parents died. I placed her for fostering with a man I trusted. I rarely saw her. A few months ago, I rode to see her—" He paused, looking down. Michaelmas noticed a muscle thumping in his cheek. "I found Brigit set out on a hill late at night, in cold winds. She had been left there deliberately. Her fostering family had died, and the old grandmother who had charge of her was convinced she was a changeling child because of her lameness."

Michael gasped. "I have heard of that custom." She frowned. "Brigit thinks that you are the king of the *daoine sìth* because you found her and took her away?"

He shrugged. "So she insists," he said. "No one can dissuade her."

Michaelmas watched him as he spoke, the naturally deep pitch of his voice musical. The candlelight turned his gray eyes to crystal, and edged the lean planes of his face and the waves of his hair with warm light. She too could believe that he had stepped from the otherworld, a warrior made of magic and dreams.

She drew a quick breath, stirring herself back to a firm, practical sense of reality. "Brigit is young," she said. "She mistook me for an angel at first. But she was very sleepy. She decided that I was a woman of the fair folk, because I said that you had brought me here." She smiled. "Young children often imagine things in curious ways."

"She often confuses angels with the fair folk. She says a prayer to Saint Brigit and to Michael the archangel each night, and asks protection from the *sìtheach* as well—just to be safe, I suppose." A twinkle glittered in his glance.

"She has a keen imagination. But she will outgrow her ideas. When I was a small child, I thought that I was a changeling too—I was adopted, and no one knew who my parents were then. And I had that strange power—" She stopped.

Diarmid smiled, the tilted lift of his mouth enchanting. Michaelas felt her heart quicken oddly. "Changeling?" he asked, so softly she hardly heard the word. "Perhaps you are one of the magic folk after all," he murmured.

"Why do you say so?" she whispered warily. She expected him to answer her with another mention of the healing touch.

"Your hair," he said. "It holds its own light, somehow." He brushed back the drift of hair that fell along her cheek, raising a subtle shiver in her. His hand rested on her shoulder for a moment. She could smell his clean male skin, and the fragrant herbs in the soap he had used. She sensed his warmth along her body, and her heart pulsed insistently in response.

She did not know what to say, how to break the spell he wove with just a look, a touch, the sound of his breath close to hers. She remained silent, waiting, remembering with a rush of yearning the wondrous feel of his lips over hers by the healing pool.

Diarmid stepped back and inclined his head. "Good night to you, Michael girl," he murmured. "Thank you for looking in on Brigit. Sleep well." He turned and walked away.

Michaelmas stood motionless, her heart hammering profoundly, while Diarmid disappeared into the shadows beyond the open door.

Chapter Eight

Diarmid leaned a shoulder against the carved wooden post at the foot of Brigit's bed and watched Michael as she spoke gently to Brigit. In the black gown and white wimple, she looked more like a chaste young nun than an experienced, capable physician.

That she was, indeed; he was certain of her skill and knowledge now. He had observed her for the past hour, ever since he had entered Brigit's chamber early that morning to greet the child, and had found Michael already there. He had seen subtle traces of fatigue in the shadows beneath Michael's blue eyes and in her pale cheeks; but she greeted him quietly and turned back to Brigit with a sweet smile.

As he watched Michael, he became certain that his decision to bring her to Dunsheen had been heaven-guided. No one better suited this task. Her manner with Brigit was calm and practical, her hands endlessly gentle. After questioning Diarmid about the child's health and diet, she had focused her complete attention on Brigit.

Diarmid stood by the bed with no thought of leaving, although much demanded his attention elsewhere. He watched silently, feeling as if time had rolled back fifteen years and he stood once again in the infirmary at Mullinch Priory, watching Brother Colum.

Whenever the elderly monk had tended to illness or injury, or to the regular bleedings of the monks, he had explained to Diarmid what he did, why, and how. Each day for two years, he had taught Diarmid about herbs and remedies. Diarmid had learned quickly and voraciously, and had committed to memory the contents of the few medical texts that the monastery owned. During that time, and through the years that followed, he had wished for more to read, more to learn, more to experience.

The hardest lessons had come on the field of battle, where he had taught himself, under duress, much of what he knew about repairing torn flesh and broken bones. But he had done little with his medical skills in the last few years, outside of helping his kin when necessary. Months ago, he had examined Brigit himself; he had scant experience with ailing children, but his knowledge of anatomy was thorough. He had found her to be in general good health, with no evidence of traumatic injury. The weakness in her limbs was puzzling for she had been a strong, active infant. He had often wondered if an illness was the cause of her lameness, although his knowledge of such conditions was limited.

He wondered what Michael would conclude. Observing her now, he was learning again. Michael's skill rekindled in him the keen fascination that he had once felt for his craft. For a moment he wished that he had not stopped practicing, but then he reminded himself that his reasons had been sound.

He leaned against the bedpost, focusing his attention once again on Michael and her quick, competent examination. She listened to the child's heartbeat by laying her head against Brigit's chest, and asked her to take deep breaths while she rested her ear against her back. She counted pulse beats for long, silent minutes; she looked carefully at the child's eyes and throat, and felt around the neck and beneath the armpits. She palpated her stomach, and rolled the child over gently to run her fingers along her spine, back, and legs.

After checking head, limbs, and trunk in detail, she asked Diarmid for a glass vial so that she could exam-

ine the child's urine, pointing out that she did not as
yet have her own instruments. Diarmid went to his
chamber and returned with the only clear glass available at Dunsheen, a Venetian cup of thick, patterned
glass banded in silver, fashioned to hold wine and once
prized by his mother. When Brigit had supplied the
necessary sample, Michael held the glass up to the
light critically, swirling and even sniffing its contents.

Then, as she had done several times during the examination, she turned away to write down a few
words, using a quill pen dipped in ink and a single
sheet of parchment, which she had managed to pro-
cure from Lilias.

"Brigit, tell me how this feels," Michael said. Supporting the child's right ankle, she lifted the leg a few
inches off the bed and held it.

"Fine," Brigit said.

Michael bent the right knee gently and pushed the
thigh toward Brigit's stomach. "And this? Fine as
well? Good. Now this." Michael rotated the upper leg
gently to test the hip joint. "Can you lower your leg
by yourself?" she asked. Brigit nodded, her mouth set
in determination. "Good girl," Michael said, beaming.
She lifted the left ankle and leg. "And how does
this feel?"

"Hurts," Brigit said, catching her breath tearfully.
Diarmid tensed inwardly when he heard the pain in
her voice.

"This?" Michael bent the knee and moved it
slowly upward.

"Hurts," Brigit gasped.

"Then I will stop. Can you move your left leg?"

Brigit grimaced with effort and barely managed to
wiggle her toes. "I cannot do it."

Michael smiled. "Ah, but you moved your toes, and
I am pleased." She held the child's flaccid left foot,
which curled inward, and flexed it gently, thoughtfully.
Once she glanced at Diarmid briefly; he saw a flash
of concern in her eyes. Then she took Brigit's left

hand. "Squeeze my fingers as hard as you can," she said.

Brigit wrinkled her nose as she tried, although her fingers barely rounded over Michael's.

"Good girl," Michael said softly. "Can you sit up?"

Brigit rolled to her left side and pushed with her right arm to lift herself to an upright position. "*Brighid* means strength," she said. "And I'm strong," she insisted.

"I see that," Michael said. "Can you stand?"

Brigit nodded and pushed her legs over the edge of the bed until her feet dangled above the floor. Diarmid stepped forward to support her as she straightened and took her weight on her right leg. Brigit stood trembling for a moment, then fell back into his waiting hands.

Michael's smile did not lighten the serious expression in her eyes. "You are indeed strong. Can you stand on your left foot?"

Supported in Diarmid's large hands, Brigit dragged her curled left foot forward with effort. Suppressing his urge to help her, Diarmid watched her struggle to take her weight on her left leg. As she tipped helplessly forward, he scooped her into his arms.

"Enough," he said brusquely, looking at Michael.

"Enough, your uncle is right," Michael said. "You are sweet to do this for me, though I know you are tired. I'll take only one more moment of your time." She stepped close to them. "Let me see your eyes once more, dear," she said, and lifted the child's eyelids to peer close. "Show me your smile, now, and then your uncle will carry you down the stairs." She tickled Brigit beneath the left armpit, and the child grinned. Michael responded with her own smile, her azure eyes lighting as if a candle flame sparked within.

When Michael glanced at Diarmid, her simple joy changed to soberness so quickly that he felt an odd sense of loss.

"Can you carry her down to the hall, please?" she

asked. "Lilias promised her a treat when we were done."

He complied with a nod, striding out of the room with Brigit clinging to his neck. Michael followed them down the twisting angle of the stone steps, her skirts swishing rhythmically.

In the great hall, he set Brigit in a chair and let Lilias fuss over arranging cushions, a blanket, and a stool for her feet. The chamber was filled with the chatter and activity of Iona MacArthur and her siblings, a younger girl and two small boys. Gilchrist sat at the harp. Diarmid stood silently by as Michael greeted his brother and was introduced to the rest of Mungo's children, Eva, Donald, and Fingal. He waited while she spoke with Lilias regarding the best foods for Brigit.

By the hearth, Gilchrist sat with his head bent over the harp, plucking strings and tuning them carefully with his small wooden key, barely looking up as girls and dogs whirled past him, working and playing. Iona scrubbed the heavy oak table, and swept the old rushes that had covered the planked floors into piles to be removed. The youngest girl dipped her hand into a bag of dried ferns and heather blooms, scattering the mixture over the clean floors and giggling while the dogs jumped and barked as if Eva made a game just for them.

Diarmid sighed and looked at Gilchrist, who shrugged as if resigned to the noise, and went back to his harp. After a moment, Diarmid folded his arms over his chest and looked at Michael, tapping his foot. She glanced at him.

"Well?" he asked expectantly.

"A moment," she said, and bent toward Brigit. "You've been an angel," she said. "And I will play a game of chess with you later, as I promised. For now I must talk with your uncle."

Brigit nodded. One of the dogs came up and licked her hand, and she laughed in delight, petting his head.

Michael smiled and smoothed a few of Brigit's tangled curls.

Diarmid gestured toward the door. "We cannot talk in here. Come outside." He took her arm and escorted her to the door, then led her toward the stairs.

Cool wind, carrying the invigorating scents of salt water and pine, struck him as he stepped out onto the stone walk of the parapet. The autumn sun warmed his face as he looked around. Beside him, Michael stepped out onto the battlement and gasped in wonder.

Fifty feet below, the base of the castle was lipped by a border of green isle, a wide swath of grass. Beyond the narrow shore, the loch glittered like sapphires and gold melted together, reflecting the sky and the autumn-colored mountains in its depths. Far in the distance lay the wide expanse of the sea.

"What are those mountains?" Michael asked.

"Mountains in the western Isles," he answered. "Mull is closest to us. Turn this way"—he took her small shoulders and shifted her—"far out there, you can see Jura."

"Beautiful," she said, smiling.

He smiled too, half to himself, standing behind her. After months of raiding with the king through mud and forest, he was home at last. He inhaled the salted air, heard the cries of seabirds overhead, heard the shush of wind and wave together, and could only smile, could only feel content, needing no words to express it. He had missed this place intensely, had needed to be here. Closing his eyes, he sensed the water, the air, the very strength of the earth and rock that supported his castle, as if he could draw their elemental, essential power into himself.

Then he opened his eyes, recalling the other reason he had come up here. He leaned against the stone wall behind him and looked down at the neat, creamy crown of Michael's veil.

"Well?" he asked.

She turned and looked up at him. The cool clarity of the autumn sunlight revealed her flawless skin. Her gaze was as azure as the sky, but a frown shadowed their color.

"She is a lovely child," she began. "Phlegmatic in nature, with a touch of the melancholic. She needs herbs suited to drying her systems, as well as to warm her. She lacks enough choleric bile, but I believe that we can help to balance her with herbs and the right foods. More chicken and broth, apples, eggs are good for her. Less grain will help. She needs thyme and dandelion and—"

"Enough of that," he said impatiently. "What about her limbs?"

"I am not certain," she said slowly. "The right side of Brigit's body seems normal, although her muscles are weak from lack of use. But the left side—" She increased the frown. "She looks somewhat like an adult who has had an apoplectic fit, although she has no impairment of speech."

"None at all," he said wryly. "She chatters like a jay."

"She has lost most of the strength in her left leg, and some in her left arm. I notice that the left side of her mouth droops a bit—"

"Cam beul," Diarmid said. "I have it too. The recent name taken by Clan Diarmid is Campbell, after *cam beul.*"

"Crooked mouth," she repeated. "What of it?"

"It is a family trait. Clan Diarmid kin, through generations, often have a wry twist to the mouth. Brigit has the crooked smile of the Dunsheens. I do as well." He grinned, mirthlessly, to show her.

"Ah," she said, nodding, and returned a sweet ghost of a smile. Something inside of him flipped crazily, but he retained his somber expression. "The slant of Brigit's lip is far more marked than yours," she said. "And her left eyelid droops."

"She is five years old," he said. "She could not have had an apoplectic fit."

"That would be unlikely," she agreed. "But other diseases can cause similar symptoms. In an adult, lameness can occur when there is an excess of one humor or another. But children tend to be more balanced in their bodily humors and in their health. Usually lameness in children is caused by injury or an accident of birth, although there are diseases that can cause stiffness in the limbs and severe crippling, even death. Ibrahim treated such illnesses in the Holy Land and in Italy and France." She paused, drawing her brows together in thought. "How long has she been like this, Diarmid? Was it evident at birth?"

He shook his head. "She was born a lusty child, strong and hearty." He stopped, unwilling to say more. He looked at his hands, turning the left one, with its smooth scars, in the cool sunlight. A flashing image of the day, the moment, of Brigit's birth rolled through his mind. He stilled its course.

"Until I brought her here, she fostered with her mother's kin, as I told you," he continued. "Mungo saw her a year past. He says she was fine and healthy then."

"Someone surely knows what happened to her."

He glanced away, fighting anguish and guilt. He would never forgive himself for leaving Brigit there. "The old grandmother told me that the child's fostering parents died of a lung fever, which the child also had. Brigit survived, of course. But the old woman insisted that the fair folk stole the healthy child away and left a sickly, crippled girl in her place."

Michael was silent for a long while. "A fever causing this? It is possible, but—until I have my medical treatises, I cannot be certain. There may be some information in there."

"In the meantime, what treatment do you propose?"

"Hot packs and herbal soaks, medicines for pain

and stiffness, and techniques to strengthen the muscles."

"I began those treatments months ago," he said.

"Of course. You would know how to treat muscle weakness."

"I know little besides the basic herbs and the need for heat. A local herb-wife prepares herbal doses for her, and Lilias gives her those and applies moist hot cloths often. The curling of her foot concerns me," he added.

"Her foot is beginning to drop, and soon those muscles will shrivel and her foot will stay limp. We can place a board in her bed to support her foot when she sleeps. But we must stretch her muscles, and she must be on her feet more often."

"On her feet?" He raised his brows. "She sits up often. We carry her down the stairs each day."

"She can stand," Michael said.

"She falls," he countered.

"She will learn to catch herself," she said decisively.

He frowned. "But her legs are fragile."

"Her muscles are beginning to atrophy," she said bluntly. "We must encourage strength rather than weakness. She is a healthy child, not a piece of Venetian glass. She will fall, but she will pick herself up."

Diarmid lowered his brows. "I brought you here to help her, not to impose harsh demands on her. I want her healed," he said, teeth clenched, "wholly and fully. I do not want her to drag herself about, lame and marked, like a freak in a city gutter."

Michael faced him, her shoulders squared. "You have asked the impossible of me. Allow me to attempt it."

He stared at her. "What do you mean?"

"I want to watch Brigit, and work with her, before I know—"

"Know what?" he demanded.

"If she will walk," she finished.

"She will," he snapped. "You will see to it."

"Then allow me my methods!" She glared at him.

He leaned down toward her. "I have told you what I want!"

"And I have told you what I can do!"

He opened his mouth to reply hotly, then paused to master his temper. "I want her healed, Michael. Quickly. Surely you understand."

Her gaze softened. "I do," she said. "You are a bit of a fool, Dunsheen, but a wonderful kind of fool."

He narrowed his eyes. "What do you mean?"

"Made simple by love for a small girl." She gave him a sweet smile, so kind that it made his heart ache. He looked into her earnest, sky-colored gaze and wanted to pour into that well a little of the agony he carried inside. She offered comfort, understanding, relief.

But sharing his grief would mean forgiving himself. He shuttered the urge quickly, looking away. "I am her guardian, and I owe her an obligation," he said curtly. "Tell me—what other methods do you plan to use to treat her?"

"Herbal poultices and infusions," she said. "I need to know what she already takes."

"I will go over the ingredients with you."

She nodded and turned as if to go, then spun back. "Can you tell me the day of her birth? Was it March, or late February?"

"Mid-March, the feast of Saint Patrick," he said, surprised.

"I thought so," she said. "She is an enchanting child, delicate and kind, with a dreamy, imaginative mind, very much like those born under the constellation of Pisces."

He rubbed his chin in dismay. "I should have known—a book-learned physician would be an astrologer too," he muttered.

"Of course," she said easily. "Those born under the sign of the Fish often have trouble with the feet," she went on. "But her legs are an area of weakness too,

so among the negative aspects of her planets, there
must be sore afflictions to Saturn and Mercury. Do
you know the hour of her birth?"

"The hour?" he repeated. He knew it too well.
"Why?"

"When Mungo brings my books, I will use my charts
to cast her natal horoscope. Then I will better understand the nature of her condition and how best to
treat it."

"Stars are for steering ships at night, and for shed-
ding light on the earth," he growled. "We had a physician here who made a natal chart and insisted it was
accurate. He said her poor Saturn made it necessary
to amputate her legs."

Michael paused. "I am sure that is not the case,"
she said. "When my belongings arrive, I can show you
how helpful a horoscope chart can be for medical
matters."

"Books will not show you what Brigit needs," he
said.

"They will be of great help—"

He leaned close. "Look at her, touch her—heal her,
Michael," he said bluntly. "You need nothing but
your hands."

"If that were true, I would be beatified before the
week was out," she snapped. She clapped a hand over
her mouth as if regretting her remark.

He scowled down at her, frustrated once again by
her tendency to do what she wanted—rather than
what he asked of her. "You would be an admirable
saint," he drawled.

She lifted her chin. "I know what I am doing. If I
can discover the planetary influences at the time of
her birth and of her illness, I will know more about
her health and about what treatment she needs," she
said. "Surely you have used astrology in your surgery experience."

"I did not learn medicine from dead mathemati-
cians."

"Will you bleed a patient during a full moon? Or perform surgery then?"

"Not by choice," he said. "Bleeding can become profuse during the days of a full moon."

"Exactly. Then you did not cut, advised by astrology."

"I was advised by plain sense."

"Charts can predict the waning and waxing of the moon for months in advance. Years," she added.

"So useful for making schedules in a city barber-surgeon's shop," he said wryly. "Income surely increases with the waning of the moon, when bleedings are safe and profitable."

The glance she shot at him fairly sizzled. "I have never used indiscriminate bleeding techniques," she said stiffly, "nor did my husband. The tradition of Arabic medicine does not advise that, but does use astrology extensively. All the celestial bodies pull upon the fluids and humors in our bodies and determine the inner balances of body and mind. When we understand that, we know more about our health and ourselves."

He watched her doubtfully. "Is this what they teach in Italy? What of bandaging methods, or medicinal treatments, or techniques of surgery and childbirth?"

"I learned those too. You, Diarmid Campbell," she said, narrowing her eyes. "I would say that you were born in the spring. Likely in mid-April."

He blinked once, twice. "The eighteenth day of April." She smiled. "You guessed by luck," he said.

"Your character told it to me. You are very much a ram—headstrong, determined, impatient, impulsive. You want others to do as you say, and do it now. Those born under the sign of Aries are quick-witted and—" She stopped.

He folded his arms. "Go on, I am fascinated."

"The ram loves to hear about himself," she said saucily.

"Quick-witted and what?" he prodded, suppressing a wide grin.

"And passionate in all endeavors," she said frankly, but Diarmid saw her cheeks pinken.

He quirked a brow. "Would you like to find out?"

She looked away quickly. "I am sure enough," she said. "I would guess that your ascending sign is in Scorpio—you have some secrets—and your moon is probably in the sign of the Bull. . . ." She studied him speculatively. "But I would have to know the time of your birth before I could know the rest."

"Moon and stars or none, you will never learn the whole of me," he said in a low voice. "Not from books." He tipped his head and looked at her critically. "I would say that you were born on the twenty-ninth day of September."

Her eyebrows shot up. "How did you know that?" She smiled. "You *do* know something of the stars."

He could not resist. Leaning forward, he tapped her chin, covered by her widow's wimple, lightly. "I know something of Saint Michael's Day," he drawled, "Michaelmas." He enunciated her name slowly, in careful English.

She looked chagrined, then laughed. He chuckled with her, feeling a burst of happiness that startled him. "Whatever I learn about you will not come from a chart," he said somberly. "It will come through being with you. Watching you. Listening to you." His voice became husky, and he leaned in close. "Touching you." He should not have said that so boldly, he knew, but just then he felt as if he could not hold back the words, or the thoughts, or the feelings she stirred in him.

She lowered her lashes as if in sudden ecstasy, and he felt its twin in himself, a plummeting rush of desire. He wanted to feel her lips pillow beneath his again, wanted to touch the silk of her hair and skin, wanted more, so much more.

And could not have it. Heart thumping heavily, he

fisted his hands against the powerful desire to take
her into his arms. Uncertain how he had gotten caught
in this current, he fought it like a drowning man.

She looked up then, and drowning or not, he drank
in the exquisite color of her eyes. "There is something
else that tells me you were born under the ram," she
said softly.

"And what is that?" he whispered.

She reached up and touched his left eyebrow with
the tip of her finger. "Head wounds," she said. "Aries
is prone to them."

He could not answer for a moment. A feeling shot
through him at her simple touch, a sensation so strong
that he sucked in his breath. Warmth like liquid fire
rushed through him, head to toe, its source the point
at which her finger met his skin.

She smiled, fleeting and soft. "Here is another, and
another." Her fingers slid along his cheek to his stubbled jaw, touching the line of a scar on his chin, tracing the thin crease of another old wound that nicked
his upper lip. His heart pounded heavily, and his body
surged, filling, desiring, changing the innocence of her
touch to something more. His breath deepened, became ragged.

"These scars tell me that the influence of Mars is
strong in your life," she murmured. "You are indeed
a warrior."

Mars be damned. For an instant, he could barely
breathe. Fascinated, drawn closer, he leaned in toward
her. He had never felt such utter pleasure in a simple
touch. He wanted to give her equal pleasure; raising
his hand, he touched her cheek tentatively.

She drew in a slow breath and lowered her lids as
if she felt the same strange pull that he did, and as if
she resisted it too. She dropped her hand quickly and
turned to walk away.

Diarmid reached out to pull her back to him, but
cold sense spilled in from somewhere. He hesitated,

summoned control, and remained still. He should not
pursue this with her.

Michael turned back, her face anxious. "Look
there," she said, pointing past the battlement toward
the loch.

He lifted his gaze. A galley, long and low, with a
gracefully curved prow and stern, glided toward the
castle. A square sail billowed out, its embroidered red
design of a lightning bolt clearly marked in the
sunlight.

"That is one of my own birlings," he said. "I own
three oared galleys—two for trade use, and one in the
service of the king. That is my largest trading galley."
He took her elbow. "Come down to the shore and
greet my brother Arthur."

Chapter Nine

"Lightning?" Michaelmas asked. She looked at the galley's wind-filled sail. As she spoke, the men on deck lowered twenty pairs of oars, jutting upward, to row closer and pull the galley into place beside the quay. "What does the design signify?"

"The lightning is for Loch *Sìan*," Diarmid answered. "Loch Sheen has long been called the loch of storms, and so lightning became the device of the Campbells of Dunsheen."

Michaelmas watched as the galley streamed toward them gracefully, then looked at the silver-blue calm of the loch, at the surrounding pines swaying green and slow, at the soft white clouds drifting overhead. They stood on a natural ridge of rock that thrust into the loch and served as a quay. Today she could not imagine strife at Dunsheen from weather or war or any other source.

"Storms? It is so peaceful here," she said.

"If you stay long enough, you will learn why it is called Loch *Sìan*," Diarmid said, watching the vessel approach. "In fact, we may have a storm very soon," he murmured.

"On such a clear day, I doubt—"

"I do not mean the weather," he answered abruptly. He stepped forward, waiting while the long galley drew closer. She thought he frowned as he looked at the two men standing together in the bow of the galley.

She watched his strong profile, his hair whipped

back by the wind off the loch, his jaw clenched as if he
dared a storm to overtake him. Suddenly Michaelmas
wanted to stay long enough to learn more about this
place—and long enough to find out more about the
powerful, enigmatic laird who held this castle on the
loch of storms.

She had seen many ships, though few as elegantly
shaped as Diarmid's birling. Large but not heavy in
its design, its graceful, powerful lines curved and swept
upward like ocean waves in a design similar to the old
Viking longships that she had seen in paintings and
stone carvings. She knew that the Islesmen favored
the old northern design over the heavier, larger European ships used elsewhere, but she had never seen
one this close at hand.

As the boat glided in beside the rocky ledge, she
studied in fascination the carved, painted detailing
along the rim of the hull and the upthrust prow and
stern ends, capped with swirled dragons' heads. The
oarsmen shipped the oars upright in the boat, and one
man tossed out a long rope. Diarmid caught it and
looped it around a jagged boulder. Michaelmas heard
the splash of an anchor.

Diarmid stepped closer, but the deep, still water
made her uneasy, and she stayed back. Two men
stepped out of the boat and down a board carved with
footholds, leaping onto the quay. One was clearly a
Highlander by his plaid, green and black like Diarmid's; the other wore a dark surcoat and cloak. He
hung back while the Highlander greeted Diarmid with
a grin and a quick hug.

"Arthur, welcome!" Diarmid said, clapping him on
the shoulder. They talked and laughed quietly.

Michaelmas immediately noticed the resemblance
between them. Arthur's hair was auburn and his eyes
were dark, and he was as tall and broad-shouldered
as Diarmid and Gilchrist. His features were amicable,
even plain, without Gilchrist's perfection or the noble
strength in Diarmid's face. But the familiar charm of

the Dunsheen Campbells emerged in full dazzle whenever Arthur smiled.

The other man appeared a little older, shorter than the Campbells but wide and muscular. Clothed in an English manner in a surcoat of slate-colored wool, belted low, beneath a hooded black cloak, he wore leather gloves and well-made leather boots.

"Raonull," Diarmid said. "Greetings." Michaelmas heard a wary note in his voice, and saw the fists he hid at his sides.

"Dunsheen." The man nodded curtly and shoved back his hood, revealing thick brown hair cropped short and a neatly trimmed brown beard. "We have matters to discuss." He spoke in a courtly form of English, his tone polite, yet with a note of coldness. "We have just returned from Ireland with a new load of exported goods, which we have deposited at my own castle."

"We will talk about the distribution of the goods, then. You are welcome to have supper with us," Diarmid said in Gaelic. "How does Sorcha?"

"Well enough," Ranald answered in English. Michaelmas glanced quickly from one man to the other, intrigued by their stubborn battle of languages.

Diarmid turned. "Lady *Micheil,* this is my brother, Arthur Campbell," he said, gesturing to the Highlander beside him.

She smiled again. Arthur gave her a lopsided grin and a half bow, and then turned to take long strides toward the open portcullis of the castle. Michaelmas heard Angus's loud, exuberant shout from inside the bailey yard.

"And this is my brother-in-law, Ranald MacSween," Diarmid said. "The captain of Glas Eilean," he added.

She stepped backward, stunned. Diarmid reached for her arm, as if to prevent her from stumbling. She pulled away.

"Ranald MacSween. I know your name and your reputation." She spoke coolly, in precise Gaelic, aware that she declared her animosity, as she sensed Diarmid had, by her choice of language.

"Lady *Micheil.*" MacSween switched easily to Gaelic then, and inclined his head courteously. "You have heard of me through the laird of Dunsheen?"

"Through my *bràthair,*" she said. "Sir Gavin Faulkener."

Whatever flickered in his eyes was instantly gone. "Ah, then, you are Lady Michaelmas of Kinglassie. I am honored to meet you at last." He looked at Diarmid. "Is her brother here?" he asked sharply.

Diarmid shook his head. "The lady is a guest at Dunsheen. She is here on my invitation, to tend to my niece's condition."

Ranald MacSween raised his eyebrows. "I did not realize that Faulkener's sister was a healer. Interesting." He smiled, thin and flat. "My lady, may I say that I have endeavored to keep the castle of Glas Eilean in your good name."

"You keep it, sir," she said, "in your own name."

He placed a hand over his heart. "I mean only to protect your property, my lady."

"You killed my brother's sergeant!" she burst out.

"A regrettable incident," MacSween murmured. "However, not uncommon in situations of war."

"Perhaps you should explain the incident to the lady." Diarmid's voice cut through the air like sharp steel.

MacSween shrugged. "Faulkener's men attacked our seaward entrance. We defended ourselves." He shook his head as if she were an erring child. "You should not trouble yourself with such matters, my lady."

"Such matters," she said, "trouble me greatly."

He inclined his head, unperturbed, watching her with deep, unreadable brown eyes. "May I inquire if your brother has found a husband for you yet?"

"I have no husband or betrothed," she said. "I will choose none."

"Is it so?" He took her hand, bowing over it as if she were a queen. "Be assured that I will hold Glas Eilean faithfully for King Robert and for you, my lady, as long as you like." His mustache and warm lips brushed over the back of her hand. A repulsive shiver ran through her. She pulled her hand away, suddenly glad for Diarmid's strong, warm presence beside her.

"If you hold Glas Eilean for me, then I ask that you give it over to my control," she said impulsively.

"*Micheil*—" Diarmid murmured, and placed a warning hand on her elbow. She shook it off and stared boldly at MacSween, her heart pounding.

Ranald dismissed her with a scant glance and looked at Diarmid. "What nonsense is this she speaks? Have you tried to influence her?"

"Not at all. The lady knows her mind," Diarmid said calmly.

MacSween turned to Michaelmas with a thin smile. "Glas Eilean has remained safe in my hands for many years. In order to hold it against English and Scots both, for many would desire to possess that castle, you would have to marry. You are wise to accept no offer, my lady. A rough Highlander or a backward Islesman as a husband might prove poor judgment indeed."

"Watch yourself, MacSween," Diarmid growled. Michaelmas felt a sharp rise in the searing tension between the two men. "The Lady Michael is my guest. She will be shown courtesy."

"I am the soul of courtesy. Your sister will attest to that," MacSween said in a smooth voice.

"Will she?" Diarmid asked coldly.

MacSween turned to Michaelmas. "As a woman— and a lovely one, my lady—you cannot possibly understand what it is you ask of me. Glas Eilean is a sentinel in the Isles. Its seaward position helps protect western Scotland."

His placating manner ignited her temper. "I know that," she snapped. "And my brother has the right to oversee my castle."

"Gavin Faulkener cannot wave me away as if I were a sergeant done with the night watch. King Robert appointed me to that post several years ago. Your name on that charter means little unless you wed a man approved by the king, a man forceful enough to hold that place." He inclined his head. "I advise you to tend to your healing simples and leave these concerns to capable men." He stepped past her and walked toward the castle.

Michaelmas scowled and started after him.

Diarmid grabbed her arm. "Let him go," he said.

She yanked away from his grip. "Glas Eilean should have been given over to Gavin last month, in peace and good spirit!"

He stepped close, his gray gaze piercing. "Then let your brother and the king solve the problem."

"They are engaged in a war in the border area. I wanted you to solve the problem." She knew she sounded petulant.

"I will not take Glas Eilean for you," he said flatly.

Her brother's men had fought and one had died at the gates of Glas Eilean, and she did not want more tragedy. "But you can negotiate with MacSween, for you are kin by marriage. You can avert much trouble for Gavin, for his men, for Robert Bruce."

He stared unblinking at the water.

"You once swore to do whatever I asked of you in exchange for a miracle," she reminded him.

"Not this," he growled. A lean muscle pounded in his cheek.

She felt as if she pushed against a solid, invisible boulder. Diarmid seemed set in stone; he would not give way. But neither would she. Folding her arms over her chest, she lifted her chin.

"That is my bargain," she said. "That is my price."

"Is it so?" The steely glint of the loch was mirrored in his steadfast eyes. "Then it seems that we will have no miracles between us." He turned and walked away.

Michaelmas stood motionless, listening to his steps

crunch over stone. His words echoed in her mind, lonely, final, disappointing.

No miracles. Thin, cold waves licked at the rocks beneath her feet, a gray chill that sucked her spirit. *No miracles.* A feeling of loss, of sorrow, swept through her.

Diarmid's grim statement had cracked the fragile new bond that had begun to form between them—a bond that she had no right, perhaps no wisdom, to desire, for he was wed, and she would be at Dunsheen for only a short while.

She drew long, steadying breaths and wondered what she would do now. She had asked him to win back her castle; he would not. He had asked her to perform a miracle; she could not.

No miracles between us.

She watched the gleaming silver skin of the water and regretted her impulsive words to Diarmid. Just days ago, she had fought against coming here. Now the thought of leaving Dunsheen Castle distressed her greatly. She wanted to help Brigit, wanted to see her strong enough to walk; she believed that it was possible with the right treatment.

And she wanted to learn more about the laird of Dunsheen, who held his secrets so close. She wanted to see that tilted smile again, hear his laughter. Feel his touch, his kiss. She sighed. None of that was for her.

Perhaps she would do best to leave this castle now and never think of the Dunsheen Campbells again. But she could not do it. She could not walk away from Brigit now.

After a while, she turned and made her way up the gentle grassy slope that led to the castle gate.

"That child should be put in a religious house," Ranald said in Gaelic. He gestured toward Brigit, holding a silver wine cup in his hand. "When will you make her an oblate?"

The web of music spun by Gilchrist's harp strings
faded. Diarmid glanced at Ranald and then at Brigit,
who sat securely in Michael's lap near the hearth. The
dogs lay beside them resting. Supper had been eaten
and cleaned up an hour ago, and Lilias, Iona, and Eva
sat with sewing tasks while they listened to Gilchrist's
harp music. Mungo's young sons, Donald and Fingal,
lay on the floor playing a game of draughts.

Diarmid turned a cool gaze on his brother-in-law.
"I refuse to make a gift of Brigit to the Church," he
answered quietly. He was certain only Ranald and
Arthur could hear him. "That is simply aban-
donment."

"The custom provides a solution for deformed
children."

"She is not deformed," Arthur said sharply, from
his seat beside Diarmid.

Ranald waved a hand impatiently. "She is hardly
normal, and is no longer an infant. Put her away and
be done with it. Let the nuns tend to her."

The harp strings sounded again, bolder this time as
Gilchrist began a quick rhythm. "I will tend to her as
I see fit," Diarmid said firmly, keeping his voice low.

"I offer sound advice. Think of her lands," Ranald
said. "She has inherited her father's castle in Argyll.
A waste. That fine fortress should be in strong hands."

"It is," Diarmid said. "Our brother Colin holds
Glenbevis for her until she marries."

"But she is not marriageable," Ranald insisted. "I
am only trying to help. You cannot want another crip-
ple to look after."

Diarmid sucked in a fast breath, quelling an urge
to grab Ranald MacSween by the embroidered neck
of his elegant English surcoat. Arthur sent Diarmid a
dark glance that showed a similar frustration, but he
too stayed silent.

Fisting a hand on the table to show Ranald its subtle
threat, Diarmid did no more. He was determined to
master his resentment for Sorcha's sake. And for the

sake of the king's plans. "What do you imply?" he asked coldly.

"I mean no disrespect," Ranald said, in a mild voice. "The Dunsheen Campbells have had ill fortune among their kin. The early deaths of your father and Fionn, and then your mother, the troubles of Sorcha, Gilchrist, Brigit—" He shrugged eloquently. "Perhaps it is just the luck of breeding. Sorcha would fare better if she were of heartier stock."

Diarmid started forward. "Say no more!" he exploded.

Ranald colored instantly, his jaw tightening. "Sorcha has lost one weak babe after another. There is no fault with the breeding tool, but with the ground it plows. She had best bear me a healthy living son this next time."

"Or what?" Diarmid asked icily. Ranald said nothing; Diarmid thought it a wise choice.

"Sorcha has risked her life six times to bear your babes," Arthur said. "When you speak of her in the hearing of her brothers, you had best praise her."

Diarmid remained silent with effort, but his fisted hand and steely glance added support to his brother's remark.

Ranald shifted uneasily and cleared his throat. "Perhaps Lady Michael should attend Sorcha. She must know something of midwifery. She is an herb-healer."

"She is a physician," Diarmid said.

Ranald looked surprised. "Indeed? Are you certain?"

"Quite."

"Then she surely knows something of women's maladies."

"I doubt she will consent to visit Glas Eilean as long as you are captain there," Arthur said.

"Is it so? A shame. I fear that Sorcha will be brought to a sorrowful bed again soon." He shrugged as if it were out of his hands entirely. "She would do well to consult a physician in this. She fears that she is incapable of bearing lusty children."

Diarmid sucked in air, striving to control his temper. As long as Sorcha could endure her anguish, then he would tolerate this arrogant man. His sister had once begged it of her brothers, reminding them that kin, including marriage kin, were respected and valued above all else in Highland custom.

"Lady Michael can tend to Sorcha here," Arthur suggested.

"I cannot allow Sorcha to travel," Ranald said. "The risk is too great."

"Our sister has hardly left Glas Eilean in the several years that she has been your wife," Arthur said. "You keep her like a prisoner."

"If she were not so weak, she would have every freedom," Ranald murmured. "But she chooses to stay isolated."

Diarmid rubbed a hand in slow frustration over his jaw, and looked sideways at Arthur, whose lean face was grim in the low light, looking as stormy as Diarmid felt himself.

No matter how angry they were, Diarmid thought, he and Arthur and the rest of their Dunsheen kin must bide time and show tolerance to Ranald. There was cause even beyond Sorcha's well-being now. But Diarmid was determined to see Ranald pay when the time was ripe for it. For now, he would consider Sorcha's needs above all else.

"How long until Sorcha reaches her term?" he asked Ranald.

"If she reaches it? Three months, I think."

Diarmid nodded. He too wanted Michael to see Sorcha, but he thought she might refuse. Nevertheless, he would ask her as nicely as he could. By now he knew that bargains and commands would not work with her. "I will speak to Lady Michael," he said, and sighed heavily.

He glanced at her. Michael watched him from her

seat by the hearth, and looked away quickly. He wondered if she had heard their conversation, and she had probably concluded that he would not help her regain Glas Eilean because Ranald MacSween was kin to him. She did not know about his determination to protect his sister.

A moment later the harp fell silent. Diarmid looked over to see Gilchrist rise to his feet and swing the wooden crutch under his arm. He murmured to the women and came toward the table.

Their youngest brother had never disguised his dislike of Ranald, rarely speaking to him at all. In fact, Gilchrist said little in general, keeping his thoughts to himself. Diarmid had noticed long ago that the depth and quality of Gilchrist's mind and emotions emerged only through the beautiful music and lyrics he composed.

He looked at Diarmid and turned his back to Ranald. "I will bid you good night," he said quietly to his brothers.

"We'll hear more of your songs on the morrow, I hope," Arthur said. Gilchrist nodded and swung away.

"So fortunate that *Gillecriosd Bacach* can play the harp," Ranald commented. "Nice skills, harping and storytelling."

Lame Gilchrist, Ranald had called him. Diarmid swore silently and half rose, tempted to take Ranald by the throat at last, and kinship be damned.

Arthur must have sensed his reaction, for he kicked Diarmid in the shin. "Skills suited to Gilchrist's brilliance," Arthur said. "He is a fine bard for Dunsheen. We are fortunate to have his talents. The king himself has praised his work."

The remarks gave Diarmid a moment to cool his temper. He lifted a ceramic jug to pour out more claret for himself. His brother had averted a disaster; a brawl, however satisfying, would create greater problems. He sipped the claret, determined to resist Ranald's manipulative baiting of his temper.

"Ranald and I have just brought back a shipment of goods from Ireland," Arthur said. "We picked up some fine steel on this trip."

"Did you?" Diarmid asked calmly.

"We traded hides and wool for broadswords of excellent Spanish steel, and German-made iron blades," Arthur said. "West Highland warriors will be well armored should King Robert require their fighting skills again soon."

Diarmid nodded. "I appreciate you and Ranald seeing to my interests in my absence. Who bought the woolfells collected from my Dunsheen tenants?"

"I met with Flemish merchants in Belfast, who were pleased to see such a large quantity of Scottish wool. At first they wanted to trade only with you, Dunsheen, but I plied them with good Danish aqua vitae until they agreed to deal with me as your representative."

"I trust the price was fair," Diarmid said. "Bruce has given the Flemish trading privileges with Scotland to encourage their support."

Ranald shrugged. "A poor price. They claimed it was inconvenient to meet in Ireland."

"Once we can trade directly with the Low Countries again, profits will improve," Arthur said. "There is a growing market among continental textile makers for Highland wool, and the fine quality of Scottish hides has Flemish and Italian leather makers asking for more."

"The English cannot blockade Scottish waters indefinitely," Diarmid remarked. "King Robert is working on another truce with England." One of the black hounds, Columba, padded over to him as if looking for table scraps. He scratched the dog's head idly as he spoke.

"You heard this news recently?" Ranald asked.

"I traveled and fought beside the king for months," Diarmid said. "He discussed the terms of the treaty with a few of us. He is aware that access to trade routes has been greatly impaired for western Scotland.

We must regain the right to sail through English waters to reach the ports where our goods are in demand."

"Until he works out a truce, we can continue to obtain goods through Irish ports, and trade our wool, hides, and timber there." Ranald twirled his cup in his hand. "I have stockpiled Spanish silk, plain woven cloth, quality leather goods, grain, almond oil, spices, and several tuns of claret and Bordeaux wines. We can trade that in Scottish ports now, and make a profit for ourselves."

"My forty-oar birling has been of great use to you while I have been gone, I see," Diarmid remarked. "I hope you intend to let Scotland profit a little from your efforts, as well as yourself."

Ranald twitched an eye. "Of course," he said blithely.

"The *White Heather* is a fine, spacious galley," Arthur said. "A joy to captain, brother. You may have pledged her to Robert Bruce as a warship, but when the crown does not need her, that birling is well suited to trading."

"Indeed, she is a fine vessel. I am having one built like her for myself," Ranald said.

"I commissioned a family of Norwegian shipbuilders on the Isle of Lewis," Diarmid said. "Their birlings are of superior design and quality. My other galleys are smaller, but just as well made."

"Indeed," Ranald said. "I prefer English oak for the hull over Norwegian. But English wood is expensive, and difficult to obtain just now." He smiled. "With a few successful shiploads, I should be able to afford it. We have more customers now among the chiefs and lairds of the western Highlands, eager to use our birlings to sail their goods to Ireland, and glad to buy the exports we acquire."

"I assume you plan to take the goods to Ayr and Glasgow, then," Diarmid said. "Use the *White Heather* for the journey, since you already have the goods loaded on board."

"I will," Ranald said. "And I will direct the oarsmen to be ready to sail at dawn. They are finishing their supper in the quarters below stairs. I appreciate your cooperation in this trading enterprise, Dunsheen. But I warn you that your part of the profits will be thin due to the lower prices offered for the wool in Ireland." He sipped from his goblet. "I have arranged a meeting with guild merchants in Ayr to discuss getting more exported goods into their markets in spite of the English blockade. Arthur has offered to attend the meeting with me. Perhaps you would care to come?"

"Arthur can go in my stead," Diarmid said. "His knowledge of the coast and his understanding of the English blockade will be helpful in those meetings."

Arthur nodded agreement. Diarmid glanced up when he heard the quiet shush of a woman's gown trailing along the floor. Michael came toward them, carrying Brigit in her arms.

She paused near the table. With her back arched slightly and her head held high, her face serenely perfect, she resembled a painted statue of the blessed Mary holding her child. Diarmid smiled to himself as he studied her quiet grace.

"Your niece is tired, Dunsheen," she said softly. "I will take her up to her chamber. Lilias and Iona are putting the other children to bed." Behind her, the others chattered softly as they withdrew from the great hall.

Diarmid rubbed a hand over his eyes, as if he needed to rouse himself out of the world of men and material concerns that had preoccupied him since supper, and enter the gentle world where women and children and matters of comfort ruled.

He rose to his feet. "Let me carry her." He came around the table and held out his arms. Brigit murmured sleepily as he took her slight, warm weight against his shoulder.

"Lilias said that she would bring the child's nightly dose," Michael said. "I hoped—you said that you would explain the remedies to me. That is—if you wish me to stay here and work with her." She looked down, as if she hesitated to meet his gaze.

Diarmid recalled the sharp words that had passed between them earlier that day. "I would be glad to explain her medicines to you," he said. "Come ahead. Pardon me, Arthur, Ranald." They both nodded an abrupt good night as he turned.

He strode out of the room with Brigit in his arms, hearing the soft susurration of Michael's gown as she followed.

Chapter Ten

"Such herbs are quite reasonable for Brigit," Michaelmas said, after Diarmid and Lilias together had explained to her the contents of the herbal electuary that Lilias had brought for Brigit to drink. "But I would suggest giving her a willow infusion early in the day, and another at night," she added. She sniffed the contents of the cup before sipping it delicately. The underlying burn of the drink made her frown. "What is used as the vehicle?"

"Claret," Lilias said.

Diarmid, standing near the bed, raised an eyebrow. "Even a little is strong for one her age. Those herbs should be mixed in something less potent."

"It's only a bit," Lilias said. "It helps her to relax."

"Chamomile added to the herb blend would be a good relaxant for her at night," Michaelmas said. "Mix her medicines in cider or warm milk, and add honey and cinnamon if she favors them. She can have some watered wine when she has pain or muscle soreness. I will write out an order for the herb-wife so that she can prepare some additional medicines. Can the woman read?"

Lilias nodded. "She is a widow who lives not far from here. She prepares simples and potions of all kinds, although I keep a good stock of herbs in our kitchen here. I may have some of what you need, but I will have Iona take the instructions to the herb-wife." Michaelmas nodded her thanks.

Lilias leaned toward Brigit, who lay tucked in her

bed. "Good night to you, dear," she said. "Be sure to say your prayers." Brigit nodded, and the old woman left the room, closing the door quietly.

Michaelmas reached out to touch the tiny head of the doll tucked in the covers beside Brigit. She smoothed the strands of silken thread hair sewn above the doll's embroidered eyes and mouth. "She is lovely," she said.

"Lilias made her for me," Brigit said. "She is my guardian angel. Her name is *Micheil.*"

Diarmid chuckled. "Ah, tonight she's Michael, is she?" he teased. Brigit grinned at him. "I thought you called her Angel because you could not decide which archangel to name her after."

"She's Michael now," Brigit said firmly. She leaned back against the pillows and folded her hands in prayer, her blond curls drifting around her small face like a halo of gold. She squeezed her eyes shut and whispered a prayer, then looked at Diarmid and Michaelmas. "You must both say them with me for the charm to work. Lilias always does."

Diarmid nodded, sending a little wry smile toward Michaelmas. He sat on the edge of the bed, while she did the same on the other side.

"May the angels of heaven shield me," Brigit began, "the angels of heaven this night, may the angels of heaven keep me, soul and body alike," she finished in a lilting singsong.

Diarmid spoke in unison with her, his voice deep and mellow beneath Brigit's light tones. Michaelmas repeated the phrases as well. Unfamiliar with the words, she recognized the cadence of a typical Gaelic prayer. "That is a lovely prayer," she said when they had finished.

Brigit began another. "I lie down this night with nine angels, nine angels at my head and feet—"

"—Saint Brigit so calm, Mary revered," Diarmid said, taking up the prayer, "and Michael my love with me."

Michaelmas's gaze flew to his. He looked at her, his eyes silver and steady in the candlelight. Glancing away, blushing, she repeated the verse and reminded herself that Diarmid spoke of the archangel Michael. But the velvet-warm tone of his voice and his direct glance had touched a deep chord within her, as if harp strings vibrated with a pulsing, excited beat.

"From the crown of my head to the soles of my feet, from the crown of my head to the soles of my feet," Brigit finished in her dulcet voice. "See, now we are blessed here, and the fair folk cannot ever come to take me away," she said.

"Ah, but I'm sure the king of all the *daoine sìth* will not let that happen," Michaelmas said lightly. She glanced at Diarmid, and saw, with surprise, that a blush stained his cheeks.

"He protects us all. And he can make magic," Brigit piped.

"Brigit," Diarmid said, with clear discomfort.

"I know you do not like others to know," Brigit whispered conspiratorially. "But Lady Michael is one of your people." She smiled at both of them as if they shared a secret. "You promised me magic to heal my legs. I hope it happens soon." Her eyes shone with trust.

Michaelmas looked at Diarmid, realizing why he had insisted that she perform a miracle for Brigit. He returned her glance reluctantly and cleared his throat. "I will do what I can," he replied. "Hush, now, and sleep. Lady Michael will rub your legs, and that should feel very nice."

Brigit snuggled under the covers, tucking the limp little doll in her arms with a few cooing, loving sounds. Michael helped her to shift to her stomach, arranging pillows beneath her. Then she began to stroke her back and shoulders gently.

Diarmid watched, still seated on the edge of the bed. "Now you know why I wanted you to come here," he murmured. "I made a foolish promise which now I must keep."

Michael nodded slowly. Turning away, she picked up a small vial of almond oil that Lilias had left for her and put a few drops in her hand, rubbing them together thoughtfully.

"You surely need some magic here," she said in a soft voice, as she began to knead Brigit's bare legs.

"We have tried everything but that. Everything. I want you to stay, Michael. Do what you can." His voice was low, soft, urgent, utterly compelling.

"Without miracles?" she murmured, remembering the bitter words that had passed between them earlier. "Without magic?"

He looked down at Brigit. "Whatever you can do," he said, "however you can do it." He looked at her. "Please."

She remembered once that he had said he was afraid he would beg her one day, and hate them both for it. She drew a long breath. "I will help her."

Diarmid let out a long, low sigh. "But I will not give up on my other request of you," he murmured.

"Stubborn Highland man," she whispered, with a warm rush of affection.

He smiled a little but did not reply. She sensed him watching her as she rubbed Brigit's tiny limbs. Deep golden firelight, warmth, and silence pervaded the chamber. The sweet scent of the almond oil on her hands filled the curtained bed space. The child, nested in soft pillows, two fingers tucked in her mouth, closed her eyes, breathing peacefully.

Michaelmas glanced at Diarmid. Low firelight edged his hair and shoulders with dark, warm color. He seemed content to stay and watch. She was pleased. His solid, silent presence was welcome to her, and the strength and capableness he emanated was deeply reassuring.

She turned her attention to the child, letting her sensitive fingers knead and test while she explored the muscles. Closing her eyes briefly, she recalled pages in her medical volumes as if they lay open in front of her. Anatomical drawings and vivid memories of animal and human physiology, observed during the many dissections she had assisted in Ibrahim's lectures, went through her mind at lightning speed.

Following the shape and contour of the child's legs, her fingers delineated the delicate structure of bones, joints, and muscles. She searched for the source of the problem, hoping that a detailed exploration would tell her more about the marked weakness along the left side of Brigit's body.

As she worked, the only sounds she heard were the snap of the peat fire and the rhythmic noises Brigit made as she sucked her fingers. Diarmid was so quiet that she did not hear him at all, although she was keenly aware that he sat only an arm's breadth away. She drew in a long breath and closed her eyes, enjoying the peace and warmth as she worked.

Within moments, she began to see images in her mind. Not memories of books and lectures, the pictures almost seemed to come from her fingertips themselves, as if her hands suddenly possessed the quality of sight. Behind her closed eyes, she saw what lay beneath Brigit's petal-soft skin.

In exquisite, beautiful detail, she saw the bones and the pink, thin muscles that wrapped around them; she saw fragile nerves tracing upward, and blood singing through lacy veins like roots carrying life.

Her hands heated quickly then, as if her fingers floated on a warm cushion of air. And for one instant, for the space of a breath, like a flash of lightning, she understood the child's ailment in its entirety. She gasped and opened her eyes—and the sweeping sense of awareness dispelled as quickly as it came. Blinking, she tried to hold her thoughts, but the images and the details of her knowledge faded like the last wisp of a dream.

"What is it?" Diarmid asked.

"I—I am certain that there is no injury here," she said. "It was the fever, Diarmid."

He frowned. "What makes you so certain?"

She shook her head, shrugged, unable to explain. "I just know it," she whispered. "I just know."

As a child, she had experienced similar spontaneous flashes of insight, with vivid images that showed her the exact break in a bone, or how deep a cut went; she had glimpsed babes carried in their mothers' wombs, knew their gender and the state of their health.

But like the healing power that had flowed from her hands, long ago, of its own mysterious accord, this inner sight was just as elusive. She sighed and moved her hands to rest on the child's back. Whatever abilities she had, they were wholly unpredictable. She frowned and tried to focus on using the medical knowledge that she had spent years acquiring, for only that was reliable.

Kneading the parallel muscles along the spine, she tried to observe, tried to think through what she found. Once Mungo arrived with her books, she would look for every bit of information on lameness. She would chart a horoscope for the girl too, hoping she could discover which constellations and planets had influenced Brigit's health at the time of her birth.

She looked up to see Diarmid watching her. He reached out then, and began to rub Brigit's small shoulders and neck with his long fingers. His large hand nearly covered her slender back. Brigit sighed and shifted her wet fingers in her mouth.

When his hand brushed against Michaelmas's fingers, the accidental touch sent a lightning shock through her. More grazing touches followed as his hand moved in languid, graceful circles.

The rhythmic motions of their hands and the quiet warmth within the enclosed bed sent delicious shivers throughout her body. She watched Diarmid's strong, gentle fingers, and suddenly realized that she had stopped thinking about Brigit's condition, had ceased to analyze what she found. Like the child, she too was relaxing gradually in the silence and the warmth of touch.

"I have been thinking about our discussion, *Micheil*," Diarmid said. Mellow, deep, hushed, the dark velvet sound of his voice was as soothing as his touch. Michaelmas felt a shiver trace through her, and recalled the brief, wondrous kiss they had shared beside the healing pool. The scent of almond oil must be an intoxicant, she thought, shaking her head to dissolve the spell and to better concentrate.

She cleared her throat. "Which discussion?" she asked.

His circling hand brushed against hers again. The contact shot through her body like solid fire. "About Brigit," he said. "Perhaps you are right—she could make an effort to stand if she had some help with it."

She watched his hand as if entranced. "How so?" she asked.

"Her legs are not strong enough to hold her weight for long," he said. "But if her knees were splinted somehow—"

"Ah!" She nodded. "In Italy we sometimes wrapped the knees of lame patients with bandages and splints. With better support, they were able to move around on crutches or with canes."

"I will see what can be done," he said.

The mention of crutches reminded her of a question she had wanted to ask. "Diarmid, what happened to Gilchrist's leg?"

"A fall, a few years ago, while hunting. Both lower bones in the right leg were badly broken, and did not set properly."

She frowned. "You did not treat him yourself?"

"I was away with the king's army. When I saw him months later, the break had healed, but the leg was misshapen."

"Poorly healed breaks can sometimes be corrected," she ventured. "Ibrahim did it. The surgeon must be very skilled, but you have the ability."

He looked at her swiftly, directly, then glanced away. "Had," he said softly. "Had." He flexed his left hand, where it rested on the bed, its scars shining pink in the dim light. Then he went back to tracing a pattern over the child's shoulders.

She touched his scarred thumb. "Have," she insisted. "You could help him. Rebreak the leg, and set it again—"

"That is a great risk," he said. "I lack the skill for it. And you lack the physical strength. Besides, Gilchrist would never agree to it." He moved his hand away. "You must think the Dunsheen Campbells a collection of weaklings and grotesques, Mistress Physician." His tone was droll but sharp-edged.

"Not at all," she replied. "I see beauty in all of you."

He looked puzzled. "Gilchrist is handsome, I know, and Brigit is a pretty child—"

"Gilchrist has the face of an angel," she agreed. "And Brigit too. But it is the protection and caring they have here that is most beautiful." Diarmid listened in silence. "I heard you tell MacSween that you refuse to put Brigit in a convent," she said. "And I saw how angry you and Arthur were when he made remarks about Gilchrist, and about your sister, who seems to have some difficulties. I hope you do not mind me overhearing some of that," she finished in a rush.

He shook his head. "I am glad you listened. I want you to consider going to see Sorcha. I know you are angry with MacSween, but I think you can help her."

She frowned. "Would you set me two miracles to perform, when I have asked but one task of you?" she asked, her tone more curt than she meant.

He held up a hand. "Peace. I just want you to see Sorcha, and help her however you judge best. I know it is difficult for you to go there, but I do not trust the old midwife that Ranald has hired for her. Sorcha needs a younger woman, a friend. That is all I ask. A few days of your time to encourage her. We all worry about her."

She was touched, as she had been at other times, by the caring and kindness that she sometimes glimpsed in him. He truly loved his kin. And he asked for only her medical expertise this time.

"I will think on it," she said. She would consider all the implications of going to Glas Eilean later.

"My thanks," he said quietly.

She nodded, and lifted her hands to tuck the blanket around Brigit. "I want her to walk as much as you do," she murmured.

"No one can want it as much as I do," he said fiercely.

"I have seen lame and crippled people treated as if they were less than dogs," she said. "In many cities in Europe, they live in the streets and beg for food. They are spurned and forgotten, and left to die by those who should show them mercy." She took Brigit's limp fingers from her mouth and tucked them under the covers. "My husband Ibrahim tried to help such beggars regain their strength. Some of his colleagues praised him as a Good Samaritan. Others criticized him for a fool."

"Was he a Saracen, your husband?"

"Ibrahim was from the Moorish part of Spain," she said. "His mother was a Christian and his father, a converted Saracen. He studied medicine and astrology in Istanbul as a young man, and later came to Bologna to practice medicine and to lecture at the university. I met him there."

"He was your teacher?" he asked, sounding surprised.

She nodded. "He taught anatomy, diseases, and astrology. He also wrote treatises on medical matters—perhaps you have read them. Ibrahim Ibn Kateb was his name."

He shook his head. "I have read few medical texts. He must have been much older than you."

"Old enough to be my grandfather, actually," she answered. "He chose me, along with a male student, to become his assistants. Ibrahim took us both into his home to teach us. I stayed to help him in his practice."

"And to marry him."

She looked away as if to protect her secrets. Diarmid's gaze was too direct, too keen. "Ibrahim was very kind to me," she said. "He encouraged me and taught me much of what I know."

"Was he aware of your healing abilities?"

She could not meet his gaze. "He—he was," she stammered. "He believed that the healing incidents were a sign from heaven that I was meant to be a physician. Ibrahim urged me to trust in empirical sciences, and to rely on what I learned through reading and experience. He . . . felt it was wise for me to abandon my healing abilities." And she felt safe just now, saying no more about what Ibrahim had done for her.

"How long were you married?"

"Four years. He died just over a year ago. His heart was not strong—although he did not let me know that until nearly the end." She bit her lip and looked away.

"You miss him," Diarmid said gently. "You loved him."

She shrugged, a vulnerable admission of her affection for Ibrahim. "I admired his kindness, his knowledge. He would have known what to do for Brigit." She looked up, uncomfortable with the direction of his probing, ready to change the focus. "And what of you?" she asked.

"What? My marriage, or my teacher? They are not one and the same, believe me," he added wryly.

She wanted to know about his marriage, but sensed he would hold his secrets back, just as she had kept hers from him. "Where did you learn the art of surgery?"

He combed his fingers through Brigit's hair, golden strands curling around his hand. "My father sent me

to Mullinch Priory in the Isles when I was thirteen,"
he said. "I was not the eldest. My older brother ran
with Wallace and died in battle when I was in the
monastery. My father wanted one of his sons to master
letters and languages and something of civilization. I
studied Latin, French, mathematics, philosophy, and
so on, learning them faster than the monks could teach
me. The rest of my time should have been filled with
prayer and meditation, but I preferred to throw rocks
and perfect my hand-grappling skills with some of the
other students. I considered myself a warrior, and no
scholar or monk."

She smiled. "The ram, ruled by Mars the warrior,"
she said. "Eager for a fair fight, and eager to win. Such
lads are keenly intelligent, but often too impatient to
be scholars."

He cocked a brow at her, amused. "Ah, is that what
it was? I wish you could have told the prior of Mullinch that. You might have spared me a few punish-
ments." She laughed. His returned grin was fleeting
and slanted, and caused her stomach to flutter oddly.

"Were you punished and dismissed?" she asked.

"The prior decided that I should do penance for my
violent urges by treating illnesses and injuries in the
infirmary. The infirmarian took me under his tutelage.
He owned two books on *materia medica* and a volume
of Galen, which I pored over until I had memorized
them. But Brother Colum was old and died when I
was nearly sixteen. I left Mullinch and pledged myself
in service to Robert Bruce, and ran with his Highland
warriors. Shortly after that, my father died, and I became Dunsheen's laird."

"When I saw you, you were young, but already a
fine surgeon."

He shrugged. "Only an empiric surgeon, without
true book-learning and academic instruction as you
have. But I learned a great deal through necessity,
added to the basics that I had learned at Mullinch."

"And now?"

He looked away. "I am done with that part of my life."

She tilted her head. "I do not believe that."

"Do you not? Is this the hand of a capable surgeon?" He waved his left hand in the shadows.

"It is a gifted hand regardless," she said firmly. The look he cast toward her was dark. She saw a warning there, as if she trod unsafe ground. "Just look at what your touch has done. Brigit is asleep." She lightened her tone deliberately.

"Ah, well." He smiled, resting his long fingers beside hers on Brigit's back, so close that Michaelmas could feel the subtle heat. "That we did together." He tilted his head. "Now, tell me why you decided to become a book-trained physician. That is an unusual education for any woman, let alone a Scotswoman. Was it because of your healing gift?"

She smiled ruefully. "I once saw a young surgeon save a man's life on a battlefield," she murmured. "From that day on, I wanted to do what he did."

He frowned. "Do not jest with me."

She shook her head. "I mean that. I watched you that day, and carried the memory of it with me for years. You were so skilled, so compassionate. I never forgot what you did."

"But you were the one—" Then he half laughed. "We each value that memory, it seems, for different reasons."

"Value it? I cherished it," she whispered. "I thought about it for years, Diarmid. My healing gift was wondrous but unpredictable. What I saw you do was masterful, based on skill. I wanted to be able to do that too."

Diarmid shifted his fingers over hers, the almond oil slippery and warm between them. "Michael," he murmured. "Thank you." He held her hand for a moment, while her heart beat an odd rhythm. Then he let go too quickly. "How did you come to attend an Italian school?"

"I have a friend from childhood, Will MacKerras—his mother married my great-uncle John. Will attended Oxford and then went to Bologna to study canon law. When he came back to Kinglassie to visit his mother and stepfather, he told me about the young women who studied alongside the men there. He said that they earned their certificates as physicians equal to the male students. I knew that Oxford and Paris would never admit a woman, so I begged Gavin to let me go to Italy. Finally he agreed, and Will escorted me there the next year. I lived there eight years in all," she added. "My life took directions that I would never have dreamed. Ibrahim was well respected. I could not have had a finer mentor."

"You had a good marriage?" he asked.

"We were suited in many ways. Not in all," she finished quietly. She looked up, the next question burning within her. "And yours?"

"My own marriage was . . . unsuitable." He paused, looked away. "We were wed five years ago. Anabel is beautiful, intelligent, and willful. She soon found that a husband who was gone for long months with the king was boring. She took a lover." He shrugged, but she sensed in his posture that he still felt the burden of that pain. "I tried to obtain a divorce, but the bishop's court declared instead that we should have a divorce *et mensa et thoro*—we are separated in bed and board, and not required to live together."

"Where is she now?" Michaelmas asked quietly.

"She lives in a convent as a lay sister. I hear little word of her. She is Ranald's cousin, and he has word of her now and then. I send coin and goods twice a year to the convent, but I never see her. And I do not ask."

"But you are still wed," she said.

He nodded once, brusquely. She saw the telltale muscle thump in his cheek, and realized that it cost him much to speak of this. "I am resigned to it, but

I do regret that I will never have sons. Dunsheen will pass to Arthur, as the eldest of my brothers."

"I am sorry," she whispered, stricken by a heaviness in her heart, as if she felt his hopelessness. A laird without a wife, without sons, and no hope for either, was sad indeed.

He smiled ruefully. "Do not be sorry for me. I made a mistake, and I am paying for it," he said. "I was young, and enchanted. Never again," he added, looking away.

She felt hope slump within herself. Until that moment she had not realized that she had even considered the possibility of marriage to the laird of Dunsheen. She reminded herself that she had a widow's secure status, and did not need to marry again. And Diarmid Campbell was virile and attractive, but far too stubborn and insistent.

She sighed and tucked the covers again around the sleeping child. "I will rub her legs tomorrow. She should have heat treatments with hot cloths soaked in herbs. I will give the instructions to Lilias."

He nodded and rose when she did. As she went toward the door, he took her arm in the shadows.

"Michael." He paused awkwardly. "Thank you. Brigit will do well in your care."

She looked at the sleeping child in the bed, so small, so fragile beneath the heavy covers. "I wish I could give her the magic she deserves. I understand why you promised it to her."

His fingers pressed her arm in a brief, comforting gesture. "I could not refuse," he answered. "Now that I have promised, I must find some way to make it happen."

She looked away. "I am sorry that I cannot be the answer to your prayers."

His thumb made heated circles on her shoulder. "You may be yet, Michael girl," he murmured. "You may be yet."

The feel of his fingers sent delicate shivers along

her throat, into her breasts, along her spine. She looked up. The warm glow of the hearth softened the hard, handsome planes of his face. He tipped his head, his gray eyes as clear as crystal.

"There is more magic in you than you know," he murmured. His touch brought back the memory of the brief, compelling kiss they had shared by the healing pool. Michaelmas suddenly wanted his lips on hers so much that she thought she would melt with the urge, thought her knees would buckle beneath her and her thumping heart pound through the silence between them.

The desire he roused in her with the slightest touch stunned her, drew her in. She had never responded to a man's touch like this. Her body, of its own accord, surged toward him, wanting the vibrancy, the promise that his hands, his body, could offer. She craved that and more, much more, as if he was water for her thirst, warmth for the cold she had felt for so long.

But she drew in a breath and fought against the strong urges of her body. He was wed, and had been hurt. She was lonely, and had been for a long time, even during the years of her marriage. But she would not behave like a wanton. Neither of them would want that, and no good could come of it past the satisfaction of the moment.

She stepped back abruptly. "Good night, Dunsheen."

He nodded in the shadows. *"Micheil,"* he said. Even his voice acted like a lodestone upon her. She loved the way he said the name he had given her. She wanted no other name now.

But she had to get away, or regret it. She went to the door, pulled it open, and stepped out into the cool dark corridor. She felt a tug in her heart as she walked away, as if a silver thread linked them together and strained a little as she left him. The length of that glittery thread had begun to spin out between them on the day she had knelt beside him to perform a miracle. Now she was caught, moored to him, and did not know how to free herself.

Chapter Eleven

"He is sodden drunk," Michael said. She frowned at Angus, who grinned back at her. "Does he do this often?"

Diarmid scratched his chin, puzzled. "Only at Yuletide," he said, wondering what lay behind his elderly cousin's unusual state. Angus was sprawled on a bench in the great hall, head down on the table, moaning. "I have never seen him do this, in the middle of the night, for no apparent reason."

"Well, we will have to convince him to tell us the reason," Michael said.

Diarmid nodded. Iona had knocked on his door quite late, during a wild storm, two days after Arthur and Ranald had left for Ayr. At first Diarmid had mistaken the frantic pounding for thunder outside the walls. Once he had gone to the door, Iona had told him that her grandfather was miserably drunk and moaning in the great hall. She had already fetched Lady Michael, who had sent Iona for Diarmid.

He sighed, and lifted Angus's arm over his shoulder. "Ho, man," he said, shifting Angus's weight until the man stood. "Come to bed, now. You've had enough *uisge beatha* for five strong men."

Angus groaned again and collapsed back down to the bench. Swiping at a wine bladder on the table, he spilled some into his mouth. Another moan, long and loud, inspired one of the dogs by the hearth to echo the mournful sound.

"He must be in pain," Iona said. "Grandfather, what is it?"

Angus and the dog howled again. The old man took another swallow from the bladder, then clapped a hand to his cheek and opened his mouth.

Diarmid leaned forward and swayed back, hit by a foul blast; the man's breath mixed good amounts of hard spirits with decay. Angus attempted to speak, his reply garbled by the effects of the drink, and by what Diarmid now saw was a swollen cheek.

"Ah," Diarmid said, nodding sagely. "Bad tooth."

Angus nodded miserably and swished more liquor around in his mouth, spitting it onto the rushes. Then he took another generous mouthful and swallowed it down.

"He's trying to numb the pain with liquor," Iona said.

"By the look of him, he should be quite numb," Michael said. She touched his shoulder gently. "Let me see, Angus."

He craned his mouth open. Michael peered inside, then felt his jaw and neck. She motioned for Iona to bring a candle and hold it high, then looked again into Angus's mouth.

"I need to probe to find the bad tooth," she said. "It will have to come out. The foul humors are causing his face to swell."

Angus moaned and shook his head, hanging it in his hands. Iona bit her lip and looked fretfully at Michael and Diarmid.

Michael glanced at Diarmid. "I will need some help."

He nodded evenly and turned to Iona. "We need hot water and a good deal more candles for light."

"Iona, does Lilias keep oil of wormwood in her kitchen supply?" Michael asked.

"I think so."

"Fetch me that, and clove oil too, if she has it."

Iona nodded at Michael's brisk order, and left the room.

Diarmid hauled a protesting Angus off the bench and situated him in the high-backed carved chair, then propped up his feet. Turning toward the hearth, he set a few pine logs on the already glowing peat coals, and coaxed the wood until it blazed brightly.

"I have some surgical tools," he said. "I'll get what you will need." Michael nodded.

Once back in his bedchamber, Diarmid opened a locked wooden chest beneath the window. He took out a leather bundle and unrolled it to reveal a silk lining and the surgical instruments that he had carried with him, years earlier, when he traveled with Robert Bruce's army as surgeon. Golden needles, silver scissors, iron pincers, steel scalpels, and small saws gleamed and chinked as he handled them. His hand trembled as he chose a pair of pincers.

When he returned to the great hall, Michael and Iona had already placed two basins of steaming water on the table. Michael sniffed the contents of a couple of small clay vials, while Iona arranged several flaming candles on the table near Angus's chair.

Diarmid handed the pincers to Michael. "Those should do well for you," he said, while she rinsed them in the water. She then soaked a small cloth in the oils from the vials and applied the wadded cloth inside Angus's mouth.

"That should help deaden the pain," she said. After several moments, she probed gently with her fingers. Angus thrashed, and she stepped back, looking, Diarmid noticed suddenly, quite unsure of herself. He was puzzled, for he had always seen her calm and certain when dealing with physical ailments. Perhaps she thought her patient too agitated for a procedure just now. Diarmid agreed; at this point, clove oil would hardly make a difference in the pain Angus felt.

"On the battlefield, *uisge beatha* was our best aid

in surgery," he said. "Perhaps he could use a little more."

"More!" she exclaimed.

"He can handle it," Diarmid said dryly. "I know him."

"Soporific sponges soaked in opium work best of all, but I have none with me," she replied. "I keep some with my medical tools, but—" She shrugged eloquently.

"We cannot delay this until Mungo returns with your trunk," Diarmid said. "His father could perish of poisoning from the tooth. The spirits will have to do." He handed the bladder to Angus and encouraged him to drink again. Angus complied, generously offering Michael and Diarmid sips, which they refused. After a while, Angus slumped into a quiet stupor, gazing at them with glazed eyes and a little smile.

"I think you can begin now," Diarmid said.

Michael's hand hovered over the iron pincers. Wondering again at her uncertainty, Diarmid supported Angus's head in a stable position and waited. Michael still hesitated.

A thought occurred to him. "Have you ever extracted a tooth?" he asked her.

She shook her head. "Never. I am not a barber-surgeon."

"I've done it several times. The procedure is simple enough." He explained it to her, and she listened, nodding. Finally she picked up the tool and leaned forward.

After several attempts to pull the tooth, her cheeks grew pink with effort and she stepped back. Shoving loose strands of hair from her eyes, she looked at Diarmid. "This needs the strength of a blacksmith," she said.

"Sometimes," he said. "Try again."

She did, without success. "The roots of the molar must be very long. It will not come loose." She braced her knee against the chair and pulled again. Then she sighed and looked up at him. "Diarmid, please, I need your help."

He shook his head. "You can do this."

"I do not have the strength." She held out the pincers. "I am afraid I will crack the tooth, and Angus will be worse off than he is now." She looked at him with full pleading in her gaze.

Diarmid glanced away, left fist clenched. "I cannot—"

"You can. You need but the one hand for this."

He sighed, then sighed again. The procedure was hardly complicated surgically, and his friend would suffer if he did not help Michael now. He clearly had small choice.

"Well," he said, "I suppose I am more of a blacksmith than you are." He accepted the tongs, then leaned forward and braced against the chair. "Only a blacksmith could pull a tooth from Angus MacArthur's head," he muttered, and applied unrelenting pressure. Finally the tooth came free, and he dropped it with a clink into the basin.

Michael swabbed Angus's mouth and inserted an herbal poultice that she had asked Iona to prepare. She stood back and glanced up at Diarmid.

"Thank you," she said.

"Easy enough to do with experience," he said.

She nodded. Her veil had fallen askew, and she pulled it free wearily. Her loosely braided hair spilled over the shoulder of her black gown like a rippled stream of moonlight. Diarmid watched, his eyes soaking in the sight of her. Dissheveled, flush-faced, she looked, to his eyes, serene and incredibly lovely.

"Thank you, Iona," she said to the girl. "Your kin will be proud of how helpful you were. Your grandfather can sleep the night in this chair. I will make sure he's comfortable. You are tired, dear. Go to bed, now."

Iona murmured her thanks and fetched a thick plaid from a bench, tucking it around her snoring grandfather. Then she picked up the used basins and bid Michael and Diarmid good night as she left.

Michael slumped down to the bench, the color drained from her face. She slipped a trembling hand through her silky hair. "I have done little surgery of any kind," she said quietly. "Ibrahim was a surgeon, but he had a male assistant, and left dentistry to the barber-surgeons. My studies and practice involved treating diseases of various kinds, and health problems of women and children. Never this sort of matter."

"Then, this was a new challenge for you. You did well." He poured the last of Angus's liquor into a wooden cup. "Drink this," he said. "You need its strength in your blood just now."

She drank, then gasped and coughed. Tears sprang to her eyes. Diarmid half sat on the edge of the table and reached over to pat her back until her breath returned.

"*Uisge beatha* is the water of life for Highlanders," he said, amused. "But I've seen it kick over someone who is not used to it."

"Another drink of that, and I might be kicked over indeed," she replied, wiping her hand over her eyes.

"You looked pale a moment ago, but no longer. Now you need to rest. Angus will sing your praises over this, and you will be very busy indeed when everyone brings their ailments to you."

She stood. "Then they should come to you, Dunsheen. You did this, not I. If not for your help, poor Angus would still be suffering."

Diarmid looked at the old man, who snored in the chair. "Angus is hardly suffering," he replied wryly. "Tomorrow is another matter, though, and I will gladly leave his care to you."

She looked at Angus critically. "We will need something quite cold to press against his jaw to help with the swelling," she said. "Cold stones will do well."

"I can fetch some stones from the loch shore for him," Diarmid said. "Go up to your chamber. You will have much to do in the morn, and it's already late.''

She nodded gratefully and turned to go, but shifted to face him. "I am not the healer you thought me, Diarmid," she said softly. "I—I am sorry for that."

He tilted his head, struck by the meekness in her tone. That hesitancy touched him deeply, like an arrow breaking through a defense; it matched his doubt in his own abilities. So much had turned in the space of a few moments—he had done surgery, and she had been the one to draw back from it. He did not want to see such insecurity in her. She had a gift, a shining, gentle power as a healer, and he wanted her to know it. He had full confidence in her abilities, book-trained and God-given.

"Dentistry is tough work, and often takes muscle," he said. "But you did well."

"I did not know what to do," she said.

"You learned a new skill," he said in encouragement. "Now you are a barber-surgeon for certain." He ran a hand through his long hair and grinned briefly. "And so you will probably charge me a hefty fee to shear this."

She gave a soft chuckle. "I would do it for free for you."

He smiled, watching her. A feeling swept through him then, so strong and potent that it rocked him to his heels.

"Come here," he murmured hoarsely.

A quizzical frown folded her brow, and she moved forward. He took her arm and drew her closer until her skirt draped against his thigh. Reaching up, he touched her face with his right hand, stroking the downy softness of her cheek, glad she had not had time to wrap her chin in the widow's wimple.

"Michael my girl," he said gently, "you are just the healer I expected, and just the one I wanted. Do not doubt that."

She stared at him. "Diarmid—"

"Hush," he breathed. Before he could stop himself, before he could think through his action, he leaned forward and touched his mouth to hers.

He had tasted her once before, on a bright day beside a pool, a kiss as quick as a wafting breeze. Now he savored her, pulling her close, sliding his fingers through the cool silken strands of her hair. She gave out a little cry and put her arms around his neck. Surrendering to the lure of her warm, soft, willing lips, and her lithe body pressed against his, he kissed her again, his heart pounding hard.

Her mouth trembled beneath his as he touched his tongue lightly to her lips. She sipped at it, opened tentatively for it, then gave out a hushed, poignant cry and pushed at his chest.

"You have a wife," she whispered. "We should not—"

Gently said, the words chilled him. There were times when he forgot the existence of the other, times when he could almost forget her face, even when he could not forget or forgive the hurt she had dealt him, or the ruin she had made of his life.

Michael had done what no other woman had: erased for long, blessed moments his awareness that the other existed, and still prevented him from reaching out for what he needed and wanted.

"I do," he admitted, letting go of her. "I am sorry." Michael stepped away, then spun and ran from the room.

Several days of rain, accompanied by fierce winds that whirled and howled past the solid walls of Dunsheen, prevented Diarmid from making the short journeys he had planned. He had meant to visit the Campbell chief and others to inquire about Ranald MacSween's activities, and he had meant to sail to Glas Eilean to visit his sister and to take the opportunity to glance around Ranald's storerooms.

Before he had left Dunsheen, Arthur had given Di-

armid several accounting sheets that he said he had
secretly taken from Ranald's cupboard. He had said
that they were significant, thus indicating to Diarmid
that his brother suspected something.

The storms gave him a chance to pore carefully over
the account rolls. As he sat in the great hall reading
the last of the rolled parchment sheets, which contained yet another list of imported goods purchased
by MacSween, he rubbed his fingers in his weary eyes.

He must need a change from the tedium, he
thought, for few of the figures he had reviewed in the
past hour made much sense to him. The day was
dreary and cold, and the storm was noisy against the
outer walls, but the hearth fire was warm beside him.
He sat back, preferring to listen to Gilchrist, who practiced a new piece of music on his harp.

Gilchrist bowed his head in somber concentration
as he plucked the harp strings in a quick rhythm. Diarmid relaxed, enjoying the new song, and glanced
toward the other end of the room. Within the privacy
of a window niche, fitted with two stone benches and
cushions, Michael sat murmuring with Lilias. A few
days ago, Michael and Lilias had spent time in the
small workroom off the kitchen, where Lilias kept her
store of herbs. Now he watched Michael scribble out
recipes for infusions and potions, which she asked Lilias to make up herself, or send out to the herb-wife.

She looked serious and beautiful as she leaned over
and spoke, then laughed suddenly with his elderly
cousin. He was content just to watch her. She seemed
to shine like a beam of sunlight in the dismal rainy
atmosphere.

Just as he had predicted, Michael had acquired several patients since Angus's quick recovery. She had
consulted with Lilias for an entire morning concerning
the catalog of the woman's aches and pains. Michael
had seen to it that Lilias began a regimen of herbal
medications, hot baths, and dietary changes to ease
her painful joints.

He had seen Iona murmuring with Michael at one point, sniffling, and Michael had nodded with her and put an arm around her. He suspected that was not medical, but had something to do with Gilchrist, for Michael gave the girl a little push toward his brother, smiling encouragement. Iona had spoken then to Gilchrist, received a one-word reply, and had run from the room.

The next day Michael had tended to Eva's persistent cough. After a long discussion with Iona, Lilias, and Eva, Michael had advised the child to stay away from the stable kittens to see if the cough would improve, to avoid nuts and cheeses, and to sip herbs in honey daily.

Donald and Fingal had tumbled down the outer steps while chasing each other, and Michael had tended to their cuts and bruises quickly, advising them to stay inside for the remainder of that day. They had played games with Brigit and had taken turns at lessons on an older harp belonging to Gilchrist. Diarmid had been surprised at the willing patience that his normally taciturn younger brother had shown the children.

He had been surprised too when Michael had sat down beside Gilchrist one day, and with his permission, began to play a lovely melody with the accomplished grace of a trained harper. She had told him that her mother was a harper who had trained her in the old style of the bards.

Diarmid had watched her often, noting her graceful hands with their bowed little fingers, somehow suited to harp playing. He had closed his eyes and listened, and wondered at the changes that seemed to be taking place within him. He was not certain what they were, but he could feel the subtle shifts in his mind and emotions, odd yearning sensations that stirred inside.

Michael had become a more necessary presence at Dunsheen with each passing day. She played the harp with Gilchrist, spent time with the children, and consulted with anyone who came to her for medical advice. The word of her skills had quickly spread among Dunsheen's tenants, and a few had begun to row over to the isle to ask for her advice.

She had even trimmed his hair as she had promised, cutting its clean length deftly with small, sharp scissors that she had taken from his surgical kit. As she had shaped and combed it, Diarmid had reveled in the luxurious, sensual shivers he had felt under her hands.

And every day and evening, with consistent patience, Michael had tended to Brigit. She rubbed the child's weakened muscles and changed the contents of the medicines; she insisted on hot baths for the child each evening, and insisted too that Brigit spend time every day standing, holding on to the chair or to any one of the willing supporters among her kin at Dunsheen.

He and Angus had made a pair of splints for Brigit with wood and silk wrappings, and she wore them over her knees, walking stiffly around the great hall, holding on to willing hands or to the dogs' thickly furred backs.

Now he looked at Gilchrist as he played the harp, and watched Brigit standing beside him, one hand grasping the arm of the large carved chair, the other on Padraig's glossy black shoulder. The dog seemed equally as rapt as the child as they listened to the music. A few feet away, Eva whirled to the rhythms, giggling as Columba circled her playfully.

Diarmid frowned slightly, his interest caught when he noticed Brigit move her left leg slightly and awkwardly in time to the music. He did not recall seeing her do that before. Perhaps Michael's strengthening treatments had begun to take effect. His heart surged inside of him. When he saw Brigit's knees wobble, saw her grip the chair, he crossed the room to pick her up and seat her in the chair.

"You are doing well," he told her. "But rest now, and listen to the music."

She looked up at him, tugging at his sleeve. "Uncle," she whispered, "I want to dance like Eva. Can you make my magic now, please? I have waited a long while for it. I have been good."

He glanced at Michael, who looked up from her seat in the window niche as if she knew he looked at her. Their gazes melded across the width of the room.

He touched Brigit's head. "*Brighid milis,*" he said. "If you keep working so hard to strengthen yourself, and take Lady Michael's medicinal potions, you will make your own magic."

"But I want to dance," she said sadly. "We have been inside all week because of the storms. Look, Padraig wants to dance too." The dog, who sat obediently by the child's chair, thumped his tail eagerly.

Struck by an unaccustomed impulse, Diarmid suddenly swept Brigit into his arms. Holding her securely, he began to spin in time to the music, making a few awkward fancy steps such as he had seen at the king's court last Yuletide. Brigit clung to his neck and giggled with delight. Eva and the two dogs circled him while he continued to bounce and spin with his niece.

He caught Gilchrist's surprised glance, and heard his brother laugh. Grinning, caught in the freedom of the moment, Diarmid laughed and spun away with Brigit. She waved her right arm and hand gracefully, her small face uplifted, eyes closed, loving the motion of his silly spinning dance.

Why had he never done this before with her, he thought, when it brought her such sweet, simple joy? When he turned again, he saw Michael and Lilias walk over to stand near Gilchrist and clap their hands to the music.

Gilchrist rang the end of the song with relish and a wide smile. Diarmid stopped spinning and held Brigit, both of them laughing.

"Now I know what I will call this new song," Gilchrist said.

"What is that?" Lilias asked.

"Dance of the King of the *Daoine Sìth*," he answered.

Michael laughed in delight, a light, clear sound that seeped into Diarmid's heart like rain on dry ground. He looked at her over Brigit's head and smiled, hearing only her laughter. He had never heard a more magical sound in his life.

That thrill was followed by a yearning unlike any he had ever felt, a longing so strong that he fisted a hand against it, bit his lip, lowered his eyes to smother it. Need, raw and burning and real, rolled in him like hunger. He realized then that he wanted Michael, needed her in some deep, elemental way that he could not comprehend. He wanted her wholly, in flesh and in spirit, two souls bonded together as one.

Startled by the depth of the craving, he became acutely aware that he had long carried within him an emptiness, a hole that he was incapable of filling. Even the joyful, laughing child in his arms did not ease the anguish he felt. He could not reach out for what he needed, no matter how brightly the light shone upon the darkness within him. Satisfaction, joy, love—dear God, he felt the strength of love within him now— were forbidden to him because of a mistake he had made years ago.

Michael walked toward him, smiling, and turned her face up to his. He glanced away from the shining brilliance in her eyes. If he returned the gaze, shared the smile, some part of him would be lost into her keeping forever. Desiring that, he saw that it was dangerous to both of them.

Magic indeed, he thought. She possessed it in every fiber of her being, and did not even know it.

She lifted a hand to touch Brigit's arm where he still held his niece, her thumb brushing over his, stirring a rapid beat in his heart. "That was a lovely dance, Brigit," she said. "None of the fair folk could have danced more gracefully than you did, sweet."

"I told you Uncle Diarmid was the king," Brigit said, smiling. "Even Uncle Gilchrist knows it."

"Ah, then, Gilchrist must be a prince, for they are brothers," Michael said. Gilchrist chuckled behind her as he adjusted the harp strings, and Lilias rang out a hearty laugh.

Diarmid, listening as he held the child, did not even smile. The profoundness of what he had just realized stunned him. He needed to consider all the aspects of his feelings for Michael when he had time and privacy to think them through.

"You look so somber now, Dunsheen," Michael said, her voice lightly teasing, still amused. "What thoughts could set the king of all the *daoine sìth* into such a dark mood?"

He looked at her then, and felt himself spin again, not in a joyful dance this time, but helplessly, into swirling blue depths, into eyes as blue as a loch in summer.

"I was thinking of magic," he said quietly, and turned away to set Brigit back in the chair.

Then he heard soft cries from Iona and Lilias, and saw Michael turn, saw Gilchrist sit up on his harper's stool. And he looked up to see Mungo enter the hall, bearing a large wooden chest on his shoulder.

"Here you are, Mistress Physician," Mungo grunted as he set the chest down heavily. "Your books and belongings, just as you asked." He wiped a forearm across his brow. Then he grinned and opened his arms to his children, who ran toward him.

Chapter Twelve

Mungo took an object from a fold of his wrapped plaid and laid it on the table. "Here is your cairngorm brooch, Dunsheen, which the laird of Perth Castle knew well, and so gave me the use of two fine horses. After that, I went back to the hospital and told them I was in need of a bed. I stayed there and groaned and complained for a few days. And I had to share the bed with a grousing old man," he added, grimacing.

Michael wanted to laugh, but stifled it. She could hardly imagine this strong, gaunt, tenacious man sharing a bed with an elderly patient. She handed him a cup of claret and pushed a plate of oatcakes close to him. "What illness did you claim?"

"Backache," he said, stretching his shoulders. "Told the prioress I could barely walk for back strain."

"You have a back like an ox," Diarmid remarked.

He grinned. "They did not know that, for I moaned loudly. The food was adequate, and the pillows were soft, and I wanted a rest after months spent running with you and the king." His small sons, Donald and Fingal, sidled close to him, and he ruffled their shining brown-haired heads. "I think the prioress was loath to let me go, and kept me," he added, wiggling a brow.

Diarmid chuckled. "And why was that?"

"*Ach,* the woman found me fascinating," he replied. "I told her she had soft hands and a fine face—though she has the face of a mule, and the cold, wet hands of a fishwife." He shrugged. "But she seemed to like my compliments. She rubbed my back with ointments, and I told her what a sacred effect she was having upon me. I even confessed to the priest to earn her goodwill. That got me extra portions of meat, and cups of good wine from the prioress's own hands." He smiled beatifically. "I always knew there was a use for prayer."

Diarmid shook his head, smiling. "But how did you get into Michael's chamber in the women's quarters to get the chest?"

"Well, I knew if I even mentioned the lady's name I would lose my privileges quick enough. I heard the prioress and the priest arguing about Lady Michael's disappearance, so I kept close about it. They seemed greatly concerned about what your brother would do when he found you missing, my lady," he added soberly. Michael nodded, wondering if Gavin yet knew that she was gone from the hospital.

"On the third night," Mungo continued, "I had had enough of rest and sickly companions, and so I stole out of bed in the middle of the night and went to the women's dormitory. No one had yet taken Lady Michael's chamber. Slipping inside to carry out the chest was easy enough. But the two young novices saw me as I was climbing over the wall."

"Marjorie and Alice?" Michael asked.

He nodded. "They were about to call the priest, but I told them I was a friend to you and told them you were safe. And I asked them to send a message to Gavin Faulkener with the king's troops in the borderlands, to tell them that you were fine and would contact him later. They let me go with good wishes."

"Thank you, Mungo," Michael said. "I owe you a great debt."

He smiled. "You have paid it," he said. "My kin have all told me how you tended their aches and pains. And my father told me how you pulled his bad tooth the other night."

"Dunsheen did that," Michael said quickly.

"Did he?" Mungo looked at Diarmid. "Pulled a tooth like a barber-surgeon, did you?"

Diarmid shrugged. "I did. Take a day of rest, Mungo. Then you and I will ride out to make some visits around Argyll."

Mungo nodded as he sipped the claret. "Have you had any news of Glas Eilean?" he asked. "News of Sorcha? How is she?"

"She is well enough," Diarmid answered. "Ranald and Arthur were here a few days past." He leaned sideways to murmur quietly of business affairs.

Michael took advantage of the change in the conversation to rise from the table and walk toward her wooden chest. She sank down on her knees beside it and freed the three strong latches, then opened the heavy lid and propped it against the wall.

Within moments she was surrounded by curious children. Eva, Donald, and Fingal fell on their knees beside her, thrusting their heads curiously into the chest to see its contents. Iona appeared too, holding Brigit's hand while Brigit gripped Padraig's leather collar and awkwardly crossed the room.

"*Dhia*!" Mungo said. "Look at her!" He laughed, a burst of disbelief and joy. Michael smiled across the room at him, and heard Diarmid explain what Brigit had begun to achieve with Michael's treatments.

She turned back toward the chest. Eva had removed a pale blue silk veil trimmed in golden braid, and was admiring it. Michael smiled. "I wore that in Italy," she said. "The days are so hot there that all we wore was silk and cotton, never wool. Try it on." She helped Eva cover her dark hair.

"May I try it too?" Brigit asked.

Michael withdrew another veil of white silk threaded with silver. "This will be lovely on you," she said, and settled it over Brigit's wild golden curls.

Michael soon found herself seated in the midst of happy pandemonium. The children were determined to examine every item in the chest. They looked with avid curiosity at the clothing and the few jewels she owned. Small hands picked up a belt of golden chain links, rings, neck chains with pendants, and swirled delicate veils with enthusiasm. The boys unfolded her two spare black gowns and two black surcoats of wool and samite and tossed them aside. Other gowns and surcoats, brightly colored, were examined by Eva and Iona, while Brigit draped herself in embroidered silk chemises in white and rich blue.

Fingal and Donald were fascinated by her instruments, handling each one in turn. She showed them probes, depressors, golden needles, scissors, steel-bladed knives, and pincers of various sizes; a gold tube used for tracheotomy, sealed ceramic jars holding rare medicines, empty glass vials, and three small folding charts of symptoms and astrological information meant to be worn on the belt.

Donald pulled a gray-and-red robe out of the bottom of the chest and thrust his sleeves into it. "Is this your night robe?" he cried, splaying his arms wide. "It's very large."

"That is a physician's robe," she explained. "The gray color and the red lining identify those who wear it as academically trained physicians."

"And this one is yours?" Donald asked. She nodded. "I like it. I want one too, when I am grown."

"Me too," Brigit said, fingering the red silk lining.

"You will have to earn robes like these," she said, sitting back on her heels. The two children looked at each other and nodded as if that task was easily accomplished.

"Ah, books!" Iona said in delight, and sank to her knees. She reached inside to touch a leather cover. "May I?"

Michael nodded, and Iona lifted out a heavy volume. While she turned its stiff parchment pages, the children gathered around her, as motley and comical as Yuletide guisers, clothed in a rainbow of veils, gowns, and jewelry. Michael smiled to see them cluster around Iona, all of them quietly looking.

"What is this?" Iona asked. "I've never seen such pictures!"

"It is a book of physiognomy," Michael said. "See, this illustration explains how the zodiac signs rule different parts of the body—Aries the ram for the head, Taurus the bull for the neck, Leo the lion for the heart, and so on." While she spoke, the children exclaimed over the detailed, colorful painting. Iona turned more folios, and stopped at a full-page illumination of a man in a loincloth, covered with open wounds, from which protruded spears, knives, arrows, axes, and a mace.

"*Ach!*" Donald cried. "What happened to him?"

"That is the Wound Man," Michael said. "Many medical texts use him to teach physicians how different weapons damage the body. The text explains how to best repair the wounds."

"I like this!" Fingal crowed, bending close. Donald sat beside him, still clothed in Michael's physician's robe, making clownish faces and clutching invisible wounds until Michael finally burst out laughing.

She heard a low chuckle, and glanced up to see Diarmid coming toward them. He squatted down on his haunches to look at the book, while the children showed him the gruesome details of the Wound Man. They exclaimed over the Vein Man, the Skeleton Man, and other illustrations, and then went on to admire paintings of the zodiac signs included in a book of astrology.

Diarmid drew a very large volume from the chest, glancing at Michael for permission. She nodded, watching his powerful hands handle its weight as if it were a prayer book. He opened the tooled leather cover and found the first page.

"*Commentaries on the works of Galen the Ancient Physician and Philosopher, as written by Ibrahim Ibn Kateb, Physician and Surgeon of Bologna,*" he read, translating the Latin title lines. He glanced at her.

"Ibrahim's expansion of Galen is well-known," Michael said. "He commissioned this copy for me when I won my degree."

"A handsome book," he said, turning the pages steadily. She watched him read passages here and there, his long fingers tracing down the neatly arranged columns, occasionally pausing beside notes in brown ink that Michael had scribbled in the margins. "You have read it thoroughly. Mullinch Priory owned one of Galen's works, and some of the writings of Hippocrates and an Arabic scholar, Razi. I read those, though it was long ago."

"Then you are familiar with the core works of academic medical knowledge. Most other writers merely interpret and elaborate on the classic works done centuries ago by Greeks and Arabics."

Diarmid flipped through Ibrahim's *Commentaries,* then replaced it in the chest and chose another volume from among several there. The next book cover was made from painted wooden boards, the book itself not very large.

"*The Booke of Cyrurgia,*" he said aloud, reading the title page. "A treatise on surgery. This is written in English," he added, sounding surprised.

"That was another gift from Ibrahim, a translation of the recent work of Lanfranchi of Milan, a surgeon whom Ibrahim greatly admired," Michael explained. "My husband added his own comments and drawings in the margins." Diarmid turned the pages, pausing at several illustrations, absorbed.

"Ibrahim had a large library," Michael told him. "Medicine, philosophy, mathematics, and astrology— over a hundred volumes. He donated them in his will to the university in Bologna. I kept only my personal books, and a few of his, which he willed to me."

Diarmid nodded, turning the crackling vellum pages, looking avidly through the book. "This explains procedures I have never even heard of," he murmured. "The drawings are incredibly detailed. Look at this method of cautery." He leaned close to study it himself.

"I hope you will look at the books whenever you wish," she said, watching him.

He closed the surgery volume briskly and set it in the bottom of the chest without replying. He stood, and Michael stood too, looking up at him, noticing a rosy stain in his cheeks and a new tightness in his jaw.

They stood silently amid a chattering gaggle of brightly clad, occupied children. Eva, Brigit, and Iona were still looking at the astrological book. Donald traded the gray and red physician's robe for a gauzy veil that Fingal was trying to look through. Fingal struggled into the heavy robe, while Donald draped the translucent cloth on his own head and began to mince around until the other children tittered with glee.

"Have this silly crew divest themselves of your finery," Diarmid said. His tone was stern, but Michael saw the fleeting smile that he smothered. "They act as if it were Yuletide. Their play cannot be good for your things."

"They will do no harm," she said. "And I wear only my widow's pleated veil and black now."

He tilted his head. "How long will you do that?"

She looked down. "I have not decided. In Italy and France, widows sometimes wear black for the rest of their lives."

"That is a long time," he said softly. He tugged gently at the wimple that covered her chin. "This is too solemn for you."

She felt herself blush. "Will you see that the chest is carried up to Brigit's chamber? There is a table and stool there. I would like to work there, if I may."

He nodded, and stepped back, narrowly missing Brigit, who sat on the floor jingling the rings and necklaces that ornamented her hands and arms. Fingal and Donald swirled around him in a circle, laughing hysterically, while Iona set the book aside to pull on a pair of

fur gloves, gasping at their softness. Eva was walking
around in a pair of delicate shoes of purple leather.

"*Ach*," Diarmid muttered. "We've had far too
much rain."

Michael read late into the night, although her eyes
felt the strain of reading by the light of one candle.
Familiar with Ibrahim's observations in his commentaries on Galen, she sought one passage in particular.
Scanning through the book, she finally found the nota-
tion, and pulled the candle closer to read.

*There is a lame fever prevalent in the Holy Land
and other hot lands,* Ibrahim had written, *which causes
lameness and often death. The disease is described by
the ancients, and begins with fever, aches, chills, and
can bring on lung fever and stiffening and withering of
the limbs. Often one side of the body is affected, and
the face sags as in apoplexy. Many victims die of the
lung fever, and those who by the grace of God survive
never walk again, but worsen with time. Some advise
amputation for these victims, and some advocate seal-
ing them in religious houses and hospitals, where their
needs can be cared for charitably.*

She sighed heavily and rubbed her fingers over her
eyes. Brigit had suffered a fever. Michael read on.
Ibrahim advised remedies for pain, and the use of heat
and rubbing the limbs to bring blood back into them.
She skimmed down the page.

*I have seen this lame fever strike knights who have
gone on Holy Crusade. Those who visit Saracen lands
and warm climates bring back the illness to their home-
lands, and so it affects others, as Galen and others say,
through sputum, and I believe through touch as well.*

Attention caught, Michael sat up to review the sen-
tence, and read further. *Lame fever is a fearsome
scourge in the Holy Land, so that some say it is a curse
upon the Infidel. But I have seen Christian men,
women, and little children with the disease, and I believe that this evil goes where it will like a hidden*

demon, carried from one land to another on the shoul-
ders of travelers. Ships are unclean, and those who sail
to far lands must bathe often, carry garlic on their per-
son, and anoint their skin with aromatic oils. . . .

She closed the heavy volume and set it aside. Still
frowning, she walked toward the bed and stared down
at Brigit, curled like a kitten beneath the covers, her
doll held tight. Padraig slept at the foot of the bed as
he often did, intent on comfort as much as on guarding
his young mistress. Michael did not disturb him.

She smoothed strands of hair from the child's brow,
then sat on the edge of the bed with a long sigh. What
she had read in Ibrahim's book gravely concerned her.
If this was indeed the source of Brigit's condition, then
Ibrahim's notes made recovery seem impossible. The
child was strong, for she had survived the initial fever
and the lung disease that often followed. But if
Ibrahim was right, she would not walk again.

Michael wanted to discuss her discovery with Diarmid, but she was certain he slept now. She pulled at
her wimple and veil wearily as she continued to think
about the implications of what Ibrahim had written.

Brigit had asked Diarmid for magic, and waited for
it with the implicit trust that children possessed. But
if she had this lame fever, then there was no cure,
no treatment.

The child moved restlessly in her sleep, whimpering
as if she was in pain. Michael rubbed her back gently.
A deep sense of sadness washed over her. She wished
that she could help her with the power that had once
flowed within her.

On impulse, she rested her hands on Brigit's knees
and waited. Warmth filled her hands quickly, as it
often did when she touched someone. She felt heat
pour through her hands, but felt no dazzling, incandes-
cent power shake the roots of her soul.

What Brigit needed was far beyond the scope of what
she could do. She bowed her head, certain that her refusal of the gift for so long had finally caused its heaven-

guided force to abandon her. With a long, regretful sigh, she stretched out on the bed and took Brigit into the circle of her arms. She drifted to sleep, feeling gentle warmth envelop her as she held the child.

When she opened her eyes, she was unsure how long she had lain in Brigit's bed. She vaguely remembered a dream about a sculpted angel with a broken wing, but could recall little of it. She glanced across the room toward the table, where the candle still glowed.

Diarmid sat there, his back to her. The candlelight formed a golden nimbus around his dark head. He was absorbed in what he read, his elbow on the table, his chin propped on his hand. Every few moments he silently turned a page. Lifting her head, she saw that he looked at the book of surgery.

Not wanting to disturb him, she lay back on the pillow and watched him. The soft rustle of parchment as he flipped the pages was a peaceful sound. She felt empty, needy, still filled with sadness, and his silent presence was comforting.

He seemed caught in his reading, careful to use her books when he thought her asleep. In a short while he closed the book and stood. She closed her eyes, pretending to sleep, not wanting him to know that in his privacy she had watched him.

Moments later she sensed him standing near the bed, and felt the warm brush of his hand and linen sleeve as he reached over her shoulder to touch Brigit's head. Then his hand brushed over her own bare head. The sensual graze of his fingertips sent a cascade of shivers through her, followed by the plummeting force of a fierce, deep yearning. She wanted him to touch her, hold her, but she lay still. After a moment he turned away.

She heard Padraig woof softly. "*Ach,* lad," Diarmid murmured. "You will wake them. Sleep, now, fellow." The dog whined, and Michael opened her eyes to see Diarmid bend to pat his head.

Diarmid saw her then. "Did he wake you? I am sorry."

"I—I should be in my own bed," she said, and sat up. "Brigit was restless, so I lay down with her."

"Lie down if you are tired. Brigit will not mind." His slanted smile was gentle and intimate.

"I am glad you are here," she said softly, and blushed. "I wanted to talk to you about Brigit." She rose from the bed and went to the table. Opening Ibrahim's book, she showed him what she had found.

He read the Latin text quickly, and straightened to glance at her, his brows drawn together. "Lame fever. I have not heard of it before. But it is similar to her symptoms."

"You spoke with the old woman who fostered her—"

"Abandoned her," he corrected tersely. "Old Morag said that her son and his wife and two others of their kin died of a fever after her son returned ill from a long journey to Berwick. Brigit became ill after they did. . . . Ships," he said suddenly.

He turned back to the book. "Sim MacLachlan was involved, as many Islesmen are, with shipping and imports. He made frequent trips to seaports—Ayr, Glasgow, and the eastern ports of Berwick and Aberdeen. He could have had contact with merchants who had been in eastern and southern countries, or, as Ibrahim says here, with men who had recently been to the Holy Land."

She sighed. "Regardless of how she became ill, Ibrahim indicates no cure for this illness."

"Your husband was a wise man in many ways," Diarmid said. "But he was wrong in that."

"Diarmid, there is no cure—"

"There is. You hold it in your hands."

She sighed, looked away, knowing what he did not: that she had already tried and failed. "Ibrahim would want me to chart Brigit's natal horoscope," she said. "That will give us some answers—it will," she insisted when Diarmid made a skeptical sound. "But I need to know the exact hour of her birth. March the seventeenth, five years past? Would you know the time of night or day? Did her mother or the midwife ever mention it?"

A shadow passed over his face. "Just before dawn," he said quietly. "No more than a quarter hour passed before the sun rose that day."

"Were you there?"

"I delivered her," he said flatly, turning away.

She stared at him in surprise. In Italy, she had known only one or two male physicians who would even consent to attend a birth, and then only when the mother was in serious danger. Diarmid stared at the bed where his tiny niece lay curled. "Brigit was born lusty and strong," he said softly. "But she lost much that day. She has little awareness of it, I think. One day I will have to be the one to tell her."

Michael waited, but he said no more, only raked his fingers through his hair. The anxious gesture tugged at her heart. "Tell her what?"

"That she has no close blood kin because of me," he ground out. "Will she think me a king, a man of magic after that, do you suppose?" he asked bitterly.

"Her mother died then?" He nodded once. "A death in childbirth is tragic, and too common. You should not blame yourself."

He laughed harshly.

"Tell me what happened," she said, touching his arm. His muscles were tense and hard beneath her fingers. Her heart beat unsteadily, dreadfully, as she waited.

He did not speak, looking at Brigit. The candlelight sputtered fitfully over the planes of his face, then burned to a sudden close. Darkness engulfed them.

"Tell me," she murmured, her voice insistent in the shadows.

He sighed. "Not here." He took her hand in the dark and pulled her through the shadows toward the door, their footsteps whispering on the rushes.

Chapter Thirteen

Michael shivered in the chilly corridor and followed Diarmid as he went toward the stairs. He moved up a few steps, then turned and sat on a wedge-shaped stair. Michael sat beside him. A watery moonlit glow shed down over their heads from the arrow-slit window above them. The space was close and private at this late hour, if voices were quiet.

She waited. Diarmid rested his elbows on his knees, clasped his hands, and looked down. "Brigit had a twin brother," he began. His voice, just above a whisper, was a velvet drift of sound. "He was stillborn just after her. Their mother died just after that." A heavy silence followed his blunt, quiet words. "I was the only one there."

"Diarmid," she breathed in sympathy. "You could not have caused any of it."

"All of it," he said flatly. He leaned his shoulders against the wall. His thigh brushed against her leg in the small space. "I blame myself for all of it." She protested, but he shook his head. "When Maire began her labor, the weather was poor, a heavy gale that kept the midwife away. I was there at Glenbevis, Fionn's castle. I had arrived a day earlier to bring him a message, but he had left for Ireland with Edward Bruce."

"Edward Bruce's invasion on Irish soil?" Michael asked. "Gavin mentioned that once. He said it was a disaster."

"It was, but the campaign had not yet fallen apart

then," he said. "The night I arrived, Maire began her labor. She was alone but for an old serving woman and the few men who had not gone with Fionn. I had planned to sail to Ireland, but I stayed to help her. The midwife could not come, and I knew the birth process, although I had never attended a woman's delivery."

"I know you did your best." Michael laid her hand on his forearm, wanting that close contact, sensing that he needed it. "If a birthing goes wrong, it is generally God's will."

He held out his palms. "Brigit was born into my hands. She took her first breath here."

Unexpected tears came to Michael's eyes. She slid her fingers over his left hand, feeling the harsh scars there. "There is a deep bond between you," she said. "That is why you love her so much, like a father. And why she adores you so."

He folded his fingers over hers. "I could do nothing for her brother, but I did all I could for Maire, who was bleeding heavily. She died so quickly—" He sucked in a breath. Michael squeezed his hand, tears in her eyes as she imagined the panic and grief he must have felt that night.

He kept a fierce hold of her hand; she felt the slight tremor in his smallest fingers. He tipped his head back against the stone wall. Moonlight rinsed his face with a misty blue light, outlined his strong throat as he swallowed heavily.

"Ah, Diarmid," she said finally, her voice thick with unshed tears. "You did not cause any of that."

"I carry that night with me still," he said in a hushed voice. "I dream about it." He looked away, his hair swinging over his cheek, hiding his expression. Michael's fingers trembled now, with his.

"The midwife came the next day and made sure to tell me how poorly I had handled the matter. We buried Maire and the child, and the midwife found a wet nurse for Brigit—her mother had named her as she died. I left for Ireland to find Fionn."

"Surely he understood," she whispered. She cradled his curled, powerful fingers in her hand, wanting to comfort him, but unsure how.

"I think Fionn knew that I had done my best," he said. He took a deep breath. "He had terrible grief and rage, but he did not blame me. We marched with the Scots, and came to a field where we met the Irish. Fionn threw himself into battle with true ferociousness, half crazed, as if he meant to let himself be killed. I went after him. Two Irish gallowglasses came at us, swords high. Fionn was cut down." He paused.

Michael said nothing, her heart pounding as she waited for him to continue.

"He might have lived, I think, if an experienced surgeon had worked on him," he said. "An Irishman's sword had sliced open my hand, and I was bleeding at the wrist. I nearly died beside my brother, but Fionn had asked me to watch over Brigit. I promised that I would. I could not let myself die, after he did."

She watched him through the sparkle of her tears. Listening to his hushed voice, she saw in her mind the two dark-haired brothers, fallen in Irish mud; she heard the gasping request, the hoarse promise. A fat, hot tear slipped down her cheek.

"I instructed one of the Scots in repairing my hand. The fellow had scant talent for surgery, as it turned out." He flexed his hand in hers and laughed harshly. "I sometimes wonder if the injury was meant as a punishment. My hell on this earth, after my incompetence."

"Never say that!" She gripped his fingers. "You did no wrong. Fionn bore no grudge against you."

"He did not," he admitted. "But I do."

She put a shaking hand over her eyes. More tears slid down. She could not stop them now. Diarmid made a soft sound, and wove her fingers gently in his. His free hand slipped over her hair.

"*Ach,* do not cry." She felt his chin press against her head. "Michael, my girl. Do not cry. Come here."

She turned into the blessedness of his arms with a little sob. He held her, rocking silently, his stubbled chin rasping against her brow. The sadness she felt began to fade as he touched her, replaced by a kind of blissful sense of sanctuary, as if his arms sheltered her from harm. Nestled against him, she pressed her wet cheek against his wool-covered shoulder and sighed into the comfort that surrounded her.

Here, in the arms of a man she hardly knew, she was home, and safe, and where she must be. The thought stunned her. Her years in Ibrahim's house had been an intellectual refuge. He had offered her teaching and friendship, but indifferent affection. She had never known the whole sense of protection and comfort that she felt in Diarmid's arms.

Remnants of the old, awful loneliness that she had so long felt gathered power inside of her. She clung to Diarmid. Meaning to offer him solace, she found herself soothed. She lifted her head and pulled away a little to look up at him.

His face was close in the moonlight, his eyes like silver, his hair dark as shadows. Still in his arms, she thought the heavy beat of her heart would shake them both.

"I did not mean to hurt you with this," he said.

"You have not hurt me," she whispered.

"Michael, my girl," he murmured. "Where were you five years back? I needed you then." A sad smile tilted one corner of his mouth. He touched her hair, sifting the wayward strands in a gentle, reflective gesture, as if he were lost in his thoughts.

"I needed you then," he repeated. "And now it is too late." He touched his lips to her brow softly, regretfully. Her knees turned weak as butter, and her eyelids floated down. Yearning for more, she sighed.

"If I had known," she said, "I would have come to you."

"*Ach Dhia,*" he breathed, and covered her mouth with his.

He had kissed her before, but not like this. Now he took her into him, possessed her, as if he breathed in her soul and kept her within him. She did not want to be released. Wrapping her arms around his neck, she returned the kiss, feeling joy and a sense of relief to be able to hold him, touch him as she had yearned to do.

He tilted his head as his lips opened over hers again and again, in a heated rhythm that plunged through her like fire, like honey, taking breath, taking thought. She could not get enough, ever, of this.

He traced his lips along her cheek, along the tender edge of her jaw toward her earlobe. Her legs wavered as if her bones melted inside. He leaned back against the wall and took her with him, settled across his lap, supported in his arms.

"Michael," he murmured against her throat. His lips played across her throat, her jaw, her mouth. She did not speak, could not, finding the slanted corner of his mouth, kissing the quirk there, tasting the salty, wine flavor of his inner lip.

He returned the exploration as if he were starved, taking her lower lip between his, letting his tongue lick open the seal of her lips. He entered her mouth sweetly, a hot, gentle, exquisite feeling.

She knew that men and women could ignite passion like this between them; she had never experienced much of it herself, but she had read about its stages, its symptoms, its dangers. She knew the theories of the humors that drove the sensual urges in the body. But she had never felt their power gather and flow through her, turning her heartbeat to thunder, her flesh to liquid heat.

His hands warmed over her, soothing, sliding, his breath deepening. She spanned her hands over his chest and felt his thumping heart beneath her touch. His fingers traced the swell of her breasts, sensitive even beneath layers of silk and black wool. His hands swept down to her waist, up again, until his thumbs found the ready buds of her nipples. She arched into him, craving now, longing, taking his mouth hungrily with hers.

Then he made a muffled sound and broke away, holding her against his chest. "Michael, forgive me. I did not mean for this to happen."

"Diarmid—" she said.

"Listen to me," he murmured. "I am not much given to talk about my troubles. The tale is a heavy burden, I know. No one knows the whole of it but you." He paused, his breath slowing, less urgent. "As for the rest—*ach*, you must think I had too much wine." His lips pressed against her brow. "Dear girl, I have not."

She wrapped her arms around him and waited for her own breath to slow, waited for the pulsing need in her lower body to calm. "I wanted to hear it," she said. "Heartfelt wounds must be cleansed, or they will never heal. And as for the rest that passed between us—" She looked up at him. "I wanted that too."

He sighed, long and deep. "We should forget this. I am wed, for all it is worth." He paused, and in that silence, her heart shattered at his feet.

"I know," she said. "I am sorry."

"Listen to me," he said urgently. "Anabel and I were given penance by the court. On pain of losing our souls to damnation, we vowed never to dishonor our marriage. It was the only way to win the separation. Michael, I cannot wed you. I can give you nothing. I do not want you to be my mistress."

Michael began to say that she would not be a mistress to any man, but she only choked back an incoherent sob. She stood quickly, spinning to run down the steps. Diarmid strode after her, but she ran along the corridor to the door of her chamber. She yanked open the door and closed it behind her, before her heart could urge her to stop, to turn, to run back.

She leaned against the thick oak, her breath heaving, fighting sobs. Hearing his knock on the door, she held herself still. She felt the press of his weight against the oak, leaning against it just as she did.

"*Micheil,*" he murmured. "Forgive me for leading you into this."

She held in a sob, waiting in silence. The thickness of the door separated them, linked them. She yearned to tell him he was forgiven, that she loved him, that she would be anything to him that he desired. Tears started in her eyes. She moved her hand to the latch.

But her fingers shook, and she stopped, swamped by fear, as if she stood at the edge of a precipice. Her heart felt newborn, needy, uncertain.

Thick oak held her apart from Diarmid, but she heard him there, mere inches away. Her heart thumped like a storm as longing and fear collided. A small, cautious inner voice told her that she was foolish to love him. She listened, and agreed.

But a deeper voice, softer, kinder, whispered that Diarmid was the source of all there was in her life, all there ever would be. Go to him, the voice urged; reach for him; find a way to be together. But she could not bring herself to move, though she might wither for lack of what she wanted.

After a few moments she felt his fist thud once, softly, against the door. And she heard him walk away.

She leaned against the door and wrapped her arms around herself. All this had come too late, as Diarmid had said. She would harden her heart against his appeal. She would not let herself love him.

She would not.

A soft, low-lying veil of mist covered the moors as Diarmid and Angus rode side by side on their return to Dunsheen. Several days of traveling had taken them from one Campbell castle to another, from the castle of the clan chief, Campbell of Lochawe, to the keeps belonging to Diarmid's cousins Neill Campbell and

Donald MacArthur, and to the hall of his own younger brother Colin Campbell of Glenbevis. He and Mungo had been shown generous Highland hospitality and had taken part in long, complex discussions that had often continued deep into the night.

The concerns of his fellow Highlanders over the political and economic situations and matters of trade had occupied Diarmid's thoughts for days. As they rode home, he and Mungo had tried to sort through what they had learned about Ranald MacSween's loyalties and activities. None of the Campbell kin suspected MacSween of treason, and none knew of subversive political moves on his part. Few, though, had expressed any praise for the man beyond his shrewd merchanting abilities. MacSween was clearly disliked, though no one seemed to hate him or consider him dangerous or evil in nature. He was merely a self-server. Any distrust of him centered there.

"What message do you wish me to take back to the king?" Mungo asked as they rode. "I assume he expects a report soon."

Diarmid sighed deeply. "No message as yet, for there is nothing to say. And Campbell of Lochawe said the king plans to visit the western Isles soon. I can tell him what I have found in an audience with him. So far, what I have heard this week neither absolves nor condemns Ranald MacSween."

"Perhaps he is only guilty of collecting a nice bit of coin for himself," Mungo said. "He does not seem responsible for harm done to the western trade routes, and he is not known to traffic with English merchants. His only transgression seems to be his grasping hold on Glas Eilean, and his explanation is a rational one— he cannot turn that fortress over to a woman."

Diarmid shrugged admittance. "True, Scotland needs a strong hand there, and an experienced Islesman would be best. Even Gavin Faulkener could not hold it as well as a western Highland laird could do. Glas Eilean sits at the gateway to the western

Isles. The English blockade of our water routes has already begun to choke the western Highlands."

"They know how dependent we are on foreign trade for basic foodstuffs, metals, cloth." Mungo shook his head. "If they want to damage us even further, they might try a direct sea assault."

"Glas Eilean is positioned to ward off an attack of that sort. MacSween is right. The king needs a strong man there."

"Ranald MacSween sits on that nest like a cat who has eaten the fledglings and dares any bird to attack him," Mungo said. "He knows his power. He manages to flourish when others suffer from high prices and scarcity of goods. Do you think he has treasonous connections with the English?"

"It is not impossible, but my brother Arthur is canny, and has his own English contacts. If Ranald had any such dealings, Arthur would have indicated it to me."

"Lochawe said that a few Scottish ships have been bold enough and fast enough to break through the English blockade," Mungo said. "Scottish pirates have recently raided English ports as far south as Holyhead and Anglesey, stealing grain shipments that later turned up in Argyll." He slid Diarmid a sideways glance. "I confess that I had an odd thought about that report."

"I did too," Diarmid said. "Arthur had command of my birlings during the months that I was gone. If he had extra time on his hands, he might have found an interesting way to fill it."

"Arthur is like you—he can coax speed and stealth from any birling," Mungo said. "He may well be one of the pirates that the English complain about. And if so, he should watch himself carefully. From what we heard, the English are looking for him."

"I do not fret about him. He will play the dull merchant in Ayr well enough. Tomorrow, Mungo, I mean to sail to Glas Eilean," Diarmid added briskly. "Ranald mentioned the high quality of the goods he exported from Ireland. I'd like to see what he has stored away there. He should be detained in Ayr for another week or two. And I want to see Sorcha."

"Then I will go with you," Mungo said. "I would like to see her too, if she does not mind a visit from a coarse man like myself." He glanced grimly at Diarmid. "Will you ask Lady Michael to sail with us?"

"She may not want to come," he replied curtly. In truth, he did not think, after their last encounter, she would even consent to stand in the same room with him, much less travel with him.

"She has a right to bear a strong grudge against Ranald MacSween," Mungo said reasonably. "But your sister needs her expert knowledge. Surely you can convince her to go."

"I have asked her already. She gave me no firm answer."

"She might, if you were charming enough. It worked in Perth." Mungo tried to look innocent.

Diarmid cast him a sour glance. "I have no plans to steal her off my own isle and toss her in a boat."

Mungo chuckled and said nothing, riding ahead. Diarmid rode more slowly, pensive. He had tried for days to keep Michael out of his thoughts. But she hovered at the back of his mind, walked through his dreams, whispered to him as he woke and went to sleep. He saw her in clouds, in fog, in sunshine, in moonlight.

Ach, he thought with mild disgust. He was as smitten as any youth with a first love. However, he was no youth, and the purity of first love had bypassed him. Life was far more complicated than in Gilchrist's harping songs.

But she haunted him, excited him, enchanted him, as if she were truly magic. He had bared his deepest hurts to her, and she had eased the awful burden of guilt he carried, dissolved hidden shadows in his heart.

What had stirred to life between them was fragile and beautiful, and he had shattered it irrevocably.

He had ridden out early the next day with Mungo, but the leagues he covered did not lessen the bond that linked him to her. Undeniably, he felt an aching, powerful physical lust, wanting to hold her, to delve into her warmth until pleasure saturated them both. But he felt a deeper need, one he did not understand as readily. He needed her in the deep well of his soul, and it frightened him.

He did not want her for his mistress. Perhaps he had said it too bluntly. What he had meant was that he did not want to dishonor her. Michael was precious to him. Had matters been otherwise, he would have made her his wife.

But the ecclesiastical court's decree made that impossible. The bishop's grant of separation in bed and board had carried with it a harsh condition, a penitential vow of chastity for both him and Anabel, as if their failed marriage had been a sin.

He felt as if his heart had torn in the last few days. He loved Michael, but he had often brought harm, somehow, to those he had loved. Now his finest hope for happiness had slipped from his grasp, and he had no right to rescue it.

When he returned, he would give her the physician's fee he had promised and send her home to her brother. She had done all that she could for Brigit; she claimed there were no miracles in her. He did not believe that, but he would try to accept it.

But first, he had one last favor to ask of her.

Michael sighed as she bent over the parchment page, a quill pen in her fingers. She sat at the long table in the hall, working on Brigit's natal horoscope. At the other side of the room, Gilchrist played a soft melody for Brigit and Eva, who listened dreamily, sleepy after a large midday meal.

Michael listened too, while she studied the design

on the page. After combing through the mathematical
figures in the *Liber Astronomicus* and another of
Ibrahim's volumes on astrology, and using a *volvex,* a
spinning chart of astronomical information, she had
prepared Brigit's chart. Drawing a neat square and
dividing it into wedged segments, she had labeled each
section carefully with the information she had found,
and then drew lines to link the planetary relationships
that became obvious.

Now she sat back, frowning as she studied the chart.
Her calculations had produced a puzzling natal design.
Mercury in the house of health was afflicted by Saturn,
and Mars negatively aspected to the sun. Pisces was
strongly represented throughout, as was Capricorn, increasing the chance of weakness in the feet and knees.
The chart showed a strong link with water, not surprising to her, but Michael also saw the positive influence
of Venus, indicating that Brigit might benefit from a
loving touch.

Touch. She drew in a breath, and worked on. The
intriguing chart showed that through hands, health
might improve. And she thought—hoped—that the afflictions to the first house, that of health and the body,
showed that Brigit's worst health problems were con-
fined to early in her life. The child had a chance of
outgrowing her condition—if Michael could find the
right healing treatment.

She sighed, growing frustrated as the subtler details
of the work eluded her. The child's natal horoscope
was more complex than she had usually seen. Ibrahim
would have understood the message in its entirety, but
he was not here to help her.

She flexed her stiff, ink-stained fingers, and glanced
at the children, so absorbed in Gilchrist's quiet music.
Then she turned back to the *Liber Astronomicus,* wondering if she had overlooked something that would
make all of this more clear.

She was not as adept at interpreting charts as she
wanted to be. Had Ibrahim lived, he would have

taught her more about the arts of astrology and medicine. Fate had not allowed her enough time to learn all that she could from him.

But if he had lived, she would never have discovered the compelling magic that Diarmid had showed her. The thought of him made her melt inside again, a shivering, excited sensation that had happened often in the past several days. That was followed, as always, by a sharp sense of loss.

She sighed and lay the quill down, rubbing her brow, unable to get Diarmid out of her mind. At first she had been relieved that he had gone away, but at night she yearned for his arms to surround her, longed to feel again the wondrous vibrance he had brought to life inside of her.

But she would shutter her desires. The laird of Dunsheen did not want the burden of her foolish heart at his feet. She would leave Dunsheen Castle. She had treated Brigit, and Lilias and Iona could continue without her supervision. She would ask Angus to send a runner to Kinglassie. Gavin was not there, but someone would come to escort her home.

Leaving Brigit and the others would hurt almost as much as leaving the laird himself. But she steeled herself against the regret and her inner protests, and returned to the chart.

When the shadows deepened, Gilchrist put away his harp and Angus came to carry Brigit up to her room. Michael continued to work in the empty hall by candlelight, vaguely aware that the dogs barked outside in the yard, and voices called.

Then she heard steady footsteps crossing the chamber and looked up, startled. Diarmid came toward her, his hair wind-tousled, his green-and-black plaid dark in the fading light, his gaze silver and vivid as it met hers.

She stood, dropping the page she held. When he was an arm's length away, he halted, eyeing her steadily.

"Lady, greetings," he said, his voice quiet and formal.

She nodded tremulously. "Dunsheen. I have been doing the horoscope," she rushed on, anxious to talk about something, anything, to keep him with her, to focus his attention somewhere else than on her eyes. She showed him the chart she had drawn. "Saturn afflicts Mercury, and there is a strong predominance of Pisces and Capricorn, but there are positive influences from Venus and the moon."

He frowned. "And what does all that mean, if anything?"

"I think she will be fine, although not for a long while yet. According to the natal design, the best method of treatment seems to be—" She stopped, blushing suddenly, hotly.

He folded his arms over his chest. "Is what?"

"Touch," she said in a small voice, glancing away.

He was silent for a long moment. Then he huffed out a low breath. "Lady," he said, "I have been thinking. You will need to gather your things for travel. You may not agree, but I—"

"I understand," she said quickly. She lifted her chin. He wanted her to leave Dunsheen; he must have decided, as she had, that it was best. "I will go," she said, firming her voice. "I will leave some instructions for Brigit's care—"

"*Tcha,*" he said, a sound of exasperation. "I want you to come with me."

She blinked. "With you?"

"I mean to sail to Glas Eilean in the morning." He frowned at her. "I know you do not want to go there, but I want you to meet my sister Sorcha."

"You want me to come with you?" She realized that she sounded like a dimwit. "To Glas Eilean?"

He nodded. "Tomorrow at dawn."

Her heart beat rapidly. He asked her to go to the lair of her enemy, her brother's enemy. But he wanted her to go with him. She caught her breath, and then remembered that he would sail there in his birling. Fear rose within her, and she bit her lip, hesitating.

"I need you there," he murmured. "Sorcha needs you. I assure you that you will be safe. The voyage is not a long one."

Something in his voice melted her resistance. "I will do it," she said in a rush, and felt as if she stepped off a cliff.

Chapter Fourteen

The world careened, and Michael clung to its last remaining edge with clawed hands. She grasped the side of the birling and groaned hoarsely, but the sound was lost beneath the roar and crash of waves and wind.

Another swell surged beneath the boat, and she lunged forward without grace or dignity to lose what little was left in her stomach. A spray of cold, salty water cleansed her face and doused her hair yet again. The chilled shock quieted her heaving, empty stomach for a while. Hands shaking, hair hanging in her eyes like rank seaweed, she leaned her arms along the rim of the birling and stared, exhausted, at the lurching sea.

Hearing repeated shouts, she carefully shifted her glance to look around. Long and narrow and fluid in design, her oak planking gleaming wet in the sunlight, the *Gabriel* rose and fell over the waves as she sped forward. Twenty-six oars were manned by the burly tenants and kin of the Dunsheen Campbells. They sat upon wooden chests and pulled steadily at the long oars outthrust from holes cut in the boat's sides. Their wide, rhythmic sweeps and the billowing sail overhead drove the vessel forward.

The calls Michael heard came from a man who also beat a drum to help the oarsmen pull in unison. Overhead, the square sail bellied and strained against the rope lines that anchored it, and the boat rocked sideways. At Diarmid's shout, a few of the oarsmen left their posts to bring the sail down, rolling it and tying it to the spar with stout rope. Michael had no idea why they chose oar over sail at this point, but thought they meant to avoid winds strong enough to blow them off course.

Diarmid stood in the bow of the boat, his stance wide and balanced, his hair winging out in the stiff breeze. Behind him, the curved spine of the wooden prow, its end curled in a spiral, thrust toward the bright blue sky. Diarmid spoke with Mungo, who stood beside him, and then walked away, stepping carefully among coils of rope and stacked wooden barrels. Michael watched him come toward her.

She turned away, curling her legs beneath her. Perched on a barrel in the stern of the boat, she clung to the rising, falling edge tightly, as she had for two hours already.

Diarmid had walked back to speak with her a few times during the voyage, but she had directed such fierce little glances at him that he had left without much comment. She knew that he stood behind her again, but she did not look up at him.

In truth, she wished that she could sink through the bottom of the boat and disappear. Her illness mortified her. Although her constitution was generally strong, she had a sensitive stomach, especially in boats. Her genuine apprehension near water stemmed, in part, from bouts of ocean sickness that she could not cure. As a physician, she sincerely thought she should exhibit perfect health. But in this, she was defeated.

"Michael," he said. "Are you any better?"

She folded her hands along the rim of the hull. "I am fine," she said. "Go away."

"Fine?" He sat on a stack of rope. "I doubt that."

"I am," she said stubbornly. "This is just the way I sail. It will pass. Go away."

"So this is why you dislike water and boats," he mused.

"In part," she mumbled, pressing her hand against her mouth.

"It is enough. Can I help?"

She shook her head and nearly fell off the barrel when a wave rolled underneath the birling. Diarmid grabbed her and steadied her.

"The winds are high today," he commented. "I feel a little ill myself, when sailing is like this."

She sent him a sour glare and shoved her hair out of her eyes. Lank and wet, it slipped down again. She was too exhausted to sweep it back once more. "Go away," she snarled.

"*Ach*, girl," he murmured gently. He kept his hand on her back, the only spot of warmth she felt in this open, cold, wet place. "Come in midships. You may feel steadier there."

"I like it here," she muttered. She was sure to hate it anywhere on board the reeling, swaying craft. And she refused to display her weakness in the wide, flat middle area, where nearly thirty men could stare at her.

"Michael, let me help."

She answered with a groan as the world went green and uncertain again, and thrust her head over the side of the ship. Diarmid held her shoulders until she had finished. She sat back, and he swept her hair out of her eyes, a soothing motion that did little to dispel her misery, her irritation, or her embarrassment.

"Go away," she muttered.

"*Ach*," he said, "I have nothing else to do but sit here."

"Sit somewhere else. I need to be alone."

"Do you?" he asked, combing his fingers through her hair. Shivers, pleasant and relaxing, rushed through her. Exhausted, she allowed herself to lean against him slightly. He provided a haven of stability in a reeling world.

"Sit where you will sit, then," she said irritably; she wanted him to stay with her, although she would not admit it. But she sighed a little when his hands began to knead the tension in her shoulders.

"Were you ill like this on the voyage from Italy?" he asked.

She nodded. "Both times, going there and coming back, though years separated the trips. The ship was a large one, French, with wooden castles at either end and a deep hold for trade goods."

"I have sailed on larger ships," he said. "My stomach bothered me quite a bit on those."

She looked at him in surprise. "You?"

He nodded. "I have been ocean sick many times, though I have learned ways to relieve it. This helps somewhat." He reached into a fold of his plaid and pulled out a small, withered bit of yellow flesh, like an old slice of apple. "Ginger," he said. "I tried to give it to you before, but you nearly took my head off with your snarl. Here, suck on it."

She grimaced. "I could not," she said.

"Try it," he said, tearing off a sliver. "Just a bit. There," he said as he slipped it between her lips.

The dried root was sharp but sweet, coated with sugar. She sucked, and waited. The boat surged, and she swung against Diarmid. He caught her and kept an arm around her shoulders. Cold salt spray drenched them both, and he slicked the water from her face with a gentle hand.

"Better?" he asked.

She wrinkled her nose. "I am not sure. Perhaps." Her stomach still hovered at the edge of upheaval, but the worst of the sensation had faded.

"It does not work for everyone, but I find it useful. I learned of it from a Venetian trader," he said. "He supplies us with sugared ginger along with other spices from the East for Dunsheen woolfells. When we can get shipments through."

She looked around the boat, at the rowers, at Mungo laughing with the drummer, who had stopped his insistent rhythm for a while. "Your birling looks like a Norwegian longship. I have only sailed on the larger European ships, and rowing boats."

He nodded proudly. "All of my birlings are Norwegian built, in the design used for centuries by Vikings. This kind of vessel is far more practical in the western Isles than the square, deep European ships, and so most Islesmen use them. Birlings are perfect for sailing among islands and coasts—light, graceful, fast, and flexible. And a great advantage in trade or in war."

"War?" She looked up at him.

"I hold my land of the king's goodwill in exchange for two birlings pledged as warships," he said. "King Robert has required their service a few times, but most of the time I use them for trading and voyaging."

She nodded, sucking on the ginger. Her stomach felt calmer, but she doubted the illness was over. Another heavy wave brought the boat high; when the prow smacked down, Michael shoved away from Diarmid to hang over the edge. After a moment, when nothing happened, she looked at him in surprise.

He smiled. "Better," he said with satisfaction.

"A little," she admitted. Her head ached viciously, and she had not lost the persistent dizziness, but her stomach was undeniably quieter. She rose shakily to her feet. "How much longer must we sail?"

He stood too, and pointed ahead. "See those mountains?" He gestured toward three blue, conical shapes that pushed against the cloud-filled sky, far in the distance. "Those are the peaks on the Isle of Jura. Beyond that lies the Isle of Isla. Glas Eilean is just off its southern tip. We will sail for another hour or so at least. Our progress is slow because of the heavy seas. Currents affect a boat like this even more than winds."

She nodded. "Is it always this rough out here?"

"Not always." He smiled a little. "There are times when the sea is like green glass," he said, "sweet and smooth and fast as ice. Other days the clouds are high as mountains, filling the sky, and the winds carry us like a dream wherever we want to go. Then there are times when the water is rough and quarrelsome. A storm often comes behind such waves. But my birlings—the larger one, the *White Heather,* a small one I call *Grace,* and this, the *Gabriel*—are nimble vessels in any weather."

She turned to glance up at him. His eyes had a silver clarity, like the sparkle of sunlight on the water, that showed his pride and his excitement. "You love the sea, and your boats," she said.

"I do," he said. He glanced at her. "But you do not, I know. We are pulling toward Isla as fast as we can, and we'll follow the shoreline on power of oars, although we must be careful of the rocks and currents."

He stood beside her for a while, silent, then put a hand on her shoulder and turned her slightly. "Listen, now," he said. "Listen carefully."

She did, frowning to concentrate. The constant rhythmic rush of waves was underscored by another sound, a deep, throaty roar. "What is that?" she asked in alarm. "An approaching storm?"

"The sound of a whirlpool—Corrievreckan, it is called—formed by the tidal currents between Jura and another island. At times that channel is calm, if tricky, but winds like these can start it turning, and storms can whip it to a dangerous frenzy. A birling like this can be swallowed in an instant."

"We are not going near there, are we?" she asked nervously.

"Not at all," he said. "We are safe." His hand still rested on her shoulder. He drew her closer, supporting her with his strong arm, peering down at her with concern. "Are you well?"

She nodded, still wobbly and uneasy, but much more in balance. The improvement might have been due to sugared ginger, but she thought that Diarmid's presence made the greatest difference. He anchored her with his steadfast support. She leaned against him like a rock in a storm.

Standing there, she could easily forget the torment of her feelings. He was with her now, and no other

life existed for either of them beyond the deck of the
birling. She glanced up at him and saw a glimpse of
his crooked smile as he met her eyes. This was what
she wanted, what she needed. She did not want to
think beyond that.

"Look out there, Michael," he said, pointing briefly,
dropping his hand back to her shoulder. "Look far
out, away from the boat, away from the waves that
break along the sides. And stand easy, with the motion
of the boat, like this"—he briefly put his hands on her
hips to demonstrate, shifting her weight subtly with
the rocking of the galley—"and you may find yourself
becoming a sailor after all. Like this," he said. "Find
your balance."

His hands shifted her, guided her so languidly that
she felt chills spiral along her spine. His voice, low
and soothing and sensual, was just as distracting as his
hands. She felt its vibration within her body, like a
kiss of sound.

She blushed and strived to gather her thoughts,
standing as he had told her, legs apart, knees flexible,
to find her balance. With his hands guiding her, she
found a better sense of stability. Then she lifted her
head to watch the distant surface of the sea, where
the water ruffled dark blue and frothy beneath the
azure sky. Out there, the tumult of wind and wave
seemed far less. She felt calmer, suddenly, and smiled
with sudden relief.

Diarmid looked up. "This wind brings a storm behind it. Those waves are long and sweeping, pushed
forward by heavy winds. We may see a gale before
long."

"Will we reach Glas Eilean before then?"

He laughed softly. "Surely," he said. "We may even
be home to Dunsheen before the storm breaks. Sometimes a gale takes days to come in." He lifted his
head, and the wind whipped back his hair. She glanced
up at the strong, whiskered line of his throat, and at
his eyes, colored like storm clouds.

He was beautiful to her, fierce and yet kind, the rock she leaned against. Standing with him as they faced the magnificent power of the sea, she felt a new resoluteness that was linked to his, as if together they created a source of infinite, enduring strength for both.

But she glanced down hastily, breaking the fantasy. She must leave when they returned to Dunsheen. His kindness out here, amid wind and water, had not changed that. No matter that her heart longed for him, that she felt strangely incomplete without him. He was not for her.

She stepped away from the shelter of his arms abruptly, and felt as if some part of her soul tore a little.

"Are you ill?" he asked behind her.

She shook her head and lifted her gaze toward the far sea. "I am fine," she said. "You need not concern yourself with me."

"But I do," he said. "I do."

She did not turn, and though Diarmid stood behind her for a long while, neither of them spoke. She looked out over the churning, cream-tipped sea as the wind beat about them both.

The world spun around her, the sea careened onward, but Michael felt changed—wary of the water still, she stood stronger to face her fears. For now her anchor, her rock, was just at hand. But she vowed that later, when he was gone, she would remember that Diarmid had showed her some of the staunchness within herself.

He stared out over the rolling blue water toward the high cliffs at the southern end of Isla. A multitude of birds—seagulls, gannets, and the white-fronted geese that flocked to the island in the winter months— sailed overhead. Pale wings fluttered as the birds glided and landed along the cliff sides that harbored their nests. He envied their freedom, suddenly.

He turned to watch Michael. She stood in the stern,

slim and straight and fine-boned. As the birling skimmed past the cliffs, she gazed upward, her face showing awe, innocence, and the strain of sea travel. Her face was pale as linen, her eyes were ringed in shadows, and her hair hung limp over her shoulders. But she stood with quiet grace, a wet, bedraggled angel in the stern of his boat.

He wanted to gather her into his arms, warm her, kiss her, but so much held him back. What burgeoned between them was still there, still powerful enough to sweep them both into its irresistible current. But he could offer her no promise, no future, no real joy. His mistake, years earlier, had created the barrier between them, and he could not tear it down.

Sighing, he looked northeast toward Jura. On a small island off its opposite coast was the nunnery where Anabel lived. Perhaps he should go there and ask her to release him. She had that power.

The ecclesiastical court had banished her to the nunnery as a lay sister, but if she ever desired to take holy vows, and agreed to donate the land she owned to the Church, the court had promised that her marriage would finally be annulled.

But Anabel MacSween was the least repentant, least pious woman he knew. She would never take holy vows, despite her exile. Until now he had not cared, but he resolved to visit her, to ask her, although he expected a refusal.

He remembered her vividly, creamy skin that flushed easily in passion, brown eyes and russet hair, a lush, strong body, a sharp, often cruel wit. She had emanated a feline sensuality, and he had found it easy to become ensnared.

The last day he had seen her on the island, she had been angry, eager to hurt him further. "I have been banished to a religious house as penance for my sins," she had said. "But I remain your wife as long as we both live. That is the prison we share, Diarmid. Mine is here on this island, and yours is everywhere that

you go. No wife to hold, no heirs for your castle." She
had turned and walked away.

He had never gone back to see her. He sent dona-
tions to the convent there, as he must, for her keep:
payment in wool and foodstuffs collected in trade. But
he never brought it himself.

Her words echoed in his mind. *Your prison is everywhere you go. No wife to hold . . . no heirs. . . .* He
could not have had a more effective enemy than Anabel MacSween, his wife.

"Diarmid!" Hearing Michael's call, he looked
toward her. She pointed south, past Isla's high cliff
sides, flocked with seabirds. Beyond lay several small,
scattered islands. On the largest of them, a castle rose
stark against the sky.

"There," he said, nodding. "That is Glas Eilean."

He heard her gasp as they drew closer to the awe-
some beauty of the island and its high keep. Glas
Eilean was a long, wedge-shaped island, its far end
rimmed in sandy beaches and green machair, its middle ground a mass of low, rolling hills, its close end a
high, raw stone cliff that plunged into the sea. Atop
the height rose the square, golden stone walls of the
castle, like a crown on the cliffside.

She pointed to the low end of the island, where
sleek gray seals clustered on rocks, and smiled as she
watched them. "Will we land on one of the beaches
and walk up to the castle?"

"There is a quicker way inside," he said, and called
orders to the crew to prepare to enter Glas Eilean.

The oarsmen changed direction and speed, and soon
sailed so close to the cliffs that Michael exclaimed
in apprehension. When they were close enough that
Diarmid could almost touch the buff-colored stone,
the prow of the ship slipped inside one of the long,
dark shadows that creased the cliff. They entered a
tall, narrow crevice.

Michael gasped, and the slight sound echoed all
around. He stepped toward her as darkness engulfed

them. The birling drifted slowly along the narrow, dark waterway, guided by the work of a few oarsmen and Mungo, who had taken the tiller.

Diarmid touched Michael's arm in the darkness. "Glas Eilean is full of caves," he said quietly, his voice ringing clear above plunging oars and the slap-slap of water. "The castle entrance is just ahead."

"I have never seen anything like this," she breathed. The tunnel widened, and amber light from wall torches high overhead shimmered on the dark water and walls. A staircase, steep and alarmingly narrow, rose into high shadows. The oarsmen guided the boat alongside the steps, mooring her with ropes to an iron ring sunk into the wall. In the darkness beyond the steps, two small boats floated, moored to other rings.

Diarmid helped to secure the galley, then leaned forward and grabbed a sheep's horn that hung on the wall. He blew three long blasts, the same distinct, plaintive notes he used at his own castle to announce that the laird of Dunsheen had arrived. Then he turned and held out a hand to Michael. Her hand was cold and trembled noticeably. She hesitated and glanced at the staircase.

"This place is easily defended," Diarmid said. "Only friends are allowed to mount those steps. A single guard can hold off a shipload of attackers, for only one person at a time can mount the stairs."

"This must be where my brother's men were defeated," she said.

"It was. But the door will be opened for us. Come ahead."

She nodded and stepped out of the boat directly onto the lowest step, which was awash in seawater. Diarmid noticed how cautiously and slowly she moved, and remembered that she would be still dizzy and exhausted from her ocean sickness, and unstable on her feet. He stepped out after her and placed his hand on her waist as she climbed ahead of him.

She faltered once or twice, and gasped when she

looked down the steep incline. In the birling, the men were stowing the ropes and preparing to mount the steps in a single line, some of them carrying sacks with the oats, barley, and plaid cloth that Diarmid had brought from Dunsheen for Sorcha.

"Easy, girl," he murmured as Michael paused again, her hand tentative on the wall. "Go up, now, you are safe."

The high, arched doorway creaked open, and a single, small figure stepped toward them on the wide upper platform. Michael attained the top step and faltered again, leaning against the wall for support.

A woman glided toward them, draped in a loose gown of gray wool, her hair like bright copper in the torchlight. With a murmur of sympathy, she opened her arms and enfolded Michael in her embrace. "Welcome," she said, and looked at Diarmid as he gained the platform. "Diarmid! Ah, brother, welcome." Her voice was light as silver bells.

He smiled. "Sorcha, you look wonderful."

She lifted her cheek for his kiss, her gray eyes sparkling in the amber light. "And who is this you've brought to visit me? She is not well, this one, and looks near to fainting."

He put out an arm swiftly to support Michael, who appeared dazed and pale. "I've brought you a physician," he said. "She'll need your care first, though. The sea is not her best means of travel."

"Come in, and she shall have whatever she needs." Sorcha turned, her natural grace uninhibited by her large, swollen belly. Together, Diarmid and his sister guided Michael over the threshold.

Chapter Fifteen

Dawn light, the plaintive cries of seabirds, and a sweet, poignant singing voice awoke Michael. She opened her eyes and turned on her side, nested in a deep feather mattress, and looked across the chamber.

Diarmid's sister Sorcha sat in a deep window niche on a cushioned stone bench. Light poured over her from the large double-arched window, its upper section filled with milky glass, its lower section unshuttered. Sorcha held a small piece of embroidery stretched on a frame, and sang as she worked the needle in and out of the fabric.

The melody was one Michael had heard Gilchrist play on his harp, but she had not heard lyrics before. She listened as the quiet voice brought her to alertness. The song told of the children of an earthly woman and a male selkie, enchanted seal children who left their mother with her blessing, and swam away with their magical father. The melody was haunting, the words wistful.

Sorcha ended her song on a pure, hovering note and turned. "Lady Michael!" she said. "Good morn. Are you feeling better?"

Michael sat up, straightening her rumpled silk chemise, all that she wore. "Much better, thank you," she said. "I ask your pardon for my sorry state when I arrived here. I think I hardly spoke to anyone, and only wanted to sleep." She swung her legs over the side of the bed. "I did not mean to be rude."

"*Ach,* you were exhausted," Sorcha said, rising from

her seat and coming forward. She lifted Michael's black woolen gown and surcoat from a wall peg and laid them on the bed. "Ocean sickness can drain the strength. You needed the rest. There will be plenty of time for us to visit." She smiled. "I hope you do not mind me coming in here while you slept. I often sit by this window and watch the sea, and the seals playing on the rocks far out."

Michael looked around the small chamber, its finest feature the window niche with stone benches overlooking an expanse of sky and sea. "This is a lovely chamber. The view of the open ocean is magnificent."

"Ranald often sleeps here, as he says he does not wish to disturb me," Sorcha said. "But since he is not at Glas Eilean now, I thought you might enjoy it."

Wondering if Sorcha knew who was true owner of Glas Eilean, Michael reminded herself of Sorcha's kindness and decided to say nothing of it to her. She stood and picked up the leather sack she had brought with a few items, which someone had carried up from the birling. She changed her chemise to one of deep blue silk, and pulled on her clothing, clean hose, and a belt of flat brass links. Then she combed her fingers through her tangled hair and went toward a tiny privy chamber curtained at one end of the room. When she returned, Sorcha looked up.

"I will order a bath prepared for you later. I want you to be comfortable and at home here."

"I would love a bath later," Michael said. "Thank you for your hospitality. I know our visit was unexpected."

"I was so happy to see my brother, I would not care if he brought the king's army with him," Sorcha answered, and laughed. She had the Dunsheen lilt in her smile, and lovely white teeth, large and square. Her braided hair, bright as polished copper, was tucked beneath a sheer white veil, and her skin had a pale, milky translucency. Michael saw that her eyes were gray and very much like Diarmid's, though lashed in delicate gold. Slim despite her pregnancy, Sorcha had a fragile, gentle quality.

"But you are a much more welcome sight than the king's army!" Sorcha continued, smiling. "I enjoyed staying up late last night to talk with Diarmid and Mungo, who tells such wonderful tales. He always did, even when we were children together at Dunsheen." Her eyes glittered, and she sounded nearly giddy. "I confess I could hardly wait for you to wake, Lady Michael. Sometimes I yearn to talk to another woman."

"Are there no women on Glas Eilean?" Michael asked in surprise. "Surely you have maidservants, and a midwife nearby to attend you."

"Ranald keeps his garrison here with male servants, and only a female laundress and cook. I have no maid-servant now, since she wed a fisherman a few months ago. Ranald's elderly cousin Giorsal has a small house on the island and acts as my midwife." She paused. "There are a few fisher wives here too, but I know them scarcely." Her voice had a brittle, lonely note.

"I met your husband at Dunsheen a few weeks ago," Michael said. Sorcha nodded pleasantly, her expression innocent, and Michael felt certain that she knew nothing of her dispute with Ranald over Glas Eilean. "I understand that he has gone to Ayr. His garrison must still be here at Glas Eilean, then."

"He took several men with him to Ayr," Sorcha said. "My brother Arthur went with them as well. Ranald's garrison is always here. You will meet some of them. I keep to my rooms most of the time. Old Giorsal is something of a watchdog when she comes to visit and check on me." Sorcha gave a sour little grimace, and Michael chuckled.

"Ranald must be glad that Diarmid is visiting you in his absence," she said.

Sorcha looked somber. "Actually Ranald would not like to hear it. Diarmid times his visits to me when Ranald is gone. They have little liking for each other, although they are tied by the kinship of marriage on both sides, and they both have trade dealings that require cooperation. Otherwise I think they would have no tolerance for each other. Arthur is not bothered by whatever stands between Diarmid and Ranald, so he attends to most of the trade matters between Glas Eilean and Dunsheen."

"What stands between them?" Michael asked curiously.

"It began when Diarmid tried to divorce Anabel, who is Ranald's cousin. Their separation and Anabel's retirement to a convent set the two of them in some silent battle. I think sometimes they hate each other, which distresses me."

Michael carefully plaited strands of her hair. "I know only a little of it, but it is none of my matter."

"Diarmid scarcely mentions it to anyone. He had only pain from his marriage. Ranald suffered too, for he is fond of his cousin." She sighed. "How long have you been at Dunsheen?"

"Only a few weeks. I expect to go home to Galloway soon."

"Diarmid told me last evening that you are a physician," Sorcha said. "How wonderful! I did not know a woman could do that. You must tell me all about yourself. He said that your treatments have been helping Brigit. Thank you, Michael."

She smiled. "Brigit does seem stronger lately. We have been working her muscles for her, hoping she will regain some strength. I think it is possible. We shall see."

"Diarmid has faith in you, Lady Michael. Great faith." Sorcha's gaze was direct. "He has a high regard for you."

Michael paused, then cleared her throat. "I have good training. My late husband was a gifted physician and scholar in Italy. He taught me much."

"To hear Diarmid speak, you have much more than education. He says you are gifted. I would have thought he spoke of a saint last night, rather than a woman no different than myself." Sorcha smiled. "All of the Dunsheen Campbells know the story of how he and Fionn met you years ago, and how you worked on Angus's leg, though you were just a child. What a wonderful knowledge and talent you must have, to save Angus as you did."

"Diarmid repaired Angus's wound, but he says little of his part in it. I helped him, but most of my training came later. I decided, the day that I met Diarmid, that I would learn to heal others as he did."

Sorcha tilted her head. "Is that all you decided that day?"

"What do you mean?"

She shrugged. "I remember seeing Diarmid shortly after that battle, when he and Fionn brought Angus back to Dunsheen. I will never forget that when he spoke of you, his eyes would shine. I thought at the time that my serious brother, who took on so many cares as the laird, had fallen in love forever. I hoped he would ask for your hand when you were older."

Michael felt a deep blush heat her cheeks. She looked away.

"Oh! I am sometimes too quick to speak my mind," Sorcha blurted. "And I have too much imagination. Forgive me."

Michael shook her head to dispel Sorcha's discomfort. "I have always admired your brother, Sorcha. But we followed different paths."

"I wish he had not followed the path he took. He would have been happy, wed to you. Or anyone else but her. Forgive me," she said hastily. "Diarmid is a stubborn man, and clings to his unhappiness like a penance. Enough, I chatter on when you must be hungry. Come to the window seat. I brought some food up here for you."

Sorcha went to the window niche and sat on a cushioned bench, and Michael sat beside her. Soon she sipped watered wine and ate baked fish and oatcakes spread with honey. While she ate, her thoughts whirled over what Sorcha had said.

Sorcha nibbled a cake and some fish, then rested her hands on the upper curve of her abdomen. "Sometimes I am so hungry," she confided, laughing. "If you knew how much I ate through the day, you would be appalled."

"You should eat what you like," Michael said, smiling. "If all is in moderation, all will be well, as my husband often said. When is your child due?"

"Two months, I think. Sometimes it is hard to be sure."

"When was the last time you were in your flowers?"

Sorcha frowned, trying to recall. "The last week of March."

Michael counted back three months on her fingertips. "Then your child will arrive in January."

"Sooner than that. My babes always come too soon."

Michael watched her soberly. "Diarmid said something to me of your trouble. But not much."

Sorcha looked down at her clasped hands. "I have lost six," she murmured. "Each one born too early."

"That is a hard burden to bear," Michael said softly.

Sorcha nodded, her eyes slick with tears. "I hope someday God will reward me rather than punish me. I think of them as my seal children," she added in a quavery voice. "I sometimes imagine that they are mer-children: half human, half magic. They are happy here inside the water of my womb"—she placed a hand on her abdomen—"but they cannot survive on the earth. So God takes them back. I love them while they are in me, but I know that they will not stay. I know that I must let them go."

Michael's eyes filled with tears. Sorcha's unquestioning love was heart-wrenching, without blame or bitterness. Michael watched her silently, awed by her acceptance, and her bottomless, endless capacity for love.

"I know my fancy about the seal children is foolishness, but it helps me to endure," Sorcha said. "God understands why this happens. I do not question it any longer." She looked up. "Diarmid thinks you can help me."

"I am well trained in women's matters," Michael answered. "I cannot promise you"—she almost said "a miracle," but held back the word—"that you will have what you most desire. But I will try." She realized that she would do anything to help this gentle, courageous woman.

Sorcha nodded. "What will you do?"

"I need to examine you, outside and inside, if you will allow it. I will be very careful, but there are some signs I want to look for. Then I will know better what to tell you."

Michael frowned slightly as she washed her hands of the almond oil she had used during her thorough examination of Sorcha. She sat down beside her on the bed, thinking. She judged the babe to be healthy and good-size, but the entrance to Sorcha's womb had already begun to open. Even if large, the child was not yet ready to be born. According to the calendar, the child needed at least ten more weeks.

She smiled at Sorcha. "Your babe is active and quick, and his heartbeat is strong."

"She," Sorcha said.

Michael blinked, then nodded. "She is fine. But your body is too eager to deliver. Do you have child pangs? Have you seen any signs of labor?"

"Sometimes, but when I rest for a day, the signs go away. But they come back again, now and then."

"Did this happen with each child?"

Sorcha nodded. "When the pains get strong, I take to bed. Giorsal gives me a potion, and the pains go away. But I have never carried to the end of my time."

"What does she give you?" Michael asked.

"Herbs to relax me. She tells me I must not complain, and Ranald agrees with her. Giorsal says I can deliver a healthy babe if I will just be stronger. Ranald thinks this would not happen if I were a heartier woman. So I try to be strong."

Michael stared at her in disbelief. "Sorcha, you should complain. And make certain Ranald hears it," she said sharply. "I want you to take to your bed and stay there for the rest of your time. Your body prepares too early to give birth, but we can delay it some."

Sorcha looked shocked. "I cannot lie in bed for months! Ranald would be angry with me. He is displeased with me already because he has no son. He has threatened to set me aside and take another wife."

Michael scowled but refrained from direct comment. "You must rest for as long as you can. Is there a wise-wife on the island who can make up some herbal medicines for you?"

"There is one on the mainland. We can send someone there to collect what you need."

"Good. Now you will go to your chamber and rest." Michael stood, helped Sorcha to her feet, and led her out of the room.

Diarmid stood near the cliff edge, watching gulls wheel and dip over the sea. On a cluster of rocks that extended out into the water, a colony of gray seals scampered playfully. He watched their antics, then turned and saw Mungo coming toward him.

"I spoke with the captain of Ranald's guard," Mungo said. "He would not allow me in the storage room on the ground floor. Ranald's orders are that no one touches it until he returns. A valuable load of spices, he said."

"Pepper and cloves come at a high price, I know, but that sort of caution is reserved for port towns, not remote Hebridean islands." Diarmid frowned. "Come on." He strode quickly toward the castle, entering by a small postern door at the back.

A dim corridor divided the ground floor into two parts, comprising garrison quarters and an enclosed byre for sheep. Walking past the guards' chambers, Diarmid and Mungo encountered a few of Ranald's men, exchanged nods, and moved past. Mungo might be unknown to some of them, but Sorcha's brother was well-known at Glas Eilean.

Diarmid quickly deceded a few steps to a door, which was locked. He glanced at Mungo. "This must be it. Go back and ask about the breed of Ranald's sheep," he said. "Make a jest or two, and laugh loudly. Tell them I'm interested in breeding my sheep with his stock." Mungo nodded and went back up the steps.

Diarmid kicked at the latch. When it gave, he lifted the torch from the wall sconce near the stairs and went inside the room. A summary glance showed him an assortment of items—coils of rope, armor, equipment for horses, and several barrels, wooden chests, and sacks heaped along one wall. He crossed the room and took out his dirk, prying loose the nails on a barrel lid.

He had always had an excellent memory for numbers and information, and used it now. As he searched the barrels and creates one after another, taking off the lids and replacing them, he recalled the account rolls that Arthur had given him.

Stored away were folded lengths of silk, gleaming splashes of color in the torchlight, along with coarser cloth woven from flax. He paused over that, fingering the humble fabric thoughtfully. Then he opened a few wooden barrels and found peppercorns and clove buds in abundance, as well as cinnamon sticks, nutmeg kernels, saffron, and dried gingerroots; two barrels held raw sugar from the East, ground to a fine powder; small casks held almond and olive oils, and several wooden tuns, marked with French stamps, contained wines and claret.

Four crates contained gleaming pieces of worked iron and steel, made into an assortment of weapons:

swords, lances, dirks, ax blades, and caltrops. Diarmid
looked at them and moved on.

Finding a pile of canvas sacks hidden in the corner,
he slit one open. Pale, milled grain spilled into his
hand. He sniffed at it, then swore under his breath.
Hearing a scrape, he turned to see Mungo enter the
room.

"I've found enough goods to stock every larder and
weapons chest in the Highlands," Diarmid said. "Most
of it was listed on the accounting sheets that Arthur
gave me."

"Most of it?"

Diarmid gestured. "That large chest holds cloth—
see what you think of its quality. And the sacks over
there contain this." He trickled dry grains into
Mungo's palm.

Mungo tasted the grains, then scowled. He knelt by
the largest wooden chest to finger the cloth inside.
"English flax and English weave. And the grains are
wheat."

"*English* wheat," Diarmid emphasized.

"Ranald prefers bread to oatcakes, just as he likes
an English cut to his tunics. He leans a bit too much
to that side, I think."

"Dangerously close. He apparently has a source for
English goods. Neither the lengths of linen nor the
wheat were listed on those inventories."

"But the English refuse to sell their wheat and cloth
to Scotland," Mungo said. "Their king has imposed
penalties against it. Could Ranald have traded for it
in Ireland?"

"Possibly," Diarmid said. "But I doubt it."

"If Arthur is one of the pirates who have broken
through the English blockade to harass English ports,
perhaps he took this."

Diarmid shook his head. "Arthur would have listed
them on his inventory of goods kept at Glas Eilean.
He said he wanted me to know everything that was

kept here. Now I know what he meant. Ranald is the one who knows best about this matter."

"Perhaps Sorcha knows something of it," Mungo said.

"I doubt my sister is a willing accomplice in a smuggling scheme."

"I doubt it too," Mungo said. "And I am loath to leave her here alone. When you go back to Dunsheen and contact the king about this, as you must, I will stay here."

Diarmid nodded. "I will not leave until I have learned more about where these English goods came from," he said. "But I would appreciate it if you watch over Sorcha when I depart."

"I would lay down my life for her," Mungo said quietly.

"I know," Diarmid said. "I have long thought that. I wish I had known it years ago, when Ranald offered for her hand, but I was too young to see what my sister needed. Ranald was the husband our father had chosen for her before he died."

Mungo said nothing, looking down at his feet. After a moment, he turned and left the storage chamber, and Diarmid followed.

Chapter Sixteen

"Tell us another tale, Mungo," Sorcha said. She reclined in her bed, propped on pillows, her body sunk deep in the feather mattress. Near the hearth, Diarmid and Mungo sat on stools, while Michael occupied an X-shaped chair with a leather sling seat, a borrowed harp leaned against her left shoulder as she played.

The four of them had gathered again in Sorcha's room for a light supper, a practice that had become a comfortable routine over several days. Often they stayed together after eating for an hour or more, talking and laughing companionably. Mungo and Sorcha told legends and tales, or chatted with Diarmid about escapades in their shared childhoods. Sometimes Michael spoke about her childhood in the hills of Galloway, or about her experiences as a student and physician in Italy.

At other times, she played soft melodies on the old harp that Diarmid had taken down from its customary place on the wall in the great hall. She discovered that Diarmid had a rich, deep singing voice, soothing and sensual, and she listened with dreamy pleasure as she plucked tunes that her mother had taught her.

Sometimes Diarmid smiled at her so kindly, so intimately, that her fingers stumbled on the strings until she focused carefully on the music. She had come to treasure their evening circle, but knew that the peace and joy was temporary. She would leave Glas Eilean and leave Dunsheen and its laird. The thought made her mood melancholic as she played the harp.

Mungo spoke and startled Michael from her thoughts. "I am not as good at telling tales as Gilchrist," he said to Sorcha.

Sorcha smiled, her eyes dancing with silvery lights. "Ah, but I like your stories best of all. Gilchrist is a fine harper and has a feel for a tragic or a brave story, but he lacks your sense of humor. You always make me laugh."

"Then I am honored," Mungo said quietly. "I liked to make you laugh even when you were a pesky little girl in long orange braids following after your brothers and me." He grinned. "But I still like your stories best. Tell us one now, if you will."

Michael, strumming the harp strings in a soft rhythm, looked from Sorcha to Mungo with a sense of astonishment. She watched Sorcha blush, saw Mungo's brown eyes linger fondly on her face. And then she knew what she had not seen until now: a well of love existed between them. Unexpressed, unfulfilled, their feelings had settled into a warm friendship.

Michael glanced at Diarmid, and saw him watch them keenly; he knew it too. Then he looked at Michael, and she smiled slightly, sadly, as if to tell him she understood. But he looked away again without changing his somber expression.

Sorcha began a tale of the selkies, the enchanted seals that roamed the seas and came ashore to wed human spouses. Michael began a soft, lilting melody on the harp strings to complement Sorcha's sweet voice. She could not help but glance often at Diarmid, almost hungrily, as if devouring his handsome appearance could satisfy her lonely heart.

He turned and looked at her again, his eyes piercing, almost demanding, as if his hunger excelled hers. She blushed and turned back to the harp. When Sorcha ended her story, Michael rang off the strings, letting the sound resonate.

Mungo watched Sorcha, his dark eyes deep with longing, his craggy face softened and vulnerable.

"That is a beautiful story," Mungo said. "I had not heard it before."

"I would like Gilchrist to make a song of it," Sorcha said. "Will you tell him the tale for me, and ask him to do that?"

"I will," Mungo said. "Though I cannot tell it as you did."

"You must come to Dunsheen yourself," Diarmid said.

Sorcha began to answer, than looked up with a startled expression on her face. The door opened, and Ranald stepped into the room, his cloak glistening with moisture. He pulled off his leather gloves as he came toward the hearth.

"What a cosy group," he said ironically, and turned to face them. "I am gone a few weeks, and I return to find my wife enthroned in bed like a queen, with her court around her."

"Ranald!" Sorcha said. "I did not expect you home—"

"I see that," he said. "There was no supper waiting for me. I have spent the past quarter hour harrying the cook for hot food. There was not even a fire in the hearth below stairs, for the cook said you have been taking your meals in your chamber. And not alone, I see. A man likes his home in order when he returns from the sea, with no unpleasant surprises."

He strode across the room as he spoke. Sorcha smiled up at him nervously. "We are all in here because I needed some rest before the babe comes," she said. "They were keeping me amused."

"You have few tasks as lady of Glas Eilean, and no children to chase after," Ranald said. "You suffer from boredom. I do not like to think that you are too fragile to fulfill what God intends for every woman. I want to see you up and about on the morrow, and no more talk of weakness. We need your hand in the managing of Glas Eilean." He patted her hand. Sorcha looked away, her cheeks pale, and said nothing.

Mungo and Diarmid rose to their feet. "She re-quires rest," Mungo said. "Leave her be."

"You are a bold ghillie, man," Ranald said with contempt. "I am the master of this place, and my wife's well-being."

"Master her no more in this matter," Diarmid said. "You risk her life to ask her to supervise this house-hold now."

"She has been cosseted her entire life," Ranald said as he removed his cloak. "Giorsal says that childbear-ing is not an illness. Sorcha must toughen herself. She loses the babes because of a female tendency to hyste-ria. She can conquer that. Can you not, my dear?"

Michael stood abruptly, stepping toward Ranald. "I ordered your lady to take to her bed," she said. "She should stay there for the rest of her confinement."

Ranald looked down at her. "I wanted you to con-sult with her, but I thought you would speak some sense to her."

"I want her counsel," Sorcha said. "She can help me birth a healthy child, I know it."

"Sorcha is right," Diarmid snapped. "Surely you do not wish to risk another child born too soon."

"Of course not," Ranald said. He sighed. "But a woman physician cannot possibly know as much as a male physician, and therefore Lady Michael differs lit-tle from any good midwife. She is welcome here, but her meddling will have to stop."

Michael opened her mouth to sputter an indignant reply, but Diarmid stepped beside her and laid a cau-tioning hand on her arm.

"As an empiric surgeon myself, a *male* surgeon, I strongly suggest that you take Michael's advice in this," he said.

Ranald scowled. "Very well. I am too weary to argue this with all of you. Sorcha, do what you will. I have other matters of importance just now. Dunsheen, why are you here? You do not normally grace my halls."

"I am concerned for my sister's welfare, just as you are," Diarmid said in a clipped, cool voice.

Ranald grunted. "No other business brought you here?" He looked suspiciously at Michael. "Did you ask him to bring you here? Have you an issue you wish to pursue with me?" His threatening tone dared her to confront him.

"You and I have little to discuss," Michael snapped.

"And what of your champion?" Ranald asked, gesturing at Diarmid. "Is he here to undermine my walls?"

"If you were not kin to me, your walls would come down fast enough," Diarmid growled. He nodded to his sister and strode toward the door, yanking it open without a backward glance. Mungo walked out behind him.

"Ranald, what is this about?" Sorcha asked.

"I am too tired to explain it. I am going to my own bed. Good night." He moved toward the door.

"Ranald, Lady Michael has your bed."

He spun. "I occupy that room."

Sorcha flushed. "You were not home. I thought it would be an acceptable arrangement."

"It is not acceptable to me."

"But it is inhospitable to ask a lady to change her guest bed. You have a bed here if you wish it," Sorcha said, her cheeks pink. "Or you can sleep in the great hall on pallets beside Diarmid and Mungo and their rowing crew."

Ranald swore under his breath. "Excuse your physician from this bedchamber, lady," he growled. "I want my rest." He began to unbuckle his belt.

"As your wife's physician, I must remind you that she is to remain undisturbed," Michael said pointedly. Sorcha looked relieved.

Ranald shot her a narrow glance. "You have disrupted much in my home and my life, Lady Michael," he said. "Consider your advice heard. Now, leave my chamber."

                          *   *   *

Late that night, Michael awoke from a deep,
dreamless sleep to blink at the dark curtains that surrounded her bed. She tried to determine what had
stirred her from sleep, but could not, and could not
summon sleep again.

She sat up, remembering that when she had gone
to bed, the peatfire in the hearth had filled the chamber with a deep orange glow. Now all was dark. The
bed curtains were closed, although she had left them
open. Leaning forward, she parted the heavy woolen
cloth carefully and peered out.

Diarmid stood between the stone benches, silhouet-
ted against the moonlight that poured in from the
open window. Hands on his hips, shoulders wide, he
truly looked like the king of the *daoine sìth,* as in
Brigit's imagination.

Her breath quickened, and she wondered vaguely if
she were dreaming. Shifting on the bed, sliding her
feet to the floor, she knew she was awake when she
felt cool, matted rushes beneath her toes. She moved
toward him like a slight shadow in silk and firelight.
He glanced at her, and looked out the window again.

"Go back to bed," he said.

"Diarmid," she whispered, coming nearer. "What
are you doing here?"

"Waiting," he said. "Just waiting. Go back to sleep.
I did not mean to disturb you." He kept his back
turned to her, and spoke over his shoulder. "Go on,
now," he said sternly. "You should not be awake, and
I should not be here. Sorcha would have my head on
a pike for this impropriety."

"I decide what is proper for me. I am not a
maiden." She folded her arms over her chest.

"I know that," he snapped. "Go on, now."

"But why are you here? Are you troubled with insomnia? Did you eat too much of the spiced meat at
supper? Let me make you a hot drink with herbs to
cool your blood and settle your stomach."

"Always the physician. And if you stand there longer, my blood will need cooling," he muttered.

She was uncertain if he meant she roused his passion or provoked his temper. She wanted the former, but expected he meant the latter. "Tell me what is wrong. Do you long for a view of the sea at night? I will not go back to bed," she said firmly when he raised his hand to point.

He sighed, gazing out the traceried window, leaning a hand on the stone frame. A cool breeze blew back the linen of his shirt, ruffled through his hair, and made Michael shiver as she waited. "At least cover yourself better than that if you mean to stand there," he said.

She turned and grabbed her black cloak, swirling its folds over her dark blue silk chemise. Diarmid shifted aside in the small space to allow her to stand in front of him.

They stood silently, her shoulder brushing his chest as they shared the view. The dark sea gleamed beneath a velvet swath of night sky, pierced by sparkling stars and a white moon. Taking in the magnificence, listening to the steady rhythm of Diarmid's breath just behind her, she felt a sense of peace. Finally she tipped her head to look up at him.

"Night air is good for insomnia, and this soothing view will help cure it as well," she murmured. "It must be crowded and noisy in the great hall where you have been sleeping. Did you come here to get away from that?" A cool wind whistled past, and she shivered slightly.

"I came here to wait."

"For what?" she asked, puzzled. "For the dawn?"

He shook his head. "I want to see what Ranald sees from this window."

She looked up at him in surprise. "Ranald?"

"When Mungo and I went down to the hall again this evening, the cook mentioned that Ranald was eager to have his supper and get to his bed. He normally sleeps in this chamber, but she said he was greatly displeased to find he had guests."

"He was annoyed with Sorcha when he found out that I had this room," Michael said. "He was adamant about being here, but Sorcha was quite firm about it. But a man must be forgiven for wanting his own bed after a long voyage."

"A man that tired will sleep anywhere and not have a temper fit like a child. He wanted to be here for other reasons. If I am right, we will see why from this window."

Michael looked out, wrapping her arms around herself. "I see only the sea, the stars, the moonlight. I doubt he is an admirer of those."

Diarmid rested his hand on her shoulder, warmth sliding through her. His fingers touched her hair briefly, sending lingering tremors through her.

"Moonlight," he whispered, his voice close at her ear.

"Moonlight? Ranald?" She looked up at him.

Diarmid chuckled softly. The sound stirred her somehow. She allowed herself to lean slightly against him, as she had on the deck of the birling.

"Michael," he said gently. "Go back to bed."

"I want to know why you are here." *And I am glad you are here,* she thought; *I am glad.*

"If I had known you would wake up, I would not have come into your room," he said, and put his hands on her shoulders to steer her away. "Go on, now."

She jerked suddenly, spinning. "I am not a child, to be ordered about by you," she burst out. "Clearly your visit here has nothing to do with me, since you only want me gone. I know that you do not want me—" she faltered, blushing. "I know you do not want me here, but—"

Diarmid smacked the flat of his hand against the window jamb, and blew out a heavy breath. "Not want you?" he asked. "Not want you? My girl, you are all I think about."

Her heart surged at the words. "Diarmid—"

"All I think about, and all I try not to think about. Now go to bed. If you stand there longer, I will not be able to do what I came here to do this night."

She stepped closer. "And what is that?"

"Not this," he growled, and took her into his arms.

With a small gasp, she melted into his embrace, tilting her head back, welcoming his lips over hers. His kiss was a demand, a plea, a gift. His hand cupped the back of her head, his fingers slid into her hair, his mouth slanted over hers. She slipped her hands around his neck, pressing close to him.

His hands stroked down to span her waist, mold her hips. Restless, warm, compelling, his touch delved beneath her cloak to shift the silk over her body, sending shivers through her. She arched into him in silent acceptance and delight, lifting on her toes to lean her hips into his. He growled low into her opening mouth and spread his hands over her hips, pressing her against him until she felt the strength of his desire through the layers of his plaid.

She moaned low and soft into his mouth and ran her hands over his chest, where his heartbeat stirred her fingertips. He parted the seam of her lips with his tongue, so gently that she thought she would melt, her lower body tingling as a deeper desire sparked within her. She gasped for the utter, wicked joy of the sensation and touched the tip of her tongue to his, soft, wet, curious, wanting more.

Diarmid groaned deep in his throat and pulled back. Cool air filled the space between them. Only his strong hands held her upright, for her legs had gone weak.

"Enough," he said hoarsely. His breath came ragged in his throat, and he set her firmly away from him, turning back to the window. "I did not mean for that to happen."

She stepped beside him, placed her hand on his arm. "It has happened before, and each time it seems stronger. So strong that it hurts, somehow."

He watched the dark sea. "I know. Soon I will not
be able to set you away from me."

"Must you?" She leaned her forehead against his
arm, her breathing rapid. She felt a kind of wildness
in her heart when he was near, when he touched her,
an urge so powerful that it pulled inside her very soul.

"*Ach, Micheil,*" he whispered, and touched her hair
gently. She loved the feel of his fingers slipping along
its length, loved the sound of her name on his lips.
"Go back to your bed and forget this. Forget me. This
is not meant to be."

She shook her head. "I cannot forget this."

He sighed. "Go on, now." He shifted her away from
him gently. "I do not want you here."

His words stabbed like a betrayal. Michael stepped
back suddenly. She had been wrong. Wrong. He did
not feel the same overwhelming love for her that she
felt for him.

Likely he felt only lust and did not wish to shame
her. He had succumbed to his bodily urges and now
meant to control them. She had stood beside him
wearing only silk and skin, had kissed him fervently.
He was no saint to resist that. But he did not want
her as she wanted him. She felt foolish. "I am sorry—"
She spun away.

He grabbed her arm. "Michael, I do not mean to
hurt you."

"Then let go," she said flatly. "For you do hurt me.
Your grip is too tight."

He complied, and she walked away, shoving open
the curtains of her bed, climbing in, pulling them shut
as the iron rings rattled over her head. She yanked
off her cloak and burrowed under the covers, pulling
them over her head to muffle the sound of the sobs
that she could not hold back.

His heart felt as if she pulled it from his chest when
she walked away from him. Diarmid sighed and
pushed a hand through his hair, turning, hoping that

the cool, salted, breeze would blow some sense into
his head, for he surely had none of his own.

He had not wanted to hurt her, but he had, and he
did not know how to repair the damage. There was
no muscle tear to seal with silk thread, no bone to
mend, no bruise to salve and bandage. He could not
even adequately repair a flesh wound, let alone a deep
gash to the soul rendered by his own words.

He felt a fierce, frustrated ache within himself, span-
ning soul and body both. Making fists, he squeezed so
tightly that his left hand began its customary, flawed
tremble. He pounded it against the wall and swore
under his breath. He had been a fool to come into
this room. Knowing he took a chance, he had tried
not to wake her. After watching her sleep peacefully,
he had closed the curtains of her bed and had gone
to the window to open the shutters.

Now he leaned a shoulder against the window frame
and watched the dark sparkle of sea and sky. The
window provided a wide vantage point. On a clear
day, the green slopes of Ireland were visible to the
west, while to the north and east rose the craggy peaks
of the Isles and the mountains of the mainland. To
the south was the wide sea leading up from England
or Ireland. A ship could be seen from here from miles
away, even on a moonlit night, if a signal flare was lit.

Diarmid suspected that Ranald had taken this room
for the view it offered rather than out of respect for
his wife's condition. He was certain that Ranald
watched for approaching ships from here.

A ship was out there tonight. He felt it in his bones,
sensed it in Ranald's return and his anxious temper.
Diarmid had to discover Ranald's intent.

But all he wanted to do was tear open the curtains
of that bed and pull Michael into his arms, devour her
sweetness with his mouth, his hands, take her, hold
her, keep her safe.

Abruptly, he turned and left the room, striding
quickly through the corridor, down the turning stairs,

past the men snoring in the great hall. With a quick
nod to the guardsman at the gate and the gift of a
silver coin for his discretion, he went through the narrow door in the portcullis and stepped outside.

The silence deepened until Michael could bear it no
longer. She slid out from under the covers and slowly
pulled aside the bed curtain to look toward the
window.

He was gone. Her hand trembled on the curtain.
Then she slipped from the bed and went to the window where he had stood, intending to close the shutters. Instead, she looked out over the dark infinity of
sea and sky, feeling numbed, ineffably sad.

She did not know how long she stood there. Gradually she became aware that one of the stars that
winked in the night was sparkling gold, and growing
larger.

And then she realized that a ship approached
Glas Eilean.

Chapter Seventeen

Surely that solitary ship was the reason Diarmid had been watching out her window, Michael thought. Whatever the reason, it had to be important to him. But now he was gone, and he might not have seen the light out on the sea. She had to tell him.

Her cheeks blazed at the thought of speaking with him so soon after his hurtful words to her. Regardless of her feelings, she must find him. She yanked her boots onto her bare feet, grabbed up her cloak from the foot of her bed, and left the room.

She dashed down the turning stairs quickly and silently, and peeked into the great hall, where the men slept, snoring and tossing, on pallets spread out near the hearth. She saw at a glance that Diarmid was not among them. She would have recognized the set of his shoulders, his thick hair, the length of his legs. Wondering if he had taken his vigil outside, she went to the gate.

The guardsman was reluctant to let her out alone, and offered to accompany her for the fresh air she claimed to need. But when she begged the guard to help her find the laird of Dunsheen, saying that his sister had sent her to look for him, the guard softened and opened the doorway in the portcullis.

"If that sweet lady wants her brother, then you go fetch him," he said kindly. "But hurry back, for Mac-Sween would have my soul for this if he knew I let anyone out of here at night."

She smiled her thanks and fled into the shadows.

As she ran along the perimeter of the outer wall, which soared immense and solid overhead, her instincts took her toward the cliffs.

The seaward side of the castle was separated from the ragged cliff edge by a span of no more than a hundred feet, and much less in some places. The wind seemed far stronger here, whipping her cloak about her legs as she ran.

Diarmid stood near the cliff edge, beyond the farthest corner of the castle. She called out his name.

He spun, saw her, and ran back to grab her shoulders. "Michael," he said hoarsely, "what in God's name—? Go inside!"

Breathless with running, she gripped his arms to steady herself against the pounding force of the wind. "I came to tell you that I saw a light from the window far out in the sea to the south. I think it was a ship. Was that why you watched from my chamber?"

He made a wordless exclamation and turned toward the cliff, keeping one hand on her shoulder. For a long moment he scanned the black horizon, and then nodded. "I can barely see it," he said at last. "From the window, higher up, you would see it sooner." He turned to her. "Thank you. Now, go back inside."

She scowled, opened her mouth to protest, then spun and walked away. A moment later, he ran up behind her, grabbed her around the waist, and began to half carry, half drag her toward the cliff. When she cried out, he put a hand over her mouth. Reaching a cluster of boulders near the edge, he shoved her down behind them, then crouched beside her.

"If you value your life or mine, keep quiet," he hissed. "Ranald is walking toward the cliffs."

She nodded, wide-eyed, and leaned against the cold rock, her heart thumping ferociously. Diarmid drew his dirk, his body shielding hers as they knelt behind the boulder. He peered cautiously around the curve of the rock. Unable to turn, Michael looked up at the glittering sky and the wafer moon, and listened to the distant shush of the sea against the cliff, hundreds of feet below.

Diarmid turned and put his finger to his lips, and ducked lower in the shadow of the boulder. He pulled up the folds of her hood, making it clear, without speaking, that her pale hair shone like a beacon. After a while, he shifted his position, seeming more relaxed.

"He's gone," he whispered. "He came out of the castle just as you walked away, and stood near the cliff edge to watch out to sea. He held a blazing torch over his head and waved it three times, then twice. After that, he went back inside."

"He signaled the ship," she said. Diarmid nodded. "What will he do now?"

He shrugged. "I am not certain. He may go down to meet them." Crouched, he began to move cautiously toward the edge of the cliff and lay prone, his hands and head extended over the cliff edge. The rim of the cliff rose in a slight incline, adding some security to his treacherous position. But Michael exclaimed in fear and scrambled after him on her hands and knees to grab his ankle.

"Get back, are you foolish?" he said, shoving her gently.

"No more than you," she said. "What are you doing?"

"Watching the ship. She is anchored out in deep water, and she's sent a rowboat toward the cliff." He turned to look again, his words partly vanished in the whistling wind.

She crawled toward the edge slowly, scraping along cold stone and thick moss, hoping her courage was enough to match her powerful curiosity, for she desperately wanted to see what Diarmid saw down there. Grasping the raw crust of the cliff, she inched her head forward.

The dizzying bird's-eye view made her gasp. She scooted back quickly and clung to the rock beneath her, breathing hard.

"Go back," Diarmid whispered.

"I cannot," she said. "Ranald will find me."

"Then go over to the rock and hide there," he said.

"I cannot," she said. "I think I am stuck."

"Stuck?" He swiveled his head to look at her.

"I cannot seem to move my legs. Or any other part of me."

"Ah," Diarmid said. "It is just the fear. Lie there until it passes."

She moaned. "I will be here until Judgment Day."

He laughed, quick and soft, and touched her shoulder. Then he returned to his vigil while she lay on her stomach. When her anxiety had eased some, she opened her eyes. In another few moments she propped herself on her elbows, although she was hardly eager to look over the edge again. "What do you see?"

Diarmid did not answer, but moved forward until his head and shoulders hung completely over the edge so that he looked straight downward. Michael gasped and grabbed hold of his thick plaid where it crossed his back.

He turned his head to look at her, the wind whipping his hair fiercely. "Michael, my girl," he said, "that will hardly hold me. If I fall, you will fall with me. Let go."

She complied, although his precarious position made her anxious. "What do you see?" she asked again, curiosity tormenting her.

"Mm? Ranald is a busy man," he said, distracted.

"*Ach,*" she ground out, knowing she would get no more detail than that from him. She crawled forward with excruciating slowness.

"The sun will rise before you get here," Diarmid observed.

"I am trying," she snapped. Nearer to the edge, she shifted closer to the warmth and security of his body. "I am looking now," she announced, and opened her eyes a bit. Diarmid chuckled beside her, and rested his arm on her back, his hand on her shoulder, heavy and solid and blessedly safe.

She sucked in a breath and forced herself to look. The wind whirled her hair into her eyes, and she inched her fingers forward to clear her sight.

Torches, and boats. She blinked, and looked again, and gradually became accustomed to the crazy, stilted view, able to look as long as she felt the solid rock beneath her, and Diarmid beside her. She saw three small boats, and a few men holding flaming torches, rowing through the waters at the cliff base.

"Look at that," Diarmid murmured, his voice deep and reassuring at her ear. "The ship has sent out a small boat with a few men, and the other carrying barrels. Ranald meets them, see—he is in the third boat."

"But why? Who are those men?"

"Smugglers, I imagine," he murmured. "Englishmen with wheat, linen, wine, wax candles, iron—whatever goods Scots need imported. But the English king has forbidden his merchants to trade with Scots. This hardly looks legitimate to me."

She gasped. "Are those English goods?"

"They must be. It seems that Ranald acquires some of his goods from English merchants willing to overlook their king's mandate. Then Ranald can charge exorbitant fees to Scottish merchants, claiming he got the goods from Irish ports and paid dearly for them. I would guess he's making a nice coin here for himself." He watched for a moment in silence. "I wonder what else he has arranged with England," he mused.

She glanced at him. "What do you mean?"

"Never mind. What the devil are they doing now?" He inched forward, and Michael looked too, feeling bolder with Diarmid's hand safely on her shoulder. They watched as the three boats disappeared, one after the other, into a deep crevice in the rugged, seamed cliff face.

"Where are they going?" she asked. "The sea cave entrance is over there."

"Apparently there is another sea cave hidden in that crevice. A perfect spot for smuggled goods."

The swirling water below the cliff reflected an eerie glow from the torchlight within the crevice. "It must be a large cave," Michael observed.

Diarmid nodded. "I would like to look around in there."

She grabbed his arm in protest. "You cannot go down there! And we must get back in the castle before Ranald sees us," she added hastily. She abhorred the thought of Diarmid going down to the sea cave while the other men were there. "Do you think the guard told Ranald we were out here? Will he know Ranald's business tonight?"

"I paid the man well to keep silent," Diarmid said. "I doubt Ranald paid him. And MacSween is alone. Likely he wants few to know his business." He shifted backward and rolled to his side to look at her. "I agree that you should get back to the castle. Will your legs work now, do you think?"

She shimmied backward. "I think so." She rose to her hands and knees, then to her feet. Diarmid stood and took her arm to run with her toward the castle. They followed the outer wall, moving against the force of the wind. Michael held on to her billowing cloak and tried to keep up with Diarmid's long, easy strides. Within a few yards of the gate, he stopped.

"Wait," he said, placing a hand on her arm. "If the guard knows why Ranald was out here tonight, he might be suspicious of us. We will need some good reason for being outside."

She looked up, worried. "What can we tell him?"

He swept an arm around her shoulders and pulled her close. "Let him think we had an assignation in the moonlight." He bent his head and nuzzled her cheek. The scrape of his beard, the warmth of his breath, made her heart pound. "Do you think he is watching?" he murmured as he drew her into step beside him.

"I do not know," she answered breathily, raising her head to his, putting her arm around his waist.

The portcullis door swung slowly open.

"Kiss me," Diarmid whispered. He lowered his face to hers. In one swift motion, he took her mouth with his, and took her heart forever.

As his mouth softened gently over hers, Michael gave herself into the kiss and felt her knees buckle beneath her. Diarmid held her firmly in his arms, dipping his head, slanting his mouth like heaven over hers. Soon, too soon, he broke away and straightened.

"Come with me," he whispered.

She would go with him anywhere, for any reason. Breathless, silent, hardly able to think, she moved alongside of him in the circle of his arm.

The guard swung the door wide and gave Diarmid a knowing grin. "Fine evening for a stroll," he said, and almost snickered.

"Fine indeed," Diarmid said. "My dear, watch your step," he murmured as Michael stumbled over the raised frame of the door.

"That one is tired," the guard said. "You had best get her to bed," he said suggestively.

Michael opened her mouth to reply indignantly, but Diarmid silenced her with a quick kiss. "Come ahead," he whispered. "Let him think what he likes."

He kissed her again to cover their retreat into the shadowed corridor that led to the great hall. Michael glanced back at the guard and saw him peer after them. Diarmid saw too, and caught her around the waist to draw her around the corner.

There, he halted and touched his mouth to hers once more, deeply, soundly, rocking a thunderous surge of desire through her. She forgot the guard, the ruse, the need to move ahead, and felt only his glorious, capable mouth on hers. All that existed was the warmth of his lips, the brace of his arms, the solid press of his body. Their curves and angles met comfortably, easily, as if shaped for each other.

Diarmid pulled back a little. "Jesu," he breathed raggedly. He dipped his head again and took her mouth greedily, as if he could not take in enough of her, then traced his lips along her cheek. "Ah, Michael," he whispered in her ear.

Michael moaned softly and tilted back her head as a wave of pure joy bubbled through her. His lips, his hands began to sweep away the hurt he had dealt her earlier. She looped her arms around his neck and smiled as his lips caressed her cheek, her eyelids, and found her mouth again. The hunger, the poignance of his kiss showed her that he too was ensnared in the magic that had caught her. She wondered if either of them could stop.

She did not want to stop, craving the feel of him, wanting more of the swirling waves of pleasure that surged through her. She would not think about whether they should pursue this. Reason would smother the wondrous joy that moved in her.

He took her hand and drew her quickly toward the stairs, and she ran lightly up the turning steps ahead of him. They hurried along the corridor, their footsteps moving in quiet, quick harmony.

Outside her door, he turned her and framed her face in his hands, then took her mouth again. The pretense that had begun outside had long since fallen away; she knew they were both caught now in the passion that stirred between them. She leaned back against the thick door and met his lips fervently, crushed against his chest, her arms high over his shoulders, fingers deep in his hair.

He sighed out and laid his cheek to hers. "What are we doing?" he whispered. "I do not think—"

"Do not think," she whispered, sliding her fingers through the richness of his hair. "Do not think, do not speak. Love me if you will."

"*Micheil,*" he whispered, and swept his arms around her, nearly drawing her off her feet to kiss her again. She circled her arms around his neck, feeling an overwhelming hunger for the touch and taste of him, each kiss deepening, quickening, until her heart pounded like a drum.

A scraping sound broke into the rhythm they made of breath and touch, and then repeated: footsteps. Michael pulled away, and Diarmid looked over her shoulder. She heard his breath, as ragged as her own, as they waited and listened.

"Ranald," he whispered, and opened the door, shoving Michael inside and slipping in after her just as Ranald's boots sounded on the upper steps.

Diarmid held the door open a crack, watching. Michael remained silent, resting her hand on his wide back, feeling the strong thud of his heart. She closed her eyes and leaned her head briefly against him.

After a few moments, he closed the door and turned to her in the dark. "He has gone into Sorcha's bedchamber," he whispered.

She breathed out a sigh of relief and looked up. The faint glow of the peat fire made an amber and black silhouette of his head and shoulders as he stood watching her. She tilted her head slightly, her heart thumping with tension, with passion.

Diarmid placed his hands on the wall, to either side of her head, and leaned forward until his brow touched hers. She waited for his kiss, tipped up to receive it, but he only watched her.

"God, I want you," he whispered. "You do not know how much. It burns inside of me."

Her heart soared. "Diarmid," she murmured, and touched her mouth to his. He groaned, faint and low, and took her mouth, then drew back, forehead to hers, his gaze steady.

"I want to carry you over to that bed . . ." He breathed deep, full, fast. "And do what I will with you."

She sighed out in ecstasy at the images those few words painted in her mind, and she arched back her head, closed her eyes. The nearness of his mouth, his breath hot on her sensitive lips, dissolved what re-

mained of her ability to stand upright. She circled her
arms around his neck for support and found his lips,
nuzzled them, pleaded silently.

"But we cannot," he murmured against her lips.

"We can," she breathed into his mouth, hardly
knowing what she said, hardly caring. She tilted her
head to deepen the kiss.

With a low groan, he delved, his tongue licking her
lips, slipping inside. She gave a wordless, joyful cry,
and tightened her arms around him. His hands fell
gently to her waist, pulling her against him, pressing
her hips to the hardened core of his body.

With nimble fingers, he undid the loop at the neck
of her cloak and shoved it aside, dropping it to the
floor. He slipped his hand over her silk-covered
breasts, drawing a quivering gasp from her as she pebbled instantly beneath his palm. His fingers stroked
one straining tip as he touched his mouth to her
throat. Then he lowered his head until his breath blew
hot and fervent through the silk.

Gasping softly, she arched, her shoulders pressed
against the stone wall, her back curved, her hips pushing instinctively against him. She felt his mouth open
hot and sweet over her nipple, and a heavy ache began
deep inside of her. Her body writhed against his in a
silent, eloquent motion of longing.

He nuzzled aside her chemise and took the raised
nub of her bare breast in his lips, wetting the pearl,
suckling there. Groaning at the exquisite shock of the
contact, she raked her fingers through his hair, fin-
gered the whorl of his ear, ran her hands along his
shoulders. Her fingertips explored his textures, the
warmth of his skin, the rasp of his beard, the rough
silk of his hair.

Wanting the contact of her skin to his, she slid her
hand inside the loose neck of his shirt. His chest was
warm, solid, its muscular smoothness softened with
hair. She found the flat nub of his nipple, and heard
him catch his breath sharply; she slid lower, her fingers

grazing over the hard, wide cage of his ribs and tight, rippled muscles.

Her heart pounded, her breath deepened as he lifted his head to kiss her again, as he shifted her arms over his neck and drove his hips against hers. She had never felt urges like this, with a craving passion that swept thought, breath, and time away, and replaced them with a torrent of pulsing sensation.

Feeling his hands graze over her waist and hips, she arched against him as he nourished the surging need inside of her. When his hand traced over her abdomen and his fingers feathered over the mound hidden beneath the silk, she made a little sound of desperate need and moved silently, eloquently.

He touched her deeply through the silk, and she moaned into the warm cave of his mouth; he stroked, silk pulling, and she twisted against him, her hands shoving at his plaid, sliding beneath to find the tight muscle of his hips.

His groan now slipped into her mouth, and he drew the silk high, shifting his hand. His fingertips found her, caressed her, raising liquid fire in her. The heat and the dance of his fingers melted her, and she quivered and dissolved in his supporting arms.

Sensing his driving hunger and his need, and feeling the urge of her own desire, she shifted her hand beneath the wool and took the warm, rigid length of him fully, languidly. He was velvet over steel in her fingers. His breath grew ragged against her mouth, and she moaned softly, arching against him, letting the sway of her body show him that she wanted him fully, desperately.

He took her mouth fervently, sliding his hands over her hips, slipping the warmed silk higher, higher. She breathed out and pushed her hips against him as a sweet demand pulsed through her, a plea of body and soul.

He felt it, too, she knew; he pressed toward her, his body achingly hard against hers. She felt the heavy

rhythm of his heart pound through her. He took her
hips and lifted her, the motion pushing silk and wool
aside. She gasped out as she felt his warm flesh against
her, and she circled her legs around him.

Her body undulated, craving a deeper joy. His kiss
immersed her in him, his hands caressed her, but that
was not enough, not now: She had to follow the thunderous tide that flowed between them. She surged
toward him on a pleading, fluid cry.

His low answering groan was anguished, soul deep.
She softened, opened for him, and he slipped inside,
and thrust. Utter pleasure rushed through her like
poured joy, and she pressed forward, circling her arms
tenderly around him.

He gasped, as if he struggled against the will of
ecstasy. His rhythm quickened within her, and she felt
the exquisite ripple of his surrender. She kissed him,
swayed with him, nurtured his need and her own with
every motion of her body.

He sighed out, a long mist of relief and something
more, a drift of sadness.

Silently, he set her gently on her feet, slipping her
chemise down to cover her legs. She held onto his
muscular arms, her legs trembling so much that she
could not stand on her own, and looked up at him.

"*Ach, Dhia,*" he murmured. "What have we done?"
Cupping her cheek in one hand, he gazed at her, his
eyes glittering deep in the low light. He drew a long
breath, and another, and slowly released it. "Michael,
I am sorry—I could not stop myself."

She touched a finger to his lips. "Hush," she said.
"Hush. Neither one of us could help what happened."

His thumb caressed her cheek. The touch sent shivers through her, a delicious echo of what had swept
through her like a thunderstorm only moments before.
"I have wanted to bed you, and I have held myself
back," he said. "But I cannot resist the feel of you. I
am lost when you are near, a drowning man." He
paused, closed his eyes, shook his head.

"Hush," she whispered. "Do not regret this. I do not."

"I do," he said huskily. "I had no right."

"I gave you the right," she murmured.

"It never should have happened," he said, leaning a hand on the wall, looking down at her. "I swear to you it will not happen again. I swear it." He moved back. Cold air swept in to chill her skin.

She looked away as the pain of his words plummeted through her. He was wed. They had both forgotten that. Passion could not be allowed to burgeon and burst between them. He meant to smother it.

"I understand," she whispered, unable to meet his gaze. "You felt lust. It is over. I am sorry." She moved away, shoving past him.

He took her arm and turned her, wrapped her in his embrace, made a husky sound in his throat. She flattened her trembling hands on his chest. The emotions that rolled and swelled between them seemed to pull her toward him, then cast her away again. She longed for a mooring rope, and had none.

"Michael mine," he whispered. "I do not know what is happening between us."

"Desire," she whispered. "And more."

"Much more." He huffed out a low, perplexed laugh. "And the rest—the rest scares me."

"I am not frightened," she said. "Deep water, boats, heights—those frighten me. But these feelings do not." She drew a breath, hid her face in his shirt. "I love you, Diarmid Campbell." She blurted the words breathlessly, dreading, hoping.

He was silent for so long that she felt him slip away from her again on another inconstant surge of the tide. "Too many things prevent this between us," he finally said.

"Your wife." She could hardly say the word, felt a surge of angry resentment for a woman she had never met, a force with a name, holding Diarmid trapped.

"*Micheil.*" He slipped a hand along her cheek, tipping her chin upward. "You are precious to me," he said. "I cannot dishonor you. I cannot ask you to love me. Can you understand that?"

She nodded, looked away, her throat tightening.

"*Ach,*" he breathed. "Listen to me. I mean this. I will never ask you to lower yourself for me. You are too fine, too good." He shifted her away from him. "This will not happen again. I promise you."

She stood there, cold and shivering in silk and skin, and watched him with all of her soul bared and vulnerable in her eyes. The hurt in his logical words cut so deep that she could not speak.

"Dawn will be here soon," he said gently. "You need to rest. And I have a task yet to be done." He turned and grabbed the door latch. "I intend to inspect Ranald's new shipment of goods." He opened the door.

A step, a breath. "Diarmid—"

He stopped, his back to her, waited.

"I love you," she whispered. "That will not change."

He did not move. Then he nodded and walked away.

She dreamed of Ibrahim, who wore his gray and red physician's robe and strolled with her through a dark, tangled forest. As they walked, they discussed the anatomy of the heart and the hand, herbal treatments for coughs and torn muscles, the stages of childbirth and the influences of the planets. She held his hand and kissed his dry, leathered cheek as she had done so often in life, and treasured his friendship and his advice.

He embraced her as they reached the edge of the forest, and told her that he was unable to go any farther. She turned and saw the rim of a cliff just at her feet. Ibrahim told her that she would be safe, that she had always been safe, and he pushed her. And she soared.

Chapter Eighteen

"*Ach Dhia,*" Mungo said in astonishment. "It's like a cathedral here." He tipped his head back to look high overhead. "A cathedral full of smuggled goods—and water."

Diarmid glanced up, and then used the oars he held to angle the narrow boat deeper into the crevice hidden in the cliff. "High as a cathedral, but the walls are dark and coated with slime. It almost looks as if we are in the belly of a dragon."

"Ugh," Mungo agreed, nodding as he held a blazing torch high. "It does have an ominous feel to it."

Diarmid propelled the boat along the channel of water that passed between glistening, soaring walls of dark rock. Overhead, the spine of the vault swayed and twisted into shadows, extending far back into the cliff. Dark stains on the rock showed how high the tide reached; above that level, hollows in the undulating wall surface provided niches for the barrels crowded there.

Everywhere, sounds echoed eerily: the creak and swoosh of the oars, the whisper of the sea as it swirled into the cave, the drip of water falling from crannies in the rock, the hushed sound of their voices.

Diarmid and Mungo had quietly taken a small boat from inside the sea entrance to Glas Eilean while the guardsmen had been engaged at the top of the staircase in a game of dice tossing. Rowing now, deep into the cave, Diarmid was not concerned with how they would get back into the castle. He only looked around, as Mungo did, in amazement.

"This cavern looks even larger than the other one," Diarmid remarked. "I wonder how far back it goes." Torchlight flickered over dark stone as the boat slipped quietly through the water. Bit by bit, the enormous cavity of rock was revealed.

"Jesu! Look there!" Mungo said.

Diarmid turned abruptly to glance over his shoulder. "I wondered what else Ranald kept in this place," he muttered.

Two long birlings, moored on sturdy ropes looped around massive iron rings in the rock, floated side by side in the huge, shadowed interior. Diarmid maneuvered the small boat toward a ledge along the wall, and he and Mungo jumped out and walked cautiously along the slippery rock shelf. Water sloshed over the toes of their boots as they peered into the first galley.

Mungo counted under his breath. "Oar holes for forty men," he announced. "Look at her design—long and low in the water, swift and quick to steer. She is a warship, not a ship designed for trade. Those boxes and barrels likely hold provisions for at least sixty men, rather than crates of trading goods."

Diarmid nodded agreement, walking along the ledge to assess the birling's features. "Her pine deck is highly polished, never yet used—and this fine hull is English oak, I think. The design is Norwegian. Ranald must have had them both built on the Isle of Lewis." He frowned as he ran his hand along the rim of the hull. "The pitch on the planking is still fresh, and the paint on the trim is new." He gestured toward the raised prow, where elaborate carving along the rim was highlighted in red and yellow paint; then he looked at the other galley. "Twenty-six oar holes over there, and just as new as this larger one. These boats are not intended to carry hides and wool sacks over to Ireland."

Mungo nodded. "Ranald would want wider, deeper

galleys for trading. War boats for certain. But what does he have in mind?"

"I do not know," Diarmid said slowly. "But I would wager that he has not pledged them in service to Robert Bruce. Perhaps the goods on board will tell us more." He stepped into the larger birling; her sides rolled gently with the movement. He walked to the middle of the deck, where the mast jutted up from the mastfish, a sail tightly furled over the spar.

He crouched down beside two long wooden chests near the mastfish, and used his dirk to open the latch on one of them. Although what he found was not unexpected, he swore under his breath. Grasping one of the long, unstrung yew bows stacked inside, he held it up to show Mungo.

"I would guess there are at least a hundred of these stacked in these chests," he said, kicking that chest and the identical one beside it.

"And the barrels?" Mungo asked.

Diarmid pried one open. "Arrows. English arrows, by their feathering. Thousands, by the count of these barrels."

"Those longbows would not be Scottish make, would they?" Mungo did not sound hopeful.

"Not a chance," Diarmid said. "We are handy with a short hunting bow, but few Highlanders have the knack of the longbow." He dropped the bow back into the chest and slammed the lid closed. Then he checked some of the other barrels and crates, finding an iron cooking kettle, wooden bowls, dried meats, kegs of wine, sacks of oats, and several small casks of oil: almond, he judged, by the pleasant smell that emanated from the wood.

He said little as he and Mungo climbed back into the small boat and rowed back toward the cave entrance. As the boat left the cave mouth, Mungo doused the torch in the water.

"Ranald has made some kind of a traitorous arrangement with the English," Diarmid said finally.

Mungo grunted. "One that has little to do with linen and wheat. Glas Eilean is in a position to protect the Inner Hebrides and the western Highlands from an attack by English."

"True. That is the crux of the matter. If English ships sail stealthily by night and come here, they could slip through Scottish waters without being seen."

"And if they bring men and archers enough to man two warships at Glas Eilean," Mungo finished, "they will get past the Campbells and MacDonalds situated along the coast. They will be deep in Scottish waters and ready to attack."

"Exactly," Diarmid said gravely. He pulled on the oars while his thoughts tumbled rapidly through the various possibilities. "Ranald will have made his fortune from this arrangement—if he can get his money from the English."

"He makes a great case of being Bruce's loyal supporter," Mungo said. "Could we be mistaken?"

"The MacSweens have a history of siding with the English," Diarmid said. "His father and his brothers before him pledged to the first Edward when he tried to take Scotland. I have never fully trusted Ranald's claim that he supports King Robert. I certainly will not trust that he keeps birlings stocked with English longbows and English arrows for use by Scotland's king."

"What will you do?" Mungo asked quietly.

"I will do what King Robert asked me to do months ago," Diarmid said grimly. "I will expose a traitor."

"Now you have something to report to the king. I will stay here with Sorcha, if I may."

"Thank you," Diarmid said. "I do not want to leave her alone here in the company of a man who plans war on his king. I must ask Michael to stay as well."

"I will look after both of them."

Diarmid nodded. He could hardly think about Michael without feeling a painful twist deep in his heart. Silently, he rowed back toward the main sea entrance and slipped the prow through the shadowed water toward the staircase that rose out of the water straight into the castle itself.

One guard paced along the upper platform. Mungo picked up the extinguished torch and flung it into the water far ahead. As the guard descended the steps to investigate, Diarmid docked the rowboat in deep shadow. Then he and Mungo raced up the stairs. Just as the guard turned back, they spun and came down the steps as if they were on their way out.

"Greetings, man," Mungo said. "We've come down to inspect the hull of Dunsheen's birling. I told him I suspected a leak, and the man just could not sleep for the thought of it."

The guard grunted in disinterest, and Diarmid and Mungo strolled past him to walk along the narrow ledge that led to the *Gabriel,* moored along the wall. A few minutes later, after looking over the boat and muttering between them, they returned, yawning, and went up the steps.

Hearing a soft knock, Michael went to the door of Sorcha's bedchamber, opened it, and caught her breath in surprise. "Diarmid!" she exclaimed, stepping back.

He murmured a greeting as he entered, and looked toward the bed. "Sorcha is asleep?" he asked softly. Michael nodded, her heart thumping hard. "Then do not wake her. Tell her I came to say farewell."

"Farewell?" She barely whispered the word.

He nodded, and crossed the room toward the window niche. Michael watched him, biting absently at her lower lip. All morning, she had struggled with the remnants of the joy and devastation that she had felt last night. Now that he stood but an arm's length away from her, she felt hope stir faintly. Hesitant, uncertain, she moved slowly toward him.

The small alcove was fitted with a single stone bench, similar to the window seat in her own bedchamber, but the view overlooked the longest part of the island. Through the partly open shutter, green hills and pale beaches stretched down toward the sea, an expanse of crumpled indigo silk beneath a cloudy sky.

"Did Sorcha sleep well last night?" he asked, looking out through the milky glass above the shutters.

"Hardly at all," Michael answered. "She said that Ranald was in and out all night, disturbing her. She had a few labor pangs, but they quieted after a while. She was very tired, so I gave her an herbal potion to help her rest."

Diarmid sat on the bench, resting his arms on his knees, hands dangling down. He glanced outside. Michael studied his lean, sculpted profile. A muscle beat in his cheek, his jaw was tight, his eyes were fatigued. She sensed too an infinite air of sadness that seemed to match her own.

"Thank you for helping Sorcha," he said quietly. "I am returning to Dunsheen Castle within the hour. Will you stay with her until I return? Mungo will be here to protect you both."

"Protect?" She sat beside him, leaning forward, careful not to touch him; she was not certain of his response if she did. "What is wrong? Does this have to do with what you found in the cave? Did you go down there after—after—" She stopped, and felt herself blush.

Looking away, he nodded. "Ranald keeps more than smuggled goods in that cave. He has two new warships there. I suspect he has agreed to help England invade the Isles."

"But—but that is treason! He holds Glas Eilean for the king!" she said in a low, urgent tone.

He nodded. "Once you asked me to take this place for you," he said. "Once you asked a miracle of me, as I did of you."

"That is over between us," she murmured.

He glanced at her, a flash of cloudy gray. "Is it?"

She twisted her hands in her lap, kept her gaze

averted, though her heart beat fiercely. "What I asked of you then was a selfish demand. Now I know why you refused to take Glas Eilean."

"What is it you understand about me?" he asked softly.

"You feared for Sorcha. I see that now."

He was silent for a long moment. "When she is safely delivered, I want you and Sorcha out of here. Then I mean to take this place from Ranald."

She looked up and touched his sleeve impulsively, and drew back. "Please, do not do this. Let my brother—"

"I will take it from him, just as you asked. I cannot tolerate the thought of him here any longer, after what I know of him now." He laughed, a harsh little huff. "According to our bargain, you will owe me a miracle if I do. Well enough. Taking Glas Eilean may require one."

His bitterness disturbed her; she felt responsible for it. "Do you leave to warn the king?"

He nodded. "And to gather men and ships."

"How long will that take?" she asked.

He shrugged. "A few weeks."

"Sorcha may deliver tomorrow, or not for several weeks yet. She must be protected from any upset."

"I will see to it," he said. She sat silently beside him, sensing the hard determination in him. After a moment, he reached over and took her hand in both of his, turning it. The warmth and strength in his fingers sent a shiver of yearning through her.

"If there was one miracle I could have of you," he said softly, "just one, I would ask you to make one for Sorcha." She curled her fingers in his, listening. "I would ask you to touch her and erase all her pain, past and future. But I know that it is an unfair burden to place on you."

Tears pricked her eyes. "Why do you think you can have but one miracle? There are endless miracles in life, Diarmid. Endless."

He stroked his thumb thoughtfully over her palm. "Are there?" he whispered.

She leaned her brow against his arm. He sat silently. "I hope so," she said.

He smiled a little, touching her hand, turning it in his as if her fingers fascinated him. She felt something bloom and open inside of her, watching him, and could not hold back the words. "I love you, Diarmid of Dunsheen," she whispered. "No matter what happens, nothing will ever change that."

"I know." He pressed her hand gently in his. "I know."

She waited, longing, hoping, to hear the words from him. But he said nothing. She felt his resistance like a sharp tug of sadness. She pulled her hand away and rose to her feet.

Diarmid stood. "I do not know when I will be back. Send word to me through Mungo when Sorcha is safely delivered."

"Farewell, then," she murmured, looking down.

He tilted her chin upward and tapped the widow's wimple that covered it. "Keep my sister safe." His gaze was even, filled with a soft gray light. "Keep yourself safe."

She nodded, closing her eyes over tears. He turned away abruptly, and left.

"Warships? I am not surprised," Arthur said.

Diarmid nodded and thanked Iona as she set supper in front of them, bowls of porridge cooked with mutton and onions. After she had refilled their ale cups and stepped away, Arthur took a sip and looked across the table at Diarmid.

"Several months ago, Ranald visited ship makers on the Isle of Lewis. He said he had commissioned two new trading vessels from them, but was hoping to get the funds to pay for them."

"He apparently got the coin from somewhere," Diarmid said as he picked up a spoon to stir his porridge.

"The two galleys hidden in that cave are well built and quite new. And stocked with English weaponry, as if ready to carry a hundred men skilled at the long-bow." He tasted the food, then glanced at Arthur. "You have seen no hint that he might be allied with the English?"

Arthur stirred his meal, sending up a drift of steam. "I have suspected it, but I was not certain. In Belfast, I know he met with two Englishmen at an inn a few times."

"In itself, that is not unusual. Merchants from several ports trade in Ireland."

"True. But Ranald was quite secretive about the meetings, refusing to share any trading information he had learned. I decided to watch him more carefully. I had no proof of my suspicions until I studied the accounting rolls in detail and compared them with what is stored at Glas Eilean. The list does not agree with the stored items, nor do its numbers make sense when examined closely. I had no chance to tell you this before, but I hoped you would catch the discrepancy on the lists."

"Then you have seen the English goods at Glas Eilean," Diarmid said. "Were you aware of the second cave?"

"Those cliffs are full of cracks and crevices, most no deeper than a few feet. I had no idea that large cave was there until you told me. It must be well hidden. As for the stored goods, Ranald did not acquire all of those himself. I obtained some of that wheat and flax from Anglesey a month or so ago. Not quite legally, I confess." He grinned sheepishly.

"Ah." Diarmid smiled. "Mungo and I wondered if you were among the Scottish pirates who have upset the English."

"They *are* displeased," Arthur agreed, pinching salt over his porridge from a dish on the table. "In fact, I would lose my head in a moment if they found me. But the *Gabriel* is as swift and sweet a vessel as I have ever sailed. We took the *Grace* out too. Only ten oars, but she glides through the water like a stone over ice." He grinned.

"I leave you in charge of Dunsheen, and you take to piracy," Diarmid said wryly, shaking his head. He looked up as Gilchrist approached the table on his crutch and sat down beside Arthur.

"Well, at least we did not lead the English home after us," Gilchrist said, reaching for one of the oatcakes stacked on a platter between the salt bowl and a dish of fresh butter.

"We?" Diarmid looked at him. "You know about this too?"

"Gilchrist is the best archer on board ship that I have ever seen," Arthur said. "He was with me on every voyage."

Diarmid blinked in astonishment, looking from one grinning brother to the other. "There is something going on here that I do not know about."

"Our brother may be lame now, but you know what a fine warrior he was before his injury," Arthur said. "He has those skills yet, in spite of a crooked leg."

Gilchrist spread butter on the oatcake. "I can still shoot a bow as well as I once did. My lack of balance on land does not seem to inhibit me on the deck of a birling. I guess I am used to swaying when I move," he added. "Arthur found me practicing in secret. Rather than pity me, he took me along on his next run into English waters."

Diarmid scratched at his chin, considering this new revelation. "And so you and Arthur both have been harrying English ports," he commented.

"When the moon was full and the winds were right, we did," Arthur said. "Our birlings are far faster than the heavier English ships. We could slip back into Scottish waters within hours, and hug the coast in the dark. The English were never able to learn who raided their ports." He sipped his ale. "Lilias and Iona appreciated the candles and the linen cloth we brought

back with us. Did you not, girl?" he asked pleasantly
as Iona came toward them again.

She placed a bowl of porridge in front of Gilchrist,
then nodded, blushing. As she bent over Gilchrist's
arm, he looked up at her, his handsome cheeks stained
as pink as hers, his brown-eyed gaze vulnerable and
adoring for an instant. He looked down quickly, and
did not see Diarmid frown as he watched.

"That I did," Iona said. "And Grandfather Angus
often says that the Dunsheen Campbells are fair trad-
ers where English are concerned. They pay a good
price for English goods—nothing at all." She smiled.
"Will you have more ale, Gilchrist?"

"I will," he said quietly, and leaned back so that
she could pour more easily. He helped her to steady
the heavy jug by placing his long, graceful hands
over hers.

Diarmid watched his youngest brother and Iona,
and did not mistake what he saw in their quick, shy
glances. Iona turned away, her cheeks more vivid, and
Gilchrist took a long sip of ale and spoke to Arthur.
Diarmid said nothing, his thoughts whirling.

He had seen similar glances shared between Mungo
and Sorcha. And the yearning that Diarmid felt for
Michael must surely show in his own eyes when he
looked at her, he thought. Even when he tried to suppress his hunger for her, his love, he knew he barely
hid it from her. He sighed and swirled his ale cup
pensively, silent while his brothers talked.

If Gilchrist and Iona loved each other as he thought
they did, he hoped that they would find the courage
to acknowledge it. Mungo and Sorcha had never admitted their feelings openly as far as he knew, but
love must have blossomed between them years ago.
Despite time gone past, and marriages for each, their
feelings still endured.

Diarmid sighed, knowing that he should have acted
on his own fascination for a gentle, gifted young girl
years ago. He could have had happiness all these

years. Instead, he had found misery in a lustful, impulsive, ill-chosen marriage.

He did not want Gilchrist and Iona to suffer and lose as he had, as Mungo and Sorcha had. Perhaps the blessing of the laird of Dunsheen would encourage Gilchrist to act. He would say something to Gilchrist at the first opportunity he found, and suggest that it was time the harper settled and took a wife. Michael would approve his plan, he was sure; imagining her delight in this scheme, he looked forward to telling her.

Then he frowned, draining the last of his ale. He would never be able to share an easy moment with her, talking and laughing and making plans together. That was a fantasy, and not for him in reality. He must be content with knowing that she truly loved him, despite his flaws. Her sincere expression of love awed him. Rare, elusive, that glimpse of love would have to be enough.

But it was not. Over the last few days, he had taken bittersweet joy in the memory of her face, her whispered words, her alluring body. He did not want to be here at Dunsheen, listening to his brothers discuss trade and traitors; he wanted to be with Michael, keeping her safe, making her his. But that would not happen unless he could release himself from the past.

He loved her, but he had held back the words. Now he realized that admitting his feelings for her would honor the love she offered him, not cause dishonor to her. She deserved to know that he loved her desperately, completely. Her love was generous, filling his heart like warm sunlight breaking through rain clouds. He owed her the same gift.

He felt unworthy of the devotion and loyalty she offered him. Even though he had refused her, hurt her, she was still willing to love him. Now, away from her, he realized how much he craved her, like a starving man. She was the nourishment his parched, hungry soul needed.

Somehow the chains that bound him, kept him from her, must be broken. He had to free himself of the burden of his meaningless marriage and claim Michael, claim his future. But in order to achieve that, he would have to plead with Anabel.

He sighed and rubbed his thumb and finger over his eyes, feeling as if a rock had settled in his gut. He feared a deep flaw in his plan—it felt hopeless—yet he was desperate to pursue it.

"Diarmid? Did you hear? They say the king will sail north and spend the Yuletide with MacDonald of the Isles," Arthur said, cutting into Diarmid's distracted thoughts. "I heard it reported in Ayr. Robert Bruce knows the value of the western Isles to Scotland, and he intends to visit the MacDonald lords of the Isles and the Campbell chief as well. He could sail as early as next week, since it is late November now."

"So if you mean to send him a message, brother, you will not find him in the Lowlands where you left him," Gilchrist said. "You will have to find him at sea, or wait until he comes into the Isles."

Diarmid looked up, his attention caught. "Did Ranald hear this news of the king as well?"

"He did," Arthur said, frowning in concern.

Diarmid sighed heavily. "Then we have little time left. Ranald has hidden those birlings away for a purpose."

"Does he mean to stop the king's progress into the Isles?" Gilchrist asked, aghast.

"I think he intends to aid the English in halting Robert Bruce's progress forever," Diarmid said.

"What should we do?" Gilchrist asked.

Diarmid's thoughts raced through the possibilities. "Arthur, take Gilchrist and Angus, and gather tenants and knights and arms enough to man the *White Heather* as a warship. I am sure the king will want her in his service soon. I will send out a runner to carry a message to the king or to Gavin Faulkener, if either of them can be found on land. And I will ride to

Campbell of Lochawe and discuss this with him. Bruce trusts him well."

"And then? Do we sail on Glas Eilean?" Arthur asked.

"I will go there first, and make certain that Sorcha is safe." *And Michael,* he thought fervently. "And I will do whatever I must to prevent Ranald from taking this course."

"In the name of peace and kinship?" Arthur asked.

"Not likely," Diarmid growled. He turned to his youngest brother. "Gilchrist, I think you know a few war marches on that harp of yours. I would suggest you practice them."

Later, Diarmid climbed the turning stairs toward his bedchamber and paused to look out the arrow-slit window. The setting sun turned the sky to gold and poured amber light through the stone fame. He watched, and thought of Michael, and wondered suddenly if she too stopped by a window in Glas Eilean to look out at the sunset. That fleeting thought warmed him, as if she stood beside him.

He climbed the stair toward the bedchambers and stopped at Brigit's door to peer inside. Since his return, he had found little chance to spend time with her. But he had already noticed she seemed to be doing exceptionally well on Michael's regimen, and he knew that Iona had taken over Brigit's care in a very competent manner. He must remember to thank her for it.

Tomorrow, before he left to speak with Campbell of Lochawe, he would do the muscle work with Brigit himself. He wanted to test how much strength she had gained. He had been pleased to see that Iona fixed to Brigit's legs the wooden and cloth braces that he and Angus had made. The child had walked stiffly around the great hall with the aid of Padraig and Columba, who flanked her calmly and protectively wherever she went.

Brigit stirred and lifted her head to look at him. "Uncle Diarmid?" she asked. "Can you sit with me?"

"Why are you still awake?" he asked gently, coming toward the bed. "Are you in pain?"

"Iona rubbed my legs tonight, just as Lady Michael showed her, and she gave me the potion in honey that Lady Michael wants me to take each night. But I am not sleepy." She hugged her cloth doll under her chin. "Michael cannot sleep either."

"She is at Glas Eilean," he said, sitting on the edge of the bed. "I think she might be ready to go to sleep soon."

"I meant my doll," Brigit said. "She cannot sleep. She misses Lady Michael. I do too."

"Do you?" He reached out to rub her feet gently as he spoke. When he picked up her left foot, he noticed a greater tension in its angle, a definite sign that Brigit's muscles were growing stronger. "I miss her too," he said softly.

"Then go back and get her," she said reasonably. "She belongs at home with us. We love her."

"You and your doll?" he asked, amused.

"You and me," she said. Her luminous gaze was oddly wise.

"Ah," he said. "So you think to know my feelings, do you?"

She gave him an elfin smile. "Are we not magic folk? And Lady Michael is like us."

He sighed. "*Brighid milis,* we are not magic—"

"We are," she insisted. "I can feel the magic working when Lady Michael touches my legs."

He stared at her. "You what?"

"I feel the magic," she said simply. "My leg tingles and gets hot when she rubs it, like it is coming alive. You promised me magic, remember? Is this a charm that will make my leg strong again?"

"I did ask her for magic," he said thoughtfully. "Brigit, when Iona or someone else rubs your legs, do you feel the same?"

She shook her head. "Not like when Lady Michael puts her hands on me. Her hands get so hot. I dreamed once that she put her hands on me and told me that I would walk. But she said it would take a long time. She said we would see little miracles, bit by bit."

He stared at her. "She said that to you in a dream?"

She nodded. "Little miracles, bit by bit, and I would walk. I do not know what she meant. But dreams can be silly."

Diarmid smiled, running a hand through his hair. Then he laughed. "Not so silly. Perhaps we should bring her back here again, and soon."

She nodded, smiling. "She is magic, like you and I. She belongs here with us."

"She does." He kneaded her tiny toes between his fingers for a moment, smiling half to himself. Then he lifted her little foot and kissed it soundly. "I will bring her back."

"Promise."

"I promise," he said.

"Then, we can have as many miracles as we like," she said with satisfaction. She gave her doll a smacking kiss and settled against the pillow.

"We can, angel," he murmured. He kissed her head, tucked her under the blankets, and turned toward the door.

The simple wisdom of a child had shown him what he wanted most. He wanted Michael with him, no matter how high and strong the barriers were between them. She was capable of miracles, and he owed her one in return: he would find a way for them to be together.

Chapter Nineteen

Michael stood near the cliff and faced the sun as it sank toward the sea. She had come outside after glimpsing the bright, beautiful sunset sky through a window, unable to resist the lure of the view. She inhaled the fresh, salted air, and lifted her head to the breeze, glad of a little time to herself.

Sorcha slept now, following another difficult afternoon filled with irregular, troublesome labor pangs. Michael had finally coaxed her to sleep with a back rub and an infusion of calming herbs. Then she had asked Mungo to sit outside Sorcha's doorway in case she awoke while Michael was gone.

The sun drifted slowly toward the horizon, washing the sky in golden light, spreading its gleam over the sea. She walked toward the edge of the cliff, cautious of the danger below her feet, but feeling no real fear. Her memories of being here with Diarmid gave her a firm sense of safety, as if he helped her to find the courage to stand alone on the cliff.

She watched in fascination as sky and sea turned to molten gold, a shining expanse broken only by the black silhouettes of small islands. Diarmid and Dunsheen Castle were out there somewhere beneath that magnificent sky, she thought. She wanted to be with him, away from the strange tension at Glas Eilean that centered around Ranald MacSween. She imagined, briefly, lying safely in Diarmid's arms, although she had tried to accept that such joy might never come to be. She wondered if he watched the sunset as she did.

The thought warmed her, and she hugged her arms around herself as she stood there.

" 'Tis cold out here," a voice said abruptly, startling her. She spun, cloak whipping around her legs, to see Ranald walking toward her. "What are you doing out here, Lady Michaelmas?" He spoke in precise, clipped English, as he so often did, though he had been born to the Gaelic.

"The sunset is brilliant tonight," she replied in English. "I only came to watch."

He stood beside her, the wind blowing the hem of his cloak, stirring his smooth brown hair. "This is a dangerous place to stand," he said. "You could fall over the edge, and we would not know of it until too late."

His odd tone sent a frisson of fear down her spine. She turned away, intending to walk back toward the castle, but he took her arm. "Hold for a moment, my lady," he said. "Stand here and watch the sky with me. 'Tis truly beautiful." He turned her as he spoke, and kept a hand on her arm. "Only in the Isles can one see these golden sunsets. Think how priceless that sky would be if it could be measured in coin."

"Will you spoil beauty with such a thought?" She shifted her arm but could not free herself from his polite grip.

"Ah, a woman of ideals. My father raised me to be practical. He taught me strictly and without mercy, and I learned well. What we gain for ourselves is the true pleasure in life."

"If we gain love from others, and family—"

He laughed curtly. "My father gained land for himself by supporting the English against the losing cause of the Scots. He gained sons of his wives and mistresses. He would think me a fool, my lady, to admire the view without thinking about the gold. He would think me a fool to father no sons, and a bigger fool to hold no fortress of my own."

She frowned. "You wish to speak to me about Glas Eilean."

"When I saw you standing out here, I knew this was a good opportunity to talk with you. We have much to discuss." He sent her a sidelong glance. "How does my wife?"

"She is asleep at the moment," she said. "Bed rest has earned another two weeks for her babe. Every day that the child stays in her womb invests in a healthy birth."

Ranald nodded briskly. "I may have been wrong about you, Lady Michael," he said. "I thought you no more than a midwife, and I have little confidence in them after so many babes lost. But perhaps you have the ability to ensure that Sorcha delivers me a healthy son."

"Or a daughter," she said irritably. "I will do my best. I can give her medicines and see that she rests. All else depends on God's will, not my abilities."

Ranald sucked in a breath. "None of my children have survived because of her weaknesses."

"Sorcha is not to blame," she retorted. "The health of this child depends on the well-being of its mother and the goodwill of heaven. We must treat Sorcha gently, with great care, and we must pray for her and the child. The herbs I have given her and the bed rest will gain time, but I do not know how long before Sorcha delivers. It may be days, or it may be two full months."

"Do what you must," he said. "Get me a child."

She frowned as she stared at the molten brightness of sea and sky. "And if the child dies?" she asked softly.

He shifted his grip on her arm, but did not let go. "I have had no sons of Sorcha Campbell, despite years of marriage. If she survives this birth, I will set her aside."

She stared at him in disbelief. "You mean to divorce her?"

He shrugged. "She may die this time. And I fear that my request for a divorce will be rejected by the ecclesiastical court in Glasgow. No matter. I can still set one wife aside and take another. Do not look so shocked, lady," he added, glancing at her. "This is done among Highland lairds more often than you know. The Church grants divorces too rarely. So most Highland lairds do not bother—they set the first one aside and choose another, and acknowledge their bastards as their rightful-born heirs. Your own champion cast aside his wife a few years back when she displeased him, although he took the slow route through the Church to do it."

She refused to look at him, though she sensed his smirking expression. "I know something of it," she said stiffly.

"Ah, but do you know all of it?" he said, leaning close. She could feel his breath on her cheek, could smell wine and meat from a past meal. "Do you know what he did, and why?"

She shook her head. "I do not want to hear it."

"But you should," he murmured, crowding her. She shifted away, but he kept his hand around her upper arm. The cliff edge seemed far more threatening and closer than before. She stepped backward, but Ranald pulled her toward him.

"Anabel was my cousin," he said. He laid an arm around her shoulders. "A beautiful girl, with dark eyes and dark red hair, and breasts and hips so full and well shaped as to drive any man wild who looked at her. Anabel wanted Diarmid Campbell, and got him," he went on, pulling Michael close. "She took him to her bed when he was troubled by his brother's death, soothed him there with her body."

The words stung deep, far deeper than Ranald knew. "I do not need to hear this—"

"She made him believe she carried his child—she may have, and lost it, I do not know for sure." He shrugged. "He wed her. He was besotted."

Michael pulled back. "I must go in now and see to Sorcha."

"Sorcha will keep," Ranald said, yanking her firmly back with an arm over her shoulders. "She has that low-born Highlander at her door like a faithful dog. Listen, now, and I will tell you what Diarmid Campbell did to his wife. So that you will not be tempted to wed him yourself."

"I could not, even if I wanted," she said. "He and Anabel are still wed."

Ranald laughed harshly. The sun had slipped below the far edge of the sea, and the golden hue faded rapidly. A bitter chill seeped into the air beneath the star-sparkled sky.

"I will tell you the truth, which even your champion does not know," he said. "Anabel and I had been lovers for years. I saw no reason to end that. Her new husband was gone for long periods of time with the king's forces. So we met, here or at Dunsheen Castle. One day he came back sooner than we thought, arriving at night. I slipped out of the room quickly, but it was obvious to him that a man had been in her bed."

"And so he tried to divorce her," she finished quickly, anxious to get away, troubled and shocked by what he had revealed. "He cannot be blamed for doing so."

"He refused to touch her again, and banished her from his house. She came to me here, upset and in need. Diarmid suspected me, I think, but he has never been sure. He sent a few of his guards away—she told him she had more than one lover, to protect me. Anabel was a loyal woman, in her way."

Michael said nothing, watching the vivid sky, wishing she did not have to hear this. And yet part of her listened, fascinated.

"The court granted them a separation in bed and board," he answered. "For her sin of adultery, they ordered Anabel exiled to a convent on an isle not far from here. And both Anabel and Dunsheen took a vow of chastity, so that neither would ever take a lover." He slid his hand up and down her arm slowly. "A shame, is it not? Perhaps he told you something of that?"

She lifted her chin and said nothing.

"For Anabel, I can tell you she did not keep that vow for long. We became lovers again. Diarmid visited her on that isle at first, but I visited her there more often. Until last year."

She looked at him, curious despite her repulsion for the tale and for the man who told it. "What happened?"

"She died," Ranald said bluntly.

Michael turned to stare at him. "Anabel is dead?" she asked, incredulous. "But Diarmid—"

"He does not know," Ranald said. He scowled, and his mouth was pinched tight, as if the topic were hard for him to speak about. "She took ill and could not be cured. The convent's prioress asked me to tell him. I have not, as yet."

"A year! She has been gone a year, and you have said nothing to him?" she demanded. "How can you be so cruel? Diarmid thinks he is not free—he thinks—" She stopped, unwilling to let Ranald know that she had any deep feelings for Diarmid.

"I have very good reason for this," he said. "If Dunsheen knew that he was a widower, he would look for a wife. A man wants a son and land, after all. But I knew he would speak to his friend, Gavin Faulkener, who has been eager to find a husband for you. I did not want that to happen, my lady," he murmured, drawing her close.

She kept herself rigid in her anger. Yet she was hopeful too, and ashamed to be relieved by Anabel's death. "Why would you care if he offered for me? I do not understand—" Then the truth became clear. "Of course. Glas Eilean."

"Glas Eilean," he agreed smoothly. "Which brings me to why I came out here to talk to you. I have decided to set Sorcha aside and take you to wife. You need a strong husband, after all, to hold this place for you."

"Marry you? That will never happen!" She shoved away from him. Ranald lunged and grabbed her arms. He dragged her the few feet toward the edge of the cliff and held her there, while the wind battered at her and she twisted in fright. She glanced at his dark gaze, fixed on her face; she had never before seen the wild glint that lurked there now.

"You could go off this cliff now, and plunge into the sea," he said. He shook her vehemently. Fear, helplessness, and anger swirled within her. She gripped his arms, her hands trembling.

"Please—" she gasped.

He smiled, rubbing her arm with his hand, holding her fiercely with the other. "If Glas Eilean's owner died, I could petition the king and gain the charter," Ranald said. "King Robert considers me his loyal liege man. But I do not want to kill you." He looked down at her, his expression softening. "And you do not want to die."

"Why are you doing this?" She tried to keep the desperation out of her voice. "Does your wife know about your cruel nature?"

He smiled thinly. "She does not know my innermost thoughts. But she fears me now, I think, where she never used to. Sorcha thinks me a heartless man, but she believes that the love of a family will soften me to a pudding. But, then, she has a simple heart herself."

"This is hateful, sinful. You are a civilized man, an educated man. You know these plans are wrong."

"My schemes will get me what I want. I commit no sin. I arrange things as I want them to be. Do you know how humiliating it is to be keeper of this castle, when a mere woman owns it? Can you imagine my shame, to have no sons and a weakling wife?"

She arched away, but he would not let her go. "You have no right to do any of this."

"Rights? I have many, for I have been wronged. Sorcha has not done her duty as a wife. The king has not rewarded me properly for the service I have given him. Glas Eilean should be mine. And Diarmid Campbell took the woman I wanted most, and divorced her. His actions led to her death. I seek my rights, and I will seek revenge for what is owed to me."

"No one meant you harm!"

He gripped her so hard that her arms felt bruised. "I have the power here," he said simply. Then he leaned her sideways over the raw crust of the cliff, still grasping her arm, so that her head and shoulders were over the cliff edge. Terrified, she clung to his arm for safety.

"I can hurl you from here, and have the castle through your death." He yanked her toward him and held her. Breathing hard, she rested her head unwillingly against him, just for a moment. "Do you want that fate, or this? Marry me, Lady Michaelmas. It will be simple enough to arrange. You need a husband. I need a wife who can give me a son." He dragged her hips to his, grinding himself against her. "I want a son."

She cried out in repulsion and pushed away. "Let me go!"

"I offer you a simple choice."

"Diarmid will never let you do this. He will take Sorcha from you! He will see that you pay for these evil plans!"

"Diarmid Campbell of Dunsheen," Ranald said precisely, "has been investigating my private matters. I will not tolerate that from any man. What has he told you of his activities here at Glas Eilean?"

"Nothing," she said flatly.

"I have made an arrangement that is delicate in nature, and requires careful timing. I suspect he has discovered part of it, but he will not live to destroy what I have planned. And he will not live to wed you himself."

"He has no interest in me," she said.

"I have watched him look at you. The man is smitten. He must not take you to wife. Has he taken you to his bed? Has he?" He shook her, but she did not answer. "When will he come back here for you?" he asked.

"I do not know."

He released her suddenly. Surprised to be freed so quickly, she stumbled backward, away from the cliff, away from him.

"Diarmid Campbell will be back for you soon, I feel it," he said. "And I will be waiting for him."

Afraid to reply, she stepped back on trembling legs. Ranald made no move to stop her. He shrugged. "Go back to the castle," he said. "I know you will not dare to speak of this to anyone. And you will not leave this island."

She felt anger overtake her fear. "You do not know what I will do!" She quaked inside, but the bold declaration felt good.

"You will keep your mouth closed," he said. "Your caring nature will not allow you to put Sorcha and the child at risk. You fear for Dunsheen's life, and so you will keep silent. You know he would come after me, and then I would have him. I know your weakness, lady," he sneered. "It is your caring heart. I do not share your kindness. I will win what I want. You will see how caring destroys a person, in the end."

She turned and broke into a run. Ranald's words haunted her, made her ill. Quickly, half stumbling, she ran into the castle and up the stairs to her chamber, where she threw herself, sobbing, to the bed.

During the following week, Michael kept Ranald's threats to herself, just as he had smugly predicted. If she had spoken of his vile plans to Sorcha or Mungo, or had sent word to Diarmid, she knew she would risk bringing harm to those she had come to love.

Ranald said no word to her about their encounter, either nodding politely to her or watching her with a

flat stare whenever she saw him in Sorcha's chamber
or in the passageways. But the strain and danger of his
presence disrupted her sleep, broke into her waking
thoughts, and took her appetite.

She stayed near Mungo as much as possible, finding
his humor and steadfastness calming. She made certain
that Mungo guarded Sorcha's room at night, and slept
better herself knowing that he lay rolled in his plaid
in the corridor. Ranald no longer slept in his wife's
bedchamber, having taken a small mural room on another level of the castle.

Several days after Ranald had made his threats, Sorcha had a particularly uncomfortable night. Michael
had been with her until well after midnight, and slept
late the next morning from sheer exhaustion. She
awoke to the raucous cries of gulls. Washing and
dressing quickly in a fresh gown and surcoat of black
serge, she pulled on her shoes, meaning to go to Sorcha's bedchamber as she did every morning.

But as she fixed a braided band of silk ribbons over
a white veil to cover her hair, she heard a knock on
her door. She opened it to admit Sorcha, barefoot and
clothed in a shapeless white woolen tunic, her face
swollen with tears. "Michael," she said, falling into
her arms. "You did not come. I waited for you all
morning—"

"I overslept. What is wrong?" Michael put an arm
around Sorcha's thick waist and walked her toward
the rumpled bed, urging her to sit down. "Has your
labor started?"

Sorcha shook her head. "Ranald came to me this
morning. He said he had to sail to Ireland for a few
days."

Michael tilted her head, puzzled. "And so the tears?
Are you sad to see your husband leave again, when
you have had so much difficulty and draw nearer
your term?"

Sorcha bit her lip. Her pale skin was blotched from
crying, her coppery hair hung lank over her shoulders,

and her lips and eyelids were puffed from tears as well as pregnancy. "He told me that I must deliver him a healthy son or he will set me aside."

Michael stopped deathly still. "What else did he say?" she asked softly.

Sorcha wiped her hand over her eyes. "He will find another wife. Someone who can give him sons." She caught back a sob.

"Lie down," Michael said sternly, and helped her, pulling the covers up and plumping the pillows.

"I knew that marriage to him would never bring me real happiness," Sorcha said. "But I hoped to be content with him. My father wanted this match, not I. The elder MacSween had English favor, and Ranald was loyal to King Robert. A position of security for me, my father thought. And Ranald wanted an alliance with the Campbell clan. He was charming, courteous—" She drew a shaking breath. "My father was dying. I wed Ranald even though he was not the man I loved." She looked away.

"I know he is not," Michael said softly, taking her hand.

"Ranald has changed. He was ambitious, intelligent, always courteous. Now he has become cruel and cold."

A blast of anger filled Michael. She knew Ranald's true nature, and hated him thoroughly in that moment for upsetting Sorcha at such a fragile time. But she reminded herself that her concern was Sorcha; she resolved to be patient and keep silent about the rest for now.

She took Sorcha's hand. "Perhaps Ranald suffers the strain of your latest confinement in his own way," she said tactfully. "You must not let his fit of conceit disturb you. There will be time enough to think on this later. Rest and be calm, and I am sure you can deliver a strong babe. Remember that is what is most important here."

Sorcha nodded, sniffling. "He wants to wed you," she said.

Michael started. "He said that?"

Sorcha shook her head. "I suspect he thinks it. I have failed him, and he told me that Glas Eilean is your property by charter. He might mean to set me aside and take you to wife."

"He could never do that," Michael insisted firmly.

"If not for Anabel, I know Diarmid would offer for your hand," Sorcha said. "I have seen the longing in his eyes."

Michael stood abruptly. "I will wed neither of them. When your babe is born, I will go home to Kinglassie. If Ranald persists in this, Diarmid will take you and your child to Dunsheen Castle with him. Do not fret, Sorcha. Please."

Sorcha nodded, her lower lip trembling. Michael turned away and paced toward the window, determined to give Sorcha no clue to her own fright. She would do whatever was necessary to protect Sorcha and Diarmid from Ranald's anger. She was the only one who knew that his threats were real.

She sighed. The world teetered on a framework of *ifs*—if Sorcha delivered a healthy son, if Michael returned to Kinglassie and gave Glas Eilean's charter to the king, if she never saw Diarmid Campbell again—she had no assurance that all would be well. But she wanted safety for these people, and she would sacrifice anything to ensure it. Even if she had to leave them.

She turned toward the window and covered her mouth to block a sob. Her heart was irrevocably lost to these Dunsheen Campbells and their laird. Leaving them was unthinkable—and imperative.

She leaned her cheek against the cool stone tracery of the window frame, and gazed at the sea below the cliff, praying for a solution to make itself clear.

The day was clear but gray. Rain clouds hung heavy in the sky, far out to sea. From her high vantage point, Michael could see a group of seals sleeping and playing on rocks near the base of the cliff. She watched, blinking back tears, as a few smaller seals swam away from their elders. They climbed onto a large jagged rock and made a kind of game of flipping in and out of the water like mischievous children. Watching them, her attention was suddenly caught.

The smallest seal climbed to the highest point of the rock and fell, unseen by the others. Michael leaned forward, narrowing her gaze, and saw the little seal floundering on a slippery ledge. It was clearly hurt, unable to crawl on its belly toward its companions. The other seals slid, one by one, into the sea and swam toward the older seals as if on some signal, leaving the little one hovering unseen on the ledge.

Michael realized she held her breath. When the tide swept in toward the cliffs, the little seal would drown. She thought about Sorcha's songs of the seal children, and her poignant conviction that she thought of her lost babes as tiny selkies, magic mer-children lost to her, but happy out there.

Tears came to her eyes as she watched the seal's dilemma. She could not turn away and go about her day. She had to help. Turning, she caught up her cloak and walked past Sorcha.

"Rest, dear," she said. "Dream of the sweet child to come. I must go outside for a while, to clear my thoughts." Sorcha nodded and curled under the covers as Michael opened the door.

As she ran down the corridor, she saw Mungo coming up the stairs. She grabbed his wrist and turned him to follow her.

"Mungo, you must take me out in a boat," she said.

"*Ach,* I cannot do that," he protested. "You were the sickest girl I ever saw the day we came here."

She pulled him along the lower passageway toward the sea entrance. "But you must row me out to sea!"

"Shall I row, or hold your head?"

"Mungo, please," she begged, running ahead of him.

"Something tells me I will regret this," Mungo grumbled as he came along behind her.

Chapter Twenty

Michael nearly regretted it herself. Once the boat glided out of the cave entrance and cut through the rolling swells, she grabbed the side and fought an onslaught of nausea and dizziness.

"Your face is green," Mungo muttered after a while as he pulled on the oars. "I knew I would be sorry. Dunsheen will have my head if he finds this out."

"This is my decision," she said. "I will not be ill."

"Luck to you, then," he said, "for you surely look as if you are losing that vow."

Michael took in slow, even breaths and trained her eyes on the far horizon, determined to maintain control over the dipping world and her protesting stomach.

Mungo shook his head. "All of this bother for a seal. Young seals are injured all the time around the rocks, from falls and from fights with larger seals. Their own kind leave them when they are badly hurt. Your heart is too tender. Fishermen club the creatures for their skins, for they fetch good prices in trade. That seal will die a more gentle death now than if he lives to be an adult."

"We must rescue him," she insisted, facing the direction of the rock that she had earlier showed him. "There! Do you see him on the ledge?"

Mungo glanced over his shoulder and steered the boat toward the small shadow on the rock. When the boat drew alongside the surface of the huge boulder and knocked against it, Michael leaned out, reaching toward the seal.

"Hold on, mistress. You are impatient and soft-hearted both, I think," Mungo said gruffly. He tossed a looped rope over a jagged part of the rock to secure the boat. Then he helped Michael climb out and stepped out with her. They moved cautiously toward the seal and squatted down.

The small pup had a mottled gray-and-black coat, large black eyes and round face, and seemed to Michael to be but a few weeks old. It lay prone on a jutting shelf of the rock, its tail flapping, its fat body swaying as it tried in vain to drag itself toward the water.

"Poor thing," Michael crooned as she crouched low. "Look at all the blood. Its left flipper is torn, and he cannot use it to crawl to the water." She stepped down, and the pup squealed and bleated as she came near.

"Careful," Mungo said. "You do not want a cow to come after you for touching her pup. They can be mean creatures, for all the pretty tales of mer-folk that you've heard."

Michael looked toward a cluster of boulders several hundred yards away, where the rest of the colony slept and played and fished. One cow barked repeatedly as she sat alone on a high point of a submerged rock.

"If that is his mother, I think she will not mind if I help her pup," Michael said calmly. She reached down and felt along the flipper carefully. "I do not know anything about their anatomy, but there are bones inside here that feel almost like a hand," she said as she touched gently. The seal barked pitifully, nudging her. Michael felt the bony structure under the flipper wobble oddly. "Ah, a break," she said with sympathy.

"He has not tried to get away." Mungo sounded astonished. "You have a gift, to be able to touch him like that."

She smiled. As a child, birds and animals had always let her handle them when no one else could come near. "Little one, we will get you back to your mother, but first we must tend to you. Mungo, there is a lot of bleeding from this gash. I will need a needle and silk thread to stitch it up."

He blinked at her. "You are going to stitch up a seal?"

She nodded. "Help me get him into the boat." She cupped her hands under the little animal's round, flaccid body.

Mungo sighed and helped her, lifting the pup easily and depositing it in the boat. He took the oars again and looked at her. "You cannot mean to bring it into the castle," he said.

She frowned. "I had not thought about it. Can we take it to the sea entrance? Will Ranald's guards trouble us?"

"Probably. I have an idea," Mungo said firmly, and began to row toward the cliff. Within minutes, he drew toward a black-shadowed crevice, out of sight of the main sea entrance.

"The smugglers' cave!" Michael breathed as they entered.

Mungo nodded. "Ranald is gone, and no one will come here. You will be safe here while I go up to the castle and fetch what you need. But you must promise to let the seal go back to its mother when you have finished mending him, no matter if he becomes another of your devoted patients."

"I will. The pup needs to be with his mother," she agreed, then looked up in awe at the high cavernous walls as the boat glided silently through the channel of water. She noted the barrels stacked in the shadows, and saw the large shapes of the two birlings at the far end of the cavern. "Leave us on that ledge, please, and go up to my bedchamber," she said. "I have a leather satchel with some medicines and instruments. I need needles and silk thread, and some bandages and ointments."

"Well, at least it is not a wooden chest you are sending me after," Mungo said as he handed her out of the boat.

Michael laughed and sat on the ledge while Mungo lifted the seal out and laid him partially, heavily, in her lap. "Thank you, Mungo," she said. "I seem to be always in your debt."

"*Ach,* well, it is a good place to be," he said. "I do not ask for much in return. And I would do anything for you, Mistress Physician." He sat and took the oars in hand.

She tilted her head curiously. "Why? Because of Angus?"

He smiled. "You did save my father's life, years past," he agreed. "But also because Dunsheen loves you dear as life, and charged me with your care in his absence. Whatever you want, that I will do. Dunsheen wants it that way." He pulled heavily on the oars, sliding the boat back toward the entrance.

Michael felt the sting of tears in her eyes. "Mungo!" she called. He looked up. "Bring me something to eat. I'm starved!" She smiled through her tears, and he waved as the boat disappeared through the narrow opening.

Dunsheen loves you dear as life. The words repeated like a refrain, warming her. She dangled her legs over the ledge, her toes just above the water, and looked down at the pup in her lap.

He lay strangely calm, perhaps suffering some shock from the injury and loss of blood, she thought. He looked up at her, his large round black eyes as tender and expressive as any human's.

"You are scared, little one," she whispered, stroking the warm, silky coat. "Do not be. I want to help you. I want you to be healthy and whole, and able to swim with your mother."

The seal bleated, a tiny, infant-like sound that firmly

caught her sympathy. She bent close and whispered to
the animal, stroking its coat. Blood stained the front
of her black gown, but she did not care. Her fingers
reddened further as she examined the gash across the
little flipper, gently probing to determine the severity
of the break. Without knowing the anatomy, she could
not be certain what was wrong.

Closing her eyes, she let her hands guide her. The
inner structure felt very much like a human hand, and
she tried to map what she felt in her mind. She probed
the healthy flipper to compare, and returned her seeking fingers to the injured one.

Then, almost as if she saw a picture of the bones
bared before her, she saw the break clearly in her
mind—much like a child's fracture, ragged at the ends,
but with time it would mend itself. Astonished by the
easy clarity of the mental image, she placed both
hands around the injured flipper and held it, speaking
soothingly to the restless seal.

The seal nosed its whiskered snout at her hand as
if asking for more petting. As she stroked it, sensing
its nervousness, she remembered hearing that seals
loved music of any sort. She began to sing one of
Sorcha's seal songs.

She did not have Sorcha's gifted voice, but the
sound echoed like small bells inside the high-walled
cave, blending with the incessant rush and lap of the
water. The seal seemed to listen to her in fascination,
staring at her as if it understood the story told in
the song.

When Michael finished, the seal nudged her arm.
"Ah, little one," she said, stroking its head. "If only
Sorcha were right about her little lost ones. How wonderful to know that they might be living and happy
with your kind."

She leaned her back against the cave wall. The
water shushed higher, wetting her feet. Feeling a moment of nervousness, she drew her legs up onto the
ledge and folded them beneath her. The expanse of

water was more threatening to her than it was peaceful, but she knew that Mungo would come soon. And
she was determined to make certain that the seal
recovered.

She stroked the seal and closed her eyes, listening
to the hushed roar of the sea as it entered the cave.
The rhythm was soothing, for she felt safe on the
ledge. Beneath her hands, the animal's body was
warm, its sides expanding and falling with rapid
breaths.

She took off her white veil and folded it over the
flipper, applying pressure, hoping to discourage the
bleeding that still continued. The warmth produced
beneath her hand grew and spread.

Soon she noticed that her palm felt as if she held it
near a hearth fire. Then, before she had time to wonder, she felt the power enter and fill her in the space
of an indrawn breath.

Tingling, swirling, the stream of heat flowed like
poured sunlight. The darkness behind her closed eyes
turned to a rainbow brilliance, and the warmth in her
hands became fire. She felt as if she floated, brimful,
as if she was a golden cup spilling over with light and
loving nourishment.

She knew the moment that the blood seeping from
the wound slowed to a trickle. An image of true clarity
told her that the tiny bone inside the flipper had begun
to mend.

Beneath her hand, the seal remained still and silent.
Michael opened her eyes and met its dark, oddly
knowing gaze. The extraordinary tales of the selkies
were not so far from truth, she thought.

"There," she whispered, stroking the small head. "It
is done, then. You will be fine." She felt weak but
clear, filled with peace, knowing that the gift of miraculous healing was still hers; she had lost it along the
way, but had found it again.

She remembered, suddenly, a moment as a child
when she had picked up a small wounded dove in the

courtyard of Gavin's castle. The bird had made no
protest as Michael held it, and she had closed her eyes
and felt the same sense of deep love flow through her
into the bird. Then she had opened her hands to let
the healed dove fly away.

That had been the moment that Gavin had discovered that she too had the strange power that he had,
the mysterious gift that ran through generations like
a vein of gold. Their mother had possessed such clarity
of power that some had called her a saint. She had
never known her mother; her father had been a gruff
English commander, and her birth illegitimate. Gavin
and her adopted mother, Christian, had nurtured her
like true parents, and had allowed her to use the gift
openly.

In Italy, however, she had discovered deep preju-
dice against her gift. The accusations, the trial, the
awful terror that followed—she drew a shaking breath
as she stroked the little seal. Ibrahim had been there
with her then. His wisdom and his influence had saved
her and sheltered her. And when he had asked her,
in the interest of her own safety, to abandon what
came so naturally to her, she had agreed out of loyalty, and out of fear.

Shunning the gift, she had tried to rely on the scientific, practical applications of her medical training. By
the time she had wed Ibrahim, she was sure that the
true fire of her power had drained out of her, leaving
but a sad flicker behind. She had secretly mourned its
loss. And then Diarmid Campbell had come into her
life, insisting on a miracle.

She felt the warmth of the seal beneath her hand,
and thought of another moment of pure healing, when
she had knelt on a misty battlefield. The compassionate, capable young surgeon she had met there had
stayed in her thoughts for years.

Her love for him had begun there, not in Perth, or
at Dunsheen. The realization hit her with a gentle

force, humbling her. She sat straighter, her hands stroking the young seal.

More than healing had been intended in the heavenly design the day she had met Diarmid. He had unknowingly led her to become a physician. And fate had brought her full circle to him again, where she had belonged all along.

Sighing, she leaned back her head, feeling the comforting warmth of the little seal, now asleep, in her lap. Daylight spread inside the cave entrance; the walls and water glittered like the inside of a dark, luminous green jewel.

She wondered how much time had passed since Mungo had left her here. The slow, steady movement of the tide had lifted the level of water in the cave considerably. Now the seawater lapped close to her folded legs, wetting part of her gown where it draped over the rock. Soon the ledge would be awash, and she would have to find another place to wait with the little seal.

She glanced around the cave. The high, irregular walls provided several niches; she could climb up there with the seal if she had to do so. But surely Mungo would be here soon.

The water rushed higher, closer, and she shuffled sideways along the inclined ledge toward a higher spot. She had sat so long with the seal, lost in her thoughts, that she had not noticed the change in the tide level. Her sense of well-being rapidly diminshed, replaced by cold fear.

Water had ever been her bane, the greatest source of fear she had known in her life. To go from a moment of safety and bliss to this sheer fright stunned her, shocked her. She drew a quivering breath and watched the encroaching tide.

"I am pleased that you have come to visit after so long," the prioress said to Diarmid. She was round, pink-cheeked, and so short that he felt awkward looking down at her. She smiled up at him, her hands folded serenely. "I had hoped that when you came to peace with this, you would come here again."

"Peace?" Diarmid asked. "I came to visit my wife."

The prioress nodded. "Of course. Come this way." She led him through the stone corridor and out a small door at the back of the convent building. He followed her through an herb garden and past a walled orchard, where a few fruit trees stood lacy-branched against the wide gray sky.

Heavy clouds hung to the west, the wind was high, and the sea that surrounded the little isle was dark and restless. His oarsmen awaited him now on the beach. He did not expect to stay long; he had a request to make of Anabel, and little else to say.

He hoped that she would listen to him fairly, but he did not expect her previously haughty, bitter attitude to have altered much. His own feelings toward her, having swept an intense range over five years from love to hatred, had finally faded to neutrality, as if she were an acquaintance and not the woman he had wed, or the woman who had betrayed him so painfully. He had not totally forgiven her, but his anger, at last, was gone.

The prioress opened a gate in the walled orchard, passing through it into a small cemetery, with stones set on a low hill that swelled above a white beach. Diarmid followed, looking around, puzzled. There was no one else here to meet them.

The prioress stopped by a smooth gray stone, cut with a Celtic cross and embedded in the turf. "Here she is," she said quietly. "Her cousin Ranald Mac-Sween had the cross made just after her death last year."

"Last—last year?" Diarmid stared at her, dumbfounded. She nodded, obviously certain that he had known about Anabel's death.

Anabel's death. He stared at the stone and read the Latin inscription: *Anabel,* he translated, *beloved, age twenty-six years in the year of our Lord 1321. Rest in peace.*

He drew in a ragged breath, then another, trying to quell the cold shock that ran through him. Anabel was dead. He rubbed a hand across his eyes in confusion, and looked at the prioress.

"What happened to her?" he asked in a low, flat tone.

"Ranald MacSween said that he told you, but I can tell you what I know. Sister Anabel took ill after she went for a walk on the beach in the rain. Her fever worsened, and went to her lungs, and she died within a few days. She went to God in peace, I think. She called your name before she died, asking your forgiveness. I assured her that you had already granted it."

Diarmid tightened his jaw against the guilt and remorse that rushed through him. "When did Ranald learn of her death?"

"He came while she was ill—he often visited her—and he was with her when she died. He told us that you were away with the king's troops, but promised to send you a message. You did not come or send word, but I understand. Grief takes many forms. We have appreciated the goods you sent in spite of knowing she was gone."

He nodded. He sent supplies twice each year to the convent as payment for his wife's keep; unaware of her death, he had ordered the goods sent as usual. "The shipments will continue, Mother Prioress, as my donation," he said quietly.

"Thank you. You and your wife were estranged, I know," the prioress said. "Perhaps you can find your peace with her now." She walked away.

He stared down at the stone, hardly seeing its graceful engravings. Anabel was gone, had been gone this whole past year. The shock of the news still reverberated through his body. He needed long moments just to allow his mind and his heart to comprehend it, to accept it.

She was dead, and with her had fallen the final barrier to his own happiness and freedom. Her bitterness and anger over his attempt to divorce her had endured, even though she had been the one who had betrayed the marriage. But he felt no relief, took no joy in her death.

She had changed, had asked for his forgiveness. He was thankful that the prioress had assured her of it. He owed Anabel that much; he had loved her once, although the bond was born of lust and blind need, rather than devotion and compassion.

Now he understood the true nature of love. Michael had taught him. He drew in a breath, looked at the flat gray horizon without seeing the approaching storm, lost in his thoughts. Michael, Sorcha, Brigit, Mungo, Gilchrist, Iona—all had shown him the generous, unrestricted nature of love. He had not realized it until now.

He glanced down at the cross that marked both a woman's passing and the fading of his own painful past. Drawing a deep breath, he felt the burden lift at last.

But he knew that he would not be entirely free until he resolved one last matter. Ranald knew of Anabel's death, and had not told him. He frowned; MacSween had been with her when she had died, and he had paid for the stone. Yet why had he kept the news from her own husband?

He stared at the Latin inscription. *Anabel . . . beloved.*

The answer hit him like a blow. The inscription had not been the requisite phrase of the absent husband. Ranald had ordered that inscription because he had loved her himself.

Diarmid knew then that Ranald had been the lover who had left Anabel's bed warm to the touch when Diarmid had arrived home unannounced one night four years ago. Ranald had been staying at Dunsheen Castle that night. Later, when Diarmid had asked Anabel to leave his household, when he had listened to the opinions of his family and friends and had gone to the ecclesiastical court to undo the marriage, she had fled to her cousin at Glas Eilean.

Diarmid had often suspected that Ranald was more than mere cousin to Anabel, but he had dismissed it as abhorrent. Now that he was sure of it, he felt a keen pain deep inside, not only for himself, but for Sorcha, who had also been betrayed.

But why would Ranald withhold the news of Anabel's death? His brother-in-law never hesitated to threaten revenge when he had been wronged, and Diarmid was sure that Ranald harbored a great deal of anger toward him for the loss of Anabel.

Ranald often acted in his own interest, in personal as well as business matters. What benefit could he gain from keeping silent about Anabel's death? How would it serve him for Diarmid to believe Anabel was still his separated wife? He shoved back his hair in frustration.

Looking up, he scanned the silver-gray sky with its burden of clouds, watched the heavy swells of the sea, studied the blurred outlines of distant islands. Glancing west in the direction of Glas Eilean, he suddenly knew the answer.

Bending down, he knelt by Anabel's grave, whispered a prayer, touched a finger to his lips and then to the center of the cross. "Let there be peace between us, Anabel," he murmured.

Turning, he strode toward the beach and the birling that waited there. He had to stop Ranald. If his suspicions were correct, both his sister and Michael were in great danger.

Chapter Twenty-One

Cold seawater pressed around her legs as Michael stood on the ledge, holding the little seal as if it were a child. The pup struggled against her and slipped out of her arms to dive into the water. Raising its slick head through the splash, it looked quizzically at her.

"I am not coming in there with you," she said firmly, and turned to make her way carefully toward a higher ledge. The water nearly swamped the entrance, making the narrow crevice opening even smaller, washing over the rough ledges there, but not yet reaching the barrels and wooden boxes stored above the water stains on the walls. She grabbed on to jutting handles of stone as she made her way toward the back of the cave, where a more accessible ledge leaned out over the water.

Stepping across the rough stone, she gained a foothold on the projection and sat, curling her legs underneath. The seal skimmed through the water beneath her, its bleating voice and playful splashes echoing around the walls of the huge cave. Michael looked down at it and pointed toward the entrance.

"Go home, little one," she said. "Your mother will be looking for you."

The seal barked insistently, as if trying to communicate its thoughts. Michael pointed toward the cave entrance again, and turned her back, expecting it to swim off toward its own kind. A moment later, she looked down and saw the little seal struggling to climb up toward her.

"*Ach*," she said reproachfully, "you are too small to climb up here. You will fall and hurt yourself again. Come on, then." She stepped down, scooped the pup's solid weight out of the water, nearly overbalancing herself, and climbed back up to the shelf. The pup waddled behind her.

"So here we are, and what shall we do?" she asked. The seal cocked its head and blinked at her, its black eyes huge in its little, speckled face. "Mungo will surely come soon to fetch us," Michael murmured, gazing toward the empty entrance. She could not imagine what delayed him so long.

She looked back into the shadowed recesses of the cave, and saw the dark bulks of the two huge birlings that floated silently there, moored to the wall. If the water rose much higher than this, she would have to climb, even swim part of the way, toward the birlings and find shelter inside one of the warships.

She dreaded the thought of slipping into the cold, dark water, which surged higher as she watched. White-capped swells rushed inside the cave with increasing force and noise. Michael flattened herself against the slimy rock wall and gathered the little pup under her arm for warmth and comfort, trying to stay calm as the water encroached relentlessly toward the ledge.

If a small boat had been available, she might have tried to row back to the sea entrance of the castle by herself, despite her fear. She had been in enough boats lately to be able to do that much. Remembering her voyage to Glas Eilean, and Diarmid's kindness while she had been ill, she realized that, while he had helped her to conquer the symptoms, he did not know the real reason for her fear.

She set the little seal down again and hovered on the ledge, trying not to watch the green depths of the water, trying not to hear the incessant echo of the waves as they swept inside, or to think about what would happen when the water level grew high enough to reach her. But the fear that she resisted finally won a hold over her.

Her hands began to shake, and soon her entire body shivered uncontrollably. The seal nosed at her, but she hardly noticed as she stared down at the deathly green gleam of the water. Her breaths became labored and tight as she fought the terror.

The seal barked, but Michael did not look up, her gaze transfixed on the water. She knew too well what it felt like to sink into such dark, cloying depths, lungs filled with the last bit of precious air that remained in the world. Her hands had been bound with rope, and her feet tied—

She cried out as the memories swamped her, choked her, drove her back against the wall, down to her knees. She covered her face with her hands and cried out again, desperately. Panic flooded her deeply and completely.

Somewhere inside, she knew she must calm herself, but could not take her hands from her face or shift her stiffened body from its cramped, frightened posture. The seal jumped and bleated, snuffling at her legs, and she could not comfort it.

Out of the rushing, whispering rhythms of the seawater, she heard a voice call her name, again and again. The seal bumped at her and barked, and she finally looked up, her glance dazed by fear and shadows, peering through deepening green-tinged light to see a dark form floating toward her through the brimming, gleaming water.

"Michael!" Diarmid called from within the small boat he rowed. "Michael!" The boat knocked against the side of the ledge, and he climbed out, moving quickly toward her, sloshing through water that swirled around his bare legs. "What is it? Did something frighten you? Come here." His hands found her in the dimness—warm, strong, safe hands. He pulled her to her feet. She sobbed out, a piteous cry, and went into his arms.

"Hush, love, I am here," he crooned, wrapping her in his embrace, resting his cheek on top of her head. "What is it? You are not in danger here. When I arrived back at Glas Eilean this morning, Mungo came in and said that you were here, waiting for him. I told him I would fetch you myself. What happened?"

She tightened her arms around him, sobbing out the wretched burden of her fear. "The water—" she choked out, and hid her face in the thick folds of his plaid.

"Ah, God. Ah, Michael," he murmured, his voice sympathetic, regretful. "You are safe, my love. You are safe." He rocked her in his arms. "I am here now. I will not leave you."

She clung to him, hearing, as if in a daze, the loving warmth in his words. The rock seemed to spin out from under her and right itself again. He loved her. She felt it, knew it. The feeling gave her enormous strength to fight the turmoil inside of her.

"Let me help you into the boat," he said.

She resisted when he wanted her to step off the ledge. She wanted only the shelter and assurance of his arms, wrapped around her like a benediction. She sighed against his chest. "Stay here with me," she whispered, clinging to him. "Just hold me. Please."

He made a gruff noise in his throat and tucked her against his heart, covering her head with his hand, sliding his fingers over the tousled skein of her thick braid. "I will hold you as long as you want," he murmured.

Michael closed her eyes in gratitude and dipped her head under the niche formed by his jaw and throat. His whiskered chin was warm, his pulse vibrant. She knew that he would hold her into infinity if she needed that.

"Michael," he whispered. "Something more than ocean sickness causes this uneasiness with water. What is it?"

She tried to summon the words, although the memories assaulted her, crowded her like squawling demons in a painting of hell. Her fingers clutched Diarmid's arm.

"It was in Italy." She spoke barely above a whisper. "The second year that I attended lectures at the university at Bologna, I was assigned to assist in a small monastery hospital, a fair distance from Bologna. Many medical students went there for a few weeks at a time."

His hands rested easily, snugly, at her waist. "Of course," he said. "When I studied with Brother Colum, I worked in the infirmary at the monastery."

She nodded. "I saw many people suffering there. Some days I could hardly stand to hear the cries for help, or see the pain on their faces." She paused. "One woman was coughing blood and was very ill. I sat with her often, and one day touched her chest and back, and felt the healing power come. She felt it too, and later said she saw lights around me in the night. She seemed to recover rapidly."

"Go on," Diarmid said gently.

"I sat with her a few times, and each time the gift came through my hands, as it had when I was a child. I did not fear using my ability then. I had often done so at home." She looked at him. "Gavin has the gift—someday I will tell you the tale."

"I want to hear it," he said. "What happened then?"

"Ibrahim visited the hospital regularly. He saw me sitting with the woman one night, and later asked me what I had done. He was kind, respectful when I explained it to him, but he told me to be careful. The woman recovered from an abscess of the lungs in three days, with greater health than she had ever had before."

"That is astonishing. Why did Ibrahim caution you?"

"He knew that she was the archbishop's mother. She spoke to her son about what I did, and he brought charges against me, even though his mother had been healed. An inquiry was called, and they found me guilty of magic and sorcery." She paused.

"Jesu," he murmured, pulling her close.

She swallowed heavily and went on. "They—they—shut me in a storage room of the monastery for days." Darkness, chill, the sounds of mice, the taste of sour milk and stale bread brought by the monks—the memories assailed her. She fisted her hands and gained control after a moment. "Then they tied me hand and foot, took me in a boat, and tossed me into the river," she said flatly. "If I rose to the surface, I would be proved innocent."

In answer, Diarmid wrapped his arms around her, silent, and rocked her gently.

Having uttered the words so bluntly, Michael struggled against tears. She heard the rush of the seawater and moaned, pressing her head against Diarmid to block out the sound.

"Where was Ibrahim during this time?" Diarmid asked gently.

She fisted and unfisted a handful of the plaid that covered his chest. "He had been in Bologna, but he rode into the village the day they took me to the river. He sent his Saracen valet into the water after me, and the man pulled me up. I was choking, nearly drowned." She stopped again, her world tipping dizzily. But Diarmid's strong arms held her up, and his hard body was the rock she leaned on in the midst of the storm.

"Michael," he murmured. "I knew none of this."

She looked up, blinded by tears. "I never even told Gavin. But I cannot forget how—how I came so near to drowning."

"You are safe now. Always." The balm of his presence dissolved the terror trapped inside of her. Parts of it vanished like fog in sunlight.

"Ibrahim told the crowd that I had risen to the surface. Many believed him, but some were angry. In the confusion, he took me away."

"I owe Ibrahim a debt," Diarmid said.

"He told the court that he had cured the woman with rare Arabic medicines," she said. "He told them that I had only comforted her with a soothing touch, and should never have been accused. He swore that I had no unearthly healing power."

"He lied for your sake. He loved you very much."

She smiled ruefully. "He was never a strongly religious man, so a lie to the ecclesiastical court meant little to him. And he did love me, in his way," she added softly.

"I envy him," Diarmind whispered.

She closed her eyes on an inward sigh, and hugged him around his waist. "Ibrahim was intrigued by my healing ability," she said slowly. "He thought that I was a good student, and he liked a curious mind, someone who challenged him. He taught me a great deal, brought me into his household, protected me. He made certain that I became a physician." She looked down, flattening her hand on his chest. "He needed a hostess and a companion, and wanted an apprentice in his last years. I agreed to marry him."

"Did you love him?" Diarmid asked.

"I was grateful to him. I was frightened, and I wanted to become a physician very much. He was a kind man, the best friend I had."

"Sometimes friendship is enough."

"It was not enough for me." A delicious warmth enveloped them, a comfort so profound that Michael wanted to stay here with him forever. She closed her eyes and sighed softly, sadly.

"You needed something more from him," he said gently.

She shrugged, half nodding in a flush of embarrassment. "He was nearly sixty when we wed," she said. "He felt that a man and wife should have a loving relationship. We did, I think, at first." She paused.

"But he had a heart illness, and kept his symptoms from me, and hid the medicines he prescribed for himself. I did not learn until too late."

Diarmid stroked her hair lightly, saying nothing.

"I know that my marriage was not ideal," she said. "But we were content with our medical discussions, our books, our patients. Ibrahim asked me never to use the healing gift again. He feared that I might have more trouble."

"Perhaps I was wrong to ask you to use it again."

She shook her head, tucked against him. "I mourned it. I thought it was gone forever. After a while, I was busy with my medical practice and my husband's failing health." She looked up at him. "When I met you in Perth, the healing power was all you wanted of me. You made me find it again."

Diarmid tipped her chin up with a crooked finger, his gaze searching hers. "If you had no healing touch, no skill at all, I would want you." He lowered his head.

Her head spun as his lips brushed over hers in a soft, exquisite kiss. Her knees seemed to melt and turn to butter as his mouth searched hers. Only his hands kept her from falling as the sweet, lingering kiss continued.

A hunger rose in her that no kiss, no words of love, would satisfy. She tightened her arms around him, pressed herself to him, but felt him stop suddenly, and pull back.

Diarmid looked down. The little seal, which had wandered away, now flapped against his feet, splashing in the shallow water on the ledge. "Your friend is anxious to be gone from her," Diarmid said wryly. "He is wise. It is cold here, and dark, and the tide is rising higher."

Michael glanced down at the pup and smiled weakly. "He wants his mother, I think."

"Mungo said you had taken charge of a badly wounded seal," Diarmid said. "He told me to bring your leather satchel, which I did—it is in the boat. But where is the wounded seal?"

Michael pulled slightly away to look up at him. "I only have one seal with me. He was wounded when he fell from a rock. His flipper was torn and bleeding, and a bone was broken inside."

Diarmid frowned. Releasing her, he squatted down to grab the pup gently and firmly to examine the flipper.

Michael looked at the dark crown of his head, at the wide angle of his shoulders and back. Watching him, she felt love pour through her, banishing the fear, the uncertainties, the dark, awful memories that had haunted her for so long.

His mellow voice, murmuring silliness to the seal pup, soothed her like sweet music. She reached out and touched his hair, trailed her fingers down to rest on his shoulder. Love filled her silently, privately, glowing inside of her like a hearth while she waited for him to look at her.

He turned at last, his gray eyes shining in the greenish light. "This wound is partly healed. The edges are drawn together, and the clot is strong. I cannot feel a broken bone inside his flipper."

"He is better," she admitted softly.

Diarmid stood slowly, his gaze never leaving her face. "What did you do, Michael?"

She looked down at the seal, looked back at him. "I touched him," she said. "I only touched him, and the power was there, suddenly, like—like lightning. The bleeding stopped, and the bone seemed to mend."

Diarmid took her hands in his, pressing them between his palms as if he held something precious. "You have the power with you constantly. But you do not realize that. Brigit told me that the heat of your touch brought feeling and life back into her lame leg."

"Brigit?" she stared at him in surprise, her hands caught in his. "But I only rubbed her legs, examined them—I never felt it pass through me into her."

"When I went back last week, she told me that she had felt magic from you. She moves around quite well now, Michael. I want you to see how much stronger she has become."

The words thrilled through her heart. He wanted her to go back to Dunsheen Castle. She smiled up at him.

"Michael mine," he said, "you have true magic within you." His lips settled over hers as gently and purely as a dove coming down from the wing. Then he gathered her against him, slanting his mouth over hers, cupping the back of her head in his long fingers, dipping his tongue into the willing recess of her opened lips. She looped her arms around his neck and arched her body into his, gladly, lovingly.

The seal barked and shoved between them, stirring the wet hem of her gown. Michael hardly noticed. But Diarmid lifted his head. "Here's Mungo," he drawled, "and we are caught." He placed his arm around her shoulders as they turned.

A second boat glided toward them, Mungo alternately pulling at the oars and waving. Diarmid waved back, and he and Michael waited until he pulled the boat nearer to the ledge.

"The seal is fine, and Diarmid is here," Michael said. "You did not need to come down. Look how well the pup is now, Mungo."

Mungo barely glanced at the seal. He looked up, his face pale and gaunt, devoid of humor. "Sorcha says she has begun her labor," he said abruptly. "She sent me to find you."

Michael started in Diarmid's arms. "Is she certain? She has had many alarms of late, but the labor has always stopped."

"Not this time," Mungo said. "Because you were out, she sent one of MacSween's guardsmen to fetch the old midwife, who came right away. The old woman says her water has broken."

Michael sent a rapid, concerned glance toward Diar-

mid. He frowned as he quickly and silently handed
her into his own rowboat. He gave Mungo the little
seal with an order to release it near the seal colony
on the rocks, and then climbed in with Michael and
took up the oars, pulling toward the narrow entrance.

Chapter Twenty-Two

"She is nearing exhaustion," Michael said quietly. "Hours of labor, and little progress." She stood in the half-open doorway, leaning against the doorjamb as she spoke to Diarmid, who had been waiting in the passageway. He had come to her side as soon as she had opened the door.

She was grateful for his steadfast presence. Diarmid and Mungo had spent most of the past ten or so hours of Sorcha's labor pacing the corridor. Mungo was not there; Michael assumed he rested, or had gone down to the great hall. "I wish I had better news for you," she added, glancing over her shoulder toward the interior of the chamber.

Sorcha lay sunk in the soft feather mattress, her back and knees propped on pillows, her distended torso covered with a blanket. She slept fitfully. Michael had taken advantage of the respite to talk with Diarmid. She turned to him, resting wearily against the door.

Diarmid leaned a hand on the jamb beside her head. "You are exhausted too." He reached out to brush at the strands of hair that slipped from beneath the clean white linen veil she wore. After returning from the sea cave, she had changed her stained, wet clothing to the other black gown and surcoat that she had brought with her. Freshened in clothing, she was not fresh in spirit, but she endeavored to hide that from Diarmid and Sorcha.

"I am fine," she answered. His tender gesture was

almost too much for her. Tired, discouraged, frightened, she needed to maintain her distance from him—or fall weeping into his arms. "The food Mungo brought up helped. Old Giorsal seemed to gain strength from it. And she has consumed most of the wine, so she is quite relaxed." She pursed her lips tensely to avoid making a less kind remark about the midwife. Spending the day with the woman had proven to be a trial of patience and goodwill.

Diarmid lifted a brow. "What have you had to eat or drink?"

She shrugged. "A little porridge, some ale, cider. Sorcha has had nothing but a hot herbal infusion and some honey, and she does not complain. Nor will I. Diarmid"—she stood straighter, remembering why she had come to him—"will you bring another infusion of the herbs I asked for earlier? Raspberry, columbine, chamomile, wormwood—"

He nodded. "I know the list. I will ask the cook to bring some more. She has kept it hot over the cook fire for you, along with kettles of broth and porridge and spiced wine. She is very concerned for her mistress, as are all the soldiers and servants in the castle. What else can I do for you?"

She hesitated, sighed. His presence outside the chamber did much for her, though he did not know that. "Only the infusion. And perhaps a little spiced wine," she added, stepping back.

He caught her forearm with his long fingers. "Michael," he said hoarsely, "let me help."

She watched him, saw the pain in his eyes. "What can you do?" she asked. "What can any of us do? We have tried to turn the babe. Now we must wait and pray."

He would not let her go. "The babe has still not turned?"

"Not yet." A few hours ago, she had reported to him that the child's poor position delayed the birth. "It still lays sideways in Sorcha's womb. Giorsal and

I have tried to turn it from the inside and from the outside. The child has shifted only a bit. They will both weaken if labor continues this slowly."

"A breech can be delivered without harm to either mother or child," Diarmid said. "Even if you can only get it to turn feet or buttocks first, it can be delivered safely."

Michael nodded, and leaned forward so that her voice would not carry. "Giorsal is certain that neither one of them will survive," she whispered miserably. She wanted his arms around her in that moment, so much. So much. Yet she remained still.

Diarmid sighed out harshly, but his fingers remained gentle on her skin. "I will get the infusion," he said. "Then I am coming in there myself."

"You cannot help," she said. "Giorsal will protest."

"*Tcha*," he said in disgust. "Sorcha is my sister. I am a surgeon." He paused. "I have attended a birth before."

As she looked at him, she saw his raw need, his determination, the awful depth of the hurt he felt. This difficult birthing brought back painful memories for him of the day Brigit was born.

"I will call you if I need you," she said. "Thank you," she added in a whisper, and pulled back, closing the door.

"*Ach,* I hope this lady has learned her lesson," Giorsal muttered as Michael walked toward the bed.

She glanced at the woman in surprise. Giorsal sat on the window bench, her heavy, almost masculine form leaned against the wall. Past middle age, she was still tall and imposing, her physique big-boned and broad, her shoulders and arms as muscular as a man's, her hips straight and her bosom large.

Her appetite was large too. Giorsal had eaten all of the food Mungo had brought in earlier, but for a small portion of porridge, and had filled herself freely with wine and ale both. A little of the *uisge beatha* that Ranald kept in a sheep's bladder in a wall cupboard had gone into the midwife too. Michael saw the glint of its effect in the woman's small blue eyes, saw the florid flush in her face.

"I think this will teach the lady," Giorsal repeated.

Michael stopped. "Teach her what?"

"She should have banished her husband from her bed long ago," Giorsal said. "A woman who suffers so with childbearing should go to a convent and live out her days in peace and content, never bearing another infant."

"Hush yourself," Michael hissed. "You should not say such things in her lying-in chamber. Has she asked for anything?"

"Only water," Giorsal said, sighing hugely and leaning back. "I told her we cannot give that to her without she delivers a babe first. I told her last year not to bear another child, after the struggle I had to pull her through her last birth. That child was even earlier than this one, small and weak as a landed fish, a girl, hardly worth the trouble I spent trying to revive it." She shook her head in a condemning way. "I told her not to do this again, on pain of her own life. She weakens each time, and suffers so after the babes die—"

"Be silent!" Michael commanded, glancing at the curtained bed. She heard only some panting, weary moans, and hoped Sorcha had not overheard the midwife's cruel remarks. "You will be out of this chamber, and out of this castle, unless you speak with respect of the dead, and of this woman's suffering!"

Giorsal hoisted her bulk to a standing position. "And who are you to tell me that, my lady?" she sneered. "I have attended all of Sorcha's births. Ranald is my cousin, and I have done my best to save his weakling offspring and his whimpering wife. And now here you come, a green thing, to tell me midwifery!" She stepped toward her. "A physician? You? No woman would be allowed that office." She turned away and shoved up her sleeves. "I will check the

position of the babe. I know well how to do that," she
muttered, and walked over to yank back the curtains.

Giorsal leaned over Sorcha, patting her shoulder.
"Time to wake up, my chick," she said, not unkindly,
and pulled down the covers to spread her large hands
on Sorcha's abdomen. She turned her hands this way
and that, and frowned deeply. "No change," she said.
"I must check her inside."

Sorcha half sat up. "Let Michael do that," she
protested.

Giorsal scowled and turned away abruptly. Michael
nodded and turned to rinse her hands in a basin of
warm water. Ibrahim, because of his Arabic training,
had always taught the virtues of clean hands. Due to
his gender, he had attended only serious, life-threaten-
ing births that often required surgery, but Michael had
studied with him long before she spent time with mid-
wives and discovered that most did not share her husband's wisdom.

Slipping almond oil over her hands, Michael approached Sorcha. "I will be very gentle. I hope we
can convince your child to turn."

Sorcha nodded weakly and allowed Michael to
probe her and place a hand on her belly. Michael felt
the bulge of a tiny head just under Sorcha's left rib-
cage, felt shoulders, bumpy knees, the mound of the
buttocks. Pushing gently, firmly, she tried to urge the
child's head downward, and felt a gentle patter of
kicks below the heel of her outer hand as the child
protested the disturbance. Sorcha cried out as a labor
pain took her. Feeling the hard strength of the growing contraction, Michael withdrew her hands.

"Let me," Giorsal said impatiently. She rubbed oil
on her hands and placed them on Sorcha's bare abdomen. "In the name of the Lord, I command you to
turn, infant," she called out in Latin. "Turn toward
my voice!" She bent down then and spoke between
Sorcha's legs, this time in Gaelic. "Here, little child,

come her. May God guide you, and the devil be done with you."

"The devil has nothing to do with my child!" Sorcha snapped. She tensed her face as a new contraction whipped through her. Michael bit back the angry retort she had for Giorsal, coaxing Sorcha patiently instead.

Just as Sorcha breathed out a long sigh that signaled her release from the grip of pain, Diarmid entered the room, carrying a tray with wooden bowls and a few cups. "Here is the infusion you asked for, and the spiced wine," he told Michael.

"Thank you," she said.

"Put it down there and leave," Giorsal said haughtily.

Diarmid ignored her. "Sorcha," he said gently, looking at his sister. "Shall I stay for a while, or shall I go?"

Sorcha reached for his hand as he approached the bed. "You should go, Diarmid," she said in a low voice. "A man does not belong in a lying-in chamber."

He leaned toward her. "I am a surgeon," he said. "None of this disturbs me. If you need me to help, I will stay."

"A man in a birthing chamber only brings bad luck," Giorsal muttered. "A surgeon would mean a poor outcome for this woman. Be gone."

Sorcha smiled weakly. "Mungo needs you, I think. He seemed very nervous earlier."

"He is concerned about you." Diarmid kissed her hand, brushed damp strands of hair away from her forehead. "I will be just outside," he said. He looked across the bed at Michael. "Call me if you need me."

She nodded silently and watched him go, her heart sinking just a little. Her own faltering strength, both physical and mental, seemed fortified when he was near.

"A comfort to have a surgeon just outside the door," Giorsal remarked when the door was closed.

"But I will pray that you will not need his services, Sorcha. Rest now. You have a long night ahead of you. We should all rest, and pray this babe is born healthy and whole by dawn."

"My child will be here by then," Sorcha said. "I know it."

Giorsal grunted. She looked at Michael. "We should not be lax with christening this one," she said. "If it comes out head first—which I doubt—I'll baptize it even before it is fully born, and put salt into its mouth to keep the demons and fair folk away. Now I mean to rest. Call me if there is any progress." She turned away to pour out a cup of the spiced wine. She drank it quickly, her swallows loud and satisfied, then went to the window seat and sank down with a sigh. Leaning back against the wall, she was soon snoring.

Michael fetched a cup of the herbal infusion for Sorcha, and held it while she sipped slowly. Sorcha seemed to relax within minutes, leaning her head back against the pillows that Michael had plumped behind her. She rested, but began to pant heavily when another contraction drove through her body.

"Michael," she whispered when it was done, reaching out. "I fear that I will die this time. Giorsal thinks—"

Michael gripped her hand. "Do not listen to her," she said. "I am here this time. Diarmid is here. You will both be fine," she said firmly. Sorcha nodded wearily and seemed to sleep.

Thinking of Diarmid, who waited outside, Michael went out into the corridor. He stepped out of the shadows and opened his arms. With a small moan, Michael leaned her head against his chest, suddenly so exhausted that she feared she would tumble over. "I only have a moment," she said. "She sleeps briefly."

"Is there any change?" He wrapped his arms around her.

She shook her head, drinking in his fresh strength

like clean water for her soul. "The child has not turned."

"Michael," he said against her hair, "use your healing touch to turn the babe."

"I will try again," she said wearily. "Giorsal has been so disagreeable, I have not had much of a chance to see if that would help." He kissed her forehead, his lips dry, gentle. The kiss made her want to cry suddenly. She stepped away from him and hurried back into Sorcha's room.

Sitting on the edge of the bed in the silent room, Michael spanned her hands over Sorcha's belly and closed her eyes. Her spirit seemed to sink into peace, into quiet, as if into a soft bed. She felt herself relax for the first time that day.

When the heat began, images came with it, surprising, distinct, filled with a warm light, golden, rosy, loving. She saw the child as it lay curled—saw its little face, pinched but serene, saw the fisted hands, the large belly, the knobby knees. She watched the head shift between tightly drawn, tiny hands, saw it kick out—and felt the kick beneath her palm.

She sucked in a surprised breath. The heat built in her hands until drops of sweat beaded on her brow, until she thought the heat would wake Sorcha. Beneath her hand, another kick, a shift, a bumping ripple of movement—she saw it even as she felt it under her hand, like a vivid dream playing out behind her closed eyes. Then the womb hardened and tightened beneath her hands, and the child stilled, curled tight, seemed to sleep.

Sorcha moaned, awoke for a few moments, fell back again into a heavy, exhausted sleep. Michael did not lift her hands, but the image of the child faded. She drew in long breaths, felt the heat, and then saw the child in her mind again, glowing, golden, tucked like a rosebud.

Wondering briefly if she dreamed this, she knew that it was part of the touching gift. She watched, and prayed, and hoped as the wondrous sight remained. Time drew out, softened, extended. She felt the womb harden again, saw the child curl, then saw it stir, felt the motion beneath her palm like the graceful passing of a fish.

The child tucked its head and surged, spun, floated in a circle. She saw its genitals, swollen and clefted, female. Tears started in her eyes.

Sorcha cried out and jerked awake. "What was that?" she breathed, putting a hand to her belly over Michael's hand.

"I think your babe has turned," Michael said, smiling a little through her tears. "I think she just turned."

Sorcha nodded, then gritted her teeth as a contraction took her. This one, Michael could see, was stronger than the rest, the result of the downward pressure as the babe's head slipped into place. Sorcha grabbed Michael's hand, grabbed the covers, and released a guttural cry.

More contractions came, each one faster, harder, fiercer than the last. Michael tried to help Sorcha through each one, rubbing her back, speaking softly, while Giorsal snored. Labor progressed so quickly, suddenly, that Michael called out to Giorsal for help, unwilling to leave Sorcha's side. But the older woman did not seem to hear her.

She wiped Sorcha's brow with a linen towel, counted the moments between pains, watched Sorcha's face, and knew that the time of birth drew near. "Giorsal!" she called again. "Wake up!"

Loud snoring was the only reply. Michael murmured to Sorcha, who thrashed and grunted with the increasing strength of the force that overtook her body. Michael ran to Giorsal and pushed at her broad shoulder. Giorsal snorted contentedly and fell over on the cushioned bench in a drunken stupor.

Michael ran to the door and yanked it open. Diarmid was there in an instant, Mungo behind him. Seeing Michael's face, Diarmid strode past her into the room. One look at Giorsal had him spinning toward Mungo. "Get her out of here!" he snapped.

Mungo, looking equally stormy, hoisted the midwife to a standing position and half dragged her from the room.

Michael supported Sorcha's back as the mother groaned with the profound urge to bring forth her child. "Help me," Michael said to Diarmid. "You must help. She is ready now. Listen to her breathing."

Sorcha moaned out, the cry ending in a grinding grunt. "Let me hold her while you deliver the child," Diarmid said, quickly kneeling on the bed to take Sorcha back against his chest.

Michael grabbed up the linen towels she had folded at the foot of the bed earlier and positioned herself between Sorcha's outspread legs. Sorcha groaned again, a primordial sound of breath and soul and blood that sent chills through Michael.

"Now, Sorcha, now!" she said.

Diarmid tilted his sister forward slightly, supporting her. "Push," he said. "Push, the time has come."

"I see the head, ah, she's lovely, push, my sweet," Michael crooned, repeating that, saying other phrases. Diarmid murmured to his sister as well, and he and Michael spoke a harmony of encouragement while Sorcha strained.

Finally Michael coaxed the head out of the passage, then the writhing shoulders, the chest. The child slipped out with a burbling sound into her spanned and waiting hands, its little body warm, slick, wondrous.

"A girl!" She wrapped the child as she spoke. "A daughter, Sorcha. A beautiful daughter." She watched the cord as it pulsed, and watched the child that lay curled and limp in her hands.

Limp. Oh, God, she thought, and looked up at Diarmid. He caught her glance, his gray eyes shining clear at first. Then he frowned and laid his sister back with a kiss to her forehead, wiping her sweaty brow. He was at Michael's side in an instant, silent, ready to help.

"Sorcha needs you," she whispered urgently. "I must try to help the child to breathe."

Diarmid bent toward his sister to help with the afterbirth. Michael focused on her task, turning her back to Sorcha, who was still connected to her child through the pearly, twisted cord. Michael sat the tiny, wrapped child upright, cradling her delicate neck and head, tipping her forward slightly, tapping her back. All the while she crooned nonsense words, loving her, pleading with her.

No cry came from the child in her hands. She rubbed her fingers over the tiny back, flicked her fingers against the bottoms of her smooth-soled foot to rouse her. The child did not respond. She laid her on the bed to examine her.

Birth blood, slick and dark in the candlelight, made it difficult for her to tell if the child had begun to breathe on her own. She pressed her ear to the tiny chest, shifted her carefully, listened to her back. She could hear the faint, slow beat of her heart—far too slow. Limp, dusky purple, slack-limbed, she had the delicate appearance of one born too soon.

Too soon, too soon, Michael thought frantically. She had called her forth, turned her in the womb, too soon. Her own heart beat in a panicked rhythm. She flipped the baby upside down and thumped her buttocks, thumped her back. Her thin arms and legs jerked.

A watery cry burst forth, wavering through the air. Michael sat the babe upright in her hands gently, hearing Sorcha sob out in joy, hearing Diarmid murmur something to his sister. Glancing at Michael, waiting for her quick nod, he cut the cord. The child was free now, and must breathe entirely on her own.

Michael held back her own joy as she washed the baby tenderly. She was pinker now, but still too deeply colored to be breathing normally. Breath and life

stirred in her, but Michael feared that she was too
weak, too early to survive long. She swathed her
quickly in silk and linen, watching her feeble movements, listened to her breathing stop, gurgle, start
again. All the while she sensed the babe's stubborn
will to live.

The child's tiny lungs labored over the unaccustomed air that burned inside of them, giving off an
odd gurgling sound. Her skin had a transparent, wrin-
kly sheen, her miniature ears were soft, still folded
from the birth passage. The child fought to breathe
and live, but was not fully prepared for life; she still
needed the safety of the womb. The spark that flickered inside of her could vanish any moment.

"How is she?" Diarmid asked, leaning toward
Michael.

"Early," she whispered. "So very early. We can only
wait, and pray that her breathing becomes regular."

"May I hold her?" Sorcha asked. "Is she
breathing?"

Michael glanced up. "She is," she said. "But let
me christen her first. What name will you give your
daughter?" As she talked, she rubbed the child's back,
held her head, warmed her against her own body,
prayed she would keep breathing long enough to have
a name, to be held by her mother. Her frail condition
alarmed Michael deeply, and she wanted to hide that
from Sorcha.

"*Aingealag,*" Sorcha said, her voice hoarse. "Her
name is Angelica. Baptize her so the demons will not
have her."

Michael nodded and dipped her fingers in warm
water from the basin. She murmured the Latin words
that bound the child to heavenly protection, and
added a short Gaelic prayer to seal the protection of
Brigit's nine angels around Angelica.

She turned away, holding the child upright,
thumping her back gently, listening to the sporadic,
frightening hiss of the tiny breaths. She turned toward

a shadowed corner of the room to hide Angelica's struggle from Sorcha.

Three times as she held her, the child lost the rhythm of her breath, sputtered, turned dark-hued. Every breath, every feeble movement, tore into Michael's heart.

Diarmid came toward her. "What is it?" he whispered.

"I am afraid Sorcha will lose this one too," she whispered, her voice cracking.

Diarmid took the bundled child. The tiny body fit in his scarred, gentle hand. "Touch her," he said urgently. "Let your healing gift flow into her. There is nothing else you can do for her now."

Michael nodded, almost relieved to be told what to do, and spread one palm over the child's torso, placing her other hand beneath Diarmid's fingers. Within seconds, she felt intense heat radiate through her hands. She knew, suddenly, that the gift had begun to flow earlier, at the moment of the birth, and had helped bring Angelica this far into life.

Diarmid and Michael held her in the cradle of their hands. Michael closed her eyes and poured her soul into the child. After several long moments, the babe rasped and mewled, lost her breath again, turned dark. Michael took her hands away, deeply frightened. She looked up at Diarmid.

"The rhythm of her breathing is not good—her lungs are too weak. Perhaps—" She could not finish the thought: perhaps this one was meant to go back to God.

"Bring her here," Sorcha called from the bed. "Bring my daughter to me." Her voice was husky, strong. She sat up.

Michael nodded sadly, and Diarmid carried the child to her, placing her in his mother's arms.

"Poor little one," Sorcha said. "Her breathing sounds like the others." Her voice had an infinitely gentle sound, like silk, like water, soft and fluid and giving. Michael watched, awed by the aura of serenity that seemed to surround Sorcha as she held her daughter. "She is beautiful," Sorcha said, and tucked her against her breast.

"Sorcha—" Michael whispered. She wanted to say that she was sorry, that she had tried, but she found that she could not speak further. She could not say that she did not expect the child to live much longer, but she could see from looking at Diarmid and Sorcha that they knew that already.

Sorcha looked at her. "You did as much as anyone could," she said. "Thank you. God will take her to be with her brothers and sisters." She looked calmly down at her child, accepting, fully loving, although her eyes held glinting tears.

Michael turned away, trembling, hardly knowing where she went as she crossed the room into the shadows. Diarmid turned away too, as if he too sensed that Sorcha needed this time with her child. Michael glanced toward Diarmid, saw him stand before the window, saw him reach forward and open the shutter.

To let out a soul, Michael thought.

Behind her, she heard Sorcha begin to sing, a melody of the seal children. She listened, strangely comforted, as the power of Sorcha's love seemed to flood the room to its brim.

Peaceful silence spilled through the room like a breath of God. And then Michael heard an exquisitely beautiful sound. A tremulous, tiny cry.

She turned. Diarmid turned.

Sorcha looked up at them, smiling, tears flowing freely down her face. The crying was louder now, a quavering, indignant sound, full of life. "Listen!" Sorcha said. "Listen!"

Diarmid walked toward the bed, and Michael followed. The child waved her hands, pumped her tiny legs, her face reddening, fists flying. Deep and impatient, her cries soon took on the strong cadence of a beating drum.

Tears stung and pooled in Michael's eyes as she watched. Sorcha looked up, smiling. A little sob escaped her lips. "I have prayed for this moment for months," she said. "For years."

Diarmid nodded silently and reached out a hand to touch Angelica's head. A tear slid down his cheek.

Michael broke then, sobbed openly, shattered by joy. Diarmid turned toward her. Sorcha looked up. The child drew another lusty cry and struggled beneath the linen cloth that impeded her legs.

"She is a miracle," Sorcha said, her eyes shining like diamonds, brilliant and deep. "For all of us. A miracle."

Michael nodded, tears streaming, feeling as if the burden of joy was almost heavier to bear, somehow, than the burden of sorrow she had expected. She wanted to go into Diarmid's arms, but held herself back, not certain why. He reached out and touched her elbow, but the caress was shy, reserved, as if he too held back.

"Diarmid, will you go tell Mungo that I have a fine daughter?" Sorcha asked. "The cook and the guards will be waiting to hear too." Diarmid nodded, kissed his sister, and left the room.

Michael took the child from Sorcha. She listened to the steady, quick thump of her little heart, measured the strong pattern of her breathing, left a kiss on her brow. She swaddled her, marveled at her, pronounced her strong and healthy, and handed her back to her mother.

After making Sorcha more comfortable, Michael gave her a little spiced wine in the herbal infusion. When Sorcha began to nurse the child, Michael sat by the window and looked out through the open shutter.

The darkness was still deep, although she thought dawn was no more than an hour away. Glistening rain pattered on stone, and a chilled breeze streamed in to cool her heated cheeks. She leaned her head against the window frame in weariness and listened to the soothing sound of the rain, felt the cool, cleansing wind on her face.

In the aftermath of a true miracle, she felt humbled, changed somehow, as fragile and delicate as a butterfly newly emerged. She watched the rain glisten like dark jewels, smelled the salt in the air. Her senses had a finer clarity, a deeper awareness of all the textures and wonders around her.

Behind her, Sorcha murmured to her child, a warm, velvet sound. Suddenly Michael wanted to hear Diarmid's soothing voice, and needed—ached—to feel his arms around her.

The door opened, and she turned eagerly to see him, ready now to run to him, where earlier she had felt overwhelmed, uncertain. But Mungo entered alone and crossed toward the bed, looking at Sorcha. His gaunt face was softened by awe and utter devotion. He loves her, Michael thought sadly, so much, and he cannot show her.

She stood and went toward the door, the urge to be with Diarmid so strong she could not resist. She had to find him.

Her expression must have given away her intent. Mungo and Sorcha both looked toward her and seemed to understand.

"You'll find him outside," Mungo said quietly.

Chapter Twenty-Three

Diarmid stood near the edge of the cliff—a tall, lean shadow in the rain. Michael gathered her dampening skirts and ran forward, then stopped as hesitancy overtook her. He did not turn, and seemed intent on his thoughts. He watched as a hint of dawn bloomed pale silver above the dark, sweeping sea.

The wind buffeted his plaid and shirt, and blew his hair back. Rain gusted over him, but he stood proud and unyielding in the midst of raw beauty and elemental force.

Sensing that he wanted privacy, Michael wondered if she should go back inside and leave him to his thoughts.

A burst of wind swept over the cliff, whipping her gown against her legs, tearing the white veil from her head. She watched it go, floating over the cliff like a pale, silken angel.

Diarmid turned and saw her, but he did not move. She approached him slowly, watching him through the dark and the slicing rain. Her love for him, her need, poured out unbidden in her gaze, like a flood that she could not hold back.

Diarmid watched her silently. Rain streamed in rivulets down his face and hair, soaked his shirt, pelted Michael's hair and gown as she returned his steady gaze.

Then he raised his arms.

Huffing out a little sob, she ran to him. He wrapped her in his embrace, kissed her brow, her cheek, the corner of her mouth. He slid his fingers through her damp, tousled hair and held her, rocked her in his arms.

She tightened her arms around his waist and clung to him, her head nestled in the curve of his neck. He was strong, warm, the haven she most needed.

When he cradled her head between his hands and touched his mouth to hers at last, a little moan of joy slipped from her mouth into his. She returned the kiss, her lips moistened by rain and the tears that slid down her cheeks.

She tasted of salt, of wind, of the clean rain that washed their faces. He kissed her hungrily, deeply, wanting her more than he ever thought possible, wanting her to be wholly his, flesh and soul, forever. Her hands supported him, her mouth nourished him, her tears were those he could not shed himself.

He had come out here to be alone, hoping to cleanse the sorrow from his heart. The grief that he carried from Brigit's birth, and the deaths that had followed it, twisted in him like a blade when he had watched Sorcha give birth and had seen Michael struggle to keep the child alive.

But in the wake of a miracle, the old sadness had finally receded, and joy flowed through his veins in its place. The rain and the silver flash of dawn over the sea, strength and majesty joined, stirred his soul profoundly. He felt as if parts of his old heart had been swept away.

He would still regret that long-ago day, but now he knew that he need no longer punish himself. The deaths of Brigit's brother and mother had been the will of heaven, and not his making—he had struggled to save them. An hour past, he had seen that heart-rending battle mirrored in Michael and Angelica.

He raised his head, drew a deep breath, and held Michael close to his heart. Another old anguish had dissolved, its last remnants of regret and anger cleared away by rain and miracles and Michael's tears. The knowledge of Anabel's death had freed him from a prison of the heart, allowing him release, granting him peace and promise.

Holding Michael in his arms, he felt joy surge anew. He had not realized, until this moment, that Michael herself was a miracle in his life. Months ago, bold and thoughtless, he had demanded one of her—and she had responded, over time, by giving him her unquestioning love. He had been a fool not to see the wonder in that.

So much to say to her, yet he kept silent and kissed her again, his lips and hands eloquent in place of words. He cherished her, and she was here, and she was his, and words would wait.

She opened her lips for him, and he delved deeply into her mouth, where she was soft, warm, wet. His body hardened, flared like a hearth fire. The wind and the rain pummeled them, but she felt warm and yielding in his arms. He dragged his lips away only to return, unable to slake his thirst for her.

Pulling her close, he felt her shiver. "You're chilled and wet," he murmured. "Where is your cloak?" Mundane words, but he was incapable of saying more just yet. His heart was too full of emotion; he could barely comprehend the scope of it. But he knew that he wanted to protect her, hold her, keep her, love her.

Love her. The impact of that thought took his breath, stirred through his heart and his body. "Come inside," he said huskily, and swept her up into his arms.

She was an easy weight to bear. He sensed her deep fatigue in the way she rode slack in his arms, draped her arm around his shoulders, rested her head against him. He strode toward the castle through the rain, and stepped in through the narrow door.

The guard was elsewhere, celebrating the birth of MacSween's new daughter with the older soldiers; Diarmid heard faint, gruff laughter from the guardroom.

Unseen, he carried Michael through the corridor and up the turning stairs.

"Put me down." She laughed softly. "Let me walk."

He did, and she took his hand to ascend the steps beside him. They had come this way together another time. The memory of those fervent kisses pounded through his body with each step he took. Michael shifted her hand in his and looked up at him; he saw in her eyes that she remembered that night too.

His heart thundered with increasing need as he went upward, still holding her hand, and led her along the shadowed upper passageway, toward the bed-chambers.

"I should look in on Sorcha," she said.

He shook his head. "You are wet and chilled," he murmured, "and far too tired. Do not fret about her—Mungo said he would wake the midwife and put her to work. You need some rest."

They passed the partially open door of Sorcha's room, where Diarmid heard the baby cry, high and lusty. The sound sparked like a flame in his heart. Sorcha murmured to her child, and Mungo made a chuckling comment, followed by the midwife's terse remark. Diarmid strode past, Michael's hand tight in his own.

No one saw them as he opened the door to Michael's chamber and latched it firmly closed behind them. Scant light streamed through the shutters and glassed windows. He looked down at Michael and saw in her face a graceful medley of silver shadows, hardly real, formed of magic and moonbeams.

He reached out with one hand and touched her damp hair, combing the strands back with his fingers. "You need dry clothing."

"Your clothing is wet too," she said, plucking at his sleeve. Her slightly amused expression was elfin and charming.

"I will change," he said. "First we shall attend to you, and get you warm. Then you need to rest."

She touched his chest, her fingertips hot through the damp cloth. "Rest with me," she said softly. "I need you here."

His loins filled, surged, his gut swirled. He tugged gently at the shoulder of her black surcoat.

In the shadows, her vivid blue eyes, gazing steadily up at him, were smudged dark. Wordlessly, she lifted her arms and allowed Diarmid to draw the damp woolen surcoat off of her. He laid it aside and turned back. Michael remained motionless as he gently undid the silver buttons at the neck of her black serge gown, and lowered his hands to unclasp the brass link belt snugged around her small waist. The belt fell with a faint jingle as he tossed it on top of the surcoat.

His palms traced the curves of her hips, his thumbs grazed the sides of her breasts as he raised his hands to loosen the neck of her gown. He pulled at the tightly fitted long sleeves and slid the gown from her body in a smooth motion.

She stood now in a chemise of pale cream silk, loose and flowing, nearly transparent. He saw the luscious mounds of her breasts beneath, pebbled with chill, or with desire. His blood pounded in him, but he kept his movements deliberately slow and calm. He had gone too fast before; now he meant to take time. Sliding his hand along her arm, touching her fingers briefly, he knelt to lift one of her feet.

She placed a hand on his shoulder for balance as he unlaced the instep closure of one narrow leather ankle shoe, tugging it from her foot, raising the other foot to remove that shoe as well. She wore lightweight woolen hose of a pale color. Her toes flexed in his hand as he slid his fingers along her leg, pushing aside the flowing skirt of the chemise to untie the silken bands around her knee. Rolling down the knitted hose, he withdrew it from her foot and tossed it aside.

Her foot was small-boned and chilly to the touch. He laid his lips against it, briefly, and set it down again. Michael sucked in her breath, and lifted her other foot. He removed that stocking as well and dropped it.

He felt her fingers in his hair, stroking his head, felt her hand drift down to trace the outline of his beard-roughened jaw. Her thumb brushed over his mouth, and now it was he who pulled in his breath. He touched his lips gently to her palm, keeping one knee on the floor, and raised his head, his hands. She glided into the circle of his arms and lowered her head.

The luxury of her resounded through his senses. Her lips were tender against his brow, her scent womanly and deep, her breasts soft, warm globes. The demand within his body grew strong enough to sweep will and thought away. Heart thundering, he stood, looking down at her, and touched her head.

"Your veil is gone," he murmured, slipping his fingers over her damp, tangled hair. "I am glad that the wind took it."

"Glad?" Her quiet voice was no more than a breath.

"The widow's pleated veil," he said. "You need it no longer." He withdrew, one by one, the small ivory pins that held her plaits in place in rolls over her ears. As the braids fell into his hands, he combed his fingers through to free the strands. Pale as moonlight, fine as silk, her hair appeared wondrous to him, full of its own light. He drew it out slowly, letting it fall, glistening, over her shoulders.

"A fair, sweet maiden," he murmured. "No widow's garb, free to choose. As I am free now. Anabel—" He stopped, gathering the difficult words needed to explain that he was a widower, that old vows no longer held him.

"I know," she whispered. "I know that she is gone." He opened his mouth in surprise, began to speak. She touched his lips. "Hush. We will speak of it later."

He frowned slightly, puzzled, but did not question her. "Later," he echoed. "Here and now, we begin anew."

She nodded, smiling tremulously, her wide, shadowed eyes watching him with understanding and perfect love. He felt humbled by the purity within her. She lifted on her toes and touched her lips to his. Her gentle kiss was so poignant that he felt the last vestiges of grief and old anger fall away into oblivion.

Silently, she undid the brooch that held his plaid on his shoulder, then slid the heavy wool down. Her fingers fumbled with the brass buckle on his wide belt. When it came loose, she dropped it on the floor and tugged gently at the thick draping around his waist. His plaid came away in her hands.

He took its weight from her and swung it behind her, netting her in its voluminous folds, pulling her to him inside the warm circle of wool. Toe to toe, thigh to thigh, his strong and obvious desire for her cradled in the silk that covered her, he kissed her.

She breathed out a sigh, swayed languidly against him. That small movement weakened his resolve to draw this out, to milk with her all the joy and pleasure possible for them. Wanting suddenly to lift her and take her in that instant, his body hardening almost painfully now, he sucked in his breath sharply, stilled his hands on her.

Michael pulled on his damp linen shirt, and he tilted his head, allowing her to draw it off of him. His skin was bared against the warm, slippery silk of her chemise, an arousing, divine sensation. He groaned under his breath and lowered his head, circling the back of her head with one hand. Her breath drifted soft over his mouth. A spark like lightning shot through him, and he was lost.

"Dear God," he breathed, low and husky. He took her mouth quickly, fiercely, deep and sure. With a little cry, she slid her arms around his neck and pressed against him. Pulsing, hungry kisses built into a cadence, stealing his breath, taking hers as well. He heard her gasp, felt her moan slip into his open mouth.

He explored the dark, sweet cave of her mouth with

his tongue, and raised his fingers to trace the delicate contours of her ear. Threads of her hair, so fine they seemed woven of air and silk, fell over his fingers. He brushed them back and grasped the cool, soft mass in one hand, slid his hand down, and took the chemise from her body in one long, languorous pull.

Her warm, yielding length pressed openly against him now, drawing another deep, breathy groan from him. The plaid was warm around them, but bothersome. He dropped it and wrapped her in his arms, his hands tracing feathery light over her back and long, loosened hair. Then he swung her up and strode the few steps toward the bed.

Stretching out beside her between cool linen sheets, he sank with her into the nest formed by the soft, thick mattress and piled pillows. Diarmid reached up and yanked the curtain closed to cocoon them intimately in silence, warmth, and darkness.

Michael rolled to him with a little sigh, seeking his mouth, slipping her leg over his. He skimmed his hands over her breasts and hips, his fingertips sensitive, caring. Kissing her deeply, he dragged his mouth away to taste her earlobe and the downy side of her cheek, to trace the graceful arch of her throat and to feel the strong, excited pulse there.

Her scent was a light, womanly sweat, and she tasted of salt and an indefinable sweetness that he could not live without. He touched his tongue to the valley between her breasts, licking gently, savoring her taste, her scent. She arched against him and he shifted, took her nipple in his mouth, swirled his tongue over the firm tip, over the ruched velvet circle around it.

"Diarmid," she moaned, a breath of air. He closed his eyes and suckled her, sliding his hand down to caress her waist, her hip, her small, flat abdomen. He knew, with a burst of awareness, that their children would someday bloom and grow there. He wondered if that had already begun. The thought paused him for an instant with wonder.

Her fingers were agile, tender, warm, and healing wherever she touched him. She slid her hands over his chest, raked through the thick dark hair that led to his hard belly. The soothing, sensual heat of her fingertips made his heart race, made his loins fill and pulse until he thought he would burst with urgency.

He took her other nipple, felt her indrawn breath, felt her back arch, her hips press forward, her hands begin to plead and guide him. He traced his fingers over her navel, down to the small nest of curls, then raised his head and took her sudden gasp in his mouth. She glided into the cradle of his palm, and welcomed his fingers inside of her. His fingertip found the trembling, heated bloom there and slicked over it slowly.

Miracles, he suddenly thought; she was made of them, her flesh soft and blissful in his hands, her breath like silk on his lips. She moaned softly, quivered beneath his touch, danced her hips toward him. He felt her small, knowing hands glide over the planes of his chest, along his waist, moving until she found his hardened core and took him into her hand.

The warmth, the loving in her slow-stroking caresses, the gentle sway of her hips begged him to come into her. He heard her breath quicken, felt the tremors begin to ripple through her body under the rhythm of his touch.

He felt her release, felt the sigh that slid through her, heard her faint, joyful laugh as she surged toward him like a wave of the sea. When she stretched her limbs languidly, gracefully, the movement undid him.

He covered her, felt her shift beneath him until she yielded him entrance. Her little soft cry roused him further, and she took him into her, her body as giving, as wondrous, as accepting as her heart.

Plunging into her deep warmth, into the honeyed silkiness inside, his breath deepened. The darkness behind his closed eyes burst into light and streams of luminous color. He heard her moan beneath him, breathy, ecstatic.

His need for her, his love, formed a new cadence that pulsed and promised within him—*forever, forever*—and he thrust forward, carried by that elemental force, until his soul swept through him and touched hers at last.

Chapter Twenty-Four

Michael opened her eyes and looked at Diarmid. He lay beside her, bedclothes tangled over his broad chest, long muscled legs half bent as he slept soundly. Feeling the warmth and firmness of him against her hip, she smiled, remembering. She touched the dark mat of hair on his chest, and slid gentle, reverent fingertips along his throat and the rough edge of his jaw. She sighed. An echo of deep pleasures still swirled within her—how long had they been lying here? she wondered.

She rolled to her side and parted the bed curtains. The light confused her at first, for she had lost touch with day or night. She slid from the bed and picked up her chemise, slipping it on, and went to the window to unlatch the shutter.

The rain had stopped. The early sky was pearled pink and silver, and the air that buffeted over her face was moist and fresh. She watched the dawn, shivering, but contented and awed. Below the soaring pastel sky, the ocean rippled toward the island like endless ells of gray-blue silk.

Michael watched the sky and the sea, and felt the sorrow, the loss and fear of the past few years finally slip away from her. A few tears stung her eyes and fell, cleansing gently, and she wiped them away.

She felt a hand on her shoulder and turned as Diarmid sat beside her on the cushioned bench and leaned his shoulders against the wall. He drew her back against his bare chest and wrapped both of them in the thick folds of his plaid. She sighed, closed her eyes, subsided into comfort and support.

"Come back to bed," he murmured beside her ear. He kissed her cheek. "We slept only a little. You need more rest."

She shook her head. "I must check on Sorcha and the babe," she whispered. "Later I will rest. Diarmid—will Sorcha and Mungo know, do you think, that we—?"

She felt him smile, his cheek against hers. "They would not condemn us for it."

She gave a small, self-conscious shrug. "We are not wed."

He sighed, long and low, tightened his arms around her. "In the Highlands, there is a custom that binds two people without benefit of clergy," he said.

She paused, her heart beating oddly fast. What he suggested raised a swirl of excitement and craving through her. She wanted him with her forever, and his soft remark told her the same.

"I know," she said, "handfasting for a year and a day."

He shook his head. "There is another, older, rarely used." His breath lingered on her cheek. "If we declare between us that we take each other in marriage—if we even so much as agree to be wed—then we are, according to ancient Celtic law. In some parts of the Highlands, it is as binding as the words of a priest."

She sat silently in his arms, resting her hands over his, watching the sun fill the sky, watching its light stream upward into the threatening overhead clouds.

"And do you want that?" she asked in a whisper.

He touched his lips to her cheek. "Very much," he murmured. "More than my life."

She watched the sky and thought, realizing that he was free to make this decision. "Ranald told me about Anabel," she said softly. "He knew, and did not tell you. I am sorry, Diarmid."

He sighed. "I mean to deal with Ranald over that matter," he said. "But for now, it is enough to know that I am no longer wed. There is nothing to prevent it—unless you do not want it." He shifted to look at her. "Will you take me as your husband?"

"I will," she whispered. "I do take you, for always."

"And I take you to wife," he murmured, his voice low, safe, strong at her ear. He held her warm against him as the cool dawn breeze fluttered in to touch them. He turned her, propped her chin on his finger, and kissed her so gently that she thought she would melt into a little stream of joy.

She smiled up at him. His eyes held the same silver tint as the dawn. "Is it done, then?" she asked.

He laughed softly. "I think it is," he said. "I think so, Michael mine." She laughed too, tilted her head, accepted the next kiss, deep, exquisite, and slow. "This wedding between us should have happened long ago," he said.

"I would not have wed you then, when you only wanted me to cure your niece and go home again," she said reproachfully.

He grinned, touching his brow to hers. "That was wretched of me," he admitted. "I meant to say that I should have wed you years ago. I was greatly tempted to ask your brother for your hand after I met you. My brother Fionn talked about it too," he added. "What you did on that battlefield those years ago not only saved Angus MacArthur's life, but caused two young men to fall in love with you."

A blush warmed her cheeks. "I never forgot meeting you and Fionn," she said. "I went to Italy two years after that. I doubt I would have accepted a marriage offer from anyone. I was determined to become a physician—because of you, Diarmid."

He smiled, a little sadly, she thought. "And when we met, you were little more than a child. Fionn and I both thought you pure, somehow, holy because of the healing gift. We were certain that you would be-

come a nun, and so each of us gave up the idea as
fancy and married others. Fionn found real love for
himself," he said, looking down. "I, on the other hand,
made a mistake."

She watched him. "Why did you wed her?"

He shrugged, looked out the window, snugged her
back against his chest. "After Brigit's birth—and while
I was recuperating from the wounds to my hand—
Anabel helped to nurse me. She was Ranald's cousin;
I had met her around the time that he and Sorcha
wed. She was beautiful, in a dark, lusty way—and she
was not a shy woman. She came to me at night, lay
with me, helped me forget. I thought I loved her,
thought I adored her. I wed her and brought her into
my home."

Michael listened, trying to understand, although a
dull pang of jealousy went through her. But she reminded herself that her love for Ibrahim had been
vastly different from her love for Diarmid. She must
trust that Diarmid felt the same.

The past was over, done for both of them. Dawn
light filtered over her hands, where they lay on top of
his, and she remembered his vow to her that he
wanted to begin anew. And so let it be, she thought.

"Anabel gave you what you needed then," she said.

"She did, but I discovered that she had a lover—a
lover I now believe she had before she wed me—" He
shook his head. Michael knew that he meant Ranald,
although he would not speak the name. "I was half
crazed with anger. I sent her from Dunsheen, rode to
the bishop's house in Glasgow, petitioned for a divorce. I could not bear her betrayal along with the
rest of the pain I felt inside. The pain she brought me
was the only hurt that I could fight, and so I did."

"The court sent her away?"

He nodded. "They banished her to a convent for
adultery, and made us both take a penitential vow of
chastity. Neither of us could have a lover so long as

the other lived. I wonder now if she kept that vow," he said quietly.

"Harsh, to punish you for her sin," Michael said.

He shrugged. "I wanted punishment of some kind, I think." He drew a long breath. "But she is gone, has been gone for a year. Even my mourning time was over before I learned I was widowed. And I do mourn her. She was not evil. She gave a great deal to me at first. But betrayal, my future stolen from me, no wife, no heirs—that I found unforgivable. Not so now."

"You feel some peace, then."

"So much," he whispered, tucking his chin on her head. "So much, my wife." She smiled, silent and content in his arms.

His scarred left hand lay on the plaid over hers, and she lifted it and kissed it, touching her lips to the old wounds. She heard him draw in his breath, felt his fingers squeeze hers.

Through the quiet, she heard the faint cry of Sorcha's little daughter. She stirred, but Diarmid held her back. "When my sister needs you, she will send someone for you," he said. She relaxed against him and listened to the crying until it stopped abruptly. "Angelica nurses now, I suspect," she said.

"Likely so," he said, holding her tightly. "Michael, when she was born, and when you fought to revive her—I felt as frightened as you, I think. But you had such strength, such caring."

"I did not save her, Diarmid. I nearly lost her."

He kissed her brow. "You kept her alive, helped her grow stronger. That was as beautiful to witness as what came after."

"Her mother's love saved that child and brought her back," she said. "Did you feel it there, filling the room?"

He nodded. "When I came back to the birth chamber with Mungo, Sorcha told me something." His voice was husky and low. "She said that when I opened a window to let the little soul out, an angel must have flown in and brought the miracle."

Tears pooled in her eyes. "Sorcha's name for the babe is more than fitting. We can never understand fully what happened. I do not think we are meant to know. Heaven granted your prayers, Diarmid Campbell." She glanced up at him. "Although the miracle you got was not the one you asked for."

"I have been a fool," he whispered against her cheek, his voice thrumming in her ear. "Forgive me."

She smiled ruefully. "When you came to find me in Perth, you loved Brigit so much that you could not see beyond what she needed most. But you were given another miracle—"

"I know," he said, tucking the plaid around her.

She smiled. "I mean you were given one of divine making, not yours, or mine."

"And a fine one it was," he said lightly. "But that is not all of my foolishness."

She turned her head to look at him, puzzled. "What, then?"

"I have not been honest with you," he said somberly.

Frowning, she watched him. "How so?"

"I should not have waited so long to tell you this," he said. "I love you, *Micheil*. God, how I love you."

She turned then, tears roused once again in her eyes. He took her fully into his arms and kissed her. Sliding her arms around him, Michael felt the first touch of the newborn sunlight as it came through the window.

Later, more loving sated her, mind and body, and revived her. While Diarmid slept, Michael dressed and went down to the kitchen. There she chatted with the cook about Sorcha's child, and ate oats cooked in broth. A little while later, she carried two bowls of porridge up the stairs. In Sorcha's room, she found the new mother asleep with her daughter tucked protectively in her arms.

Mungo slouched in a high-backed chair watching them. He started when Michael entered the room, and sat upright. Michael smiled at him and gave him one of the bowls with a wooden spoon, setting the other down. He grinned sheepishly at her.

"I should not be here, I know," he admitted. "This is a woman's duty, to watch over the newborn and the mother, but Giorsal said she was too exhausted to stay longer, and went to find a corner to nap. I did not want to disturb you and Diarmid last night. . . ." He stopped. Michael blushed. "I just wanted to guard them while they slept. Sorcha refused to let Angelica lie in the cradle alone. I wanted to be certain they were both safe."

Michael smiled. "She would not mind you being here. I was tired too. I am sorry—I should have come back to help sooner."

Mungo stirred the porridge, swallowed some, stirred again. "*Ach,* well," he said. "You had an important matter elsewhere, I think." She saw him smile as he took another mouthful.

Her cheeks grew hotter. "We—we are wed now," she said softly, knowing Diarmid would not mind if she told Mungo first. "We said the vows ourselves." She smiled shyly.

Mungo grinned again. "What a night we have had here, eh? A birth and a wedding. And those vows were none too soon," he teased. She blinked, feeling her whole face go fiery. "Yesterday morning, Diarmid told me about Anabel's death," Mungo went on somberly. "I wondered then how long it would take before he wed you. He has been anxious for it, I think."

She lifted a brow. "Before now?" she asked.

He nodded. "When he came back yesterday, he told me that he had gone to the convent to ask Anabel to finally release him from the marriage. She could have taken holy orders, but had refused to do it. He meant

to beg her if he had to. Did you know that he wanted
to wed you years back?" He glanced at her with a
little smile, then scraped up porridge with his spoon.

"I know," she said. The awareness of Diarmid's
love for her glowed inside of her, a constant sense of
safety and wonder.

Then the baby whimpered and awoke, and Sorcha
opened her eyes and smiled down at her. Michael
shooed Mungo gently from the room, reminding him
that certain tasks were best left to women.

"Three nights," Michael murmured as she stood beside Diarmid. "For three nights you have lingered beside this window, watching the sea. Will you not come
to bed this night, at least?"

He put his arm out to draw her close. "I have had
plenty of rest these last few days," he said, kissing the
top of her head. She turned her head, taking in a
drift of the lavender herb bath, which they had shared
earlier; she smiled at the memory. "That is, when we
have not been occupied with other matters," he
added. She laughed softly and slid her arms around
his waist.

"What makes you so certain that an English ship
will come?" she asked quietly, knowing why he
watched so often by this window.

"Ranald would not keep those birlings hidden in
the sea cave for long without using them," he answered. "They are stocked with weapons and ready to
be manned. And from what I heard from the Campbell chief, King Robert plans to sail toward the Isles
soon. And I would wager that the English will not be
far behind. I suspect Ranald means to help them inter-
cept Bruce's peaceful progress through the Isles."

"But Ranald is not here," she protested. "Would
he not be here if he knew the English were coming?"

"If I am correct, Ranald will return in time to meet
an English ship, and that ship will be carrying extra
English sailors to man the warships he has hidden

away," Diarmid said. "But in fairness to my sister's husband, I could be wrong."

A feeling of cold dread slid through Michael as she listened. She frowned, remembering those awful moments on the cliff when Ranald had made his vile threats. The joy of the last few days had allowed her to forget that danger, but now she could not erase the images, the words, from her thoughts. She had said nothing to Diarmid out of fear of Ranald's reprisal. But now she knew that her silence could create even more danger for Diarmid.

"You are not wrong in your suspicions," she began. "When Ranald was here last, he—he told me that he meant to cast Sorcha aside. He said that he intended to wed me when she was gone."

"The bastard means to gain Glas Eilean for himself," he growled. "I feared this, but thought he would not dare to go so far."

"He wants sons as well, to hold it forever. He is certain that Sorcha cannot give him a son. He thinks that I will."

Diarmid hugged her close. "Did he touch you? I will kill him," he muttered.

She shook her head vehemently. "I am fine. But now that you are my husband, you hold Glas Eilean according to the king's law. Ranald will want revenge for that. He told me that he means to kill you—he said that he did not want you to know of Anabel's death because he feared you would try to wed the widowed owner of Glas Eilean."

"He thinks that I share his wretched goals," Diarmid said. "He has always suspected me of conspiring to take this castle from him. As I took Anabel from him," he added thoughtfully.

"Ranald has a wicked heart, Diarmid. Be careful." Michael clenched the fabric of his shirt anxiously. "Keep away from him. Please. Go back to Dunsheen Castle before he comes back."

Diarmid tightened his arm around her. "You and Sorcha are the ones who should leave," he said grimly.

"Sorcha is not able to travel yet, and the babe is far too fragile to be exposed to winds and cold. Diarmid, I am frightened. Ranald will return soon, and he will surely try to destroy you. Leave, I beg you."

He shook his head slowly. "King Robert and Gavin assigned me to watch Ranald and determine if he was involved in any sort of treason. The king's life and the safety of the Isles could depend on what happens here at Glas Eilean. And I expect my brothers to arrive with my own birling soon. I must stay here." He stared out through the open window at the dark, empty horizon. "And I have some private matters to discuss with MacSween. He will not disgrace my sister, or threaten my wife and live."

Michael frowned. Diarmid's grim tone and hard grip on her shoulder alerted her to the depth of his anger. He would seek his own revenge. "Ranald seems to want to hurt you through the women in your life," she said. "Why?"

"I had not thought of it, but it seems that he does. It may all go back to Anabel," he mused. "I think he might have wed her himself, years past, if they had not been within consanguinity."

"Diarmid, please leave here. Ranald does not trust you. He will blame you for all if any of his plans go wrong."

"Then the blame will be wisely placed. Let him think what he likes, let him try what he likes," he said flatly. "I mean to await these ships and to await him. And believe me, dear girl, Ranald will never see his plans come to be."

"Is that a storm brewing?" Michael asked, glancing through the glass window in Sorcha's bedchamber at the steel-colored sea. Gray daylight streamed into the room, and heavy winds rocked the shutters. "Those clouds are large and dark, and the waves are getting high."

"The sea is high, and the clouds are fast and heavy," Sorcha admitted from her reclining position on the bed. "A gale might blow toward us from the west. But such storms can take days to reach us."

Michael nodded and strummed the harp propped against her shoulder, endeavoring to play a soothing tune. The weather increased the anxious sense that had disturbed her all morning. Her fears had begun last night, while she and Diarmid had spoken of Ranald. Now she could not lose the heavy sense of an approaching threat.

Early that morning, Sorcha had mentioned that Ranald must surely have completed his business in Ireland by now, and would return home soon. Michael could not keep her gaze from straying nervously to the window again and again.

Sorcha began to sing the poetic verses that Gilchrist had written for the melody Michael now played. She watched Sorcha gaze at her infant daughter while she sang. Diarmid's sister had donned a blue woolen gown and rested on the bed against pillows, with Angelica bundled in her arms. Her coppery hair was wound in braids framing her face, and covered by a simple linen veil. Her gray eyes sparkled with happiness. Michael smiled as she played, determined to hide from Sorcha the uneasiness that crawled inside of her.

Diarmid and Mungo had gone out early that day in Diarmid's birling, taking the twenty-six oarsmen from Dunsheen who had, Mungo reported, been complaining about their days of inactivity. Diarmid told Michael that he meant to sail a circuitous route, watching for the approach of any ships.

But in his absence, Michael felt uncertain, as if she stood on the deck of a careening ship. Bonded closely to Diarmid now, she could not bear to be separated from him for long.

Giorsal had been with them earlier to bathe the

child, then drink a good portion of morning ale. She had announced that she had sat the night with mother and child and deserved to rest during the day. Michael felt little comfort in the woman's presence, but once Giorsal had gone, Michael's fears increased. She and Sorcha were alone.

Ranald's guards filled the ground level of the castle, but none of them came to the upper level. The few servants and the cook stayed in the kitchen and lower rooms. Although the cook's young son had brought a breakfast tray for Sorcha, he had scampered away quickly.

Michael continued to play as Sorcha sang and then cooed to her babe. Angelica was wide awake, her dark blue eyes bright and keen as she looked up at her mother. Sorcha and Michael laughed with delight, spoke in wondering tones about her tiny, perfect face, her soft pale hair, her strong cry. Michael managed to forget some of her unease as they talked.

When she stood and set the harp aside, she heard heavy footsteps. Startled, she looked toward the door as it swept open.

Ranald crossed the threshold, hardly glancing at her as he strode toward the bed. Michael's heart pounded in her chest, and she stepped back.

"Where is my daughter?" he demanded. "My cousin Giorsal greeted me in the great hall as I came in from the sea entrance. Let me see the child!" He looked down at his wife and child, unsmiling.

"She is healthy and strong," Sorcha said, peeling back the wrappings to display the child's face. "I have named her *Aingealag,* for that is how she came to us—through the angels."

Ranald reached forward with a finger to touch the child's cheek. "You can give a daughter any name you like," he said.

"I am sorry that I did not give you a son," Sorcha murmured. "I hoped you would be pleased with her health."

"I am pleased enough to have a better outcome this time," Ranald said gruffly. With Sorcha's coaxing, he tentatively lifted the small bundle in his hands, with such gentleness that Michael felt a sense of surprise. She had been afraid of this man, as if he were some demon; now she saw only a man, humbled by the sight of his newborn child. Ranald was silent for a long moment, studying his daughter's face. Then he looked down at Sorcha.

"You are well?" he asked.

"Very well," she replied, smiling.

"Giorsal told me the child nearly died, and that some sort of miracle occurred here," Ranald said. "What did she mean?"

"We owe our daughter's life to Michael," Sorcha said. "Without her skill, Angelica would not have survived."

"Her life is owed to the grace of angels, as Sorcha said," Michael insisted.

"Either way, I thank you for your help," Ranald said. "Much has happened in my absence."

"There is something else too," Sorcha said. "Diarmid was here earlier—he and Mungo are out on the sea today. Ranald, he said that Anabel died a while ago—did you know that?"

Ranald gave the child back to Sorcha, and slid a glance at Michael. "I did not know," he said precisely. "How sad."

Michael narrowed her eyes and watched him warily. She nearly spoke, knowing his bold lie, but Sorcha's tremulous smile kept her silent. But Sorcha's hands, fluttering nervously over the babe's swaddling, revealed Sorcha's own trepidation.

"Now that he is a widower, Diarmid took Michael to wife," Sorcha continued. "They said their own vows, and now are wed by grace of God and their own wishes. Though we will call in a priest as soon as we can, both to oversee their vows again and to baptize the child once more." She looked up at her hus-

band, then glanced quickly at Michael. Her grim gaze
somehow communicated, as effectively as words, that
she had told Ranald about the marriage to deflect his
anger and blame to herself, and away from Michael
and Diarmid.

Ranald grew pale, his mouth a grim line. "Married?" His voice was even and far too smooth. Michael's heart slammed with dread. "Married?" he
asked again.

Michael felt a cold frisson of fear whirl through her,
as if danger radiated from Ranald suddenly. He turned
to look at her with narrowed, darkened eyes. The
stormy anger in his gaze made her gasp silently.

He looked down at Sorcha, hands fisted on his hips.
"What greetings I get when I come home. First a
daughter—by God, if you were to bear a healthy infant, it should have been a son! And then this news—
do you realize what this mans? Michaelmas holds the
charter to Glas Eilean! It reverts to her husband's
possession!"

"Surely the king will grant you property for your
loyalty in holding Glas Eilean," Sorcha protested.

Ranald seemed not to hear her. "Diarmid Campbell
covets whatever I hold! He will not have Glas
Eilean!" he snarled. The child startled in her mother's
arms and began to cry, loud and reedy. Ranald
scowled and spun on his heel to stomp toward the
door. "He will regret his actions against me! You say
he is out on the ocean? My birling can go out again,
no matter how weary my oarsmen claim to be!" He
yanked open the door.

With a frightened glance in Sorcha's direction, Michael ran out into the corridor after him. "Ranald!"
she cried. "Ranald!"

He whirled as she approached. "I will gain my
revenge!"

"You must not do this," she said. "Diarmid has
done nothing malicious to you."

"He wed you," he snarled, and took a long step

toward her. She faltered, backing away as she saw the fierce expression in his dark eyes. As he advanced, she retreated, until her heel struck the wall behind her.

"Our marriage is no threat to you," she said. "Diarmid never thought to harm you when he said vows with me."

"He must have planned all along to wed you and take this castle from me. You have been used." Ranald came closer, until Michael pressed her back against the cold stone wall. "Just as he took Anabel from me!" He hovered over her, his eyes wild, truly frightening. "I have long owed Diarmid revenge for that—and now he has done this! I swear to you, he will not have Glas Eilean!" He took her by the shoulders in a hard grip. "I would not give it up to Gavin Faulkener, and by God I will not let Diarmid Campbell take it by right of marriage. If he had a thousand men at my gates, I would not give up this place! Do you understand?" He shook her violently. "Do you?"

Her head slammed hard against the wall. For an instant, pain swamped her. "I—I understand," she gasped. "But, Ranald—consider what you do."

"I have considered it. I mean to kill Diarmid Campbell. He has made it an easy task. I will find his birling and sink it."

"The *Gabriel* is far too hardy," she said. "You could not destroy it."

"Watch and see," he said, taking her by the upper arm and dragging her along the corridor with him. "Come with me. I want your new husband to see that I now have what he wants most. I have you. Once he sees you with me, he will not dare to fight."

Michael stumbled along after him, resisting, protesting. Ranald growled and slapped her face hard enough to make her fall to one knee. He dragged her to feet, but she pulled away. He snatched at her and got a grip of her linen veil, ripping its folds from her head. Her braids tumbled down, and he grabbed again, yanking her hair, forcing her to come forward.

When she fell toward him, he gripped her arm painfully.

"The seas are rough today," he said as he pulled her down the turning steps toward the sea entrance. "Nearly anything could happen out there, my lady. A challenge for a sturdy boat and a strong master. I know you are eager to go out with me to see just who shall take the day."

Chapter Twenty-Five

"The winds are getting stronger!" Mungo called to Diarmid. "We should turn back!" A cold blast of air tore the words from his mouth, but Diarmid nodded in understanding.

As the birling rolled precariously with the cresting waves, Diarmid cautiously made his way toward the prow, where Mungo stood. He walked between the two rows of oarsmen and stepped over coiled ropes, around barrels, and past the creaking mast spar, where the square canvas sail bellied in the wind.

Mungo pointed toward dark clouds heaped high overhead. "There's a gale coming for certain," he said. "We are foolish to stay out here longer. The *Gabriel* is a fine birling, but her merits will be tested in a gale."

Cold, vigorous air pummeled Diarmid, blowing his hair back from his brow, flattening his shirt against him. He nodded at Mungo. "No point in sailing farther south—no English ship would continue in this direction once they see those clouds."

"Nor will the king be sailing," Mungo added. "He'll wait out the storm in some Highland hall."

Diarmid shouted an order to the man at the tiller to turn the birling back toward Glas Eilean. The man sat on a wooden chest in the stern, gripping the handle of a wooden rudder. He nodded to Diarmid and called out to the oarsmen to veer the boat's course.

Diarmid rested a hand on the high upsweep of the prow, and watched the rocking ocean and its empty horizon. They had headed south that morning out of

Glas Eilean's sea entrance, looking for ships that might approach from English waters, but so far had sighted only a few fishing boats.

An hour, heading northeast, brought them close enough to see the high, pale cliffs of Glas Eilean, crowned by its castle of golden stone. Soon he would see Michael again and hold her in his arms. The desolate, wild ocean and the chill winds made him long for her comfort, and the warmth of a fire and hot food.

He smiled to himself, remembering the voyage he and Michael had taken from Dunsheen to Glas Eilean. Much had happened since that day to change his life. He was not the same man he had been even a few weeks ago. The love he felt for Michael, and the new measure of contentment that she had brought into his life, had cleansed him, strengthened him. Only his anger toward Ranald MacSween lingered, bitter and heavy.

A sudden blast whipped past him, and he looked up at the sail, now overfilled. If the winds grew stronger, the sail would have to come down or the birling could be blown off course. He turned to signal a few of the men to pick up the oars they had shipped earlier. The winds and strong currents carried the ship northeast too swiftly; unless the winds slowed, every hand was needed to prevent them from being swept past Glas Eilean.

He turned as he heard Mungo shout, and saw him point toward the island of Glas Eilean, closer now. Diarmid saw a birling coming from that direction, sleek and graceful, though its sides dipped dangerously as it cut recklessly across the wind. Several pairs of oars rose and dipped in a steady rhythm. Diarmid narrowed his eyes.

"That's Ranald!" he called to Mungo. "What the devil—"

"By the saints!" Mungo shouted. "Look there, in the stern!"

Diarmid had already seen. Hunched low in the stern

of the other birling was a small form with pale golden hair. After another moment, Diarmid saw her face and slender shoulders above the rim of the hull. He swore aloud.

Mungo stepped close to Diarmid. "Knowing how little your lady loves sailing, I doubt she is a willing passenger."

"Ranald is a fool," Diarmid growled, watching the birling speed toward them. Even from this distance, he could see that some of the men aboard the other birling were armed with bows and arrows.

"Jesu! He's come in pursuit of us," Mungo said.

"Tell six men to drop oars and take up arms. There are bows and arrows in those chests over there. I thought to be prepared in case the English attacked us. I never expected this."

"But Michael is on board! She could be hurt!"

"I have no other choice!" Diarmid bellowed. His fear mounted rapidly, heart pounding harder than the helmsman's drum. The thought of endangering Michael cut into him like a blade. Yet if he did not order a counterattack, Ranald would kill his men or himself, even sink his boat, while Michael watched.

"I am sorry," Mungo said quietly. "I know you have no choice." He walked toward mid-ship, calling out the orders.

Diarmid turned back, squinting as he watched. Several moments passed before Mungo returned to hold out a bow and a thick bunch of arrows. Diarmid took them wordlessly. Grim anger filled him, as frigid and dangerous as the coming gale. His left hand trembled, and he made a fist, pounding it white-knuckled against the prow. Then he swore vehemently as he saw Michael lurch forward to grip the low-lying rim of the hull.

"She's sick," he said.

"She's a poor sailor," Mungo said. "Ranald will have a task of it if he wants her to do anything but hang over the side."

Diarmid crammed the arrows into his belt. "At least she'll stay low and out of the way." He never shifted his gaze from the birling that rode closer through the waves. Michael curled in the stern, her hair glinting bright and blowing loose, her face deathly pale. She looked up then, and seemed to see him. Even at this distance, he could tell that her eyes were filled with fear. She raised a limp hand and gestured to him to flee.

His gut wrenched, and his heart thundered as he watched Michael. The need to take her from that birling burned within him like a fire, capable of consuming his reason. He drew a deep breath to summon control and glanced away; if he looked at her longer, he might act too impulsively. He needed his battle sense intact just now.

MacSween stood in the prow of his ship, glaring defiantly at Diarmid, still too far away to shout or waste an arrow shot. "Eighteen men," Diarmid told Mungo. "Seven of them with bows held ready."

"But that is a twenty-six–oar trading boat," Mungo said. "He does not even have enough men to man the oars in these winds. He may attack us, but he cannot defeat us!"

"Pray that you are right, my friend," Diarmid said grimly. He nocked an arrow in his own bow, and held it down and ready. "Tell the men to avoid striking Michael once I give the order to shoot."

The open oarlocks in the stern of the birling spouted cold salt water in her face every time the hull dipped. Michael wiped the moisture away weakly and struggled to resist the awful sensations roiling in her stomach and head. Dizzy, ill, and deeply frightened, she gripped the carved rim and thought longingly, ridiculously, of Diarmid's slice of dried ginger.

She raised her head, shoving her hair out of her eyes, and watched Diarmid's birling approach. The high, graceful prow and the flaring sides undulated over the wild swells, coming ever closer. She saw Dunsheen's insigne, a streak of red lightning, clearly marked on the ballooned sail. Twenty-six oars stirred the waves in a fast cadence.

For a moment, her dazed mind saw a great dragon flying forward over the wild seas, the high-curved prow its head, the sail its wings, the oars its legs. And standing beside the head of that dragon, she saw Diarmid, tall and wide-shouldered in the prow, his hair tossed back, his plaid and shirt flattened against him, his stance unyielding, his gaze fierce. She felt the pure force of his presence as keenly as if he stood beside her.

Watching him, she drew strength from the sight. She roused herself enough to raise her hand and signal him to turn back, beg him to turn back. But he looked away as if he had not seen—or chose to ignore—her attempt to warn him.

A series of rolling waves pitched Ranald's birling violently up and smacked it down again, over and over. Michael cried out, grabbed for support on a free oar locked in an oar hole, and felt her stomach heave. She leaned over the side as the boat rocked precariously in a trough, and was drenched in wash.

She looked up, wiping her streaming hair back, to see Ranald standing over her. "Get up," he said. "Come with me." He leaned down and yanked her to her feet.

Weakened by seasickness, she wobbled and sank back down. Ranald grabbed her under the arms and dragged her the length of the boat toward the prow.

"Stand there and let Dunsheen see you," he said, pushing her forward. "I want him to know that I have what he most wants."

She gripped the flared edge of the prow with shaking hands. Diarmid stared at her, motionless, fearsome. Ranald stood behind her and held her shoulders. She jerked away from his grip and stood on her own, refusing to let her legs give way.

342   *Susan King*

Wind shipped at her, cold and violent, and the heavy beat of the oarsman's drum thundered through her body. But she stood firm and straight, remembering that Diarmid had once told her to stand and sway in rhythm with the motion of the boat; look far out to sea, he had said that day. She widened her stance as she gripped the edge of the prow, and lifted her head high.

But she could look no farther than Diarmid. His gaze was like a beacon. She held herself proud and fearless, for she did not want him to fear on her behalf. A fountain of love poured forth from her, her own heart streaming out a silver light to touch his. That invisible strand of feeling anchored her to him, her stalwart rock. He supported her with his gaze, with his steadfastness, with his love.

She felt the illness begin to diminish, as if their locked gazes produced a healing, sustaining force. Ranald grabbed her arm, but she raised her chin, squared her shoulders, firmed her back. He let go. She stepped forward away from him.

Diarmid's birling rocked on the waves, each rise and drop bringing him closer to her—three hundred yards, two hundred, half that. The distance lessened rapidly as Diarmid's oarsmen pulled, despite strong currents and merciless winds.

Behind her, Ranald shouted a command. She turned and saw his men raise their bows, saw the arrows fly upward, saw them arc in the sky and fall like a hail of thorns toward Diarmid and his men. She leaped toward Ranald, as if she could stop the order by pulling at him. He knocked her away and lifted his own bow, calling out again. Another volley of arrows lifted on the wind.

The world fell into mad chaos around her—careening ship, howling winds, shining arrows. The boat lurched, and she stumbled toward the prow. The sickness came over her again. But she could not give into weakness now. She clung to the rim of the birling and looked for Diarmid.

He was in the prow still, gesturing to her; she thought he mimicked pulling something over his head. Then he lifted his bow, his men gathering on the deck to do the same. Michael frowned and turned, then noticed several round targe shields lashed to the inside of the hull. She snatched one loose and hunkered down, pulling it over her to protect her head and back.

Peering out, she saw Diarmid lift his arm to signal his men. He aimed his own bow toward Ranald's birling, and they shot in unison. High winds knocked the released arrows awry, no matter how true the aim. Many fell in the sea, but most hurtled toward the birling, smacking into wood, ripping the sail, sinking into flesh. She heard someone scream out horribly. Gasping, she crouched under the targe as arrowheads struck it noisily.

Ranald's men fired another volley. Michael peeked out from under the shield, frightened, confused, never sure which way to turn, to move, to glance. The rocking of the sea knocked her to her side, tossed her, rolled her around on the slippery, narrow deck. She staggered drunkenly to her knees, snatched at the shield's handgrip, and curled like a snail in its shell.

Arrows thwacked around her, and the winds and sea howled. Ill, terrified, she sank so deeply into misery that the careening world became oddly normal to her. She scrambled to her hands and knees, hanging on to the shield, and crawled forward with one goal: she had to see Diarmid.

Lifting her head, she peered out. The daylight had faded rapidly, darkened by heavy clouds. She felt the sting of a few cold raindrops on her hand. Glancing around, she saw Diarmid's birling, but he was out of sight; unable to find him with a quick glance, she rose higher to look again.

Hands snatched her around the waist. "Come here, mistress," one of the oarsmen said, pulling her backward. "MacSween wants you. He's been arrow shot. This way, if you will."

She half crawled after the Highlander toward midship. Ranald sat propped against the mast, two arrows protruding from his body, one sticking in his lower back, the other bloodying the front of his tunic.

"Take them out," Ranald gasped, his face green-tinged. "Repair the wounds. I have a task to do."

"You have only revenge in mind." She knelt beside him. "Perhaps your injuries will stop you now, if nothing else can."

"Pull the arrows out!" he snapped, through gritted teeth.

Tightening her jaw, she did not reply, reaching out to test the arrow in his back. The oarsmen who had fetched her, an older man, large and muscular, sat beside her. She asked for a knife and cloth, and within moments he had produced both, ripping his own shirt beneath his dirty plaid and handing her his sharp dirk.

She slit into Ranald's thick dark woolen surcoat and pulled it away from his back, then cut through the brown serge tunic and the linen shirt beneath, exposing part of his smoothly muscled torso. The wound in his back was cleanly made, the arrow bed shallow.

She steeled herself, paused, and yanked out the iron tip. Ranald screamed and jerked. Michael pressed wadded cloth against the wound and wrapped a strip around his waist to hold it.

Then she carefully peeled away the bloodied cloth over his abdomen. The second arrow had penetrated deep into his belly. She frowned; this wound was far more dangerous than the first. Directing the Highlander beside her to lay Ranald flat, she cut his shirt more thoroughly and examined the wound. Then she pressed a cloth over it, careful not to pull at the arrow shaft.

The need to help a wounded man, no matter his identity, somehow righted the reeling world. Concentrating on her work, already adapting to the chaos that surrounded her, she nearly forgot her fears, though arrows struck down in a wicked, whipping hail. She propped the shield against her upright back and ducked down, feeling strangely calm now that she had purpose.

"Let me help you, mistress," the old man said beside her. "I can pull that arrow out, or bandage a wound if need be."

"What is your name?" she asked.

"Domhnull," he said. "Domhnull MacSween. Ranald's cousin."

She peered at the wound as he spoke. "Domhnull, I need more cloth." She heard him tear his shirt, felt the warm linen as it dropped in her lap. She grabbed it up, discarding the reddened one she held. "One more favor," she said. "Tell me if you see Diarmid Campbell on the other galley."

The man craned his head. "I see him," he said after a moment. "He's in the stern, bent over one of his men."

"Is he unharmed?" she asked.

"I cannot tell. Wait, there is blood on his shirt. He seems well enough in spite of it. *Ach*!" Domhnull swore viciously as an arrow narrowly missed his leg. "I need one of those shields too," he joked as she leaned low beneath her shield to work on Ranald. "What a brave woman, without fear. Serene as an angel, you are."

Michael smiled grimly at the irony. She had never been more terrified in her life.

Ranald raised his head and gripped her arm. "Take the second arrow out too. Now," he said hoarsely.

"Ranald, the tip may have cut through the intestine," she said. "You will do better if I leave it for now. It acts as a plug. We must go back to Glas Eilean so that I can tend to it properly."

"It cannot be that bad," he rasped. "I feel strong enough to finish this fight. Take it out and bandage

me up." He gestured toward one of his men. "Keep
shooting!" he yelled. "Do not stop! Do not let him
get away!" He gritted his teeth and groaned.

"Ranald, we must go back," she said. "You could
die."

He turned a ferocious gaze on her. "I will not die
until Diarmid Campbell pays for what he has done."

"And what of his lady, MacSween?" the old man
asked suddenly. Michael turned in surprise. "Do not
forget that she saved the life of your child days ago.
You owe her for that. And now she is trying to save
your own hide. Learn forgiveness from her, man. Give
the order to cease and turn back."

Ranald glared at him. "I need no advice from you,
Domhnull," he snarled, then raised his hand. "Shoot!"
he screamed. "Use flame arrows!"

Michael looked up in alarm. Two of Ranald's men
had wrapped oiled cloth around the ends of their
arrows, and now lit them with a flint. Michael
screamed in protest, wrenching around to get up. The
men shot the flaming missiles, one after another. The
arrows streaked red and orange across the darkening
sky.

Domhnull grabbed her. "You cannot stop this. He
is truly crazed, I suspect." He pulled her back. "Protect yourself."

She sobbed out as she watched the flames bite into
the square sail of Diarmid's birling. Another hit inside
the boat, and still more hit the sail. She watched the
canvas catch fire slowly, smoking heavily, until orange
flames erupted around the jutting tip of the mast and
began to blaze along the lines.

She saw Diarmid beat out a small fire at the base
of the mast, saw him look upward toward the higher
flames, with no way to reach them. The old man
pulled at her arm.

"Come away, now," he said gruffly. "I do not want
you to watch your man die. A fire on a birling is a

serious thing. You may have to be stronger than you have ever been before."

She curled forward in agony. Domhnull laid a hand on her shoulder. Within moments, she felt wet drops on her hands and face, on her arms and back. "Rain!" she cried, looking up as the towering dark clouds unleashed a torrent. "Rain!" she sobbed gratefully, heedless of the downpour that soaked her.

Domhnull grinned. "Another miracle for you. I heard you helped bring one in for Lady Sorcha's child. You must have angels following you, lady." He laughed, gap-toothed and whiskery, rain streaming down his face. "Your man will be fine if he can get his ship to land as fast as possible. Ranald's men will fire no more volleys. The rain has ended this battle."

She nodded, tears sliding down her face, and saw through the rain that Diarmid searched for her, his hand shielding his brow, his shoulder reddened. She waved to him frantically, trying to plead to him to go back. Mungo stepped over to him then and pointed as if telling Diarmid something dire.

Finally Diarmid turned away, and the smoking birling moved obliquely to maneuver around. Michael watched the oars lift and dip rapidly as the vessel pulled away into the sheeting rain. She bit her lip and wiped the wetness from her face.

"They will be back," Domhnull said. He gripped her arm, steadying her on the undulating deck. "I vow it pains him deep to leave you. But I am here, lady, if you need me. I saw MacSween's treatment of you. Believe me, I did not plan to let it continue."

She nodded, his reassurance that Diarmid would be back for her repeating like a litany in her mind. Determined to make certain of that, she turned to Ranald.

"Diarmid is returning to Glas Eilean," she said. "Enough of this. We must go back too."

"I did not win," he growled, wincing as he placed a hand on his stomach.

"You did not," she said.

"Pull out the arrow," he barked.

She shook her head. "When we return to the castle, it will be done properly. Tell your men to turn the galley around."

"Remove the arrow now," he said, grasping the shaft with a bloody hand, "or I will do it myself. I am not done with Diarmid Campbell. I will turn back and pursue him. Pull it out and bandage me. I need to take command of this vessel."

She sank to her knees and placed her hands over his. "Stop. You will kill yourself."

"Let go," Ranald growled.

"Ranald," she said. "Remember that you will need a skillful surgeon if you hope to survive this wound. Leave Diarmid in peace, I beg you."

He snarled incoherently, tried to yank, and groaned.

Michael pressed her hands over his to prevent him from pulling out the arrow tip. As if a flame sparked unexpectedly, she felt heat flow from her hands into his, joined around the shaft. She sat in a rocking ship in the aftermath of a battle, in the cold biting rain and howling wind, and felt a warm, loving peace descend into her.

She gazed at Ranald and saw into his brown eyes, where fear lurked, where his needs were hidden. Sympathy for him, a mute understanding, filled her without words. Heat poured through her hands, and she felt her fear, her anger toward him dissolve.

Ranald stared at her and slowly released his hands. "What—what are you doing?" he asked. "The heat—the pain is gone." He struggled to sit up. "What did you do?"

"Helped you, Ranald," she said quietly. "Only that."

"Jesu," he breathed, staring at her. "By all the saints." He shook his head as if in a daze.

"We must go back," Michael said.

"We must," he said. "I feel stronger now. I am not done with Diarmid."

"You are a fool, Ranald MacSween," Domhnull snapped. "Think of what you owe this woman! You have a daughter now—think of that child, if no one else!"

Ranald rubbed a hand over his face. "I have a daughter, but none to carry on my name."

"There are plenty to carry on the name of Mac-Sween," Domhnull said. "Because of this woman, you have a child to carry on your blood."

Ranald hesitated, looking at Michael, looking at his elder cousin. Then he grimaced, grabbed the arrow shaft, and tore it from his abdomen. Screaming out, he fell sideways. Domhnull leaned forward to lay him down.

"Ranald—" Michael grabbed his arm. "Go easy. Let me see." Domhnull handed her a cloth and she wadded it against the gushing wound. "Now he will need Diarmid Campbell's skill for certain," she said quietly to Domhnull. "I cannot repair such serious damage alone."

"I must have my satisfaction against Diarmid," Ranald gasped out. "You do not know how much he has taken from me."

"Never meaning to, Ranald." She held the wadded cloth against him, tried to summon the heat, the power again. "Never meaning to."

Around her, she heard shouts. Men scrambled to take up the oars, screaming to one another through the furious sound of the storm. Domhnull turned. "Seek safety, lady," he said. "Hold on to the mast."

"What is it?" she cried.

"The currents have carried us northeast, well past Glas Eilean and Isla. Look there." He pointed through the curtain of rain. "Those mountains are on the Isle of Jura."

"Jura!" Ranald shouted. "How far up its coast are we?"

"Too far," Domhnull replied. "Too far!"

"What is wrong?" Michael cried, alarmed.

"Listen!" Domhnull shouted above the deafening howl.

Diarmid had said that to her once, at sea. *Listen.* She did, and heard an agonized roar, like a monster caught in the deep, and remembered what Diarmid had told her then. No storm alone could make that hideous, black-hearted sound.

Ranald lurched to his feet, clutching his belly. "The currents have driven us toward Jura's northern channel. We must turn—*row!*" he screamed. "*Row!* Your lives depend on it. Turn back!"

Michael looked at Domhnull, dreading, knowing.

"The whirlpool," he said. "It has come to life, just ahead."

Chapter Twenty-Six

"The *Gabriel* can be repaired," Diarmid said as he sat heavily on a wooden chest. "Her mast is partly burned, the sail is gone, and she has a few leaks. But we made it back whole, with all the men aboard."

"We can ask for no more than that," Mungo grunted.

"We can ask for Michael's safety," Diarmid said, and winced as he shifted his arm. The arrow wound seared like fire whenever he moved his shoulder; he knew it had cut deep into the muscle. He had removed the arrow and bound it tightly, knowing that would have to do.

Mungo nodded. He looked up. "This was a brilliant idea, Dunsheen," he pronounced. "What a fine birling this is. Look at her—shining new, forty oars, even filled with provisions and weapons! We lack for nothing, except enough men to man these oars." He grimaced. "Twenty-six will have to do. Twenty-eight, with the two of us rowing. But in a storm we need a full crew."

"We have no choice but to try," Diarmid said grimly. "We must get Michael from off that birling."

"Row!" Mungo called. "Row! To the northeast, with the winds, in the direction of the storm!"

Diarmid placed a hand on the prow of Ranald's proud new galley, propped a foot on a low wooden chest, and watched silently as his oarsmen slid her out of the sea cave and headed for the heart of the storm.

Despite furious winds and sporadic rain showers,

the voyage took far less time than earlier, when his men had taken the limping, damaged *Gabriel* back to Glas Eilean, leaving her in the hidden sea cave. The new birling rode the waves like a dolphin, low and sleek and built for speed and endurance.

"Not even your own forty-oared *White Heather* is as fine and fast as this one," Mungo said. "I wonder if she has a name. If she were mine, I would name her *Sea Dragon*."

"A fitting name. Someday you will have one like her."

Mungo shrugged and looked ahead. "Surely Ranald saw the foolishness of staying out in this storm, and is turning back."

"He will, if only to pursue me," Diarmid replied. "We will meet them soon." He scanned the wild, choppy seas. When several minutes passed, then longer, he darted grim, worried glances at Mungo. No birling appeared on the horizon.

"Perhaps we veered in the wrong direction," Mungo said. "I did not think they would have gone this far north."

"The currents are wickedly strong," Diarmid said, watching the rushing waves that pushed the birling relentlessly forward. He looked to the side, and saw the vague conical shapes of mountains through the drizzle. "Jura, so soon? These currents are more powerful than I thought. Together with the gale winds, they could drive a ship far off its course—" He frowned suddenly, and ran toward the prow. "Mungo—the currents will push us toward the channel at the north end of Jura!"

"*Ach Dhia!*" Mungo stepped beside him. "It cannot be!"

"Do you not hear the proof of it? Listen to that roar!"

"But that sound can be heard for miles. The whirlpool's roar does not mean that we are in imminent danger."

"Look at those mountains, man! We are heading for the channel for certain!"

Mungo swore. "Do you think Ranald's galley was blown as far northeast as this? Our *Sea Dragon* handles well, but no galley can resist a storm like this."

"If Ranald's vessel was blown toward the whirlpool, pray God we catch them before they go down," Diarmid said.

Mungo frowned. "Listen. It is close, too close. We will have to choose whether to risk going ahead, or to turn back."

One of the oarsmen shouted as the scream of the whirlpool rose over the winds. Around him, others began to take up the cry to turn around.

"Row on!" Diarmid shouted. "Row ahead!"

Mungo grabbed his arm. "Are you a madman as well? We have to turn back while we can!"

"Michael may have gone this way!" Diarmid said. "We can veer toward Jura and leave those who do not wish to take the risk. But I will find her!" He glared at Mungo. "If she is at the bottom of the sea, by God, I will find her!"

He turned away, his fists clenched, his heart slamming. Michael hated water. For a moment, it was all he could think about. She was frightened of the water. He had to find her.

"Too late," Mungo said behind him. "The currents have us now. We have no choice but to go where the sea takes us."

"Tie down what you can!" Diarmid shouted, turning. "Dowse the sail! The wind will rip it to shreds!" He scrambled to help his men, then found a chest by an oar hole and sat, taking up the oar. "Pull!" he screamed, dragging on the oar with all of his strength. They had to resist the force of the eddy, or die within its grasp.

The roar increased steadily in furor. Ahead, Diarmid saw a swirling mass of water where currents came from two directions to collide. He felt a chill of fear unlike anything he had ever known. He had heard the heavy moan of Corrievreckan before, from a distance. But no one ever risked negotiating through this channel at the height of a storm. Now the enormous power of the sea carried their sleek galley there, tossing her like a fragile toy.

The sight that lay beyond the crashing waves was terrible in its power, a gaping, black, monstrous mouth. The bellowing of the vortex was deeper, grander, louder, more horrifying than Diarmid could ever have imagined.

Mungo sat down across from him, taking up another empty oar. Twenty-eight men strained with every measure of strength that they had, joining together in a massive effort to hold the galley away from the mouth of the whirlpool.

What Diarmid saw next turned his soul to ice. Ranald's birling swept around the edges of the revolving current, rocking precariously as she went. In the mix of spray and rain that nearly obscured his vision, Diarmid sighted Michael.

She clung to the mast with two men, her hair whipping out in the wind. Diarmid's heart sank, broke. He cried out from his gut in anguish. Ranald's birling was caught in the wild whirl, and no power of mankind would stop its course.

He prayed then, muttering in anger, in terror, in pleading as he rowed, rolling Latin prayers and Gaelic chants off his tongue as if he could wring magic from them. His thoughts centered on Michael, then expanded to beg for all of their lives, nearly fifty men and one woman between the two galleys.

He prayed like a martyred saint, but he rowed as if the demons of hell had hold of the oar with him, sweeping it with superhuman effort through the water. If they could just stay outside the edges of the pool, they would not be sucked into the heart of the black well that sang for their souls.

And if they could stay out of it themselves, they

might be able to throw lines to Ranald's ship—might be able, through sheer strength, to pull it back from the maelstrom. If they had an anchor of some sort—he looked around anxiously.

Then he saw a rock behind them, glistening like onyx in the storm, jutting several feet above the cresting waves. He dove from his seat and took up a coil of rope. Swinging the line, he tossed it. Missed. He swung again, tossed, only to see the line swallowed by the sea.

Beside him, in front of him, he saw two of his men grab lines and throw them toward the rock. Diarmid hauled back the rope and looped it, swung it, threw it again, though the effort seemed to tear his wounded shoulder from its socket.

His line caught, held. Another man's line snagged the rock as well. Diarmid and the oarsman grinned at one another, then fixed the lines around the wide mast.

Running to the stern of the boat, Diarmid took up the tiller, swerving the rudder to steer away from the spinning grip of the water. The moor lines held to the anchoring rock, holding the galley back. Diarmid ran the length of the slippery deck toward the prow and scanned through the rain and the spraying, foaming waves for Ranald's birling.

They were still upright, still trapped in the swirling current, following it helplessly. Diarmid saw a man on board Ranald's galley attempt to toss a line toward the other birling, but the rope was too short. Diarmid turned.

"Let out some slack!" he shouted. "We need to go closer!"

He heard no protest. Two men ran to unwind some of the length of the mooring lines, allowing the galley to swoop over the water, closer to the lip of the vortex.

"If the waves were not so fierce—" Mungo shouted. He hollered a sound of inspiration and lifted one of the casks of almond oil high. Knocking it against the side of the boat, he smashed its end. Diarmid watched in amazement as his friend poured the oil into the water.

Running across the deck to peer over the side, Diarmid saw the effect: the waves quieted noticeably, then swirled again. He picked up another cask of oil, broke it open, poured it into the foam. Mungo did the same, until they had emptied several casks into the surrounding water. Diarmid looked down in astonishment.

The waves crashed into the side of his birling more slowly, cresting with less strength. He bellowed with joy, and heard Mungo scream like an elated lunatic.

"How did you know that would work?" Diarmid shouted.

"An old fisherman on Glas Eilean told me the trick!" Mungo yelled. "I have spent a good deal of time on that island, with little to do but talk to folk!" Diarmid grinned, and they both turned to take hold of ropes and toss them toward Ranald's floundering galley.

Throwing again and again without success, they had to wait at one point as Ranald's boat circled the far side of the maelstrom and came back. Diarmid held his breath every second that the vessel was out of reach, never taking his gaze from the pale, slight form clinging to the mast.

The water would soon swallow them into its terrible depths. Michael tightened her arms around the mast until her whole body ached with the strain. She would never see Diarmid again, never feel his arms around her, or hear his voice at her ear. Sobbing, she leaned against the post, drained, flattened there by the force of the winds.

Beside her, Ranald clung too, so weak that Domhnull held him up with one large arm while he circled the mast with the other. During the endless moments while they circled the upper edge of the whirlpool, Michael had first seen Diarmid's galley—a new one, a larger one, sleek as a sea eagle—riding the outer lip of the vortex.

She could hardly bear to look toward him now. The sight of his galley, so out of reach, so beyond her hope, hurt her unutterably. She did not want to see his stricken face as she spun away from him again. She did not want him to watch her die.

Soon the whirlpool would pull them lower, and there would be no prayer of survival. They would go down, down, gripping frail wood, until the endless water sucked them into its soul. Diarmid could not stop it, yet Michael knew he would try, and she feared his death as well.

She bowed her head against the force of the rain and wind, listening to the scream of the monstrous force beneath them, and prayed, imploring heaven to show mercy to all of them.

Ranald gripped her arm. "Look," he said hoarsely. "Look there. Your man still comes for you. He does not give up."

She raised her head and saw the other birling riding close, saw the line snake out, saw it fall limp into the swelling water. Diarmid threw the line again.

"He comes for all of us," she called back.

"But we are doomed," Ranald groaned. "Michael— I want to—I need to thank you. For my daughter. She will live on after me."

She stared at him. He looked away, rain and water washing over his contorted face.

Moments later, one of Ranald's oarsmen shouted as he grasped and held the writhing loop that crossed from the other birling. Several men scrambled to help him hold the line.

A small hope of salvation, fragile and unsure, sparked within her as she watched the men struggle. She moved away from the mast as they wound the rope to its base. Falling to her knees, she crawled toward the stern to hold on, and watched, through mist and rain, as Diarmid's men pulled and strained to draw them from the grip of the current.

A crest of water surged upward and flung the galley back, closer to the other boat, so blessedly close suddenly that both hulls knocked together for an instant. Michael could almost reach out and touch the prow. Behind her, a few men stumbled over to join her, but then shouted for the others to stay back. The galley was beginning to tip, her prow rising high, her stern dipping.

Diarmid's birling bumped theirs again. She turned, saw him, and cried out. He was so close that he could have grabbed her, but the two hulls kept sliding apart. He tossed another line over the gap. Michael leaped for it herself, missing it.

Ranald and Domhnull came toward the stern, Ranald's weakness so severe now that he could barely stand upright. He fell to his knees on the slick deck and looked at her silently, his eyes wild, his face gray. She laid a hand on his shoulder as the men around them worked to release the galley from the hell of the whirlpool.

Another rope whipped out, and Domhnull caught it this time, his massive strength sufficient to draw them nearer yet to the other boat. Diarmid leaned over the side, arms extended.

"Michael!" he yelled. "Michael!" He reached toward her.

The vortex roared then, impossibly louder, and a new blast of wind tore between the two boats. Domhnull lurched, strained, held on as if he were made of oak. Diarmid's oarsmen did the same, but the current threatened to devour them all.

Ranald grabbed Michael's arm with surprising strength. She looked at him, terror resurging. The prow of the other galley slammed against their stern, swept away, slammed again. Diarmid reached out, shouting.

Ranald lifted Michael and dragged her toward the undulating, uncertain gap between the two boats.

"Go!" he screamed. "Go to him! I owe you this!"

He held her legs until Diarmid's hands closed around her. When he grabbed her under the arms, Ranald let go.

She fell against Diarmid, gasping. His arms closed around her like a benediction, a moment of inexpressible bliss. Then he released her and turned back to help the others.

Michael stepped out of the way and fell hard to her knees as a wave rocked the deck. She stayed low and watched as Mungo and two other oarsmen crowded into the bow to help the others come over the side. The lines that anchored Diarmid's boat to the rock creaked and stretched, and the ropes connecting the two boats tightened, while the whirlpool sucked and screamed. But within minutes, men crowded the deck of the newer galley.

"The ropes are dragging us into the eddy!" Mungo shouted. "The mooring to the rock will not hold against the pull!"

"The rock will not let us go," Diarmid replied calmly. He turned back toward the deserted ship as Michael watched. She gasped when she saw Domhnull still standing in the stern with Ranald lifted in his arms.

Michael bolted to her feet and pushed through the cluster of oarsmen. "Come on!" she yelled. "Come on! Domhnull! Ranald!"

Domhnull looked directly at her as if time and the furious vortex were no threat. "He is dead." She barely heard him over the roar of the black, bottomless well. "He is dead."

She sagged downward in sudden shock, grasping the side of the boat, staring in disbelief. Diarmid moved swiftly.

"Push him toward us!" Together, between his strength and Domhnull's, Diarmid pulled the limp

body of his kinsman into his arms. He laid him on the
deck and turned to Domhnull, grasping his wrists to
yank him forward. Domhnull leaped, fell to the tipping deck, and rose to his feet.

Michael felt dazed and empty, without thought,
without sensation. She watched as Diarmid and another man cut the ropes, watched as Ranald's birling
spun away and disappeared, prow first, into the mouth
of the whirlpool. Diarmid watched too, then turned
away quickly to test the strength of the ropes that
held fast to the rock. She staggered to her feet and
moved toward Ranald's body, limp and drenched on
the floor of the boat.

She sat beside him and lifted his cold hand, so pale,
drained of blood and life, and sat with him as if in
vigil. He had been grateful for his new daughter—
Sorcha would want to know that. And she would want
to know that he had saved Michael at the cost of his
own strength. The change in his withered heart had
been profound, and too late. She felt hot tears slip
down her cheeks. Someone tossed a cloak toward her,
and she covered him with its damp folds.

Around her, men pulled at the oars, strained on the
ropes, drawing the galley ever backward toward the
steadfast rock, until the lip of the vortex released them
at last. She watched in mild astonishment as Mungo
and Diarmid emptied casks into the water, and heard
them shout victoriously as the birling edged around,
veering, dipping, turning. Finally, the prow faced outward. Diarmid ran toward the two lines that anchored
them to safety and sliced them through.

He shouted orders to row, and sat down to grab an
oar and pull mightily with the others. Full forty men
now worked together to free the boat from the wild
grip of the water.

Michael sat beside Ranald, oddly feeling no ocean
sickness, no fear. As the wind tore past her and the
rain lessened around her, she bowed her head and put
a trembling hand over her face.

A pair of hands, strong, scarred, loving, took her then, lifted her. Diarmid wrapped her in the circle of his arms and held her fiercely. He murmured words she did not catch, his lips warm and infinitely gentle where they touched her brow, her cheeks, her mouth. "You taste of salt," he said, half laughing.

She lifted her face and held onto him, her rock, her comfort, her joy. The sorrow and bliss that mingled within her was complex, poignant, beautiful; unable to dissect her feelings with inaccurate words, she stayed silent and held him tightly. His hands dipped and swirled over her, pulling her close. She rested her head against him with a sigh.

Finally she spoke. "Ranald . . . Ranald saved me. He was arrow shot through the gut. I cannot bear to think—"

"You did not cause his death," Diarmid said. "He gave his life freely for you—just as I would have done."

She sank against him, moved beyond words, and held him.

"Come, my girl," he said after a moment. "If you are not too weary, I have a task for you." He took her hand and led her toward a chest beside an unmanned oar.

"I think it's time you learned a little of rowing," he said, and sat her down on the chest. "Just now we need every hand at work to take us home."

She eyed the oar doubtfully, and placed her hands around it, pulling. It hardly budged. "Can I do this alone?" she asked. "Is there a skill to it?"

Diarmid sat down beside her. "Try," he said. "That is the skill. Just try."

She pushed, then pulled, and felt the paddle shove through the water slightly. She smiled, pleased, repeated the motion.

"Good," Diarmid said. "You will be my finest sailor yet."

She laughed outright at that. Diarmid rounded his

long fingers over the oar and pulled with her. "Together now," he murmured. "Always together, and we can do whatever we must."

She smiled and moved in an easy rhythm with him, and the boat surged toward home.

Epilogue

"A wedding," Michael said, "is joyous enough, but to have more than one, together with a christening and the New Year—it is almost too much happiness to bear!" She laughed in delight and looked up at Diarmid.

"Too much, Michael mine?" he murmured, taking her hand. "Not at all." Too much and not enough, he thought, watching her; never enough. The sparkle in her summer-sky eyes, the moonlight glint in her hair, made the gleam of the gold-and-jeweled brooch at her shoulder seem dull indeed. He would never have his fill of looking at her, touching her, loving her.

"A wedding on New Year's Day is said to bring great luck to the couple," she said, pressing his hand with her slim fingers.

He reached out and touched the golden circlet pinned to the shoulder of her indigo surcoat. "You once told me that this brought you luck too."

"It has," she said softly, watching him.

He smiled, a contented quirk of his lip, as he sat on the bench beside her and watched the happy chaos around them. Glas Eilean's walls had never hosted this kind of celebration before, he was sure. Not only had he and Michael stood before a priest that morning to take solemn, binding wedding vows, but Gilchrist and Iona, and Mungo and Sorcha had joined hands and spoken their own marriage vows as well.

After that, the priest had christened Angelica, who had fussed in Michael's arms and spit up on her own silk swaddling clothes. Then she had christened her adoptive father in turn by wetting his new shirt. Diarmid grinned at the memory of the laughter that had accompanied Angelica's formal welcome into the world, so different from the moments that had surrounded her birth.

He tightened his hand over Michael's and felt the gentle vibration in her body as she tapped her foot in time to the music of Gilchrist's harp. His Dunsheen kin had arrived by birling a few days earlier: Gilchrist and Iona, Arthur, Angus, Lilias, Brigit, and Mungo's children, Eva, Donald, and Fingal, were all at Glas Eilean now, eager to celebrate the New Year, and the joining and welcome of their loved ones. Little mention was made of the small, quiet funeral that had been held at Glas Eilean a few weeks earlier. Sorcha had insisted that prayers be said for Ranald's soul at the wedding mass this morning, and a long, respectful silence had been given him.

Now, hours later, they laughed and teased one another, danced and ate and listened to music, while Diarmid sat apart, content to watch them. Michael had joined him a few moments ago, sipping from his wine as if it were her own, picking at the leftover bits of the honeyed oatcake on his platter in a familiar manner that pleased him somehow. He reached out and rubbed her shoulder lovingly, lazily.

"They want you to dance with them," Michael said, leaning toward him. "Look, Brigit is waving to you, and still you sit here. You are in a solitary mood, for a man who is at his own wedding supper," she teased.

He smiled, a little crooked pull of his mouth, and waved to Brigit. "She knows how to dance without me," he murmured.

Brigit waited for Diarmid, and when he would not rise from his seat, she slowly began to sway and turn in a dance of her own making. Stiff-legged but upright, shuffling one foot more quickly, dragging the other, she followed her own rhythm.

Gilchrist changed the cadence of his song to a softer, slower beat as Brigit swirled and turned. She laughed, her golden curls flying outward, and nearly tipped over. Righting herself with Arthur's willing hand quickly thrust out to catch her, she beckoned to Diarmid.

"Go on," Michael whispered.

But he sat, smiling at Brigit, watching her spin, sway, move her arms gracefully like a rosebud opening its petals. He wanted her to have this moment alone. Then he would twirl her until she was dizzy if she wanted it.

"She has come so far," Michael murmured.

For a moment, Diarmid's throat tightened as he continued to watch his niece. Her legs were stronger, her muscles more developed, her pain less and less each night. Diarmid had sailed to Dunsheen Castle just after Ranald's death to meet with Arthur and Gilchrist, and to convey a message to the king. When that was done, he had brought Brigit back with him to Glas Eilean, with the others' promises that they would follow soon.

Michael and Diarmid had worked together with Brigit each day and each evening since then, rubbing her legs, helping her to stretch and move and walk, placing her in hot, soaking herb baths. And every night Michael sat with her and let the magic, as Brigit called it, come through her hands, warming, soothing, healing.

"She is much better," he agreed. "We have seen little miracles with her, bit by bit, each day a new one." He lifted Michael's hand, safe in his, to his lips and kissed her fingers. She glanced at him silently, smiling, her eyes brimful of tears, and looked back at Brigit swaying like a flower in a garden.

Diarmid saw Mungo standing in a shadowed corner, watching Brigit with a tender expression on his face. Sorcha walked over to him, and he put his arm protectively around her as she held her infant daughter.

They stood together, so different in appearance and yet somehow the same, a quality of kindness and peace shared between them now that their love could grow at last. She would love Mungo's children well.

Both devastated and touched by Ranald's heroic death, Sorcha had made a quick recovery from grief as well as childbirth. She had confessed to Diarmid that she felt released from years of unhappiness. She began to spend more and more time with Mungo, talking with him in private corners, walking with him on the cliffs, rowing out to watch the seals at play. Diarmid had not been surprised when they had announced that they too would wed at the New Year with Diarmid and Michael.

"Why waste the priest's visit?" Mungo had reasoned. "He will not be back this way for months and months." Diarmid was glad that Sorcha did not wait long to claim happiness for herself, and he was pleased that she never wore black.

Michael had cast aside her black gown, and her widow's pleated veil and chin-shrouding wimple, in favor of a soft rainbow of colored silks and wools that suited her far better. He liked best to see her in blue, which added a sparkle to her eyes, or in mulberry, which glowed in her cheeks. He liked her even better in nothing at all, or cream silk, but he had kept that opinion to himself, not wanting to spoil her sweet delight in a changed wardrobe.

She glanced at him now, her cheeks flushed and lovely, her gold-tipped lashes fluttering down over vivid blue eyes. "We have had so many miracles lately, Diarmid," she murmured.

"When I decide I want a miracle done, believe me, it gets done," he said, and grinned slowly.

She laughed and touched a fingertip to the corner of his mouth. "I love the way you smile," she said. "Do you want to hear about two more miracles that are going to happen?"

He blinked. "Two? Are you a prophetess, as well

as a healer? What are they?" He pinched back a smile.
"I think I know what one might be."

She tilted her head. "Now you are a prophet. What
is it?"

"You, my wife, have been unable to set foot in a
boat for the last two weeks," he told her, touching the
tip of her nose. "Your stomach cannot take even the
slightest rocking on the water, with or without dried
ginger. You nap every afternoon. I am a trained
healer, and I assure you that this will be cured," he
said, "in several months." He grinned as her blush
deepened.

"Ah," she said softly. "And then what will
happen?"

He leaned toward her. "And then I expect to have
my shirt christened by a new Dunsheen Campbell,"
he said in a low voice.

"With a crooked smile," she added.

"Undoubtedly." He kissed her languidly, sliding his
fingers into the silk of her hair, wanting to lose himself
in her sweetness, in the wonder and joy that her body
held. He lifted his lips from her reluctantly, and
looked at her.

"What of the second miracle?" he asked. "Who else
among us will be adding to our clan?"

She smiled, shook her head. "I have been spending
some time with Gilchrist. I thought you should
know—"

"I have seen the two of you together often in the
past few days, playing at the harp," he said. "I thought
you were learning new tunes from him. What else
could it be but that?" He felt no twinge of suspicion,
and never would, knowing that his wife's loyalty and
love were beyond question.

"I have convinced him to let us do surgery on his
leg."

He frowned. "Us?"

She nodded. "It is a simple procedure of rebreaking

the bones in the same location, and resetting the break
to straighten the leg."

"Simple? Have you ever done this before?"

"Ibrahim did it," she said.

"Breaking a man's leg bone takes enormous
strength and accuracy."

"You can do that. A small iron hammer is used,
and padding to cushion—"

He twisted his mouth at her scientific eagerness.
"Such a procedure would be incredibly painful."

"I have soporific sponges, soaked in small amounts
of henbane and opium, kept dry and sealed in a jar in
my chest. The patient breathes through the moistened
sponge, and goes to sleep for at least an hour." When
he tipped a brow skeptically, she nodded. "The sleeping medicine truly works, and much more reliably than
a sheep's bladder full of *uisge beatha.* Although it is
not a medication that can be used often," she
admitted.

He scowled mildly. "He could come out of such a
repair more lame than he is now. Did you explain that
to him?"

"I told him there was a chance of that."

He still frowned. "Then why did he agree?"

"Because he trusts you, Diarmid."

He glanced away. "We do not know the nature of
the original break. This is too risky."

"I can tell you just where the scars are on the bones.
I can, Diarmid." She smiled. "I held his leg in my
hands yesterday, and I am sure of the problem inside.
I can show you now if you like. It is just here, with a
jagged angle that goes this way—" She bent to show
him on his own leg.

He watched her hands circle his shin, heard her explain in detail what she knew about Gilchrist's old
injury. She was a wonder, and he was nearly defeated
in spite of himself. He was all out of protests but one.

"Michael," he said softly. "I cannot do this."

She looked at him, her eyes wide, blue, deep as heaven. "You can," she breathed.

He flexed his left hand, where it lay on the table, shook his head mutely. Michael touched his hand, took it in her own, turned it to look at the ugly scars across the wrist and thumb.

"You can do this," she said. "Please."

He huffed out a bitter little laugh. "You are asking for another miracle, girl," he whispered hoarsely.

"I am," she said. "I told you there would be two." She lifted his hand to her lips and kissed each small scar slowly, gently, kissed his thumb, his fingers, the center of his palm.

The feeling plummeted deep into his groin, swirled there, surged and heated within him until he thought he would have to grab her and haul her from the room to look for privacy.

"Michael," he groaned, so low it was no more than a breath. He pulled her to him, kissing her mouth. "Is that how you intend to make another miracle? My sweet girl, the one we just made has yet to be born. But we can try as often as you like."

She laughed, a silver sound. "The second miracle will happen like this," she said, and lifted his left hand in hers, palm to palm, fingers woven. "Our hands together, working to help Gilchrist."

He looked at her, felt her warm hand pressed to his, and his heart opened even further under the endless measure of her love. "You would be my left hand?"

"I would be your eye, your ear, the very heart that beats in your chest, Diarmid Campbell, if you wanted it of me," she whispered, staring up at him.

He nodded slowly, so filled in his soul that he could not speak. He tucked her hand in his, kissed her small, pale knuckles, waited a moment. "When did you tell Gilchrist we would do this?" he asked huskily.

She smiled. "Whenever you wish, Dunsheen."

"We will let him decide," he answered, and drew

her to her feet. "But I think he will give us plenty of time."

"Time for what?" she asked as he pulled her along.

He stopped, turned, leaned down. "To make some small miracles," he murmured.

Author's Note

Medieval women healers usually practiced an empiric art, that is, using knowledge and skills learned from generations of other women healers, generally in the areas of herbal medicine and midwifery. Some women, however, received academic training and became physicians and surgeons alongside their male peers.

Surviving documents name several medieval women who were awarded full medical degrees from universities in Italy, particularly Salerno and Bologna, while Oxford, Paris, and Montpellier refused women entrance. Michaelmas's education is based on what is known about the studies offered in Italian medical colleges, among the finest in the world at the time.

The illnesses and treatments suggested in this novel are based on reasonable possibilities for the time and place. Michaelmas's training in the Arabic medical traditions allowed for better cleanliness and common sense than was generally the case in the Western tradition alone. Brigit's lameness could easily have been the result of a poliovirus, quite common in the ancient as well as the medieval world, although not understood as an illness until the eighteenth century. The childbirth process, along with its accompanying problems and joys, has changed little over the centuries; although modern techniques are far better, the basics are still the same.

Finally, a note about boats: the kind of galleys sailed by medieval Scots seems to have differed between the east coast, which tended to use a more European-style galley, and the west coast, where Norwegian influence was still strong. Documentary references to multi-oared birlings pledged in service to Robert Bruce, and images on contemporary Scottish carvings, indicate that the boats used in the Western Isles were very similar to Viking longships. I owe thanks to Dr. Ed Furgol, naval historian, and Dr. Shelley Wachsmann, nautical archaeologist, for taking time to discuss this with me.

I sincerely hope you enjoyed *Lady Miracle*. Please watch for my novella in *A Stockingful of Joy*, on sale from Onyx in November 1997. My next novel will be set in fourteenth-century Scotland, and will tell the story of a forest outlaw and a prophetess.

I'd love to hear from you. Please write to me (enclosing an SASE) at P.O. Box 356, Damascus, MD 20872.

If you enjoyed *Lady Miracle,*
you'll love Susan King's
wonderful new novel set in Scotland,
filled with the magic of the land
and the passion of its people.
Turn the page for a special preview!

The Border Hawk
by Susan King

Coming soon from Topaz

Scotland, the Lowlands
Spring 1306

The sandstone walls of the castle glowed rosy and brilliant in the sunset as Isabel Seton climbed the steps to the battlement. She went steadily and resolutely, her head held high, her trembling hands clenched in tight fists. Hunger and fatigue weakened her, she told herself firmly; not fear. Never fear. She could not let anyone see that in her.

She moved along the wall-walk toward the crenellations built over the foregate. Each day at set of sun, through the ten weeks of the siege, she had walked this path to show the English that she was still here, still unharmed—and still defiant.

Isabel looked down through an embrasure. Vivid sunset light poured over the only access to Aberlady Castle: a rocky slope pitted with ditches. Along that treacherous incline, nearly a hundred English soldiers gathered near cookfires and tents, or hunkered down behind crude wooden palisades set up for protection. Their weapons would be close at hand, she knew, although the day's fighting had quieted a few hours ago.

Her father's men—her younger brother Adam's men, she corrected herself, for Sir John Seton was gone now—watched from sheltered positions along the wall-walk. Eleven Scotsmen remained of Aberlady's garrison, though over sixty had manned the battlements ten weeks past. A few of the men glanced at her as she passed, their bows held ready, their faces gaunt and grim.

But they knew, as Isabel did, that their mistress was safe wherever she stood. The English would not fire their arrows or missiles at Black Isabel, the prophetess of Aberlady.

Her value, rather than her mystery, protected her: The

English commander had shouted up to her that King Edward wanted her brought to him, whole and unarmed. The English king, she had been told, knew that Black Isabel of Aberlady had predicted the defeat of the Scots at Falkirk, the fall of Stirling Castle to the English, and the capture and execution of the freedom fighter William Wallace. King Edward approved of such prophecies, and was eager to hear the Scotswoman foretell another English victory.

A cool breeze stirred past, lifting her unbound hair and spreading it out like a glossy black banner. She raised her chin. Prophecies came to her spontaneously; she could not control them. And as long as breath stirred in her body, she would never use her gift to benefit the English.

She stood still and proud, heart pounding, as she stared down at the English encampment. Below, the English soldiers milled about on the slope. Some looked up at her, while the rest repaired weapons and armor, or packed the ditches leading to the castle gates with bracken and tree branches. A few English soldiers constructed the wooden framework of yet another siege engine with which to battle the thick walls.

The delicious smell of charred meat roasting over English cookfires made Isabel's stomach rumble miserably. Their hauberks and helmets glimmered in the sunset as the enemy soldiers ate and chatted and settled for the night. In the morning they would begin another battle, perhaps the last. The defenders of Aberlady were weakened by hunger, and far too few in number to withstand another onslaught from the English garrison.

Isabel turned away to gaze over the bailey yard and beyond, to the high enclosing walls. The keep and walls of Aberlady Castle rested upon a high dark crag that rose out of a flat plain. Surrounded by sheer cliffs on three sides and a steep incline on the fourth, the fortress was said to be impenetrable. No enemy had ever reached its walls.

Aberlady was impervious to all but starvation, Isabel thought. She sighed as she walked, trailing a hand along the gritty sandstone.

"Come awa' from the wall, now, Isabel." She glanced up to see Eustace Gifford, her father's bailie, step out

of the shadows. As the burly man held out his hand
toward her, his chain mail sleeve caught a red glint from
the sun.

"Stay back, Eustace," she said. "They will shoot i
they catch sight of you."

A smile touched his grim, weathered face. "They've
loosed their pebbles and thorns at me for weeks now
and I'm still here. Come on, 'tis time you were inside
the keep." He guided her toward the steps leading down
to the yard. As she went, Isabel heard the familiar whine
and thwack of an arrow bolt hitting the outer wall, close
to where Eustace had stood a moment earlier.

"By the Rood," he muttered, "they usually give you
more time to leave the battlement before they fire
upon us."

Isabel turned and climbed back to the wall-walk, de
spite Eustace's protests. She pulled a white silk cloth
from inside her sleeve and leaned deep into the embra
sure. With an exaggerated motion, she wiped at the fresh
scar on the outer wall, then shook the stone dust from
the cloth, and stood back.

Shouts rose from the English troops, cheers mixed
with a few loud jeers. Isabel inclined her head regally
and turned toward the steps. Eustace followed her, shak
ing his head.

" 'Tis John Seton's lass, you are," he said with a half
laugh. "Your father would have been proud to know
that his daughter defends his castle with wit and back
bone both."

"If my father were here now, he would never surren
der. Nor will I, nor any of us. The English have no right
to try to take Adam's inheritance."

"And that lad would surely be on the battlement i
we allowed it," Eustace said. "Your brother is too eager
by far to catch an English arrow. Moggy Shaw near tied
him hand and foot today just to keep him in the safety
o' the keep. Come ahead, now. Moggy has a fine kettle
o' soup simmering in the kitchen."

Isabel nodded, knowing that the soup was a thin blend
of well water and a little barley. When the grain was
finally gone, they would face their darkest, strongest
enemy: starvation.

Another English bolt smacked into the side of the

attlement above them, and sounds of laughter floated
toward them from the English camp. Eustace lifted a
and to deter the Scotsmen on the battlement from re-
urning the shot. He raised a brow in warning toward
abel, but she only sighed wearily and shook her head.

"I wish this was over," she said softly. "I dreamed last
ight that help came to us, and we walked out of here
to freedom, under a bright sunset."

"Is that a prophecy?" he asked as they moved down
ne steps.

"Just hope," she said. "Only hope." She looked at the
.y, where the reddish brilliance had faded to indigo
usk. If the dream had been prophetic, as her dreams
ometimes were, then help would come another day.

A shiver rippled through her, as if a hand rested gen-
y on her shoulder. She glanced around, knowing Eus-
.ce had not touched her. But she felt a presence, silent
nd strong, as if someone watched her keenly through
ne gathering shadows. She examined the deserted bailey
ard, but saw no one.

"Did Moggy measure out the oats and barley?" Eus-
.ce asked.

Isabel turned. "She said there are no oats left, and
ne last of the barley is in the soup—Eustace, what is
?" She saw him grab the hilt of his sword and scowl
nrough the dusk.

"Look there," he murmured, "in the far corner of the
ard, beyond the stable."

Isabel looked, and gasped. A group of men—six,
:ven, she counted hastily—emerged out of the shadows
eneath the back wall of the enclosure, and walked
oldly toward the bailey. They paused in the middle of
ne yard and looked at Isabel and Eustace on the steps,
nd at the Scotsmen on the battlements, who now stood
ith their bows held ready, aimed at them.

Isabel blinked at the newcomers in shock and disbe-
ef, then glanced at Eustace. Calmly, he raised a hand
o his men in a clear, silent order that no arrow should
e loosed yet.

Isabel turned back to stare at the seven men. They
ere not English soldiers, she was sure; their ragged tu-
ics and worn cloaks gave them the appearance of poor
armers or herdsmen, although they carried fine bows,

staffs, and broadswords as if they were knights. She won
dered if the men were rebel Scots, or even Englis
sympathizers.

At that thought, her heart pounded heavily and he
vision wavered, as if all the strain of the past week
weighed down upon her at once. "Dear God," she whis
pered hoarsely, "who are they?"

"Hush," Eustace hissed, his gaze fixed on th
strangers.

A man stepped forward, taller than most of his com
panions, his shoulders wide, his legs long and lean. H
brown tunic and the faded green cloak draped over on
shoulder were well-worn, even ragged, and his dark ha
and beard needed shearing. But his gaze was sharp an
penetrating, even at a distance, and his silent presenc
seemed to charge the air like lightning.

He walked toward the parapet staircase with smooth
agile grace, holding his unstrung longbow like a staf
and halted a few yards away. The nod he directe
toward Eustace and Isabel was courteous and brief, th
gesture of a nobleman.

"Isabel of Aberlady." His voice was deep and quie
like the dusky shadows that filled the yard. "We hav
come to rescue you and yours."

She stared at him, fascinated, drawn into the momen
The stranger possessed a wild beauty, his eyes glitterin
deep, his hands, gripping the bow, finely made but pow
erful. He seemed somehow beyond the ordinary realm
as if he had stepped out of the mists, out of legends c
the ancient race and the fair folk. Isabel looked at hin
unable to summon an answer, feeling almost bespelle
but the pleasant, peaceful sensation quickly vanished.

His gaze seemed to assess her from her hair and gow
to the roots of her soul. She pulled in a breath and lifte
her chin, determined to yield none of her thoughts
him. He offered rescue, but she could not trust tha
unsure if he was friend or foe. Her inner sense, usuall
keen, told her only that a current of danger surrounde
this man. Somehow, though, she felt that he was mor
likely the target of the threat than its source.

"Who are you?" she asked calmly, although she qui
ered with apprehension, and an odd, raw excitemen
"How did you get inside Aberlady's walls?"

"Through the postern gate in the north wall."

Isabel gaped at him. "But that small door is hidden by scrub and rocks, and overlooks a cliff nearly a hundred feet high. How did you reach it?"

"That took some time," he said simply.

"Who are you?" she asked again. She saw that his eyes were a dark, deep blue, like the twilight sky. Keen intelligence gleamed there, as if he constantly examined all that he saw. She wondered, suddenly, what else he intended here beyond aid.

"I am James Lindsay," he said in that soft, commanding voice. Beside her, she heard Eustace draw in his breath, but the name meant nothing to her. "At times," the man continued, "I am called the Border Hawk."

"Jesu," Eustace breathed out.

Isabel gasped softly. She had heard that name. The Border Hawk was a renegade Scotsman who hid from English and Scots alike in the vast lands of the Ettrick Forest. His arrival inside Aberlady could mean salvation—or complete defeat for all of them. His loyalties, of late, were known only to himself.

Reports alternately said that the Border Hawk fled north, west, south, even out to sea; that he was a sorcerer who changed his form at will; that he was alive, that he was dead; and that he was immortal, born of the air race.

"James Lindsay," Eustace said. "I know the name. You are welcome here if your purpose is fair-minded. If is not—we still outnumber you by a few men." He indicated the wall-walk, where ten men trained halfdrawn bows on the newcomers.

Lindsay nodded. "We are here to help Aberlady's defenders. And we bring some food." He beckoned, and one of his men stepped forward, pulling three dead hares and a grouse from a sack. "I assume a meal would be to your liking."

"It would," Eustace said. "Our thanks. The cook is in the kitchen—she'll welcome the meat." Lindsay's comrade nodded and turned to run toward the keep.

"I have heard that the Border Hawk has an army of bole men hiding in Ettrick Forest," Isabel said. "Are they outside, ready to attack the English?"

"These six men are all who run with me," Lindsa
said. "But we can get you to safety with scant trouble

"Six men!" Isabel burst out. "There are nearly a hu
dred English outside the gates!"

Eustace looked at her. " 'Tis said that a Scotti
knight is never truly tested until he has flown wi' th
Border Hawk. These men may be few, but doubtle
clever and highly skilled."

James Lindsay inclined his head at the complimer
"They used to say that, but nae more," he murmure
"Six men are all that fly with me now. We can take a
of you out of here the way we came up, after you hav
eaten, and the darkness is deeper."

"We canna leave Aberlady," Isabel said firmly. "Th
English would take the castle."

"Then we willna leave it to them." He looked at Eu
tace. " 'Tis old Scottish practice, and our new king
wishes, that Scottish castles be made unavailable for E
glish use. Either a castle is held by force of arms, «
destroyed."

"Destroyed!" Isabel gasped, horrified.

James Lindsay glanced at her wordlessly, then bega
to climb the steps toward the wall-walk, brushing pa
her. Eustace shot her a grim look and turned to follov
Isabel grabbed her skirts and ran up the steps behir
them.

Eustace stopped. "Go back to the keep, Isabel."

"But he means to ruin Aberlady!"

"Isabel." Eustace sighed heavily. "We have a chanc
to walk out o' here alive. If James Lindsay hadna com
we would have starved to death inside these walls. W
my last dying effort, I would have set fire to Aberla
myself, to prevent the English from taking it."

She stared at him, stunned. Eustace turned an
walked away to join James Lindsay, who stood behir
a merlon stone, scanning the English garrison. Isab
moved toward them, halting by an embrasure in fu
view of the English.

Lindsay lashed out and grabbed her arm, pulling h
behind the shelter of the merlon. She shoved at him, b
he held her firmly. "Are you a dimwit, to stand there?
he asked.

"The English willna harm me," she said.

"If you believe that, then you are not much of a ophetess," he snapped, as he held her fast.

"Look," Eustace said to Lindsay, from his position veral feet away. "The English have filled those ditches ith branches to smooth the incline for their siege en- nes. But each time they pack the ditches, we set em afire."

He called to two guards, who prepared fire arrows ith cloth, pine pitch, and a torch, materials already arby for that purpose. The two men loosed flaming rows that sailed through the darkness and fell into the tches, setting them ablaze.

Isabel, held in the iron curve of Lindsay's arm, craned r neck and watched the fires spark and blossom. She w Lindsay's six men, their bows strung, mount the eps and arrange themselves along the battlements with berlady's scant garrison.

"Now that we've shot at them, they'll return it," she id.

"Aye. When I let you go," Lindsay murmured, his ce close to hers, his soft voice creating shivers in her, want you to crawl along the wall-walk to that corner wer over there."

"When you let me go," she said between her teeth, will go where I please."

"Isabel, do as he says," Eustace pleaded, as he loaded crossbow. "Och, now it begins." He ducked as an row whined overhead and slammed into the wall-walk, llowed by two more that clattered on stone and fell ide. "They dinna see you up here, lass, so they think safe to fire upon the walls. You must get away from e battlement."

Lindsay released her. "Go on. Stay low." He began string his bow and drew an arrow from the quiver at s back.

Isabel stood, quickly and boldly, and stepped in front the embrasure. She knew that her appearance on the ttlement could deter the fighting; Aberlady's men ere weary, and much-needed food awaited them in the tchens by now.

As she stood, a bolt slammed into her shoulder with ch force that she spun sideways and fell backward ainst James Lindsay. She cried out, stiffening against

the searing pain. Lindsay swore softly and crouched lov
supporting her with one arm while he pulled aside th
torn fabric around the arrowshaft.

"Isabel!" Eustace called gruffly. "Dear God, the
didna see the lass—Isabel!"

" 'Tisna serious." Lindsay's voice was cool and sootl
ing through the haze of bright pain that filled her. Deftl
he cracked the long shaft protruding from her shoulde
leaving the bolt embedded in the muscle. "I'll tend to
properly later, if you can stand the pain for now."

She winced and nodded. Arrows fell around them lik
cruel rain, smacking and clattering into stone and woo
Another bolt bit hard into her leg and fell aside. Isab
flinched and cried out again, struggling in Lindsay
arms.

"Let me up," she gasped, panicking, aware only that
she stood, the arrow storm would stop. "I must get up!

"You willna," he said. "I'll take you to the tower.
He kept low and half dragged her along the wall-wal
until they reached the door of a round tower. Kickin
the door open, he pulled her inside, while arrows whine
through the air.

Once inside the quiet, bare room, he set her down o
the wooden floor and crouched beside her. Using h
dirk, he cut a strip of wool from the hem of her gow
and wadded it against her bleeding shoulder. She too
the silk cloth from inside her sleeve and pressed it t
the tender cut in her lower leg.

"Arrow wounds are painful, I know," he said, "bu
these are simple enough, and will heal quickly."

She nodded, drawing in a sharp breath as he applie
more pressure to her shoulder. She watched him throug
the darkness. "James Lindsay," she said after a momen
"tell me why you came to Aberlady. More than rescu
brought you here, I think."

He frowned, folding the cloth to a clean side. "I cam
here," he said softly, ominously, "to find Black Isabe
the prophetess of Aberlady."

She narrowed her eyes. "King Edward sent you!"

He shook his head and glanced at her, his eyes mic
night deep in the shadows. Suddenly she sensed ange
in him, and strong purpose. A chill spiraled through he

"We have business, you and I," he murmured.

"But I dinna know you—though you seem to know me."

"Let me make a prediction, Black Isabel." He stood and looked down at her. "You will come to know me well," he said. "And you will come to regret what you have done to me and mine." He turned toward the door. "I will be back to tend to you properly. You will be safe here for now." Then he stepped into a hail of falling arrows.

Isabel stared after him, and wondered just how safe he was.